Praise for Caitlin Kittredge's Nocturne City series

PURE BLOOD

"*Pure Blood* pounds along hard on the heels of *Night Life*, and is every bit as much fun as the first in the series. With a gutsy, likable protagonist and a well-made fantasy world, *Pure Blood* is real enough to make you think twice about locking your doors at night. A swiftly paced plot, a growing cast of solid supporting characters, and a lead character you can actually care about—Kittredge is a winner."
—Jim Butcher

"With enough supernatural death and romance to keep readers glued to the pages…Jump in with both feet and hang on tight because *Pure Blood* is an emotion-filled ride."
—*Darque Reviews*

"The pacing is rapid and the peril imminent…This is a series and an author that are definitely going places!"
—*Romantic Times BOOKreviews*

"The unexpected plot twists and high-octane action of *Pure Blood* kept me turning the pages until the wee hours of the morning."
—*Romance Junkies*

NIGHT LIFE

"Dark and cutting-edge."   —*Romantic Times BOOKreviews*

"I loved the mystery and the smart, gutsy heroine."
—Karen Chance, *New York Times* bestselling author of *Claimed by Shadow*

MORE…

St. Martin's Paperbacks Titles by

Caitlin Kittredge

BLACK LONDON SERIES

Street Magic

Demon Bound

NOCTURNE CITY SERIES

Night Life

Pure Blood

Second Skin

Witch Craft

Demon Bound

CAITLIN KITTREDGE

St. Martin's Paperbacks

DEMON BOUND

Copyright © 2009 by Caitlin Kittredge.

All rights reserved.

For information address St. Martin's Press, 175 Fifth Avenue, New York, NY 10010.

ISBN 978-0-312-94363-9

Printed in the United States of America

St. Martin's Paperbacks edition / December 2009

St. Martin's Paperbacks are published by St. Martin's Press, 175 Fifth Avenue, New York, NY 10010.

10 9 8 7 6 5 4 3 2 1

PART I

Clockwork

Listen to the army march across my coffin lid
Fire in the east and sunrise in the west
I'm just a dead man, walking with the rest

—The Poor Dead Bastards,
"Dead Man Marching"

Chapter One

A crow sat on the dead branch of the dead tree that watched over two gravestones in the corner of Brompton Cemetery. It watched Jack Winter with its black eyes like beads, and he watched the crow in turn, with eyes that most people called ice, but that he called simply blue.

Jack drew a Parliament out of the air and touched his finger to the tip. He sucked a lungful of smoke and blew it at the crow, which flapped its wings and snapped its beak in irritation. "Fuck off, then," Jack told it. "Not like I want you hanging about."

"Leave that bird alone," said his companion. "If the map I got from tourist information is right, the graves are close by here." Her circular ramble through the headstones came to a stop next to Jack. "Oh. You found them."

"Mary and Stuart Poole," Jack said, flicking his fag at Mary's headstone. "Who says the gods don't have the occasional bout of humor?"

Pete Caldecott gave Jack what he'd describe as a dirty look, and not dirty in the manner that led to being naked and sweaty. She strode over and picked up his litter, shoving it into her coat pocket. "You're a bloody child, you know that? Emotionally twelve. Thirteen at the most."

Jack shrugged. "Been accused of worse." He felt in the inside pocket of his motorbike jacket for another Parliament, but thought better of it when Pete put a hand on her hip.

"We've a job to do, and if we don't do it, we don't get paid, so are you going to stand there all day with your thumb in your arse or are you going to get to work?"

Jack withdrew his hand from his coat slowly, feeling rather like a nun had caught him with a dirty magazine. Pete was, at the first look, not a She Who Must Be Obeyed sort, but Jack knew better. Shorter than him by a head, she had green eyes straight from the Emerald Isle, and dark hair and sun-shy skin that turned her to Snow White in torn denim and an army jacket. Lips plump like rubyfruit, a body that a bloke could spend hours on and still feel like he was starving for it.

But at moments like now, when she glared at him and tapped her foot on the dead grass over the Pooles' final rest, Jack had learned he was better off doing as he was told. Unless he felt like a smack in the head, and it was too early in the day for kinky foreplay.

Jack picked up the black canvas tote they'd brought along and crouched between the Pooles' headstones. The entire practice of raising the dead for things like "closure" and "peace" was a load of bollocks, but Pete's Irish temper kept him from articulating the thought, and she was right, besides—they did have a job.

"'S still a bloody stupid request from the family," Jack told her. "Just like I said when you took them on."

Pete folded her arms. "I spent near a decade of my life pushing paper around a desk at the Metropolitan Police, so once you've dealt with expense reports and a DCI who thinks that equipment that works is a luxury, not a necessity, you can jabber on about bloody stupid, all right?"

Jack grimaced. "I'm not a party trick, luv. This here is my talent and using it thusly . . . well . . . frankly, it's demeaning."

Pete pointed down at the grave. "Get to work, Winter. Before I lay you a smack."

"I should have been a fucking fortune teller," Jack grumbled. "The future is an open book compared to this shite." He heaved a sigh for effect while he unzipped the satchel and pulled out his spirit heart. Pete merely folded her arms, her expression ever the impassive copper.

In Jack's hand, the clockwork contraption weighed no more than a melon and was of comparable size. Round, made from brass, and hung from a chain, the spirit heart held a small hollowed-out chamber in its bottom. Jack dug the plastic baggie of galangal root out of the satchel and breathed on a pinch of the stuff.

Just a touch of sorcery, just enough to wake up the strands of magic that lived in the galangal. Jack rubbed the pinch between his fingers and tamped it into the chamber of the spirit heart. A stab of pressure hit him in the temple and he rubbed his forehead before standing. His talent knew what was coming, even if his mind didn't, and Jack braced himself to take the punch of spirit energy the galangal root conducted.

Pete reached out and touched him on the arm, the lightest of touches, on his leathers no less, but he still felt it, dancing down through his blood and nerves to his bones. Her own talent felt like gooseflesh, like being touched by a girl you fancied for the first time, every time. It was different from his own slippery, slithering magic as a tube tunnel from a sewer. Similar functions, separated by miles of intent.

"You all right, Jack?" she said.

He lied to her with a small, tight nod and a smile. His head throbbed harder. "Close enough for horseshoes and hand grenades, luv. Let's have this over with."

Pete wasn't fooled, and the twin lines between her eyes said so, but she had the grace to step back and pretend that Jack was as skillful a liar as he claimed.

Jack supposed if he had any sense, he'd be worried. Using magic wasn't supposed to hurt. Not him, not a mage of the *Fiach Dubh*. The brothers of the crow were the rock stars of a magic trade often fraught with blood and blackness, hard and wicked men whom no one crossed.

Many of them were that. Jack was not. And if he *did* have sense, he'd stop before his talent burned a hole in him.

No one had ever accused him of having sense, though. Of being a wanker, yes. A thief, a sinner, and a murderer, certainly. But sensible, no. Jack thought that the day someone *did* accuse him of sense, it would likely be time to hang up his spurs.

"All right, you dusty lot," he murmured, so low only the dead could hear. "Come and give me a haunt."

Pete drew her small digital video kit from the bag and readied it, training the lens on Jack and the graves.

For his part, Jack held the spirit heart straight out above the earth, arm rigid as a divining rod. The clockwork pendulum swung gently, aimlessly. Jack inhaled and held the air. Panic chewed on the ends of his guts, scratched at his neck, and wormed into his brain. His body knew what he was about to do, and it was screaming.

Times like this, Jack felt the longing for a fix like the grasp of a familiar lover—tight, hot, gathered behind his eyes, knotting him up, making him cold, telling him, *I have what you need. Take it and warm yourself, save yourself, taste the golden delights of the floating world.*

The hiss of need had only grown louder since he'd kicked heroin, begging and pleading to have a chance, just one more chance to make it right.

All Jack could do was tighten his grip on the spirit heart, the cold brass warming to the same degree as his palm, and drown the murmuring of the fix in a tide of other whispers, crying and shouting, faint and fierce, buried and so old no one knew they were buried any longer.

The dead came to Jack as they always came, and he let himself see, do what he'd started fixing to avoid in the first place. Sight was his curse, and the one thing he could never fully erase.

In his hands, the spirit heart gave a *tick*.

Jack's second sight found ghosts, thick here as a crowd in Trafalgar Square. They stood, for the most part, silent and staring at the living intruder in their pale, witch-lit world. A few hissed at him, black-eyed revenants with their flesh hanging off their bones. Revenants fed on the malice of their lives, which followed them in death like a shroud of black, twisting magic, spots on celluloid film.

Pete moved nearer to him. She couldn't see what he saw, but she knew all the same, perhaps better than Jack, the chill of having the dead always just out of view. "Want me to start it?" she asked quietly. Giving him a way out, a way to pretend that merely looking through his sight wasn't causing him the sort of headache normally found only after strong whiskey and passing out on something hard.

The spirit heart gave another *tick*, louder, stronger, and Jack nodded. "Wake them up."

"Mary and Stuart Poole." Pete raised her voice and pitched it sharp. Jack flinched as a ghost drifted closer to Pete, a girl with dark wet hair still tangled with the garbage she'd drowned in. The salt-sour stink of the Thames at low tide tickled his nostrils.

The girl ran her hand longingly across Pete's cheek. Jack narrowed his eyes. "Oi. Shove off, miss. That's not yours to take."

Pete shivered, but continued. "Mary and Stuart Poole, we call you to this resting place. Come back to your bones."

The drowned ghost drifted away, her torn dress and

lank hair trailing behind her in a remembered river current. Jack felt a pull at his arm, and the spirit heart began to tick faster and faster, clockwork innards spinning like the earth was revolving too fast. He planted his feet and concentrated on staying merely upright. It shouldn't be a task during a simple spirit raising

"Mary and Stuart Poole," Pete said again. "Come back to your bones."

There was power in triplets. Jack had taught her that. Pete never forgot something when you told her once.

A tug on his arm warned Jack that his insistence on going ahead while his magic was spinning out of control may have cost him his arse. The spirit heart was twirling now, as if someone had spun a globe and walked away. The brass caught the low afternoon sun and threw off light, the whirring of the clockwork like a bird's heartbeat. Too fast. Too fast and too soon. The Pooles were coming to his summons, and they could get loose if he didn't rein the power in.

Jack pushed against the swirl of enticement generated by the beating clockwork, forced it into a shape. A focus like the heart, or salt, or stone was important—raw magic pulled from something like a spirit could blow your insides out surely as a shotgun blast.

A halo, black, gathered around the spirit heart, touched it experimentally, the lightest of caresses, while the spirit heart shot blue sparks through the realm of the dead. Pete couldn't see them, but she stepped back all the same. "They coming, then?"

"If I have any say," Jack answered, and tugged ever so gently at the curiosity, the suggestion of minds and bodies that floated from the graves, and guided them to the spirit heart. Coaxed them, teased them, but never ordered them. Ghosts didn't like being pushed about.

Jack had learned that rule the hard way.

In his hand, the spirit heart stopped.

It gave a last *click*, and the sides opened to allow the Pooles' residual energies in. Jack released his grip on the chain, and the spirit heart floated under its own steam, turning gently in the passage of power from the awakened ghosts.

"Yes? Hello?" Mary Poole stood partly in the earth, ankles cut off by the grave. Her burial clothes clung to her frame in tatters. "Hello, yes? Can you hear me?"

"What do you want?" Stuart Poole was heavy, a heavy face full of jowls sitting on top of a heavy mound of body. "Who are you?"

"Jack Winter," Jack said. "This here's Petunia Caldecott."

He flinched when Pete fetched him a punch in the shoulder. "Tosser." She faced the ghost, pleasant and pointed as if Stuart Poole were a banker she suspected of defrauding his clientele. "Mr. Poole, we're here on behalf of your children. Jayne and Stuart, the junior?"

"Hello?" Mary Poole said. "Yes? Can you hear me?"

"Repeater," Jack said at Pete's questioning eyebrow. "Just a fragment of a spirit left behind with the bones. Mary Poole's been taken on to her eternal reward, if you believe that bollocks."

"Comforting to know what's waiting when I shuffle loose the mortal coil," Pete muttered.

"Pardon me, but I've asked a question—*who* in blazes *are* you?" Stuart Poole demanded. "This is most irregular."

"Pete," Pete said. "And that's Jack, like we've established. Your children have some questions about your will, Mr. Poole. Seems they're absent from it?"

"Your beloved offspring were wondering if perhaps there was some mistake there," Jack expanded. The dead pressed closer behind him, and he heard the wings, like wind through a grove of trees, but they were wings. He knew the sound. It was familiar, old, as much a part of him as his tattoos or the vertical scar on his right cheek from the business end of a smashed witch bottle.

Jack supposed he had stolen that necromancer's Hand of Glory, and his wife, but he still thought the bloke had over-reacted.

Scars faded, but the rush of wings never did. They always circled back, always came to him when he talked to the dead. A living walker in death's realm always called to them, the eyes and wings of the Underworld. The crows of Death.

"Jack . . . ," Pete said, right on cue. She didn't have the sight, but she did have a connection he didn't, to the push and pull of power under the world, the constant tide of the Black under their feet.

"I know, I know," he snapped. "Wrapping up—how is it, Stu? You cut your brats out of the will, or was it all a terrible misunderstanding that will be resolved with tears and hugging and vows to be a better sort of person because it's what Mum and Dad would have wanted if they hadn't kicked off in that lorry collision?"

Stuart Poole puffed up, his silvery insubstantial form spreading out over the graves. "It most certainly was not a misunderstanding. Jayne and my son were miscreants—Stuart with his embezzling and Jayne with her women."

Jack cocked an eyebrow at Pete. "The very nerve."

"They're not getting a penny!" Stuart Poole bellowed. "Not a single cold shilling, you understand?"

"Perfectly." Jack dropped a wink at Stuart Poole. "Hope you're less of a miserable sod in the afterlife, guv."

"I never heard such . . . ," Poole began, but Jack let go of the thin thread of spirit he'd caught, and Stuart sputtered out like a run-down torch.

The wings were much closer now, ruffling the leaves and

the grass around their feet, filling up the air with hisses and cries.

"Hello?" Mary Poole said. "Yes? Hello?"

"Shove off, luv," Jack said. "Your ticket's pulled. Run on and frolic up in God's heaven, now."

"Jack, honestly," Pete said, rolling her eyes. She snapped the camera shut and tucked it back into the bag.

Jack reached out and gently cradled the heart as the clockwork slowed to nothing. The sound of ghosts leaving the living was almost never a howl, an explosion, or a dramatic dying gasp. Like most things, the dead just faded away.

The wings went with them. The ravens of the Bleak Gates, the guards of the entrance to death, had found their quarry, and it hadn't been him. Today.

"Good job of that," Pete said. "Quick and quiet, and the Poole family can't dispute it."

"Pete, people will always dispute what they don't want to hear," Jack said. "Although if you're desperate enough to call on a shady ghost-raising sod like meself, I really don't think you can dispute much of anything. Certainly not that you're a tosser."

"And I thought I was a pessimist." Pete folded the camera into its case and handed him the bag. Jack shoved his spirit heart inside and shouldered the weight. He'd never had to drag around a bloody satchel when he was living as a mage. A little salt and chalk in the pocket, a sliver of mirror or silver, and it was enough to curse or hex his way out of and into most trouble. He'd carried more kit to shoot up than to work magic.

"Let's call on the Pooles and get this over with, shall we?" he asked Pete, ignoring her last comment. You couldn't spend any time at all in the Black and not lose faith in men, gods, and basic decency. The only ones who didn't were the prize idiots who soon got themselves topped, if the older, hungrier citizens of his world were merciful.

"Now we're eager to work?" Pete shoved her hands into her jacket. "This isn't going to be a pleasant scene, you know."

"Yes, well. The less time I have to spend doing parlor tricks for rich twats, the better off we'll all be." Jack added extra weight to his step as they reached Old Brompton Road and started for the tube station. His jackboots rang against the pavement like funeral knells.

Pete let the twat remark pass, and for that Jack was grateful. His temper had returned with a vengeance when he kicked his habit, and lost the thing keeping his sight at bay. The sight was no longer intermittent and faulty, forcing him to live rough and desperate as he used to keep the dead where the dead belonged. Now it was raw, like a fire eating through the paper of his mind, and it played hell with his control.

Pete got the brunt of it, and though she bore it with sharpness and a frown like a Victorian nursemaid, she didn't deserve it. The heroin hadn't eaten away enough of his brain to mask that fact. He was a twat himself for the things he said and did to her, but she'd chosen to stay with him, chosen the Black over her old, safe life, and Jack wasn't so noble he would force her away for her own good.

The truth was, if he didn't have the fix he needed her. And needing anything wasn't a luxury a mage of his situation could afford.

But it was the truth, and Jack knew that in the Black, there was no changing truth.

Chapter Two

The Pooles lived in Kensington, in a million-pound row house that Jack would have happily vandalized at a point in the not-so-distant past. Pete stepped up and rang the bell, the camera dangling from her fist. "Let me talk to them, right? Let's have a minimum of interrupting and an absence of swearing until the check's in hand."

Jack sighed, irritation spiking like acid in his guts. "I know how to play nicely, Pete. I'm not going to steal the silver or insult the Queen."

"The Pooles' kids are not going to be pleased," Pete said. "The last thing I need is you making things worse."

"Oi, who's the teacher and who's the apprentice, luv?" Jack said. "I've been raising ghosts since you were in nappies."

"You're the teacher, it's true and you're brilliant," Pete said, with that deceptively sweet smile, the one that would take your head off like a razor if you got too close to it. "But you have the social skills of a chimpanzee on match day, and I'll be doing the talking."

"Well and good," Jack grumbled in assent, since he'd

probably say something to get the police called with the mood his headache and the effort of raising the spirits had fetched.

Jayne Poole opened the door and drew back, like one did when they found salesmen on the stoop. "Oh," she said. "You've found something?" Jayne Poole had a pinched, anxious air to her, like a thin, nervous dog with thin, nervous blood.

"We did, Ms. Poole," Pete said. "May we come in?"

Jayne Poole stepped aside and gestured them into the dank bowels of the house, which still smelled like her parents even after the nearly full year since their deaths. Jack couldn't blame her entirely for the grim memorializing that was going on—death by runaway beer lorry wasn't the most dignified end a couple of posh twats could come to.

Pete walked ahead of Jayne Poole, who moved slow and sloppy with pills or gin, or both. Jack would wager there was a regular Sid and Nancy doing a dance in her bloodstream.

"We made contact with your mum and dad," Pete said, "and spoke about the issue of the will. . . ."

"Yes?" Jayne Poole chewed on her bloodless lower lip, one long square nail tapping her overbite. All that money, Jack thought, and the Pooles couldn't fix their daughter's traditional English teeth.

"I'm terribly sorry," Pete said. Jayne Poole put her hand on her throat, covering the large emerald pendant that sat in the hollow like a wart on a wicked witch.

"What on earth is that supposed to mean, Miss Caldecott? I was Father's favorite. I paid you good money . . ."

Jack cleared his throat. "Not to split hairs, but your brother paid us, and it don't change the result—you and he both get nothing. And incidentally, the old man? Not such a fan of yours."

Jayne Poole's mouth flapped open, snapped shut, and

she jabbed her finger at Pete. "How dare he speak to me that way? How dare the both of you take our money and deliver this . . . this . . . *shite?*"

Pete opened the camcorder and pressed the playback. Stuart Poole's voice rattled through the sitting room, the windy, eldritch sound that ghosts on film took on.

Two heat flowers blossomed on Jayne Poole's cheeks. "It's fake," she said hotly. "You must have faked it. Father would never say such things. Patently ridiculous."

"Ms. Poole, we've done the job you paid us for," Pete said, "and we'd like the rest of the money now."

Jayne Poole clopped over to the door on her spiked shoes, heels digging divots out of the soft wood floors. Jack thought of his flesh, and flinched. "Get out," Jayne Poole snapped, flinging the door wide to let in the muted daytime sounds of Kensington. "You'll get not one red cent from me, and you'll be hearing from my solicitor."

"Ms. Poole," Pete warned, her eyes going jewel-hard. "I advise you to think carefully before you decide not to pay us."

"What are you going to do?" Jayne Poole's horsey lip curled back. "Put a curse on me?"

"Don't bloody tempt me," Jack muttered, and grunted at the sharp pain when Pete jabbed him in the ribs.

"I'll deal with this," she said, low. "Ms. Poole . . ."

"Out!" Jayne Poole cried. "Out, right now, before I call the police."

Pete threw up her hands. "I would *love* to see you do that," she told Jayne Poole. She shut the camera with a slap and shoved it into the bag. "Come on, Jack. We're finished."

Jack followed Pete to the door, stopping on the threshold and turning his eyes back to Jayne Poole, who stood in the center of the foyer huffing like a well-coiffed freight train. "Your father hated you," he told Jayne. "Right down to your greedy, rotten core, and it's easy to see why. You'll see him again sooner than you think, so perhaps you should spend your remaining years trying to become a bit less of a cunt."

Jayne Poole's fists curled, and she let out a sound of fury, but Jack ducked out before she could land a blow. "You take care, now, Ms. Poole."

Pete rubbed her forehead as the door slammed behind them, leaving them with curious looks from the pavement population, tourists and posh types browsing in the nearby antique shop. Jack glared at the nearest group. "Take a photo or piss off."

"Must you do that?" Pete said. "To everyone we meet? Must you play the villain?"

"Jayne Poole? That rotted-out bitch had it coming," Jack said. He went around to the street and climbed in the passenger side of Pete's battered Mini Cooper. Pete climbed behind the wheel, slinging the bag into the rear seat with force. The spirit heart rattled, reminding Jack with a few ticks of clockwork how badly the day so far had gone, and warning it wasn't over yet. He stood by his words, though. The Jayne Pooles of the world did have it coming, the fate they thought couldn't apply to them rushing up from the next life. Jack knew better than most that Death could tread your tracks for a very long time, until you got tired and gave out. He'd seen Death do that very thing, to a score of people a far better class of soul than Jayne Poole.

"We *needed* that money," Pete said, her fingers tight on the steering. "As if I needed the reminder, my savings are nearly out and you've got the shirt on your back, if that." She cast a look at the red slogan splashed across Jack's chest, the one that read NAZI PUNKS FUCK OFF. "And did it have to be *that* shirt, in particular?"

"Hasn't got any holes," Jack protested. "No visible stains. What's wrong with it?"

"Forget I said it," Pete muttered, jamming the Mini into

gear and lurching into traffic with a wheeze of abused cylinders. Jack thought better of saying anything else, like they may *need* Jayne Poole's bloody money but he'd be fucked by a priest, face-first up against the confessional, if he *wanted* anything to do with this spooks-for-hire business at all. It was risky, and silly, and it was only going to end with somebody getting their head jammed up their arse by an angry ghost.

Pete headed them back across the city toward Whitechapel, and Jack sat still in the passenger seat, not saying all of the bitter things sitting on his tongue. They'd dissolve eventually, as they always did, and he'd swallow them back down and let them rot his guts a bit more.

Chapter Three

Pete parked in the alley next to Jack's flat in the Mile End Road, and went inside without a word to him. Jack sat on the Mini's bonnet and lit a fag, drawing it deep into his lungs, feeling the hiss and whisper of the Black fade in the face of something darker, more present.

Roman citizens burned their dead on the fields of Whitechapel, to the east of the City walls. Eighty thousand souls crouched there during the reign of Victoria, all of them steeped in magic and misery as Jack the Ripper stalked among them, blood trickling through his fingers to the smooth-rubbed cobblestones, while just behind him, the far larger and more terrifying specter of poverty and a smoke-tinged, stinking death marched, implacable and inexorable.

Whitechapel was the only place in London where Jack found a little relief from his sight. The dark and bloody veins of power that ran through the place masked the vibrations of the Black, put the volume down so he could at least sleep, if he had a fix in him. He'd first found the place going on twenty years ago, fresh off the train from Manchester and sleeping rough.

Whitechapel became home, an odd sort of home, dirty and sooty and filled up with past misery. But you didn't choose where you rested your bones, the place chose you. Whitechapel was in Jack's blood surely as the fix had once been.

Jack worked a hand under his collar and scratched at the tattoo on his left collarbone, one of the twin eyes of Horus resting under his skin. Pete had imbued them with power, the kind only someone of her talent could draw to a thing. And it held, mostly. The ink did as the skag had before it. But never enough, never as completely nor as quietly, never with the feeling of wrapping cotton wool over his third eye.

Shutting his eyes, Jack let the sounds of the real London, the real world, cover him. Slamming doors from his building, shouts in Urdu from his neighbor's children, the flow of traffic on Mile End Road, the rumble of a train in the Hammersmith & City Line under his feet.

A window slid open four landings above, and Pete stuck her head out. "Jack, you coming up?"

He exhaled a last halo of blue smoke and ground the burning butt out under his boot. "In a minute, yeah."

"You fancy tea?" Pete, though she lived here, in what many still considered a slum, with him, who most would consider a bum, kept her middle-class habits. Jack found his mouth quirking. The fact that she assumed civility of him was oddly charming, though he'd put a boot in the face of anyone who suggested such a thing.

"I suppose," Jack said.

"I'll get something in from Tesco, then," Pete said, and disappeared, shutting the window. Jack felt her power waver away from him, descend the lift, and drift up the street to the Tesco Express before it slipped away, so much sand through fingertips. Jack ran a hand over his face. Told himself the noise of the street and the muted dark heartbeat of Whitechapel was all he heard.

It helped, for the moment, but it was always temporary. Always, the Black clawed at his mind, and the dead, which came to Jack because he radiated power like a torn electrical cable, hovered. The madness that had caused him to shove a needle in his arm in the first place sat in the corner with its face hidden, and it laughed.

The laughter turned and twisted, lapped back on itself until it bounced off the brick around his head, and Jack felt a sharp pain like a hot iron blade cut through his skull, behind his eyes.

He had enough time to think, *This isn't right.*

Briefly, he was seventeen again and face-down on a carpet that smelled like dust and pipe tobacco as the dead danced around him, a funeral procession for any shred of his mind that remained protected from the sight. For a single clock tick, the dead reached out their hands and begged Jack to join them as they had that day.

The Black couldn't invade consciousness, couldn't move him from one place to another, up and down through time. Jack ground his knuckles into his forehead, hoping pain would bring him back to the present.

He was in the alley behind his flat.

He was thirty-eight years old.

And he was clean. The things the Black showed him weren't real, they were only memories birthed from dreams.

Even though he whispered the mantra to himself, over and over—*Not real, not real, I'm clean, I'm clean*—the laughter became corporeal, a velvet touch on the back of his neck.

Belatedly, Jack knew the pain for what it was, and anger burned the panic out of him. Panic was for common people, those who had never touched the Black. Panic was death. He recognized the pain in his skull, greeted the sensation as one he'd hoped never to feel again.

"You've got a lot of nerve crawling up out of Hell in me backyard, whoever you are," he told the demon.

"Always a kind word for your friends, Jack," the demon purred, and Jack felt his admittedly ill-used heart give a jump against his bones. The voice, the voice that came out of the haze in his head, through the memory of blood gone cold against skin, and of broken bones that pressed against nerve.

The voice. When Jack dreamed of the deed, he dreamed of the voice. The voice that whispered secrets, terrible secrets into his ear, and called him . . .

"Jack," the demon said again, running black-painted nails over a black silk tie. Its shirt was white, too white for the real London, its suit coal, eyes and hair to match. In them an ember burned, the flicker of visible power Jack recognized from his own eyes. The demon's were crimson with corruption, like oil fire floating on a darkened sea.

"Jack," the demon said a third time, because it knew the power of names and of triads, had taught them to the first member of the *Fiach Dubh* a thousand years past. It drew its bloodied lips back over twin, pointed front teeth. "Don't say you're surprised to see me."

Chapter Four

For all he prided himself on quick reflexes and quicker wits, Jack froze. He froze like a man caught out, with his sins on display like scars.

"You thought we wouldn't meet, on the eve of the deed?" the demon questioned. He took a step toward Jack, his gait gliding as if he moved on a snake's belly. Jack felt his heartbeat slow, his blood thump through his ears like the bass on stage during one of his sets with the Poor Dead Bastards, back in the bad old days. The edges of the world smoothed out, and he felt a cold, empty well open up behind his eyes.

"It's been thirteen years for you, Jack Winter," the demon said. Its tongue flicked its lips, crimson like it had just been dipped in blood. "Or nearly so."

Jack didn't allow himself the luxury of more than a few seconds of shock. That was all you got, and then the bastards ripped your spine out because you'd stood there catching flies, insensible with fear.

He dug deep, grabbed a great handful of magic, and flung it outward, toward the demon.

The protection hex came to life in a flare of blue witchfire, the excess energy curling around Jack's hands like tongues of flame around a tree branch. The air between the demon and himself rippled as the hex took hold. It wasn't elegant and it wasn't solid, but it was strong and rolled over the demon like a wave on rock.

The demon shook its head as if it had been caught up in a nest of cobwebs, and gave Jack a reproachful frown. "Still the same old Jack, jumping at shadows." It glided forward again, like the snap of a camera lens—one heartbeat, one flicker of movement, and the demon was close enough to embrace him. Jack felt its thick, smoky aura brush up against his hex, heavy and dense. It was a fiftyfifty shot as to whether the hex would hold. Jack was mortal, and the demon was a creature of Hell. A thing made of magic against a bag of flesh with an unusual talent. This was usually the bit where the mage died horribly.

"If I didn't know you so well, Jackie, I'd feel insulted," the demon said. It smoothed a hand over its tie. The veins under the flesh stood out black as roads on a map. "But I do know you, boy. Paranoid as a schizophrenic on the corner. Impotent as a rapist with a bird who fights back."

The demon chuckled to itself, and Jack found his voice. "I have time."

"Ah, true," the demon purred. "But how much? Have you counted? Have you marked a thick black X across the remaining days?"

"I have time," Jack repeated. "And you and I have no business before that day. Threaten me again and you'll find exactly how unpleasant I can be when some sulfur-scented bastard comes onto me home turf."

"Your better half appears absent," said the demon. "You won't be able to do to me as you did to poor, foolish Talshebeth." It sucked on its teeth, whistling against the air. "Pity, that is. Rumor has it she's soft, supple, and willing. That true, Winter?"

Jack knew that the demon was toying with him, down in the hard and rational part of himself that kept him from getting into fights he couldn't win over exactly this—a girl, an insult, or a petty threat. The demon was only exacting torment for Jack and Pete's banishment of its mate, Talshebeth. Jack had called the demon of lost things to find a little girl who'd been stolen by the hungry ghost of Algernon Treadwell. Treadwell hadn't taken kindly to this, and Talshebeth had tried to make Jack into a meal when their arrangement went pear shaped.

Jack knew this, but the witchfire around his hands flared and the hex vibrated like it had been struck. Black rage boiled up, filling the space between the demon and Jack, hot and throbbing on his skin like he'd hit a brick wall at full speed. The rage chased away rationality, and Jack started talking before he fully knew the words. "You don't fucking speak about her. I'll peel your skin off, roll it up, and shove it down your fucking throat, you cunt."

Twin flames in its eyes dancing, the demon laughed again. Jack felt his hex waver as his rage warred with his concentration. His own arse was one thing, but Pete . . . enough of the Black already wanted the both of them on spikes. The demon would not touch Pete while Jack was drawing down air.

"Jack?" She appeared at the end of the alley like he'd summoned her, a plastic Tesco sack dangling from her hand. "Who are you talking to?"

He whipped back toward the demon, and found only empty air wavering beyond his protection hex. Jack let out his breath and massaged the center of his forehead. "No one, luv. Just no one."

Pete raised one eyebrow in a dainty, disbelieving arch. "So you just decided to hex the alley for the fun of it, then?"

"What sort of tea did you get?" Jack slipped the new subject in like he'd dip into an unwary pocket for a wallet.

Pete favored him with a look that said she wasn't put off in the least by his bullshit. "Cranberry sandwiches, and I popped by the off-license for some good Belgian lager. Thought we both deserved a treat after that wretched scene at the Pooles'."

"I've half a mind to go back and curse that woman so her ugly teeth fall out," Jack said, glad she'd let the matter drop where it was. Pete couldn't know about the demon. Not yet, at least. If Jack failed at great swaths of life, he could at least keep a fucking secret. It was a point of mage pride—the good ones became paranoid bastards in short order, so that no one learned their tricks.

"Mm-hmm," Pete said. They walked into the stairwell of Jack's flat. "And wouldn't that be brilliant for business, what little of it we have."

"Oi," Jack said, slinging his arm over her shoulders. "It was your *brilliant* idea that we become a bloody ITV special made flesh, so don't give me any of your sass."

Pete favored him with a half smile. "However much you complain, Jack, us exorcising spirits and raising the same put this tea on the table, and if you've got a better solution for both of us being skint broke and nigh unemployable, I'd love to hear it."

"No dice, Petunia," he said. "Everyone knows you're the brains of this little operation." They mounted the narrow stairs, the tread shifting under Jack's weight. The lift was unreliable at best and Jack preferred the narrow, dim stairway even with lifelong smoker's lungs. The lift was closed, gated, trapped. If an entity manifested, he'd have nowhere to go, no recourse to banish it, trapped within four walls of iron.

Living with the sight taught you quickly and with great finality what sorts of places to avoid if you expected to live to next week. At least, to live in the sorts of places that didn't have bars on the windows and serve Thorazine smoothies.

"Stop calling me Petunia," Pete said. She shrugged off his arm as they reached the second-floor landing. "And don't think I've forgotten about that display in the alley."

Jack finished the climb to his flat in silence and waited while Pete unlocked the door. "I told you, it weren't nothing." He could shrug off one incident as his own jumpiness now that only tenuous ink, flesh, and a pinch of magic held back his sight. He'd have to be more careful when the demon came back.

Because it was most definitely fucking *when*, not *if*.

Pete slammed the doors of the kitchen cabinets as she brought out plates, glasses, and napkins. "You have to talk to me sooner or later, Jack. Are you seeing things again? Have you been lying to me since we did the ink?"

"I'm not bothered by the sight," Jack said honestly. *Just bedeviled by a demon . . .*

Pete let out a small *humph*. "I was a copper. I know when you're lying to me, Jack Winter." She ripped the packaging off her sandwich and sat down, gesturing for him to join her.

What Jack really wanted was a smoke, needed it with every jangling nerve at the ends of his body, but he forced himself to sit at the dinette table across from Pete, open his tea, and take a bite. He consumed the sandwich in less time than he could have counted. Casting the hex had left him drained. It was a new sensation to be hungry—before, he just wandered the streets nerve-jangled and sleepless until he found a hit and a bed to take it in. His body was like a wrung sponge, magic soaking up his every reserve. And yet now, when he'd kicked, gained weight, and even had someone feeding him, the magic hurt more.

It was a problem, but not the one set to rip his head off at the moment, so Jack pushed it to the back of his mind.

"I'm not, luv," he said after he'd wiped away bits of Brie and cranberry with the back of his hand. "Lying to you. I swear it." He needed a shave, needed to sleep.

Needed a fix, needed it like a drowning man needs oxygen . . .

"All right," Pete said, lighting a cigarette and tapping ash onto her sandwich crust, "if you want to shut me out it's your own bloody funeral."

"Isn't that the bloody truth." Jack shoved the last of the sandwich into his mouth so he wouldn't have to look her in the eye. No magic let Pete detect untruths—just a life as a copper and a copper's daughter before it.

"If you feel like talking about it, I'll listen," she said at length, her cigarette growing a long crown of ash as she failed to draw on it.

Jack heard the need to keep pulling, keep interrogating in her voice, but Pete merely reached across the table and slid her hand over his, small and warm. "You know I would, about anything. The truth, heavens forfend. You haven't scared me off yet, Jack."

Jack shut his eyes, pulled his hand from under Pete's, and pushed back from the table. "I'm going to catch some kip," he told her. "Been a long day already."

Pete whipped her hand back to her side as if she'd only intended to brush away crumbs. "I'll leave you the washing up, then, since I got the tea."

"As long as you don't mind it taking place at some future date," Jack said, as he retreated to the flat's only bedroom. His and Pete's sleep was cyclical enough that one bed was all they needed, even if she hadn't agreed to share with him yet. Her last words were lost to the door slamming.

Jack leaned against the backside, an ancient Poor Dead Bastards poster crinkling against his head. He felt sick, the sandwich having its revenge on him, sight chipping in with a throb at the center of his forehead. His heart accelerated as he remembered the pop of the Black, the way the demon was just *there* with nary a warning whisper in his mind.

That could have meant he was dead. That was a serious problem for the longevity of Jack Winter, cock-up mage.

Sweat broke out along Jack's spine, his shoulders, all of the lines of his bones, and he grabbed for a fag, lit it with his finger with a savage snap, and inhaled so deeply that he started to choke.

He sat on the bed and lay back, setting the smoke in the ashtray, where a thin trail of blue curled toward the stained ceiling, yellow flakes of plaster hanging on like scales.

Pain in his head redoubled. His magic curled and howled inside his head, clawing for release, and perhaps it was a memory or perhaps it was a whisper, but again Jack heard and felt the wings of the crows, the inexorable wings and eyes of Death.

The memory of being cold, bloodless, immobile, with stone digging into his back and pain through every inch of him, hit Jack like a boot in the mouth. He pressed his hands over his face, breathing shallowly. It didn't help. Not one bit.

Jack banged open the bedroom door and made a beeline for the loo, dropping his head over the toilet and vomiting until his throat burned and his abdomen ached like he'd just taken a fist to the belly.

"Jack?" Pete's feet rumbled up beside him, her hands went to his neck, his shoulder, fingers grazing through the bleached and ragged edges of his hair. "Luv, are you all right?"

Gasping, Jack swiped his hand across his mouth. He should push Pete away, tell her there was nothing wrong with him past a bad sandwich. Should, and didn't. Story of his bloody life.

"I . . ." He looked up and caught sight of them in the mirror. Pete pressed her forehead against his temple, stroking the back of his neck. Jack's own eyes stared accusingly back at him even as he turned into her touch.

The demon had come back to him. Jack's thirteen years were nearly up.

Bent over the bog, he considered facts. It was as good a spot as any to do so. He owed the demon a demon's bargain, and when Pete found out the particulars she'd try to work him out of it. She was stubborn, and clever, and still thought that counted for more than it did in a place like the Black. She'd convince Jack he could find his way out of his entanglement, that Hell could be tricked, wheedled, or softened.

And because it was a creature of Hell, and cruel, the demon would end her without a second thought when Jack tried. Or take her as his very own curiosity, the *soft, supple, willing* Petunia Caldecott, with her talent that let her talk to the Black and to the worlds beyond, to the Land of the Dead and even Hell itself.

As Pete murmured in his ear, her breath warm and her hands cool, her presence bringing him equilibrium like he was the wheel and she was the spoke, Jack's own eyes in the mirror told him that Pete could never know the truth.

Chapter Five

Pounding on the front door of the flat broke the spell. Pete heaved a sigh. "Bollocks, if it's that neighbor brat from 402 again, I'm going to feed him his Transformer toys." She grabbed a rag, ran water over it, and placed it on the back of Jack's neck. "Stay put. Back in two ticks."

That was Pete, quick and commanding and certain. Never wavered, never doubted that she'd solve everything and set it right side up again.

Jack pressed his forehead against the rim of the toilet bowl. He'd been low when he was shooting junk, but never as low as this. His lies had been small lies, of survival, cowardice, or necessity. The black dog treading in his footprints had never mattered, because no one else had ever been in range of its jaws. And now, just when the dog was close enough that Jack could feel breath on his neck, it mattered. Pete was an innocent, someone who hadn't come to the Black willingly and borne the terrible price it exacted from anyone human. All the scars she bore were dream-scars, a set of nightmares about him and their time together, when she'd been barely sixteen. About the visitation of Algernon Treadwell and the hunger of Talshebeth, but the Black had left her relatively untouched. She was its child, a speaker for magic. She wasn't a citizen of its bleak, hungry streets and alleys on sufferance, like Jack.

Pete hadn't paid the price Jack and his brethren had, and she wasn't going to if he could still draw a breath into his useless lungs. Jack was skilled at lying to himself as he was to anyone else, but he admitted that Pete being here, being close enough for the demon to use against him, was his fault. Entirely his.

His stomach clenched again, but nothing came up. He was empty, hollowed out, ready to be filled by the demon's bargain.

But not yet. He had time. Enough time to put things right and to keep the one who'd pulled him from the Pit from harm. He owed a second debt, an unspoken one, to Pete. He owed her at least the decency of staying alive to teach her to survive the vagaries of a life with a talent. They'd barely begun. He couldn't leave yet.

"Pete," he called, standing up and slinging the cloth into the basin. No reply echoed from the front of the flat. "Pete!" he said again, padding into the narrow hallway. "Petunia, where've you gone to?"

She turned away from the flat's front door, beyond which Jack could see, standing, the sort of man who would have told Jack to *Find a job, you miserable cunt* when he was sleeping on the streets, shaking in the dead of winter and thirty pounds underweight. The visitor wore a black sport coat, black sweater, and soft heather trousers. His hair was trimmed over his ears, expensively, and his eyes were soft brown. A trustworthy soft, a grasping, sinking soft. Jack disliked him instantly.

"What sod's this, then?" he demanded, letting the full

burr of a Manchester childhood creep into his voice. Nothing like a reminder of factories, dirty hands, and steel boots to warn off a ponce at the door.

"Mr. Naughton," Pete said, shooting Jack her customary *Shut up afore I kill you* look, "this is my associate, Jack Winter. Please, come in."

Naughton smiled at Pete, and she smiled back. Jack felt his jaw twitch. He didn't get tetchy or jealous easily, because birds were the cause of nearly all of life's avoidable ills, but this was Pete, and she was giving the nonce her *real* smile, the one that curled up one side of her mouth more than the other, that spread into her eyes.

"Thank you, miss," Naughton said. He looked between Jack and Pete, feigning polite confusion. "It is *Miss* Caldecott?"

"You can call me Pete," she said. "Would you like a cuppa? We were just having tea."

Naughton nodded his assent and then stuck out his hand to Jack. "Nicholas Naughton, Mr. Winter."

Jack watched his eyes follow Pete's rear end, showcased in black denim as it was, into the kitchen, and shoved his hands into his pockets. "I don't shake hands," he explained. "Might get a look at something both you and me don't want eyes on."

It was a better class of rudeness than Jack's first impulse, which was to pull the smarmy git close and kick him in the balls.

But Pete'd rip his tackle off if Jack insinuated her honor needed defending, and so he settled for staring at Naughton until the other man backed up a step. And then another. Sweat worked in a fat drop down his neck, into the collar of his cashmere.

Staring was a vastly underrated talent to Jack's mind—fix a bloke with a dead man's stare, put the full force of your magic behind it, and watch him piss his pants for reasons even he can't entirely explain.

Naughton had practically climbed up into the crown molding of the front hall by the time Pete returned with tea. "Jack," she scolded, "at least offer him a place to sit down." She gestured at Naughton. "In the front room, please, sir. We can discuss your problem there."

"Call me Nicholas," he said, the charm crawling back into play like a rodent curling up in a warm place. He shot a glance back at Jack, who'd brought up the rear. Jack dropped him a wink, and put some power behind it. Nothing fancy, just nightmare fodder for the next few weeks. Eyes, fire, secret black places, perhaps a touch of the old Oedipal complex.

It was petty, but after the day he'd had, Jack felt he'd behaved with remarkable restraint.

Chapter Six

Naughton sat on the sofa and Pete took the armchair, leaving Jack to perch on the wide windowsill. He nudged it open and lit a cigarette to cover the taste of vomit in the back of his throat.

"I'll get to the point," Naughton said, fidgeting as he cast an eye at the peeling plaster and meager furniture. The only thing Jack spent any hard cash on was books, and they were in evidence, in multitude, where furniture and *objets d'art* should be. "My family home is experiencing some extremely . . . unusual phenomena, and I need it stopped."

" 'Unusual.' 'S a bit general—care to expand on that?" Pete said. She reached into the pile of books and papers on the end table and withdrew a pad and pen. Pete, for all her crispness, was as much a pack rat as Jack when it came to books and notes. If Jack were the sort of teacher who put store in memorizing spells and conjury by rote, he and Pete could have had a fine time ensconced in his library. Unfortunately, a book could never prepare one for the first sight of a ghost. Or a demon. Or hell, a ruddy *tanuki* with its bollocks swinging free. Jack knew more than one mage who'd pissed himself at the sight of the Black's citizens in flesh and blood. Or ichor. Or vapor.

Words couldn't prepare you for the embrace of magic. Only magic could do it, and sometimes a mind wasn't meant to see. Those who couldn't handle it lost their grip, became the screaming psychotics in state hospitals or gibbering madmen on street corners. The junkies with the needles and the hollowed-out eyes.

Naughton sighed, in the seat that should be Jack's, and took an irritable sip of his tea.

"I have to admit, this isn't what I expected when I came calling on a couple of ghost hunters."

Jack exhaled, flicking ash onto the fire escape. "What were you expecting, then? Foot rub to go along with your tea? Happy ending with the sandwiches and cakes?"

"*Jack*," Pete hissed at him, and then gave Naughton another one of the smiles that Jack knew were to be hoarded like treasures, but that Naughton lapped up as if they were his due. "You'll have to excuse my colleague."

"It's no matter," said Naughton, moving closer to her. "I've heard Jack Winter could help me, and you're just a pleasant surprise."

Pete cocked an eyebrow, and crossed her legs primly at the ankle. "What seems to be your problem, Mr. Naughton?"

"Please," he said. "It's Nicholas, or Nick."

"Nick, then," Pete said, tapping her pen irritably against her chin. "The question stands."

Jack pinched out the end of his smoke and disappeared it back into a pocket. "Here's how it works, Nicky boy," he told Naughton. "You give us your story of old Gran knocking about up in the attic, waking the baby and frightening the missus, we take care of the problem, if you're not just jerking us off, and you pay. If you *are* jerking us off, well . . ."

"What Mr. Winter is trying to say," Pete said, reaching over and whacking Jack on the knee with her notepad, "is that we take this seriously and we expect you to as well."

"My family owns a country home in the Dartmoor forest," Nick said. "It's always been a spooky, dank old place since my brother Danny and I would summer there as children, but lately . . ." He sighed. "It's not right there, Miss Caldecott. I live in the city home, taking care of Mother, and Danny . . . well. Danny was in charge of the estate."

Jack watched Nick Naughton's mask peel away in layers as he talked, the charm and the breeding and the manners stripping back to reveal something thin and desperate, the kind of deep fear that only people who had touched the Black and not understood it possessed. Naughton may be a ponce, but he wasn't lying.

Pete's pen scratched away, ever the Detective Inspector. "And you and your brother each witnessed phenomena at your estate?"

"Voices," Nick said quietly, as if he were relaying bad news. "Cold spots, writing on the wall, sooty handprints that appear and disappear. Laughing. Danny's always been the drinker, the odd party drug or two, so at first I thought he was getting worse. Then I saw and heard it—them—too."

"Right," Pete said, scratching notes absently along the margins of the pad. "This is how we conduct an investigation, Nick: we'll need access to your estate to do some research, and we discuss payment when we've determined what we're dealing with. Should you want us to proceed with an exorcism, or if more investigation is needed, payment is half up front and half when the case is . . . resolved. Plus a retainer now."

"And you might want to let your brother know we're coming," Jack said, "in case he wants to set up the bleeding walls and rattling chains in advance."

Pete mimed stabbing him with her pen, but Naughton didn't rise to the bait.

"There's no need of that," he said. "Danny hanged himself two weeks ago from the crossbeams in the attic. He's dead."

Chapter Seven

After Nick Naughton finally quit the flat, leaving behind a check for five hundred pounds and the key to his family's Dartmoor estate, Jack watched a crow land on the wires outside the flat block and stare at him with one black, reflective eye. *Psychopomps*, his treacherous rote memory recited. *Harbingers of death and war. Ushers to the Land of the Dead.* The crow preened its feathers and tucked its head down against its breast. It could ferry souls to the Bleak Gates, but now it was content to merely stare a hole through Jack.

It took Jack several seconds of glaring back at the crow to realize Pete was talking to him. "Sorry, luv. What's that?"

Pete took the check, folded it in precise quarters, and slipped it into her hip pocket. "I said, what do you think?"

Jack shook his head. "Dodgy, at best. Ghosts don't just cause a bloke to hang himself for no good reason. They don't stir up like a mixed drink after a hundred years of silence, either. Personally, I'd give Sir Ponce his check back and tell him to sod off."

"Personally, would you happen to take exception to Naughton being a wealthy and attractive man?" Pete inquired.

"I take exception to liars," Jack said. "Rich, poor, fuck-ugly, or otherwise." Although really, today Jack and Naughton were just alike. Minus the fuck-ugly bit on Jack's part.

Pete came over and put her hands on Jack's shoulders. "I'm not an idiot, you know," she said. Her touch was cool, vibrating with power, not altogether unpleasant. Jack had a flash of second sight, of lips crushed against his and pale, pale skin turning rosy under his hands.

He shifted so Pete wouldn't see his face or any other traitorous part of him. "I know that, Petunia," he said softly.

"Then tell me what the bloody hell is wrong with you. You're pale as a ghost, you're puking in the loo, you're surly to a paying client—surly for *you*, and that's saying something, and now you don't want a job you would have jumped on with a rugby tackle a few weeks ago." Her mouth lifted at one side. "You're Jack fucking Winter. You chase the monsters, not vice versa."

Jack felt Death's specter following him patiently, ticking off the seconds on the gears that unfurled the Bleak Gates to allow a new soul through. Jack would stop the clock as long as he could, had to, even if it meant becoming ten times worse a liar than Naughton.

"Nothing's wrong, Pete," he said, making sure not to look her directly in the eye, nor look away. The stare of Truth, practiced over a hundred arrests and a hundred more dodgy meetings with mages and Fae in the Black. "Tea was past its date, or I could be catching the flu—as for Naughton, I think he's a sanctimonious cunt and nothing more. There's no monsters in his mansion. Bats in the belfry, maybe. You know how the landed gentry love their inbreeding."

Pete rolled her eyes and went on tiptoe to brush her lips

across his forehead. "He's giving us five hundred quid to go chase his bats, so speak for yourself, but I'm packing up and heading to Dartmoor tomorrow. Just as soon as I check with my friend in the murder squad about Danny Naughton."

Jack lifted one shoulder. The money was the thing—he was flat broke and Pete's savings were what you'd expect from an ex-civil servant. If he wanted to keep his new-found habit of eating, Nancy Naughton was his meal ticket. He'd just have to deal with the demon afterward. And Pete would need the money, if he was gone . . .

Not if, the fix whispered. *When, Jack. When.*

"Guess there's no harm in it," he said. Famous last words. *No harm in it.* How many disasters had he preceded with just those words?

"And you *were* the one whingeing about parlor tricks and useless jobs," Pete said. "This might be real. Think of that. A real spook-house instead of this inheritance and last wishes tripe, which, I admit, gets on my last nerve as much as yours."

"Bloody Algernon Treadwell all over again," Jack muttered, rubbing at the center of his forehead. The pain had retreated a little, but only a little.

Pete sobered immediately.

"I didn't mean it like that. Jack, I don't blame . . ."

He held up his hand to stop her. "Go cash the check before Duke Nancy changes his mind. I'll round up a few exorcism tools from Lawrence while you check with CID."

Pete nodded her assent and backed out of the room too quickly. She grabbed her bag and her jumper, and a moment later the door slammed. She was fleeing a discussion of Algernon Treadwell and her ghost sickness, and Jack didn't blame her in the slightest.

He went to the kitchen, fishing in the cramped cabinets

for a bottle of vinegar. Pete wouldn't allow hard liquor in the flat since she'd moved in. All roads led to the fix.

Jack personally thought it was bloody stupid—he'd been a junkie, not an alcoholic, and right now he'd murder a pint of anything. But he washed his mouth out and pulled on his leather to go visit Lawrence in Bayswater Road. He thought walking to the tube station might shake the breath of the demon off his neck, but he saw the blank-eyed face in every passerby and felt the inexorable tide of the Black stronger than ever under the dark heartbeat of Whitechapel.

He walked through the street market outside the Whitechapel tube station, hunched old women in saris picking over fruit, men in long caftans shouting in three different languages, competing with the white newsagent bleating about the latest footballer scandal and the music drifting out from the kebab shops and money changer's.

A breath of hot wind on his face, a whisper of sand, and Jack turned his head to see a man in a stall selling knock-off handbags stare back at him with flaming eyes, his skin flowing from brown to burnished gold. "Have a care, crow-mage," he said. "They've been here. Searching for you."

Jack blinked as a pair of Japanese tourists who'd undoubtedly gotten off at entirely the wrong stop on their way to the British Museum jostled past him, and when he could see again the djinn was gone, just a swirl of gold dust dislodged into the gutter and flung asunder by a passing lorry.

"Well," Jack said to no one in the cacophony outside the tube station, "bollocks."

Chapter Eight

He felt eyes on him the entire way to Bayswater. You didn't have to walk up to a bloke and knock him one in the teeth to make him feel uncomfortable. Jack knew there were things in the train tunnels, things that liked the dark, that waited and watched for the scraps and leavings of humanity to fall down to them.

He knew that if they were hungry enough, sometimes they wouldn't wait at all. The older the tube stations got, the more he sweated inside his jacket. At one time—too long ago to be anything but a middle-aged sot and his nostalgia—the pyramid spikes and patches and hand-painted slogans had been his armor, a clear warning to anything even half-human that he wasn't to be fucked with. He wore the boots, the leather, and the black hair bleached startling blond everywhere but the roots still, but the hungry things were older and wiser, too, and they saw behind his mask.

Jack just felt older in that moment, and wrung out. He hated being underground. It reminded him too much of when he'd taken peyote on his single trip to the United

States, when he'd seen the Bleak Gates, stood in front of them and felt the terrible weight of the dead on his inner mind, his mage's mind, and knew that his sight and his magic were linked in a way that wasn't normal or natural, even for the Black. Hated being underground. Too close to the dead for comfort, entirely.

Baker Street passed, and he caught a skittering on the train roof over the clatter of the track, small nails and paws, and the hiss of tongues that couldn't form words any human ear understood.

Jack closed his hand around the flick-knife in his pocket, closed his mind around a protection hex, waited.

The next station passed, tunnels growing newer and shallower, and the whispers retreated. They hadn't been hungry enough, in broad daylight, but they'd known he was there and that was bad enough.

"Fucking demons," Jack muttered aloud, garnering a look from the girl in the nearest seat. She was holding a guidebook, her thumb loosely marking her page, and had short red hair and large eyes, like a fey creature. A bit of blood, long ago, Jack thought, when her family still lived in the Isles. "Where are you going, then?" he asked her.

"Tower Bridge," she said. "Meeting my friend." Her accent was American, the rounded vowels of the Midwest. Jack had never seen a place so flat, or so devoid of decent drugs.

"You want the next, then," he said out loud. "Change to the Circle Line and it'll take you straight over."

"Thanks!" the girl said brightly, tucking her guidebook into her canvas bag. "You take care."

Jack watched her long legs and shapely back end exit the car, and felt only the barest interest. Americans were like fish in a barrel, and he wasn't even going after her to find out why she'd come to the UK, where she was staying, if she had a boyfriend and whether she was open to experimenting with a bloke who could say *bloody hell, football* and *fancy a shag?* authentically.

It wasn't like he was married to Pete.

Jack swapped for the District Line, pressed up against the window amid a gaggle of be-knapsacked Germans.

It wasn't like he'd done *anything* to Pete, except a single kiss, sitting on the edge of a swamp in Blackpool. A fine kiss, to be sure, probably one of the best since he'd still been new enough at it to find them all fine, but still. There was no ribbon around their hands. And Pete had made it crystal clear that she wasn't keen to pick up her old flirtation with a middle-aged junkie ex-boyfriend, which Jack wouldn't blame her for even if he could and not be a great bloody hypocrite.

It wasn't Pete, he argued. The old days of the chase, the hunt, and the parade of women were just that—old. He wasn't that Jack Winter any longer. The demon and the smack had made sure of that.

The tube doors slid shut with a sigh and a breath of coal-scented air, and the train moved on.

Everything and everyone in the Black knew what happened when a debt to Hell went unpaid, and they knew better what happened when the debtor tried to be clever and weasel out in any of the usual ways. Jack could try to be a clever boy, but it would be a try and nothing else.

Clever boys' bodies ended up in gutters. Their souls ended up on trial before the three ruling demons of Hell for breaking a bond as sacred as any church vow. No one who owed a demon a bargain was stupid enough to risk it.

But Jack still got off the train at Queensway and walked to Lawrence's flat, taking comfort in the crush of tourists and foreigners working the cheap souvenir shops and chain restaurants, and in the smell of sweat, smoke, diesel fumes, and humans. The feeling of being watched retreated, but only a little. Jack had to get out of London before someone or -thing decided to speed his bargain along to the main event by putting claws or a bullet in his back.

Jack guessed that Nancy Naughton had been good for something, after all.

Chapter Eight

Lawrence folded his arms when he answered Jack's knock, eyes glittering hard as gems. "Jack Winter, why you always bringin' trouble to my door?"

Jack took a step back, out of choking distance. "I've only just bloody gotten here, Lawrence. Give me a few minutes to work up a proper trouble for you."

Lawrence's face broke into a grin. "Come you in, Jack. Always did like to take the piss from you, old devil."

"No such thing," Jack said, returning the smile, not meaning it. Lawrence stepped aside and let Jack in. There were no protection hexes in his flat, none of the dove-gray magic Jack trafficked in. Lawrence's hearth magic enfolded his flat, created a glimmering wall of power that ugly and hungry things in the Black could never claw through. Being a white witch did have its rewards.

Jack shut the door after himself while Lawrence went to take the needle off his record. Jack stood in the center of Lawrence's smothered living room, rugs and books and hunched furniture giving the place the air of a fussy old woman, not a six-foot-odd Rastafarian.

"You be wanting a beer?" Lawrence said, shuffling into his pocket-sized kitchen and rooting in the icebox.

Jack grinned. "Is the Pope a skin-changing incubus?"

Lawrence tossed him a bottle of Newcastle. Jack unscrewed the top with the tail of his shirt and sank into Lawrence's armchair, downing the beer faster than was strictly gentle to his empty stomach.

"So tell me, Jack Winter, what trouble be vexing you this fine day?" Lawrence opened his own bottle and changed the record. Soft strains of Al Green floated through the thick air of the flat, scented with incense and high-quality marijuana. Jack grimaced around his mouthful of ale.

"You trying to calm me down, Lawrence? Keep me from doing something foolish?" Lawrence's spell was subtle, smell, sound, and tactile sensation, but it was there, pressing on him gently as a helping hand.

"Anyone got eyes can see you wound up tight, boy," Lawrence said calmly. "You clean now, I can't offer you a toke, so I'm doing you the favor. Be gracious, now."

"Trust me, you're the only bastard who cares about that," Jack said. "The cleanliness or lack thereof of my bloodstream." He rubbed his chin. He still needed the shave. "I may be fucked, Lawrence." The spell made it easy to talk, a safe sound booth with the world locked out.

Lawrence rolled his bottle in his hands. "Wouldn't be him first time, being fucked."

"Not this way," Jack muttered darkly. "Not this hard."

"True?" Lawrence said. "Tell me."

Jack sighed. Lawrence was a stand-up white witch, and he operated strictly on the daylit side of the Black. Jack might well get himself punched in the balls and thrown out of the flat when he told Lawrence his problem. Hearth witches didn't deal with demons. In the bad times, the bloody times, they'd hunted those who did by the side of the witchfinders. Jack rolled his bottle across the back of his neck. The flat was close and too warm, smothering him all at once. That had been war. This was Lawrence. Lawrence had to at least hear him out. Jack hoped.

"What would you say if I told you I owed a very bad bloke?" he asked Lawrence. "The kind who doesn't fuck about."

Lawrence lifted one shoulder. "How bad we talking, mate?"

"Peel the skin off of adorable household pets in front of your kiddies, bad," Jack said. "And not patient, and not kind."

Lawrence nodded once, slowly. "Bad, yes. That is. Three times bad for you, Jack Winter."

"He's put the word on the infernal wires," Jack said. "So I can't even try to reason with . . . him." Demons favored certain bodies, but Jack had never known one with a definite set of gear. "I've got my bloody foot clamped right in a bear trap," he told Lawrence, "and I can't see my way to chewing it off."

Lawrence set his beer down, pressed his hands together like he was in church. He didn't look at Jack until he finally asked, "How much time you got?"

"Some," Jack said. "Not enough."

"Let's Stay Together" ended and the record hissed softly in the space between music.

"I had ideas, mind," Lawrence said. "You got a duppy on you back, Jack Winter, sure as any man I ever met. I seen the hints, little things you say and do."

"Like go shambling around London stoned to me gills?" Jack quirked a grin, an entirely fake one. Lawrence didn't return it.

The telephone buzzed from under a pile of Aramaic scrolls, and on the third ring Lawrence stirred himself and plucked the old rotary handset from the mess. "Hail."

After a moment he passed the set to Jack. "It's your woman."

"She's not my anything," Jack said. "Oi, Pete."

Pete's voice came from far away, down a well full of other souls. In the background Jack heard the cool female robot of the Underground announce, *"This is a Hammersmith & City Line to Hammersmith."*

"I spoke with Inspector Patel at New Scotland Yard," Pete said. A bus horn blatted in the background as she ascended from tube sounds to traffic sounds.

"Where are you?" Jack said, tucking the phone under his chin.

"Paddington," Pete said. "Just fetching a bite before I go home. It was a suicide, Jack. The local coppers cleared it last week."

"Doesn't mean a ghost," he insisted. "Sometimes a hanging is just a hanging."

Pete huffed. "Fine. Do you want to give back the five hundred quid, or should I?"

"It's a questionable job, Pete, and I'm not bounding over the Moor like sodding Heathcliff on some nonce's say-so," he said.

Lawrence shook his head, drawing a finger across his throat. Jack threw him the bird while Pete muttered something on the line. It might have been "Tosser."

"Meet me at the station and we'll go home, then," she snapped. "Since you know bloody everything today."

The phone gave a pathetic click when she rang off, and Jack hung up the set.

"You a braver man than I," Lawrence said, chuckling. "I spoke to my lady so, she'd cut me head off and put it in a flowerpot."

"It ain't like that," Jack said, irritation crawling all over him like a swarm of ants.

"She could be right." Lawrence fixed Jack with a hard

stare. "The Smoke be no place for you until this is settled. Too many eyes watchin', too many tongues waggin'. Country air clears the mind. Even inside your thick skull."

"Bugger off," Jack muttered. "You want to be my mum, put on an apron and fix me a meat pie."

Lawrence stood and went to the door, flipping the bolt and opening it enough for someone skinny as Jack to slip out. "I have sympathy for what you done, Jack. But now the truth be known, I can't be your sanctuary."

Jack stood. He didn't feel angry or betrayed, or any of the things you were supposed to feel when one friend of only a few turned his back on you. In a lifetime of doors slamming in his face, the novelty wore off quickly. The stone in his chest just grew a bit heavier. "Thanks for not turning me in, at any rate."

"I am a worthy witch," Lawrence growled. "I bow to no demon's order."

"In a few months we'll have a pint and a laugh about this," Jack promised, stepping into the hallway. The Black rushed back, flowing around Lawrence's flat like water around a bridge piling in the Thames.

"Jack." Lawrence bowed his head. "You know you don't go making promises you can't keep. How bad is it?"

"I bargained for my life," Jack said shortly. "And a life is what I owe it. It's bad business, Lawrence. Bad all around, up, down, and sideways. But don't worry your pretty head." Jack dropped Lawrence a wink. "I'll get it sorted. I'm still planning on being here at thirteen years and a day."

"Don't you take up no fortune-telling, boy," Lawrence said. "The future, she not your strong point."

Chapter Nine

The rain had started when Jack's boots hit the pavement, the thin miserable midwinter rain that foreigners thought of when they thought of England. Jack hunched inside his leather, and felt ice slide down his shoulders into the curve of his spine.

He wound through side streets like a maze rat until the porticoes of Paddington loomed up, and the rain finally ceased.

Pete waited beside a ticket machine near the National Rail tracks, under the grimy iron braces and the blackened ceiling of the station's top floor. Being inside Paddington was like being inside a giant lung, black and tarred over from decades of smoke and the resultant soot.

Pete stood still and watchful in the way that only coppers and psychopaths excelled at. Hands in pockets, head thrown back to give the appearance of indifference, eyes unblinking and sharp as they skipped from the kiosks selling pastries and noodles to the groups of anxious foreign travelers gathered under the bank of National Rail schedule boards to the heavily peroxided Londoner stuffed like an anemic sausage into her slim dungarees, designer boots, and fur jacket.

"It was *awful,* just *awful,*" the woman intoned into her mobile. "Not a proper vodka tonic anywhere in the hotel. That's bloody France for you."

Jack considered taking a dip inside her handbag, one of those enormous blue sharkskin types that a family of refugees could live inside comfortably for some months, but gave it up in favor of watching Pete.

She hadn't seen him yet. One small hand went to her neck, worked the kinks free. Pete's old gig with the Met had made her a hand at blending, but in recent weeks she'd scuttled her wool pea coat for the canvas army jacket and had begun wearing her hair down instead of in a practical knot at the back of her skull. Little touches—pink lip gloss rather than plain, black nails like the very first time Jack had seen her, a dozen years ago at an underground club in Soho.

Not a dozen. Nearly thirteen. The weight of the demon's smile washed away the odd sort of calm Pete carried with her. She had the demeanor of a battlefield nurse, unyielding but a comfort nonetheless simply because she'd ventured into the corpses and laid a hand against your cheek.

She's too good for the likes of you, the fix whispered. *Come with me, luv. I'll never tell you no.*

The pressure of a rotten and magic-riddled day built up behind Jack's eyes. At least Paddington was so crushed with life and strapped with iron that the sight was silent.

He took a step forward, raised a hand. "Pete."

The woman with the mobile smacked into him, shoulder to shoulder. Hers was even bonier than Jack's.

"Watch *out,*" she snarled. "I've a mind to call the policeman over here, you."

"Eat a curry, luv, and cheer up," Jack returned. "Unless you're keeping so slim because your bloke fancies a bit of necrophilia."

"Cretin!" the woman snapped, and stomped away, boot heels clacking like bones on the station's tile floor.

"I think she likes you," Pete said. "The two of you could share bleaching tips."

"Sod off," Jack said, and Pete rewarded him by smiling. No Naughton, this time. Just him.

The secret of the demon grew larger and sharper, pushing on Jack's heart and his guts.

"What is it?" Pete said. "You look peaked."

"Nothing," Jack said. "Just fancy a fag, is all."

"Can it wait?" Pete worried the zip on her jacket. "We should get to driving if we want to make Naughton's by midnight."

"'Course." Jack shrugged. He could do apathetic, do it well. He'd been a punk frontman, after all.

Pete slipped her arm through his and her sudden proximity, her smell of clean linen shampoo and perfume and a little sweat, nearly made him stagger. He rolled his eyes upward in an effort to stave off a word, or a touch, or fuck it, a thought that would betray him as nowhere near cool and in control, the diametric opposite of what Pete and the world at large thought him. He was nearly forty—he shouldn't be fainting at a girl's touch. But the problem came again: it wasn't a girl. It was Pete.

When Jack opened his eyes, the crow sat on the crossbeams of the station roof, and flicked its beak behind Jack as if to say, *Watch your arse, old son.*

In the same moment, his sight flared, like someone had put a pipe across the back of his skull.

Jack spun back the way he'd come, so quickly that he dragged Pete around in a drunken dance with him.

Two figures moved through the crowd disgorged from a Bristol train, two men in workman's coveralls when he looked straight on, and emaciated forms with black, bleeding holes for eyes when he blinked.

Jack skidded to a stop, Pete stumbling against him. "Fuck."

Pete's eyes widened. "What is it? What's happened?"

"Those two." Jack jerked his chin. The figures passed by and through travelers, and where they touched, faces fell and eyes narrowed in anger. Travelers shoved. Babies shrieked. A woman in a green wool coat slapped her lover and ran off in the direction of the loo, sobbing.

"Yeah?" Pete let go of him, dropping her shoulders and curling her fists, like a small but determined bulldog. Jack had witnessed her drop men twice her size, but these were not men. The cold encroachment of their energy prickled the hair on his arms, made the ink in his tattoos dance, made the Black spin in front of his eyes as his sight screamed to show him the true faces of the things before him.

"Sluagh," he said.

"Gesundheit?" Pete said hopefully. Jack shook his head. An entry from one of Seth McBride's diaries swam up into his mind. *Sluagh. Restless spirits.*

Seth may have been a wanker, the bastard child of con man, mage, and roaring Irish drunk, but he knew ghosts, knew them better than any man besides Jack himself. He'd taught Jack enough to stay alive for another nineteen-odd years, at least.

"The restless dead," Jack said aloud. "Sent away from the Bleak Gates to trouble the living."

The twinned ghosts opened their mouths in a single, silent scream, and in unison raised arms of dessicated flesh and bone tipped with black nails that curled over with graveyard growth. They pointed at Jack, eyes and teeth spilling black pollution across the psychic space of Paddington.

"I gather they're not here to have a pint and a laugh?" Pete said.

"No," Jack said. "The sluagh appear at the moment of a person's death." He turned in a slow circle, watching more and more of the silent, howling, and pointing figures appear in the crowd. "And they always travel in packs."

"They're here for you?" Pete snugged close against his side, their arms touching along the length. She wasn't asking him the question except as a courtesy, and Jack was relieved he didn't have to answer. As a mage, whatever horrid thing crawled from under a rock was most likely there for you and your skin, and Pete had at least learned that much.

Jack watched the sluagh by turns, counted them, felt the chill abrasion of the dead against his sight.

They advanced, in flickers and slithers, leaving a black trail across the floor of Paddington. Cold stole across Jack's cheeks and burned his lungs, and the sluagh watched, pointed, marked him as the death they'd come to claim.

"Jack!" He became aware of Pete shouting, in a harsh whisper to avoid passersby noticing her panic. Still tight against him, like they were twins sharing a heart. "Shield hex?" she mouthed.

The sluagh were close enough to touch now, if he'd been a madman with a death wish. "No," Jack said tightly. "No bloody good." The dead were not tempered or repelled by living magic. Unwanted, the memory of Algernon Treadwell and his overweening hunger came to Jack, borne on the cold air ruffled by the passage of the sluagh.

Don't just stand there like a knob. Not the fix, now. A little of Seth, a little of Pete, a little of his own survival instinct, battered and bloodied as it was.

Only blood could sate a spirit, and only dead blood could sate the sluagh.

Jack snatched Pete's hand, and the jolt of her magic, the sight, and his own talent nearly unbalanced him again. "Run," he ordered. "Run and don't look back."

With his free hand, he fumbled in his pocket and pulled forth his flick knife. The blade popped, a gleam of quicksilver obscured by crimson as Jack turned the knife to slice through the back of his opposite hand.

Blood fell to the dirty, mud-crusted floor of the station. One drop, two, three.

"Go dtáthaí mé tú," Jack muttered, and the gray tendrils of the spell feebly sought out the sluagh. It wasn't enough, wasn't nearly enough. Jack needed more blood and more time to keep the dead away.

But it was *his* spell, the ghost box, his strongest magic. As the blood fell, Jack wove the cage of power and sight, holding the spirits back, keeping the dead at bay for just a little longer. The ghost box was the first spell he'd learned, the first, desperate magic that he'd tried when he wasn't sure that he wasn't simply succumbing to the same kind of delusion that made his mother talk to her plaster figurine of the Virgin Mary. Jack had first felt the Black enter him alone on the floor of a filthy, leaking squat on the outskirts of Manchester. He'd poxed it up, and was lucky he hadn't died then and there, but the ghost box, straight from a mouldering "ye olde chaos magicke" tome at the library, had held.

Jack hoped fervently, with a jump of nerves in his chest that hadn't happened in years, that it held now.

The sluagh drew back from the entanglement of blood magic, their silent mouths growing long, ghostly white teeth.

Jack ducked through a gap in their ranks and ran, towing Pete behind him. She hadn't obeyed his order to run, but he hadn't expected her to. Pete was too stubborn to run even for her own bloody good.

Jack took the stairs to the Underground lines two at a time, shoving passengers out of the way. He let go of Pete and vaulted the fare gates, a transit worker shouting at him, just a blur of blue and life next to the overwhelming, encroaching flock of sluagh.

Jack veered into the tunnel for the Bakerloo Line, his heart pulsating like to break his ribs. He had a moment of *This is it, you've blown your wad* as his vision blacked, and then he was on the platform and a train was roaring into the tunnel and Pete snatched his arm and kept him from going over the edge onto the tracks.

The doors sprang open, disgorging their human load, and Jack shoved his way inside.

"*Please stand clear of the doors,*" the robot announced. "*This is a Bakerloo Line train to Elephant and Castle.*"

Jack slumped against the train window as the car pulled out of the station. The sluagh stood on the platform in a cluster of nightmares, hollowed-out eyes following him until the train rounded a corner and they were lost to blackness and reflection.

"Too much iron," Jack rasped. The need for a fag was vicious, and had claws. "Even for them."

"What did they want with you?" Pete said. She rubbed her hands up and down her arms, palms making a soft hiss against the leather.

"Me dead, I suppose," Jack said. "''S the only thing sluagh ever want."

"Because they're restless?" Pete stepped to the door as the train pulled into the next station, at Edgeware Road. "Unfinished business or some bollocks?"

"Not likely," Jack said. "The restless dead are them too full of malice and hunger even for the Land of the Dead." Sluagh were wild spirits, feral dogs feeding on the souls and deaths of the living. Picking spectral bones, until there was nothing left.

They came into the day, out of the tunnels at last, and Jack breathed in a lungful of cold, damp air. It was nearly as good as nicotine. "They're hungry, plain and simple," he told Pete. "And they've been pointed at me to feed themselves."

"Maybe we should put off this job." Pete worried her bottom lip with her teeth. "I could tell Naughton something's come up."

Jack hunched inside his leather. The rain had ceased, but the thick iron clouds crouched overhead promised a proper storm when they'd finished massing. "No," he said. "We should take the fucking job."

Pete cocked one eyebrow, and Jack spread his hands in return. "We need it, yeah?"

The scene in Paddington had cemented his resolve to leave London until he could figure out what to do with the demon. Lawrence was right, as Lawrence often was—the Smoke wasn't his place now, not while he was marked so.

"Well, if you're so keen all of a sudden," Pete said, "the car's this way."

Chapter Ten

In Pete's Mini, with the window down, Jack let the air wash over him, keep him awake. Keep him from drifting. His fag flared as the wind caught it, trailing ash along the M5.

"You've barely said a word since we left," Pete said. "Long face for such a little person, my da would say."

Jack crinkled his nose. " 'M not little."

"Something's on your mind all the same," Pete replied. "What is it?"

"Not a thing, luv," Jack lied. Lying was easy when only your own reflection was staring back.

The Black rippled and churned as they drew farther and farther from the tangled and teeming knot of energies, ghosts, and monsters that was London. City of plague pits and cemeteries, of iron, smoke, and bells. All of it faded, like a radio station under the shadow of a hill.

"All right." Pete hit the flat of her hand against the wheel. "You don't want to talk to me, suit yourself. Don't come whingeing to me when your dark magely secrecy bites you in the arse, all right?"

"Believe me," Jack snapped, "You're the last person I'll be whingeing to."

"Good," Pete said, and turned the dial on the Mini's ancient stereo. "Good Times Bad Times" floated around Jack and closed him off in a wall of sound.

"Good," he agreed, unheard.

He'd had a 78 turntable when he was ten or twelve, from a jumble sale at the church his mum sometimes stumbled into. His Uncle Ned took it when no one wanted it, and gave it to Jack. No one wanted records, either—it was all bootleg Walkman tapes and CDs if you didn't live in the rotting council flats beside the church, as Jack did. Jack took custody of his mother's few albums that she hadn't pawned, and played them over and over until Kev, the pimp boyfriend and man of the house—as he never tired of telling Jack—took them out in the car park and smashed them.

Jack had owned albums since, master tapes for the Bastards, free CDs from friends with recording contracts, but he never forgot the hiss and scratch of the needle on the vinyl, the particular magic of wringing sound from a thin slice of nothing.

He touched his head to the now-cool glass of the Mini's window, looked into the depths of the passing darkness. Something loped beside the car, long and lean with teeth that caught the moonlight. Jack's skin went cold, needles and pins all over like it should have with the sluagh, in the station.

That wasn't his fault. Too much iron and distraction. A desire not to see or think about what waited for him making him careless. Didn't mean he was slipping loose from his power as the thirteen years came closer, that using magic was agony as his talent shut down and that even his sight was giving him up for dead.

The demon wasn't waiting. It would drag Jack to its side by any means. And Pete would be there when it came to collect him, and she'd know. She'd see his sins, count them by turns, and cast him out.

Or the demon would kill her, drain her, use her like Algernon Treadwell had tried to use her, the ancient and terrible talent of the Weirs and their line to the old gods a sweet too tempting to resist.

Jack slid a fingernail under the plaster on his cut, scratched. Wished for a fag. Looked over at Pete. She hid a yawn as the motorway unfurled in the Mini's headlamps.

"I could drive for a bit," he suggested. "Let you catch some kip."

"Jack, you haven't a license," Pete protested. "What was the last thing you drove?"

"A Maserati," Jack said. "For nearly six blocks."

Pete cocked her eyebrow. "*You* had a Maserati?"

"Nah, it belonged to some Italian bloke. Wasn't using it at the time."

Lefty Nottingham, the Bastards' roadie and later—much later—Jack's first smack connection, had bet him he wouldn't. He'd flashed the flat roll of foil, eyed the sports car idling at the curb like an eager beast, and rumbled in his smoker's *basso,* like the selfsame needle dropping onto a 78, "*Bet you wouldn't for a day's worth of hits, Winter.*"

The Maserati ended its life with a post box in the bonnet and Jack walked away with that flat roll of foil in his pocket. And a concussion, but that wasn't the sort of thing you worried over when there was half a gram of skag burning a hole in your denim.

Pete chuckled softly. "I'll take my chances, I think."

Jack put his head back against the rest, trying to drain the tension of Pete's company from his neck. He preferred birds he could compartmentalize. Friend, fuck, foe. Pete was a combination of all, or none. She wasn't easy, and the old Jack didn't like that. The present Jack just felt like a useless wanker for having to lie.

He didn't think he could sleep, but the draft of warm air from the heating vents, combined with blood loss and exhaustion, dropped him into a drowse.

He woke to Pete's shaking. She pointed out the windscreen and Jack saw black turrets, dead trees, and a slice of sky tarnished silver by moonlight.

"That's the place?" he said. "Christ, where's the lightning and the sinister albino butler?"

He put his hand on the door, and it was far as he got.

The Black shuddered and pulsed around the house, and Jack grabbed his head as a spike of pain split the front of his skull. The Black wasn't just around the house, it was in the house, a part of it as much as beams and mortar, a great swirling well of magic, dragging him under, dragging him to drowning . . .

"Jack!" A small cool hand slapped him across the face, and the sting was enough to quiet the scream of the void.

He'd fallen out of the car and onto damp gravel. The stones dug divots in the side of his face, and a finger-light mist kissed his eyelashes with droplets.

Pete helped him sit up, and when he looked at the house again it was perfectly silent, just a house surrounded by overgrown gardens and backed by the sweep of the moor. "Fucking hell," Jack muttered, brushing mud off his cheek.

"Everything all right?" Pete crouched down with hands on knees to examine his eyes and breathing, like they taught you in a first-aid course.

"Not sure." Jack shook himself, shrugging off the last vestiges of the Black. It slithered reluctantly back into the small, secret place inside his head where his talent resided, hissing as it coiled up and went back to sleep.

Pull yourself together, Winter, the fix whispered. *Until you can't any longer, and you come begging for a taste.*

"Fuck off," Jack grumbled. Pete cocked her head.

"Excuse me?"

"Not you," Jack said. He pulled his boots under him and climbed up to his feet. The maneuver took him several more steps than it had even five years ago. Jack decided creaky knees and a back permanently out of line from sleeping rough on squat floors were the least of his worries at the moment. He could be a vain sod when his head wasn't breaking apart like an egg. "Let's get on with this sorry endeavor and see what skeletons Naughton has rattling around his family manse."

Chapter Eleven

The interior of Nicholas Naughton's mansion was much like the exterior—grim, dusty, and unwelcoming. Pete hit the light inside the double front door, igniting exactly two bulbs in the fifty-lamp chandelier looking down on a marble entry so thick with dust even Pete's petite frame left footprints.

A grand stairway lead up to a landing of peeling wallpaper and rotting carpet, and two hallways trailed deeper into Naughton's residence like dark, clotted veins. The place smelled of rot and damp—cemetery smells, with the musical accompaniment of rats and bugs scuttling over the decaying bones in holes Jack couldn't see.

He took in the shrouded furniture, the third-rate landscapes hanging from the picture rails in the narrow front parlor, the stained walls and cracked mirrors that reflected jagged, mismatched Jacks back to his gaze. "This is what Danny Naughton lived with? Cross and crow, I'd hang meself within the week."

"Kitchen's this way, looks like," Pete said, flipping another switch. The lights along the hall flickered ominously. One bulb exploded in a blue cacophony of sparks.

"Not that I'm terribly keen to see the state of it," Jack said. Something slithered, fluttered, across the underside of his mind and then the mansion settled, went as quiet as a coffin.

A house shouldn't echo so silently in the unseen spaces. All things had a footprint in the Black. The Naughton manse was a void, a space into which you could fall and lose yourself.

"Jack." Pete waggled her fingers in front of his face, expression letting him know he'd gone to the vacant place like an addled teenager chewing on mushrooms. "You coming?"

"Yeah," Jack said, moving himself along. The fluctuations of energy around the house could be nothing special—or they could be why Danny Naughton had strung himself up. For a sensitive who didn't know his own power, such a place would be unbearable. That feeling, of your head too full and your heart pumping too hard, Jack knew firsthand. It whispered, *Come to me* like a siren on the rocks, searing the compulsion into a psychic's mind until the psychic would do anything to make it stop. Booze. Smack. Chisel to the forehead. Jack knew this firsthand, too.

He just hoped Pete wouldn't pry into it overmuch. Jack's head and his heart that still beat out of sequence after the shock in the drive weren't putting him in a confessional mood.

The kitchen was no better than the rest of the place—Jack wagered it was even worse than his own pre-war one burner/one kettle setup in Whitechapel. At least nothing furry was alive in his sink drain.

Pete wrinkled her nose at the mice scuttling around the baseboards and the mold blossoming everywhere else. "He might have had it cleaned before he sent us here. Jesus."

"Somehow I think Naughton is more the flashy type than the one to grab a mop, luv." Jack dropped the tattered kit he'd packed in a rush back at the flat on the kitchen table. He'd leave the discovery of every casting implement and important bit and bob he'd forgotten in his hurry until tomorrow. "I'm off to find a bed without anything residing in it."

"Best of luck," Pete said, hiding a yawn with the back of her hand.

"Tomorrow we'll take a proper look around," Jack said. "See if this wasn't all a laugh cooked up by Nancy Lad to make Danny Boy hang himself."

"Why would Naughton want his brother dead?" Pete sighed.

"That's your department, luv," he said. "I just exorcise the ghosts. Assuming there are actual spirits and not just bloody great rats in this place."

"I'll go pay respects to the local constabulary tomorrow," Pete said. "I saw a sign for Princetown back at the last fork. They'll have proper police to check on the Naughton's history and see if Nick lied to me."

"As if that'd be a bloody surprise," Jack said, more to himself than Pete. She rolled her eyes at the kitchen ceiling, stained with browned and mellowed continents of unknown origin.

"This possessive streak is becoming less and less attractive, Jack."

"Just looking out for you," he protested. Pete held up a hand.

"You made it clear after Blackpool we're not anything, Jack. So don't pretend this is for my benefit and not to make yourself feel bigger."

The silence ran long and thin, and Jack contemplated whether he should put his fist through the wall or merely break Naughton's tacky family china against it. He didn't have much pride, but he had enough to dislike it when attractive women called him on his shite. Jack discarded all of his arguments while his blood beat in his ears. Pete had heard them all at least once. Finally he decided it was simpler to change the subject entirely. Blackpool was months past, and seemed like an eternity. There was no point in standing under the storm it had stirred in him when he could be indoors.

"Princetown, you say?" Jack rubbed his chin. Had to do something about the beard before he started looking like a fucking hippie.

"That's what the sign read," Pete said, dropping her own luggage. She found and mounted the servants' stairs, which lead them to a back hall and a warren of rooms filled with boxes, naked dressmaker's dummies, and camp cots for the eponymous servants.

The bedrooms for the gentry were numerous and nearly as cluttered.

"Danny was a bit of a pack rat," Pete said.

"Crazier than a bowl of bar nuts, you mean," Jack said, as they encountered one room filled entirely with back issues of *Penthouse*, stacked neatly by year, and jar upon jar of kosher pickles, also arranged by year.

"That as well," Pete agreed. She found the master suite, a great oppressive four-poster dominating the scene like the set of a particularly dull vintage porno film. "This will do for me."

"And you're welcome to it," Jack said. Even the colors of the room, muted bloody purples and bruised blues, depressed him. "Don't let the ghosties bite."

"Jack." Pete put her hand on his arm. "Do you know someone in Princetown?"

"Why?" Jack said. "Jealous?"

"No, but when I said the name you reacted like someone had stuck a hat pin in your arse." Pete took her hand away. "You owe another gangster money?"

Jack blew out a breath. It was a fair question, and had it

been anyone besides Pete asking he might have shrugged, even made a joke of it. "That's all you think of me? Bad man with bad debts?" The words came out far harsher than he'd intended.

"I didn't mean . . . ," Pete said. Then her face set, hollowed out and as tired as his own must be. "Let's face facts, Jack. You've a lot of carnage in your wake and I like to know what I'm getting into when I'm with you."

"There's nothing sinister in Princetown," Jack snapped. "Just another lot of musty old ghosts, like this place." And because it was Pete and not anyone else, he felt compelled to twist the knife he'd landed. "You have sweet dreams, luv, since you're so bloody innocent."

Jack slammed the door on Pete's thin-lipped face and stomped down the grand staircase, wanting to break his fist on something vulnerable but settling for a smoke instead.

He stopped on the landing, breathed out, lit the fag, breathed in. Sweet, blessed nicotine. Every addict's pity fuck.

A shape shimmered in the broken mirror, over Jack's left shoulder. His own profile half obscured by smoke, he fixated on the spot, unsure if he'd even seen it.

Wasn't that every poxy haunting he'd ever seen on telly? Smoke, shadow, and no substance?

Jack exhaled at his reflection. The mirror sucked all the color out of its view, drained everything but his face down a black whirlpool.

"Come on then," Jack sneered. "No cameras. No whimpering psychics. Just you and me, a pair of mean old bastards."

Nothing moved beyond him in the glass. Jack shut his eyes and rubbed his temples. Mirrors were useful, but not this water-spotted mess. Old mirrors, made with silver, were what attracted spirits. New glass just served to spook over-tired mages.

Jack opened his eyes, resolved to have one more fag and then bed, when a pair of hands grabbed him by the shoulders and threw him down the stairs.

Chapter Twelve

He landed on his back, on the stone, and saw stars as all of his air escaped in a last, mocking puff of blue smoke.

Jack choked, unable to do anything except flop like a hooked mackerel while his mind screamed at him from the primal place of blood and birth to *Run, run you stupid cunt, get free before it kills you.*

He pushed the panic away, focused on his various bits, the quick mental check one developed after one had taken a few beatings. No lancing pain in his sides, his hands, or his legs, no bone scraping muscle anywhere, but he'd had the wind knocked out of him, properly.

"Jack?" Pete appeared at the top of the stairs, barefooted and barelegged, wearing a stretched Siouxsie shirt as a nightie. "Jack!" She took the steps two at a time, landing next to him on the cold floor, able fingers feeling his pulse and checking his pupils. "What happened? Did you black out? It's a miracle you're not gushing blood all across the floor." Her words blended together, skipped and flowed over one another like water over rocks and mingled with the current ringing in his skull.

Jack shut his eyes because it seemed a remarkably good plan. Enough beatings also taught that sometimes, you didn't want to get up. You just lay there and bled until the hurt passed and whoever had put you down in the first place lost interest.

The plan worked well, until Pete slapped him hard across the face. "The nearest hospital is thirty-five kilometers away and if you think I'm driving you there in my night things, you're bloody stoned."

Jack forced himself back to the surface of waking. Everything was quiet again. No shapes fluttered in the mirrors and no great howling morass cried to him across the Black. The Naughton mansion was, to his senses, dead as a doornail once more.

Pete laid the back of her hand on his forehead, cradling his skull on her knees. Her nightshirt was cut out in the collar and from his vantage Jack could see the top curves of her breasts, Snow White skin dusted with a helping of Black Irish freckles. He gave what he hoped was a sickly but courageous smile.

"That feels good, luv."

Pete followed his eyes and huffed. "Sit up, you wanker."

Jack did as he was told, with great reluctance on the part of his swimming vision and screaming muscles. Pete went and fetched her penlight from her kit, shining it in his eyes.

"Your pupils are the same size," Pete said. "Your head isn't bleeding badly. Just don't go to sleep for a few hours." She held out her hand and Jack let her pull him up. The Naughton's foyer swayed agreeably, like he'd chased the fag with some high-grade opium.

He held on to Pete. "I'm spent, luv." He brushed his thumb over the back of her knuckles. "Though you could always keep me awake."

"Fuck off." Pete gave him a gentle shove with her free hand.

Jack swapped his grip for her waist under the nightshirt, fingers slotting between Pete's ribs, pulling her flush against him. They were a good fit.

"'M not joking, Pete." The terrible thing was, he wasn't. If Pete had, in that moment, put her hands on him in return, Jack wouldn't have stopped himself.

Not for the demon, not because Pete was an innocent in matters of the Black. Jack knew one thing surely about himself and that was, he was rubbish against temptation. Pete was flame and he was paper, and if he touched her he'd burn. No question about the matter.

"Get some rest," Pete said softly. "I'm sure the ghosts will keep until morning."

Jack rubbed the back of his skull, where a lump roughly the size of the Isle of Man was rising. His back would be a mass of bruises by morning, if the ache along his shoulder blades was anything to go by. "Not this one," he said. "Pushy bastard. Quite literally."

Pete's brow wrinkled. "Will you be all right?"

Jack flashed her a grin. It was a cold comfort as she stepped away and adjusted the shirt to cover the flash and curve of skin on her exposed shoulder. "'Course. Go back to bed, darling. I'll sit up for a bit to make sure me brain stays inside its house."

Pete started up the stairs, and then turned back and went on tiptoe, planting a kiss on his bruised cheek.

Jack watched her go and then shut off the arthritic light and sat on the stairs in the dark, watching the ember of his last fag glow like a dying, faraway sun.

In a way, the poltergeist shoving him arse over teakettle had been a gift. It meant there was something in Naughton's house, something dead and full of screaming, clawing rage. The dead silence lied to him, just as he was lying to Pete. It hid the thing that crept and crawled in the Black, exposed itself and vanished again like a movie-screen phantom. The intermittent magic of the Naughton house was a puzzle, but it wasn't one that could distract him from exorcising a poltergeist. Poltergeists were solid, a good fight and good practice for exorcism. Plus, he could ratchet the charge into the stratosphere for that cunt Naughton, if only to make up for nearly turning his brain into pudding in the man's grand entry.

Jack exhaled and watched the smoke rise and curl its fingers around the air until it disappeared, his own small spirit that was soon vanquished.

The ghost meant he was needed, for at least a little longer. It meant the company of the dead, the only presence Jack had relied on since he was fourteen years old. He had its scent, and even though his sight was changeable and treacherous in this curious vortex of Black and nothing, Jack was going to run it to ground.

If nothing else, the ghost meant he wasn't alone.

Chapter Thirteen

Pete moved under him, her body arched against the iron shackles that held her wrists above her head, flush against the stone. The air tingled, chill, drops of dew collecting in the hollows of her clavicle, the planes of her stomach, crowning her nipples in crystal tears.

A ring of torches and a ring of watchers closed Jack and Pete inside surely as a lover's embrace. On the stone within a circle of stones, Jack touched her, put his mouth on her skin, tasted sweat and bitterness from the blue woad the women had painted on her, before she was brought to him, in the circle, on the stone, with the scent of rowan in the air.

Pete met his eyes, her slim pale thighs bruising under the pressure of his hands. Jack knew this place, in the primal sense memory of his magic, and from the same memory the ritual power curled around him, whispered what it wanted, begged him to close the circle.

Pete struggled as Jack moved her legs akimbo, gasped as he placed himself against her, warm wet burning him against the cold contrast of the stone.

Pete held his gaze, her own eyes wide and pooling. "Please. Please, Jack . . ."

The chanting crested, the power of the place with it, and Jack fell over the edge, into the swirling vortex of the Black . . .

The Mini's car horn cut through the fog of sleep, and Jack winced as light and sound hooked their claws in his consciousness and dragged him into the waking world.

He felt wrung out and stiff, hungover without the fuzzy memory or naked bird in his bed to make it at all worthwhile.

"Jack!" Pete shouted at him from mansion drive. "It's not a bloody hotel, so rouse yourself before noon, if it pleases you, and let's get this done!"

He stumbled to the window and saw Pete standing with her hand in the car window. She hit the horn again. Jack slid up the sash and stuck his head out.

"One fucking moment, Your Highness! Some of us don't roll from slumber ready for telly!"

"Hurry up!" Pete shouted. "I'm starving and the Naughtons hadn't any food."

"I'd be a deal faster if you'd stop blowing that fucking horn," Jack returned, and shut the window. He had aches in every part of his torso, a throbbing in his head, and a raging hard-on. A morning at some point in the distant past might have started off worse, but Jack couldn't think of it offhand.

He pulled on boots, dungarees, decided the undershirt he'd worn the day before—and the day before that—was still in service. He rooted through the drawers for something to keep out the cold.

The last occupant of the room had lived in the mansion during a time when lapels had sat wide enough to take flight and ties were made to blind oncoming pedestrians, but Jack found a flannel that smelled of stale tobacco and staler pot, shrugged his leather over it. Flick-knife, fags, lighter. The essential kit Jack Winter required to face the cold, cruel world.

Briefly, he debated asking for Pete's help with the hard-on, and decided it would only get him smacked in his already tender head.

"Jack!" More of the horn. "I'm not a taxi!"

Before he left, Jack risked a look into the bedroom mirror. Nothing stared back at him except his bruised reflection, and that was terrifying enough.

He limped down the stairs and out to Pete, collapsing into the Mini with a grateful sigh. Normally, he despised the little car that folded up his more than generous legs like he was inside a Christmas cracker, but today it was a chariot of the gods moving him toward caffeine and civilization.

"Sleep all right?" Pete said, once they were out of the drive and on a road that could have doubled as a ride at Euro Disney. In the daylight, hedgerows stripped of foliage bent over the car, scraping the Mini's paint job like bone fingers.

"Slept like the dead," Jack lied.

"I had terrible nightmares, myself," Pete said. Jack watched her profile as she downshifted to take them up a hill and around a hairpin turn, where the road narrowed from something chancy to drive to a route that should only be traversed by hobbits.

"Nothing like . . ." He winced as the wheels pitched them sideways into the ditch that grooved next to the road. "Nothing like the ghost dreams?"

"No," Pete said quietly. "Not like that. Cold eyes, mostly. Silver eyes, pairs and pairs of them just . . . staring. Not blinking. Like they were waiting."

Weirs like Pete could see the truth in dreams, and Jack

was gratified that her dream-sense, at least, also believed the mansion was bedeviled by a haunt.

"It wasn't anything like the things Treadwell made me see, but it was damn spooky," Pete continued. "So much cold, predatory attention . . ." She stomped on the brake pedal as a lorry materialized from around a bend. "*Fuck!*"

Jack ricocheted off the dash, which set his aches aflame anew. "How does anyone bloody *live* here without becoming a statistic?"

"They're fucking hermits, I suppose," Pete fumed, reversing until she found a pull-off to let the lorry by. "No wonder Heathcliff went mad."

After a time, during which Jack found himself gripping his seat in panic more than he'd ever admit to in public, they arrived in Princetown.

"There's the police station," Pete said. "I'll go introduce myself and you—" she looked Jack over. He looked at the trickle of morning shoppers in turn, most in windcheaters and wellington boots, checkered caps or overcoats. He stood out like a Sikh at a skinhead rally.

"I'll try not to set any fires," he promised.

Pete crossed the street and entered the small tan police headquarters. As soon as she was out of sight, Jack unfolded himself from the Mini's interior and lit a fag, leaning on the fender.

Princetown held a small market square, the usual compliment of pubs and a chip shop, the Jubilee and Memorial Railway Inn, which looked like a fine place to get yourself murdered in a cozy mystery on the BBC, and a tourist information center manned by a teenage girl with blue stripes in her hair and a surly look on her face.

Jack checked for cars, and quickly crossed the square, slipping down a side street. If he was quick, he could be back before Pete knew he'd been gone. This wasn't the sort of social call he wanted to explain to anyone, least of all her. And honestly, Jack thought, asking him to sit in the car like a sidekick in a place like Princetown was simply cruel and unusual.

He walked past house after house topped with damp thatch, surrounded by dead flowers, and populated by stony-eyed moor folk who glared at the platinum blond sore thumb from behind faded sprigged curtains. No cinema, no decent pub, and not even a newsagent's where one could indulge in the bored country vices of smoking, cheap lager, and porno mags.

"Cruel, Pete," he said. "Definitely cruel."

The house Jack sought out was how he remembered it, perhaps a little sadder, a little more sag along the roof line and a few more feet of dead, tangled grass in the front garden.

Sidestepping a drift of newspapers and mail, Jack mounted the steps and pounded on the door with the flat of his fist.

A youth in an overcoat, iPod buds dangling from his ears, opened the door and stared Jack over with bloodshot eyes before he shifted the wad of gum in his mouth and spoke. "Yeah? What do you want, then?"

Jack flicked his fag into the bushes. "Looking for Elsie. Her folks still live here?"

"Nope," said the youth. "They kicked."

"Simon!" A voice that could pierce a pit full of drunken punks twenty men thick echoed from inside the house. "Who's at the door?"

"Oi, Elsie!" Jack shouted, shoving the youth out of the way. "Elsie Dinsmore!"

"Jack?" Elsie came barreling from somewhere in the shadowed interior, beyond the beaded curtains and head-high stacks of magazines. Her shawl and layers of skirt flapped behind her and enveloped him as she threw her arms around his neck. It was rather like being embraced by an enthusiastic parrot. "Jack fucking Winter! Always knew you weren't dead, you sly skinny bastard!"

"Elsie Dinsmore," Jack said with a grin. "You still look beautiful as when you wore your hair three feet high and wrapped yourself in DIY tape."

She laughed from deep in smoke-scraped lungs. "You're a flatterer, you are, but it's Elsie Boote now. Haven't used that shite stage name in ages."

Elsie took Jack's face between her hands, turned his head from side to side. "But you're still Jack Winter, aren't you?"

"Some of us are rubbish at moving on," Jack said.

"Well don't just stand there like a knob!" Elsie cried, grabbing his arm. "Come have yourself seat. *SIMON!*" she bellowed at earsplitting volume. "Put on the kettle for our guest and get some of them chocolate biscuits I bought on a plate."

Jack let himself be gently dragged into a sitting room smothered in tapestries and furniture made entirely out of pillows braced on wooden frames. Herbs hung in dusty clusters, so thick the ceiling beams looked like furrows of earth. Dozens of birdcages blocked the light from the window, full of dead birds with glass eyes that stared balefully at Jack.

The only bare surface in the entire space was a round table covered in purple velvet. A box made of carved bone sat at the center, scenes of nymphs and harvest orgies parading around the edge of its lid.

Elsie settled herself with a groan into an armchair opposite the table. Jack perched on the edge of the pillows and tried not to lose his balance or sneeze at the overwhelming cinnamon incense that blanketed the room in a sticky amber miasma.

"Jack, Jack, Jack." Elsie grinned at him. "Tell me everything about you. Last time we were together . . ."

"Leeds, 1997," Jack said.

Elsie nodded. "You were down the rabbit hole, lovie." Her gravel-pit voice and avalanche of platinum hair, the two assets that made her the post-apocalyptic stunner vocalist for the Razor Babies a dozen years before, were both present now but greatly diminished. Her hair was long, knotted, going gray at the roots, and she'd covered herself in the same garish gypsy getup as her snug house.

She was a far cry from the girl who wrapped herself in tape and cut it off with razor blades throughout the set, for certain. The shine was still in her eyes, though, and the smirk still on her lips. Elsie hadn't lost her fire and Jack was relieved, because he needed something burned.

"Only climbed out recently," he admitted. "Spent too many years in Wonderland, I suppose."

Elsie shifted her bulk, which had grown considerably in the intervening years. Jack supposed that was fair—he'd diminished nearly as much.

"I don't think you'd be here at the family sprawl on a social call, once I've considered." Her mouth turned down. "You'd never come by just to see old Elsie getting on." She snorted. "Then again, neither would I."

Simon skulked in and set down a tray of tea and biscuits.

"Your mum and dad gone away, then?" Jack asked. Simon simply stood, in his overcoat and fingerless gloves, staring dumbly at Jack.

"Far away," Elsie said. "Mum passed nearly five years ago now. Dad followed her."

"I'm sorry."

"No, you ain't." Elsie hooted. "You weren't sorry when Death crossed your path, Jack. Not once."

"Things change," he said shortly, and turned his worst glare on Simon. "You need something, my son, or are you just holding up that bit of wall?"

"He's harmless," Elsie assured Jack. "Got a snip of talent and not much of a brain. Simon, go feed the cats and take in the wash. There's a fog brewing up."

Simon shuffled away like an enormous carrion bird, and Jack turned his eyes back to Elsie.

"I need you to read for me."

Elsie's tea stopped halfway to her lips. "Thought you didn't believe in the future, Jack. You said there was no point."

"And I told you, things change." Jack reached out and put his hand on the bone box. "Afraid of my future, Elsie?"

"You had any sense, wanker, you'd be afraid, too." Elsie set down her teacup with a bone-on-bone clink. "Give it here. Of course I'll read for you. One old conjurer to another."

She opened the bone box and drew out her tarot cards. Elsie hadn't had much beyond a filthy shirt, ripped tights, and a skirt that barely kept her decent when Jack had met her, but she'd had the cards, rolled in purple velvet in her knapsack. She'd had the magic to make them dance under her stubby fingers, to unfurl the future with the ink and paper and quicksilver dance of the seventy-two images that she turned into windows on the mind and soul.

Elsie shuffled once, twice, thrice. No ceremony—she was fast and hard as a dealer in Monte Carlo. She slapped the cards in front of Jack. "Cut."

Jack did as she said, making sure to touch the cards only with his fingertips. They weren't a new-age scam that you could buy in any Waterstone's. Elsie's deck was at least a hundred and fifty years old, stiff paper inked by hand. A Death's deck, every card a representation of the Bleak Gates, the Land of the Dead, or Death itself, in all its guises from Thanatos to the pale Horseman.

In her band days, Elsie claimed the deck was inked in sorcerer's ink and colored in human blood. Feeling the pinprick shock of foreign magic, old magic that did not brook disturbance, Jack was only half sure she'd been jerking him off.

Elsie held the cards between her palms and then with a snap, laid the first one face up on the velvet.

"Death," Jack said. "Shocking, I tell you."

"Death right side up is a change," Elsie said. "Transition. Evolution. The painful birth of the new."

"And the Fool card is a stubborn sod and the Lovers mean everybody hug," Jack muttered. Crystals and tarot and candles only served to allow the weak talents to think they had more than their share, and the non-talents to fuck about where they had no business. Objects of magic threw Jack off balance, made his stomach lurch and his skin crawl. They were never good omens, and frequently the harbinger of a royal cocking-up on the part of the owner.

Elsie flipped the next card. The Devil leered up at Jack as he copulated with a pale-skinned virgin on a funeral pyre.

"Well," she said. "You're off to a strong fucking start, my darling. Death and destruction."

"Just another day, luv." Jack shrugged, although a faint prickle of unease crawled through him. The Black woven through Elsie's smothering house grew restless, like ghostly wings against his cheeks, and the dead birds swayed in their cages as a wind blew in.

"Storm's coming!" Simon shouted from the kitchen, slamming a door and a basket. "Laundry's all gone to shit."

Elsie didn't stir. Her eyes were distant, gray mist drifting across the surface of her pupils while her fingers, nubby with arthritis, communed with her cards. Jack's eyes did something similar when he was in the throes of a spell. Pete said it made him look "like one of those bloody kids from that spooky village movie."

The next card flipped, and Jack's breath stopped.

Death, his skeletal form standing atop the highest tower in the Land of the Dead.

Death stared him down with hollow eyes.

"No," Elsie rasped. "No, no . . ." Her eyes snapped back in her head, and the fog of energy stole her gaze until something fathomless and old, something Not-Elsie stared out.

Her fingers moved of their own accord, laying down card after card. Death, and the Devil. Across the velvet they marched, death and destruction cutting a swath like an execution squad.

Jack reached out and grabbed Elsie's wrist. "That's enough."

Elsie's lip curled back and she snarled, hands continuing to twitch spasmodically, card after card after card glaring up at Jack from the velvet. Skull and horn. Death and the Devil.

"Oi." Jack grabbed her by the shoulder, shook her. "Elsie!"

She slammed the last card down with a bang and stared into his eyes. Her face was a skull with skin stretched over bone like a death masque. Her eyes were storm clouds hiding lightning.

"No escape," Elsie croaked. "Not for you."

Her voice was the demon's voice. Jack jerked, his knee slamming the underside of the table, sending it tumbling. Seventy-two Deaths and Devil fluttered to the floor like autumn leaves.

"Run, Jack." The demon grinned at him as Elsie shuddered, head thrown back and legs twitching in convulsion as the demon rode her body. "Run while you still can."

Chapter Fourteen

Pete was at the car when he returned, leaning on the bonnet, arms and ankles crossed. Jack slowed his feet, slowed his breathing, composed his face into a mask. "Waiting long?"

Pete sliced him with her gaze. "Where the bloody hell were you?"

Jack waved a pack of Parliaments. "I was out. Went over to the pub."

His heart hammered loudly enough that he was sure they could hear him in the next county, and cold sweat clung to his skin under his clothes. The demon's message was clear as a churchbell: *No escape. Not for you.*

"You look pale as the dead," Pete said. "Are you sure you just went for fags?"

"'Course I'm sure," Jack said. The words didn't slide off his tongue easily this time, and Pete's pretense of believing it cracked as she jerked the car door open and jammed her keys into the Mini's ignition. Jack climbed in, shut the door, and nearly had his head whipped off as Pete kicked the little car into motion.

"The locals didn't have much to add," she said once they'd left the square. The moors rose on either side of the ribbon of road, a petrified sea that could fold over your head and swallow you down.

"He topped himself?" Jack said. Pete nodded.

"No medical examiner here, of course, and no proper morgue, but he most definitely suffocated. Naughton called the locals immediately and the sergeant I spoke to—Hogan—said Danny was in the attic on the crossbeam. 'Swingin' like a Christmas ornament' is how he put it, I believe."

Jack watched the tops of the moors slowly fade away as fog crept over the crest and down the hillside, the sky turning from the peculiar empty blue-white of open spaces to the hard gray iron of rain and storm. "Could explain the poltergeist. Suicide doesn't usually leave Casper the Friendly Fucking Ghost behind."

"So?" Pete slowed at a junction and squinted at the signs. Fingers of fog obscured the miles to the next town.

"So, what?" Jack cast a glance at her. They were alone now, just the road and the fog and a bit of stone wall separating them from the windswept nothingness of the Dartmoor.

"What do we do now?" Pete asked, going left. "If it's only a poltergeist and not a real haunting?" The Mini jolted as the road turned abruptly from paved to gravel.

"Cleanse the house," Jack said. "If it doesn't take care of Danny Boy it will at least tell me what I'm dealing with." Jack wasn't convinced the great, grasping void of the Naughton estate was simple resonance from a suicide. The power that had taken a crowbar to his sight wasn't natural, as much as anything in the Black was ever natural.

"What we're dealing with," Pete said.

Jack rubbed the center of his forehead. "Yeah. 'Course."

Pete gritted her teeth as the Mini's undercarriage scraped the track. "It is *we*, you know."

Jack debated with himself, and then nodded agreement. He was crap at looking contrite, so he patted himself down for a light but found nothing useful. "You're right, luv. 'We' it is. Forgive me?"

Pete hissed through her teeth. "I'd be a deal more inclined to forgive the sins of the world at large if I knew where the bloody hell we were."

The road was nearly invisible beyond the Mini's bonnet, and Jack shivered as the fog formed vines and tangles outside the windscreen. They were alone, closed off, and the road narrowed and turned back on itself.

Pete stopped and set the emergency brake, turning off the car. "I'm lost."

Jack looked behind them, but there was only fathomless gray, like the mists outside the walls of the Land of the Dead. Endless, cold, and full of lost souls.

"Must have taken a wrong turn in the muck," he suggested. "It's all right. All of us get lost at one time or another. The trick is getting found again."

Pete drummed her fingers on the wheel. "I guess there's nowhere to go but forward. Have to come out somewhere."

Jack joined in her drumming, the bass line to "Shut Up and Fuck Off" springing up under his fingers. He'd written the song with Dix McGowan, the Poor Dead Bastards' drummer, after a night sitting up with more bottles of whiskey than comfortably fit in the bin of Dix's minuscule flat. Dix was newly dumped, Jack was pissed, and he felt good enough about being too drunk to see the dead that he wrote a song. It hadn't gone on the Bastards' single LP, and only hit a few set lists in their club gigs, but it was Jack's favorite. Simple, uncomplicated. *Shut up, fuck off, I'm not your Prince Charming, I'm not your broken heart.*

"Jack." Pete tapped him on the back of his hand. "You with us?" She turned the ignition key, and the Mini coughed and shuddered.

He folded up the memory and put it with all the others that lived in a rat-eaten cardboard box marked Before the Fix. In the Mini, there was no warmth and no biting scent of whiskey, no guitar neck under his hands. Jack felt as if a finger of fog and damp had slipped in and placed a hand on the back of his neck. "Try it again," he said to Pete, trying to keep the low urgency from his voice even as his chest felt as if a giant had closed its fist about him.

The Black boiled, in the wake of something passing through, large and ancient, that set all of Jack's mental alarms to screaming.

Pete jiggled the key and then hit the dash. "Bollocks! I *knew* that bloke who replaced the alternator was dodgy."

Jack put his fingertips against the Mini's window. His prints turned the mist to droplets and they slid down the glass, turning his handprint into nothing but streaks on a pane.

Outside, on a lone telephone wire, a crow landed, and stared at him. It darted a gaze left and right, and then took wing, cawing madly.

Magic prickled up and down Jack's body, and he shivered as the crow's call faded into nothingness along with all else.

The Black of the Dartmoor was not the Black of London. There were layers in the city, ley lines of abandoned tunnel and underground river, the cool sting of iron railway tracks and bridges binding the wild power of the Thames. London breathed, it fluttered and shouted, wriggled and screamed. A million energies spread across the Black, slithering through smoke and stone, caressing his sight like a lover's insistent hand.

Here, the moor was simply alive, an open wound. Raw power from the Black trickled through Jack's consciousness, undiluted and primal. The tors and pagan sites scattered across the landscape were like torches in a vast darkness, floating on a sea of raw power.

It was an ancient place, a place of wild magic, and Jack watched his breath make a cloud when he exhaled. Even though it was freezing in the Mini, sweat broke all over Jack's skin, under his leather. His pulse jittered, and his nerves crept up and down his flesh. The Black of the Dartmoor felt like nothing so much as ghost sickness. Jack shut his eyes, tried to push against the tide of the sight. Had to, because if he left Pete alone out here by checking out they'd both be fucked.

"I'm going to check the motor," Pete said, climbing out. "Open the bonnet, would you?"

Jack did as she asked and followed her. They were in pea soup now, and Jack smelled the icy, freshwater scent of rain on the breeze.

"We shouldn't linger," he said. The waves of power only worsened, outside the protective steel bubble of the Mini.

Pete poked at the innards of the engine, while Jack lit a fag. "You know," she said, "you should be doing this, you being the man and all."

"Sorry, luv," Jack told her. "My manly prowess is confined to picking locks, smoking, and being ridiculously good looking."

"You're bent." Pete shook her head, fighting a smile.

Jack returned it. Seeing Pete smile started a small fire under his stomach, and it helped mute the buzzing of the Black, for a moment. "I don't hear you disagreeing, luv."

Pete sighed, at him or the car, he wasn't sure, and shut the bonnet. "Well, it's buggered." She pulled out her Black-Berry and held it up to the sky. "No service, either. We either walk, or wait to be pancaked by a lorry."

Jack looked into the fog, where he knew the hills were watching them. Gathering magic. Waiting.

"How far can it be?" he said gamely. Pete got her bag and jacket, locked the Mini, and joined him on the edge of the road.

"Hopefully not so far my shoes start leaking. I'm in a foul enough mood already."

Jack shoved his hands into his pockets, keeping a few steps ahead of Pete. He swept the hills from one side of the road to the other, steps hard and sharp on the gravel, heartbeat sharper. Whatever was out there in the fog stared back. Jack could see nothing except the phantoms of mist wandering aimlessly among the hedges and the hills, but he felt it. His skin went colder than the air, and he curled his fists inside his leather, scrabbling for a little magic to throw behind a shield hex. He wasn't going to be dragged away like a sod in a fairy tale. Whatever had stalked them to this deserted spot clearly didn't know what sort of a mood he was in.

Nothing sprang at him as they walked away from the Mini, but the wild power of the moor followed, and the watcher followed with it. Jack resigned himself to a game of seeing which of them broke nerve first—the mage, or the creature.

"You know," Pete said as they squelched through the dead grass on the shoulder of the road, "this reminds me of that night. You remember the one, where you played the set at Club Bleu . . ."

"And your sister got herself pissed on tequila," Jack remembered. Pete's sister MG was a vision in black lace, long Bettie Page curls, wide eyes, and lips made for blow jobs All of which hid a mind that would have done the bunny-boiler from *Fatal Attraction* proud. In other words, she was just Jack's—old Jack, Bastards frontman Jack—type. If there wasn't a chance a bird would come at you with a kitchen knife, where was the laugh?

"Right, and she made us walk for miles at three in the morning looking for a curry." Pete picked up the thread.

"Not just any curry," Jack said.

"A *green* curry." They mimicked MG's put-on posh accent together.

"Thank God they only made one of her." Pete sighed. "That's what our Da used to say."

Jack had first seen Pete standing at the edge of the pit in Fiver's, a hole in the wall shitebox, far from Club Bleu as she was from her sister, even though they'd arrived together. Where MG dominated every room she entered, Pete stayed small and pale, worrying a full pint glass between her hands. There was no great lightning bolt, no flash of recognition from past lives. She looked at him, and he looked at her, while the music played.

And suddenly, MG had been the furthest person from his thoughts.

"I . . ." Jack swallowed his words. Whatever he'd seen in the dirty basement club that night was gone now. Now, there was a demon, and a dozen years of growing older and harder in between.

"Yes?" Pete turned back to face him. They were standing close as they'd ever been, save for the night Jack had pulled Pete out of Highgate Cemetery, bleeding for trying to keep him from being swallowed by the hungry ghost of Algernon Treadwell.

Closer even than when she'd kissed him.

Jack reached out and brushed the droplets of mist from her hair. "Not a thing, luv." He dropped his hand, and stepped back. "Not a bloody thing."

Behind Pete, in the fog, something moved. Jack didn't see it, not really. His headache spiked and his skin numbed as if a north wind had blown across his face, and a shadow flicked in and out of his vision faster than the shadow from a nightmare.

Hulking and dark, it moved across his sight, parting the mist. A long, low howl echoed between the hills, lower than the wail of the *bansidhe* or the scream of the *bean nighe*.

Pete whipped her head around. Her sixth sense, the part of her connected to the Black, felt it—the soul-stealing cold, the oppressive weight of a creature of magic breaking the barrier between worlds.

"Jack." She reached back and grabbed for his hand without taking her eyes off the spot where the thing stood. It was indistinct, the size of a small horse, just a black blur of fog surrounded by lighter mist. Whatever Jack had imagined coming when he'd felt the magic of the moor awaken, he hadn't imagined it would be quite as large.

Or seem quite as slagged off.

"Pete," he said in return, to let her know he was still there, wasn't running.

The thing snarled, a sound that cut through his ribs straight to his heart. Twin golden globes blossomed in the fog, as if the creature were all flame inside. Eyes, golden and round, staring at Jack and through him, straight down to the bone.

"Pete," Jack repeated. "We need to get back to the car."

The creature in the fog took a step forward, its power brushing up against Jack's. The creature was cold, the cold of dead skin and frozen iron. Its magic was hard and unyielding, power borne of the Underworld.

It could cut through Jack's shield hex like a razor through a wrist.

He wasn't up for debating the point, either. Maybe twenty years ago, when he was stupid and carried a death wish with him like a scar. But not today. He was too old and too bastard-clever now to engage with something that had crawled straight up from the Land of the Dead. Particularly when that something so clearly wanted to gnaw his bones.

Pete twined her fingers in his, and he felt the flutter of the gateway she carried in her talent. A Weir possessed a direct line to the oldest, sharpest, bloodiest part of the Black. It promised a mage like him power beyond imagination, if only he were willing to burn himself to ash and Pete, too, in the process. When a Weir and a mage met, the uncontrolled magic could eat you alive. Terrible catastrophes had resulted, and the sweet, overwhelming desire to let the magic take him was the reason.

Jack yanked his hand free. He wasn't that desperate. Not yet.

Running was nearly always a better option than dying, so Jack turned and pelted for the Mini as if the coppers were chasing him and he had open warrants.

The thing gave chase, cold breath on his back, panting in his ear, and the howl that could rend flesh ululating across the moor.

Jack's fingers fumbled for the Mini's door, scrabbled uselessly as Pete dove across the driver's seat and sprang the latch.

Jack fell in, his sight shrieking, and slammed the door.

"What the bloody fuck is that thing?" Pete shouted, but he barely heard her. She was down a long tunnel, back in the living world. The Black boiled up around him, threatening to drag him under, take him to that primal bloodlust that flowed under the moor. Under the hill, to the old races that waited there.

Jack had seen what lived under the hill.

He wouldn't go back.

The cut on his hand from Paddington was raw and weeping still, but he turned the flick-knife on the same digits, his off hand. If he needed to work a spell or, fuck, pick a pocket, he needed his left.

He sliced the fat of his palm deep, felt the cold bite of metal and the serpent sting.

The air was so cold now from the encroach of the creature that his blood steamed when it hit the glass. Jack smeared his palm down the car window, leaving a ruddy streak, and when he had enough blood began to draw.

Sigils weren't something the *Fiach Dubh* had much faith in. Their magic was gut-deep, physical, the shield hex and the summoning circle. *Pretty drawings are for pretty faeries, boy.* Seth McBride's voice, roughened by cigarettes and hard magic, crept in as Jack tried to push magic into the blood. Seth had taught Jack the hard and fast, boot-to-the-bollocks rules. The ways and wicked tricks of the Brothers of the Crow. He came back, unbidden, most often when Jack had gotten himself into a situation that would end either with him a corpse or royally fucked.

"Shut your gob, Seth. Crusty old Mick," Jack muttered as he finished the cycle. Picked it from the notebook of Declan Disher, a Vatican-trained exorcist who found Wicca and swanned about in a hippie shirt and pentacle until a gang of Stygian Brothers cut out his liver one night in a dark pub washroom and used it as a ceremonial offering to Nergal. Or perhaps Dagon. Jack got the two mixed up sometimes.

Declan had always been a git, but he was a hand with markings. The sigil had saved Jack's arse before, and now it would save him and Pete one more time.

It had to, because if the creature broke through, he was out of brilliant ideas.

"Jack. Jack!" Pete grabbed his shoulder and shook. "There's something out there and it's not stopping for a chat!"

"Give me half a fucking second," he gritted. The symbols were slippery, transient, escaping his attempt to infuse them with power. Concentration shot, panic rising, wild magic threatening to claw his brain apart—never the best time to draw a complex magical wotsit.

Pete stilled herself with effort, effort that manifested in the widening of her pupils, the cords in her neck pulled taut by fear. "All right. All right. Just tell me what you need me to do."

Jack put his hand against the symbols. They flopped with faint energy, like dying goldfish. Outside, the creature prowled, circling the car, scenting for life and magic.

Fuck it, he couldn't take the chance that the sigil would crumble under the creature's onslaught. He couldn't chance visiting the Bleak Gates, not when the demon was walking in his shadow. Jack turned to Pete.

"What you can do is take my hand."

She put her palm in his without hesitation. Warm, sure, alive. Trusting.

Like he'd spun a tap, power rushed through him, making his fingers and toes and everything else tingle. The sigil cycle glowed and then it lapped up his magic, strengthening, locking out the malevolent Black that crawled beyond the glass.

He felt the vast well of the Weir, the doorway to the old magics, the blood and bone and sex magics. It was sweet as bubbling spring water, hot as coal. It filled Jack with the high that only the Black could give.

The creature outside snarled, and then whined. It circled the Mini once more and then with a final throaty growl, it retreated, great fog lamps of eyes fading into the mist.

The power of the moor leached away at a far slower pace—whatever had gotten it up in the first place, called the creature, was strong enough to bend the raw Black to its will, to command a thin space between the worlds to appear and release its denizens.

Jack let out his first breath in what he swore was hours, felt his lungs burn and his head lighten. Pete let go of him. Her face was drawn and she was panting a little, grim circles standing out around her eyes and veins crawling up her face.

The first time her Weir talent had touched his magic, she'd passed out cold on the floor of his flat. This was an improvement, if not a vast one.

He brushed the backs of his knuckles over her cheek,

reflexively. Make sure she was still warm and still had blood beating in her. "You all right, luv?"

She took in a breath, let it out, hands gripping her knees, wrinkling the denim hard enough to whiten her knuckles. "Fine. What in fucking hell was that thing?"

The mist blew onward, wind rocking the Mini, and behind the mist came the rain, in soft gray sheets that wafted across the moor like wraiths chasing witchfire across the lowland bogs near Seth's farmhouse in County Cork.

"Nasty," Jack murmured. "A hungry, nasty creature of the Black." His blood was drying to sticky paste on the window, and his palm ached. Pushing magic through his own blood always left him cold, fever-achy, and drained like he'd passed out in a pub loo and woken with a crick in his neck.

It left too the faint craving for that floating, golden place where his talent met Pete's Weir. He wished to drink down every last drop of Pete's power, ride it forever.

One fix or another, it made no difference.

"That's it?" Pete jiggled the key and the Mini started on the first crank, purring contentedly as always. "Usually you talk my ear off, Professor. Have you ever seen something like it before?"

"Once," Jack said, as they turned back onto the paved road and crawled back through the thinning fog to the junction.

He could still hear the howl, echoing off the low stone wall and thatch roof of Seth McBride's farmhouse. He'd climbed up on the roof and lit a fag, watching the enormous spectral creature pad on four feet across the fields, a purpose in its step so terrible and deliberate that even though the night was warm and soft, the height of an Irish summer, Jack had felt bone-chilled.

The creature had looked at him, great blazing eyes staring across the distance and searing him body and sight. Then it had walked on, over the rise and into the valley, where Seth's closest neighbors resided.

In the morning an ambulance bumped over the dirt track and into the same valley, left again with cargo wrapped in a yellow hazmat bag.

You got yourself under stone when you heard a *cu sith* at bay. The black dog scented for blood, and the blood of the soul he'd come for was the only blood that would do.

It was the first time Jack felt real fear toward a creature of the Black. Demons could swallow you down into Hell and Fae could bargain your memories away for a song, but they had rules. They could be tricked. No one bargained with the *cu sith*, the hound of Death. No mortal could make it see reason, no matter how clever a bastard he might be. Jack didn't like fear—fear was useless in the Black, the stealthy, laughing killer that made you freeze, forget your hexing words, and piss yourself before something bit your head off.

The *cu sith* was a subject of fear, of the inexorable human fate that conjured it. You couldn't look into its lantern eyes and not see death staring back, unblinking and untenable.

"It's a *cu sith*," Jack said. "Lots of names besides the Irish—black dog, in English. Harbinger of death. Chases down souls and drags them through the Gates."

They pulled into the circular drive of the Naughton house and Jack had the peculiar sensation again of falling into a vortex, the Black swirling and concentrating in this spot. After the *cu sith*, though, the state of Naughton's psychic real estate seemed a minor concern.

"Any particular souls?" Pete climbed out and approached the sucking void, but Jack blinked and it was just a rotted-out, rundown estate again.

"Any it can get its jaws around," he said. Pete bit her lip

as if she wanted to press him, but she merely collected her keys and bag and went inside.

Jack stayed for a moment, reluctant to walk back into Naughton's eldritch problem.

If the *cu sith* had only been hungry, it might have happened upon him by accident.

But he was a mage and this was the Black and there weren't any accidents or fucking coincidences. The *cu sith* had come for him, had seen the brand of the demon hovering just out of view. Marked for bloody death, and a *cu sith*'s favorite snack. Jack had the cold comfort that the *cu sith* was stepping onto the demon's turf and that the demon made short work of those who tried to play with its toys.

The only downside to the equation was Jack being the toy.

He watched the crow land on the finial of Naughton's roof and caw, spreading its wings and widening its beak until it looked grotesque, as if it were trying to answer Pete's query.

Any particular soul?

Only mine, Jack replied. *Jack fucking Winter, dead man bloody walking.*

Chapter Fifteen

Jack didn't believe in dwelling on the inevitable. Try to change the future, and the future would just fuck you back, bent over and proper. Instead, he went into the Naughton house, went to his room, and checked his kit for graveyard dirt, coffin nails, herbs, and his scrying mirror. Matches, chalk, and copper wire. The essential tools of Jack Winter, exorcist. Much different than Jack Winter, wrung-out junkie, and much preferable. It gave him something to think about other than the demon's bargain. He was good at exorcisms, sure of them and himself when he was performing them. If he could solve Naughton's poxy problem and get Pete some cash in the doing, so much the better.

"Cleansing will take an hour or so," he told Pete when she came to the door and propped herself against the jamb by her shoulder, watching him lay out his kit. "Got to find a setup spot where the poltergeist can't fling any crockery at me head."

"I'm going to look in Danny's room in the meantime," she said. "See if there's anything Nick missed."

"Might be a good spot," Jack decided. *Nick.* Christ on a bike. Nothing but bloody Nick. "Close to but not too close to where he kicked off." Setting up a cleansing on a suicide's last breathing spot was just asking to have your lungs ripped through your nose by an angry spirit.

Jack gathered his tools and followed Pete to Danny's room, a large back bedroom that looked out on the rotting, soggy gardens. The rain lashed down in earnest outside, and wind crawled under the slanted eaves of the Naughton house, moaning low and lost. Day outside darkened to the half-night of storms and dreams.

Jack wiggled his eyebrows at Pete when a bad gust rattled the windows. "How apropos. Always did like a bit of mood weather."

Now, with the job, he could put the *cu sith* and the ghosts in Paddington out of his mind. At least for the few moments it took to cleanse Danny's sad, wandering spirit.

The room Danny Naughton had chosen was worse than Jack's own flat, if that were possible—the peeling plaster and warped floors, the chipped war-era furniture, all attached to a crumbling en suite equipped with the sort of plumbing American comedians cracked jokes about.

The bed was stripped bare, a stained mattress the only sign anyone had recently slept atop it. Drawers stood half open, clothes trailing out and across the floor like shed skin. Nancy Nick had been in a whirlwind hurry to get out of the place after Danny hung himself, Jack thought. That or he'd been keen to erase evidence of something before the emergency crew showed themselves. Jack'd cleaned up enough mates who'd overdosed to know the signs.

A massive mirror opposite the bed was covered with a sheet, and Pete moved to snatch it off. Jack stopped her with a hand up.

"Leave it. Mirrors could let something watch us that we don't want."

Pete frowned. "Do you think he knew? Danny? That this place was off?"

Jack kicked an empty plastic bottle, and it rolled to join three more fellows under the bed. "I think he liked his vodka cheap and by the quart."

Pete examined the empty closet, jangling wire hangers the only residents. She was methodical, sifting through the detritus atop the dresser and each drawer with quick, professional fingers. Jack could imagine her in a pants suit and blue nitrile gloves, standing in this same room while white-suited crime scene technicians moved around her like explorers on a foreign moon.

Her hair would be pulled back in the low, efficient ballerina twist she'd worn during her time at the Met. Her warrant card and badge clipped to her belt along with handcuffs and pepper spray. A low heel, nothing flashy or trampy, just enough to elevate her petite frame to eye level with the male detectives of the squad.

"You're staring at me," Pete said. "Keep it up and I'm going to think I have something growing out of my forehead."

She wriggled the bedside drawer. "This one's locked."

"Let me," Jack said. He passed his fingers over the lock, and then pulled his ring of skeleton keys from his leather. They wore an enchantment, just the smallest charm to conduct a spell. Jack found them years ago at a bazaar in Leeds, mixed in with a box of mundane junk. He sometimes wondered about the mage who'd lost such a valuable tool, but not often.

Jack stuck the smallest key into the lock and whispered the words inscribed around the hilt and down the shaft of each skeleton key.

There was a click and the drawer popped open, overflowing with small squares of paper.

"You should teach me that one," Pete said.

"You wouldn't want it," Jack said. Pete took a handful of the slips and shuffled through them.

"Wouldn't I?"

"Lockpicking is transmutation. Transmutation is black magic," Jack said. "You don't want to have that on your first try, luv."

Pete cocked her eyebrow. "You do it. I've seen you crack open a lock a dozen times."

Jack lifted his shoulder. "I've got an affinity for breaking and entering, luv. Has more to do with nicking things when I was a stupid kid than magic, truth be told."

"Of course," Pete snapped. "You have the ease of everything. I'd just pox it up, like some *stupid kid*. Not like bloody Jack Winter." She crumpled the slips viciously.

"You know that's not what I meant," Jack protested. Pete's temper, like her freckles, was Irish and her glare could have cut glass. "You have an affinity, luv. You find things like no one I've ever seen." Jack stepped back and let Pete examine the drawer. "Lost papers. Lost children." He swallowed, his tongue dry in the closed-up room. "Lost souls."

Pete's anger faded, replaced by half of a small smile. "I suppose it's what I'm good at," she said at last. Jack nodded.

"It's the truth. What have you found, then?"

"They're betting slips," Pete said. "From all over the country. *Losing* bets, mostly."

"So Danny boy spent the time he wasn't getting pissed and seeing ghosts betting on the ponies?" Jack said. As far as skeletons in a rich twat's closet went, it was fairly mundane. Nobody was even wearing lady's underthings. "Nicky might have mentioned that," he murmured. "Seems quite a thing to omit."

"He might not have known," Pete said. "You'd be surprised what families can keep from one another. Met a bloke once, had a mistress living one flat block over from his wife and children. They used to pass each other in the street and nod hello. Did it for *years*."

"Why'd you get involved, then?" Jack dropped to one knee and started setting up his supplies. Ritual was familiarity as much as magic. Setting out the tools of exorcism quieted the mind, readied it for the things an exorcist would see pulling in wayward ghosts.

"His wife puzzled it out and blew his head off with a skeet rifle," Pete said. "Can't say I blamed her overly much."

"That's a secret for you," Jack said. "Like vicious little dogs. Never know when they'll turn around and bite."

Pete stopped her searching and cast her gaze on him. Her eyes could cut you like broken green glass if she meant to get the truth.

"Indeed," was all she said.

Jack put out his scrying mirror, a black ceramic bowl, and matches for burning herbs, a nub of chalk for the circle. He sat down cross-legged even though he felt a groan in the hinges of his knees and fingered a piece of chalk, deciding what to draw into the varnish-bubbled floorboards. Spells and hexes ran wild in a mage's blood, scrawled on car windows and dripped onto tube station floors, but exorcisms had to be orderly.

Seth had shown him the results when they weren't orderly and measured. When an exorcist lost his cool.

Once Jack had finished vomiting his breakfast into Seth's loo, he'd paid attention to the lessons, and he hadn't let a ghost get over on him yet. Until Algernon Treadwell's ghost. But that time, Pete had been there. She'd yanked him back from the Gates with her talent, and anchored him to the living world.

He owed Pete a favor, no question. And such a favor wasn't lying about the demon's bargain. Jack could deceive others with ease but lying to Pete always took on a hollow quality, made him feel rotted and twisted up inside like a car wreck.

"Find anything else? More rattling skeletons?" he asked as Pete poked about in the wardrobe, so that she wouldn't take his silence for what it was and ask him, in the manner of nosy coppers, what he was thinking about.

"Aside from a baggie of extraordinarily mediocre pot and the slips? No." Pete sat on the edge of the mattress. "Just the usual leftovers of life."

"Pot?" Jack perked up. "Mediocre or not, at least the lad wasn't completely boring." He winked at Pete. "Give it here."

"Not a chance." Pete stuffed the dusty baggie into her jeans.

"You don't have the slightest idea what to do with that stuff," Jack teased her.

Pete rolled her eyes. "Please. I went to university."

"Did you, now." Jack found the black silk squares and cord at the bottom of his bag. "Smoking marijuana, getting up to mischief—if you tell me there was inexperienced but enthusiastic lesbian experimentation, I could die a happy man."

One of Danny Naughton's worn-out loafers narrowly missed his head. "You're a sod," Pete said, but she was chewing her lip to mask the smile.

Jack grabbed his baggies of exorcism herbs and patted the spot next to him on the floor. "Come here, luv. First things first." *Protect yourself before you even think about ghosts. An unguarded exorcism was akin to painting yourself with honey and insulting a grizzly bear's mum.*

Pete folded up into a seat across from him. "If this is anything perverted and unnatural . . ."

Jack folded the herbs into the silk—camphor, white pine, and garlic root drifting past his nose in waves—and tied them up with a red ribbon. "Perverted and unnatural comes later." He winked. "This is just a conjure bag. Keeps the ghosts from doing . . . what Treadwell did."

"This smells like a Pizza Express," Pete complained.

"Lawrence taught it to me," Jack said, preparing his own bag and slipping it around his neck. "His grandmother uses them back home to keep away the duppies."

Pete softened at the mention of Lawrence, and put the cord over her head. "Jack, it's not going to happen again. Treadwell. Going to the thin spaces. Any of it." She grabbed his hand, unexpectedly. He'd been shivering since they saw the *cu sith*, colder than the air around him, but her touch warmed.

"I'm stronger now," Pete whispered. "And so are you. It'll never happen again, Jack. I won't let it."

Jack's memory of the night in Highgate came back in snatches. Treadwell had tried to take his flesh, to cast out Jack's spirit into the thin spaces, the mists outside the walls of the Underworld. A reverse exorcism, Jack supposed. Throw out the living git and move into his empty meat sack.

He hadn't seen anything in the thin spaces besides his own life parading past in reverse, but it had been bad enough.

Jack knew what was waiting for him, when the clock wound back to zero.

And then Pete had come, and she'd pulled him back, and she'd banished Treadwell back through the Bleak Gates. Lain bleeding by the gravestones afterward, blood staining the white linen of her shirtfront, eyes clouded over with the pure white of the Weir.

His palms had gone cold. Blood was supposed to be warm, but when it soaked his fingers it was chill.

Jack had never had fear like that moment since. Not the kind that put claws into your throat and drained all the hardness and wickedness out of a person.

In the present, far from the bloody grass of Highgate Cemetery, Pete squeezed his fingers between hers, and Jack nearly told her everything. The only thing that stopped him was the thought that Pete wouldn't understand she had to leave him, get as far away as possible once she'd heard the true story.

She'd stay and try to face the demon. And it would end just like it had the first time.

"I won't let it," Pete said again, and Jack heard the desperate strain creep into her voice.

"Pete . . ." He sighed, but there weren't words for it. No words could explain that after he'd been walking dead for a decade, she breathed life back into him. No way to explain that Pete was in every heartbeat since the day they'd found each other again, in a filthy Bloomsbury hotel room.

She made him solid. Pete was the thing keeping the world real. And no one, no matter how hard-bitten and capable they thought they were, deserved to hear that. No woman deserved the responsibility of keeping Jack Winter in one piece.

Pete's tongue darted out, licked her lips. "What, Jack? What's the matter?" In the pale halfling light of the storm, her skin was translucent and her eyes drowning deep. When she looked at him like that, Jack's fine thread of control snapped at last.

"Fuck it," he muttered, pulling her close by their connected hand, his other taking the back of her neck, wrapping his fingers in her hair.

It was nothing like the kiss in the marsh, not hesitant and not slow. Pete's lips were warm, parted, and breathless. Jack could have drunk her, every drop, and still been parched.

Her hands, trapped as they were against his chest, pushed him back, and they broke apart as abruptly as they'd come together, Pete's taste in Jack's mouth, melting and dissolving. Nothing he could do to save it. The bitterness returned when Pete stood up, cheeks flushed to roses and breath ragged.

"I shouldn't have done that." She flexed her fingers, fists and not, over and over. "Shit. I really shouldn't have."

"Too right," Jack murmured, though he wasn't talking about Pete. His own heart was thrumming, speeding along like he'd just choked down a handful of uppers. The drug was power, and the fix was Pete. How he wanted to taste her again, throw her down on the dirty mattress, expose that snow-petal skin, make the blood rush to the surface as she took away his pain quick as any needle.

"It's not . . . I mean, it wasn't . . ." Pete slammed her fist against the wall. Plaster dust sifted down from the ceiling. "Bloody hell, Jack. I know there's something you're not saying. Until you trust me, I can't. I'm sorry, but I can't."

Quick as it had come upon him, the need subsided and left the same small dirty knot Jack felt in his chest when he stole from Lawrence, or nicked pensioners' prescriptions, or woke up in a filthy squat with no memory of how he'd come to be there.

Before, the solution was simple—get high again and bollocks to guilt and shame.

Jack rolled the kinks out of his neck and picked up his chalk, short savage slashes on the polished floor drawing the beginnings of his circle. "Let's just get this done and get back to the city, yeah?"

"Best, I suppose," Pete said. "What should I do?"

"Just stay out of the way, if you please," he snapped. Pete's eyes narrowed and then she took a large, deliberate step back to the window that overlooked the fields beyond the back garden.

"You git," she said softly.

Jack's chalk snapped in half from the force of his stroke. "Never claimed I was Prince Charming, did I?"

Pete shook her head, but she stayed where she was, rain lashing the glass behind her. Jack focused on the circle blossoming under his chalk stub, the grit between his fingers and the soft scratch on the wood. It didn't make him less of a wanker, but it helped dull the facts.

Ghosts were thin and slippery creatures, and a circle for an exorcism was about control more than power. Demons a sorcerer summoned needed power, drank it and craved it. Ghosts a mage tangled with were inevitably hungry and desperate, and they would rush the electric fence until it broke.

The exorcism circle required precision, focus, clarity. The trifecta of things Jack Winter didn't have and had never held in any quantity.

You're a selfish little knob, Jackie boy, Seth rasped. *No thought and no control for anything, including yourself. Bloody good thing you've got charm to spare.*

"You're right," he said. The magic words. Bollocks to *I love you* or *You look beautiful. You're right* had gotten him off the sofa a hundred times over.

Pete sniffed. "Of course I am."

"When we've done what we came here to do," Jack said slowly, "I promise I'll tell you why I've been . . ."

"A complete and utter cock-stain?" Pete supplied.

"That," Jack said. "But it won't matter if we're out on the street for want of cash, and right now I need to concentrate. Can we put a hold on the couple drama, please, until I kick this poltergeist back beyond the beyond?"

He expected an argument or maybe a slap—Pete was the kind of woman who slapped rather than sulked—but instead she frowned a little, and then her shoulders dropped and her fists relaxed.

"You called us a couple."

Jack felt one side of his mouth curl. "Did I? Must have inhaled some of that shite pot you found."

The baggie smacked him in the side of the head. "Arsehole." Pete glared at him as he worked, the circle growing and expanding and building on itself, a framework intricate as any clock, ready to hold the power of cleansing spells.

Jack finished the circle, checked the symbols to make sure he hadn't cocked up, and dumped incense into the bowl. He added a pinch of galangal to draw any lingering spirits to the smoke. His lighter clicked thrice before he called a flame and touched it to the pile of dry herbs.

The house held its breath, stayed silent and still. Nothing inside his head except echoes and nothing before his sight except darkness.

"Feels normal," Pete said. "Just a dusty old house."

"That's bothersome," Jack said. "Old place, shouldn't be so quiet. Old homes, old bones. Echoes."

"Not every place is a backdrop for *Masters of Horror*," Pete said. "The Naughtons may have been happy."

"Can you look at Sir Nicholas and honestly tell me you believe that sack of wank-leavings was ever happy, for a single moment in his life?" Jack slipped his scrying mirror from the velvet. He set it gently on the floor and pointed at his bag. "Hand me that white candle, would you?"

Pete found it and passed it across, keeping well clear of his chalk markings. Jack lit the white candle and placed it west, the direction of the dead. He set his mirror on the floor and sat, fingers on the glass.

Waited.

The Naughton house was curiously blank, like a dead station on the radio, not music, not static. Just silence, eerie in its stillness and breadth. Jack's skin crawled all up and down his body.

"Daniel Naughton," he said, putting a push behind the words. "Master of this house. Come to me, spirit. To the circle, you are called. *Tar do mo fhuil beo.*"

Pete shifted. "Where is he?"

"It's not a summoning spell," Jack said shortly. "Ghost summoning's what put us here to start, luv, and I don't fancy another Treadwell."

"Still . . . if this is a haunting shouldn't he be doing . . . hauntish things?" Pete glared at all the corners of the room, brow wrinkling like she could will Danny into being.

Jack took in a breath, tried again. "Daniel Naughton. Master of this house. Come, spirit. By the power of circle and crow, come."

Rain fell, battered the windowpanes. Jack's heart pumped blood against his ears, all of his extremities vibrating against the power of the spell. His nose detected the sticky-sweet of the incense and the tang of the galangal, and for one perfect moment, his sight and the Black were utterly silent and still.

Then the mirror in the corner shattered into ten thousand snowflakes of glass, scattering across the floor. A piece of glass kissed his cheek, a hot sting and a lick of blood.

"Bloody hell!" Pete shrieked, swiping at the scratches on her own face.

From all the corners of the room a low giggle burbled, scratchy as a needle across vinyl, mad and grating against Jack's ears.

"Daniel Naughton," Jack gritted. "By the power of iron and smoke. By the power of the binding words. Show yourself. And quit fucking about," he added as the sounds of madness increased, the bulbs in the lamp overhead flickering madly.

Jack could see his own breath as the ghost crawled around the perimeter of the circle, drawn by the ritual but too strong to allow the markings to drag it down. Yet.

"Pete," Jack said. "You try."

She dabbed at her cheek, lined with thin deep scratches

that leaked blood. "Me? I haven't got a thing to say to the bastard ghost."

"You're a speaker for the magic," Jack said. He felt his power struggling to grasp the ghost, like picking up handfuls of mud, cold and dead and futile.

The sounds rose in pitch, and more voices joined them. One by one the bulbs in the lamps blew, showering down sparks.

Jack could see his breath as he commanded Pete, "Call him! Before something gets in here and fucks me proper!"

"Daniel Naughton." Pete drew her spine straight. Her eyes were wide and her body was strung with wire, but Jack gave her credit—her voice was sure and strong. "Master of this house. Come, spirit. Appear and be heard."

Danny boy can't play right now. The voice slithered up out of the Black, and on the wall opposite Jack he saw black handprints blossom, bleeding into the plaster as they fought their way toward the shattered mirror's frame, finger marks and handprints in remembered blood, chromatic as an old horror film.

"Who speaks?" Jack demanded. This part he knew like lines in a well-rehearsed stage play. He'd done plenty of séances when he was skint, and a mage willing to commune with an unknown spirit, to risk possession and ghost sickness, was worth enough coin for a bed and a few weeks of the fix.

"Who calls from the arch of the Bleak Gates?" he said. "Tell me your name."

You'll know my name soon enough, crow-mage. The voice wasn't the sibilant rasp of a fully formed ghost. It was small and high, playful in the way of a child who enjoyed killing small furry things.

In the pit of his stomach, Jack felt a twist. The twist of needing the fix and the twist of a guilty secret. If he were being honest, he'd call it fear, the same fear that came upon him in Highgate. The bastard fear that chewed him up. This voice, this crawling evil on his shoulder, wasn't a simple poltergeist. There was something else in the house, and it had come out to play with him.

He stiffened his fingers on the mirror. He wouldn't shake and he wouldn't show it the fear, not an ounce. "How do you know that name?"

The giggling increased tenfold. *Wouldn't you like to know, grumpy old man.*

"Tell me or I exorcise you on the spot," Jack growled. "I don't need a name and a lock of hair to do it, and you're on me last nerve, cunt. Polite or otherwise."

Pete pointed over his shoulder. "Jack."

A spirit stood in front of the mirror, framed by jagged reflections of Jack and Pete's faces. The spirit looked like a girl, in an old-style sailor dress, hair curled into painfully tight sausages against her scalp. Her eyes were black, bleeding hollows and she grinned at him. Laughed at him.

You should mind your tongue, before I take a notion to cut it out.

The walls were covered in the black miasma now, the air choked with malignant strands of the Black. It spread like water stains, and Jack smelled decay as the temperature dropped, the too-sweet stench of rotted orchids.

Such a funny man you are, the spirit hissed. *So much fun to cut you open and see what clockwork makes you walk and talk.*

She started for him, hollow eyes reaching down into the black howling depths, and Jack felt again the tug on his skull, the vortex of Black energy gathering and swelling until it threatened to burst the bonds of the circle.

"You are not welcome in this house," Jack said. "Go. Last chance, little one."

I belong here, the ghost snarled. We *belong here*. You're *the nasty trespassers.*

All around the circle Jack saw more shapes, struggling to form, twisted spirit figures bathed in the same wicked-smelling magic as the little girl.

A man in a waistcoat with a dark slash across his neck that dripped blood. A woman in an apron with burns bubbling across her arms and face. A boy, tall and rangy-limbed with the first spurt of growth, legs twisted to unrecognizable sticks as he pulled himself across the floor on his hands with the sickening *thud-thunk* of flesh hitting wood.

Jack didn't grace them with a look. Didn't even grace them with a sharpening of breath. If you wanted a ghost to obey, it couldn't see anything except your contempt and your magic. It sure as fuck couldn't get its teeth into your roiling, rollicking panic.

Jack stared at his mirror. He said, "Pete. Salt."

She grabbed the leather sack from his bag and tossed it to him. Jack took a handful and flung it in a careless circle. The ghosts drew back, all except the little girl.

You think that's enough? she mewled. *I'll trim your wings, crow-mage, and chop off your feet to make my curse bags.*

"Too much talk, luv," Jack said. "And no substance." He threw a fat handful of salt on the ghost and she melted away into nothing with a scream, like a Black-ridden garden slug.

Jack let go of the mirror, let himself slump and feel as if his strings had gotten cut. His muscles trembled and the echoes of the ghosts scraped nails through his skull. Vomit welled in the back of his throat but he breathed, fought the feeling down, and pulled his spine upright at last.

"I don't think we're dealing with just a suicide," Pete said finally. Jack laughed. It came out high and hysterical.

"Do you think so, really?"

"All of them were murdered," Pete said. "Or they died right quick and nasty."

Jack extinguished the herbs and opened a window. The rain landed on his face, cold like old tears. It felt good after the touch of the dead. "No arguments. And four of them, plus Danny's chain-knocker. Lots more than dear old Nancy let on." He swiped the water from his skin, through his hair where it wilted his usual crop of spikes. "Inbred liar, just like I fancied him."

"This isn't Naughton's fault," Pete snapped. "This place *is* terribly haunted, just as he said. Spirits don't just find a house and say 'My, this looks lovely. And such a wonderful garden. I think I'll stay and drive the owner to hang himself.'"

Thunder rolled from the moors, back and forth like the rumble of a cell door.

Jack shut the window and kept his hands on the sash until his fingers could open a lock or lift a wallet again. The shaking retreated—mostly.

"No," he said. "They surely don't."

He left the circle, left the room with its echoes of ghosts and the cloying scent of decay. He wanted fresh air and to be outside the walls of the Naughton's house.

Pete followed him, as he shoved the front door open and went to the Mini. He held out a hand to her. "Keys."

She frowned. "What's wrong with you? You look like you're fixing to kill something."

Jack unlocked the boot and pulled a crowbar from the mess of Pete's tools, blankets, and a battered picnic hamper.

He turned back to the mansion. The deadness of the Black tickled the back of his mind—the Black didn't simply fade and then flood. It was constant, a current through his brain straight to his core. It was a comfort and a torment, but always, it flowed.

Jack had felt the flow die once before, faced with a necromancer in the United States. The man fancied himself a warlock, one of the city masters of old, who bent themselves over for a demon. He'd eaten up the Black of Savannah, the city of moss and necropolises in Georgia, until he'd knotted the ghosts of the place so tightly that they tore him apart when Jack took his clay necromancy tablets and burned them in a cleansing fire of sage and cedar wood.

What had been the man's name? Clemens, or Collins. A small man with small delusions who'd managed to grab himself a great gob of power. He'd given Jack a fight, but not a very large one. Not many men, professed wicked men or no, could stare the hungry dead in the eye for long.

Pete grabbed his arm as he re-entered the house. "Are you going to tell me what you're doing stalking around like bloody Jason Voorhees with that thing?"

Jack stomped back up the stairs, taking pleasure at the black marks his boots left on the wood and the plaster that sifted down around him from impact. "You said it yourself—too many ghosts. Things that hungry are territorial, and here there's at least four all sharing nice as you please." He kicked open the door to Danny's bedroom. The doorknob left a fist-sized dent in the wall.

"Spirits like what I called up are bound to a place whether they fancy it or not," Jack said, "and there's only a few sure ways I know to do such a thing."

Jack had dabbled in black magic, of course. Stuck a hand in the water, felt the currents and the pull of dark, old things, but he'd never immersed himself. Once you were under that water, it filled up your lungs and you drowned. Sorcerers were gits with a short life expectancy and shorter ambitions—they wanted magic. Or money. Or sex. But he'd never met a sorcerer worth the curses he spat. The *Fiach Dubh* made sure one of theirs could kick the legs out from under a sorcerer without a second thought.

Still, binding ghosts was the work of a soul shot through with desire, the desire for control or the belief that they could outrun Death. And if any sorcerer he'd met had held real knowledge and truth instead of a load of bollocks and a taste for black clothing and theatrical overstatement, Jack would have swung down the path of sorcery in a heartbeat, and bugger Seth and all his lessons.

But you couldn't outwit Death. It was the single constant of magic and mortality. A thread, a measuring, and a cut. Anyone who thought they were a special case was a bloody fool.

Jack swung the crowbar and bashed through the plaster of the wall behind the great mirror. Dust swirled up, a pale imitation of a spirit. Pete coughed and Jack joined her, the horsehair plaster and wooden slats crumbling under his assault.

"I hope there's a point to this," Pete choked out. "Because that's vile dust."

"Mixed it with arsenic and horsehair in the day," Jack said. "Lovely stuff." The wall was rotted through, and he cleared away debris, half hoping he'd find nothing behind the plaster. He'd never be so lucky, though.

Pete held her sleeve over her nose and mouth. "There's something back there. In the joists."

Jack stuck his hand into the blank space between the studs and closed around dusty glass, sealed with wax. He drew out the small blue bottle, and another, and another, four in all for the quadrant of spirits his exorcism attempt had attracted. "Yeah. There is," he growled. The bottles rolled in his hand, clinking in discordant notes with each other.

He held one up to the light, watched the liquid inside slosh back and forth. "Corpse water," he told Pete. "Used to wash the bodies before burial. Before formaldehyde and all of that shit."

Pete plucked one of the bottles from his hand. "And this binds the ghosts?"

Jack set the bottles in a row amidst the broken glass and

crouched before them. "It's a very old trick. A nasty one. Keep the last thing you touched in this world close and keep you from the Underworld."

Pete knelt next to him. "Did you ever do anything like this?"

Jack shook his head. "No. Never fancied keeping a ghost that close to me." The thought of attracting a ghost on purpose was laughable. They'd found good old Jack Winter all on their own.

Jack had thought he was simply going crazy. Madness would have been a welcome reprieve from the chill, breathless feeling that overcame him when the dead reached out, tried to make him see, to make him their instrument to finish whatever scraps of life they'd left behind.

He'd found magic first in books and then as a failed experiment to make the voices and the sight stop. He hadn't properly understood until he'd met Seth that the ability to speak with the dead marked him as a servant of the crow. Seth had taught him about things like corpse water, bound spirits, and how Jack Winter would never stop seeing—he could only hope to keep the dead at bay until the crow woman came for him, as well.

Seth wasn't one to paint a rosy future where only ash existed.

He stayed silent, staring at the little bottles for long enough that Pete chewed on her lip. "Well, what now? We get rid of them, yeah?"

Jack stood, his boots crushing the mirror shards to sand. His immediate reaction was to flee the Naughton house and never come back, but that was the boy in him, the death-fear that sat on his shoulder and whispered in the demon's voice. More than half of being a successful exorcist was simply not cutting and fleeing like your arse was on fire when the spook show started.

"These specters died here, on the grounds," he said. "And whoever bound them was here, on the grounds."

Pete looked relieved to be back in a domain she understood. "I can check with the local council about suspicious deaths, get a record of property ownership to see if this place always belonged to Naughton."

"That's fine," Jack said. "But this wasn't recent, some spousal dust-up or a kiddie-fiddler hiding his shame. Going by the clothes alone, we're looking at fifty or sixty years gone for the newest."

"Except for Danny," Pete reminded him. Jack looked at the mirror, ten fractured images staring back where glass clung to the frame.

"You'd think Naughton might have mentioned wholesale murder going on amongst the family heirlooms," he grumbled.

"I'm sure he didn't know," Pete protested. Jack felt a surge of heat against his heart that she was in any way defending the ponce. He didn't think it was irrational—when a woman like Pete stepped in for a waste of flesh like Nicholas Naughton, Jack thought his feelings were entirely fucking rational.

"I'll drop you wherever it is you need to go," Pete said, jingling the Mini's keys.

"Town," Jack said, turning his back on the reflections. Jealousy wouldn't matter for much longer, if the demon had his way. Nothing that Jack currently held dear would. Demons thrived on stripping you down to the bone, when they bargained with you, stealing a life and leaving you hollowed out for Hell to fill back up.

Jack said to Pete, "I've got some more ghosts to talk with."

Chapter Sixteen

St. Michael and All Angels crouched on a hillock staring down upon the hulk of Dartmoor Prison. The mica in the cell house stones gleamed in the sunlight after the rain, and Jack squinted and turned his back on the grim edifice. He'd heard that they'd faced the windows toward the moor deliberately, so that a prisoner could contemplate the great heather-choked nothingness and despair of ever leaving the place alive.

The church itself was disused, friendly plaques posted by the Anglicans explaining that services were now held in the next town due to budgetary concerns.

Jack wasn't interested in churches. There hadn't been a time, even a sliver of a second, when he'd truly believed a benevolent God would lift him out of Manchester, away from his mother, her pills, and the endless parade of dingy council flats and dingier boyfriends. What could an invisible man in the sky do against thrown bottles, drunken rages, fists and words and touches that did their level best to reduce him to a shadow?

Bloody nothing, that was what. And all the while the

church charities that came to the Winter flat wearing their good hats and shoes, carrying their boxes of musty hand-me-downs, had told him, *God helps those who help themselves.* A grand fucking joke if he'd ever heard one.

The graveyard around the church was what drew Jack to the place. Overgrown with shaggy weeds, toothy gravestones poking every which way from the dirt, right up to the edges of the church wall, the place seethed with spirit energy. A grotesque of life, a mockery of the feeling he got in a crowded tube or shoving along Oxford Street at holiday time.

Teeming ghosts meant at least one chatty soul in the mix, and Jack drew out his spirit heart over a likely-looking grave. The name was nearly washed from the limestone from forty years of winter rain and year-round wind howling off the moor, but Jack brushed the moss away and spoke it loud.

"Jonathan Lovett."

The spirit heart began to spin instantly. The ghosts in the churchyard, bound by the iron fence, were bored and restless and any hint of magic drew them in like flies on flayed skin.

Jonathan Lovett, plump and serious in life, appeared in a blue uniform and peaked cap that didn't entirely hide a gaping black dent full of hair and brains in his ethereal skull. "Yes? You want something, boy?"

Jack grimaced. A bloody prison guard. Just his luck.

"Thought maybe you could help a bloke with a bit of knowledge," Jack said. Lovett's face crinkled.

"I'll have you know I don't care for Northerners. One of 'em stove my skull in, winter of 1966. A thrice-damned Geordie."

"Can't imagine why he'd want to go and do a thing like that," Jack muttered. "Anyway, I hail from Manchester, so we've nothing to fuss about."

Lovett huffed. His cheeks rippled, like he was made out of sail cloth. "I suppose. Get on with it."

Jack let the chain of the spirit heart twine in his fingers, but he kept it between himself and the spirit. Even cordial ghosts could turn. The mage who thought they couldn't was the mage who had a spirit reach into his chest and stop his heart like a cheap watch.

"You know a house, about twelve miles from here as the crow flies?" Jack asked Lovett. "The Naughton estate?"

Lovett shivered. "I certainly do, and I wouldn't go up that lane if you paid me."

"Oh?" Jack feigned disinterest. "And why is that?"

"When I was . . . how d'you say . . ." The spirit chewed on its lower lip.

"Alive?" Jack prompted.

Lovett twitched his cuffs in irritation. "Yes, well. All sorts of stories about the place back then. Sacrifices, naked dancing about bonfires, screams in the night. Old women around town said Aleister Crowley himself came and stayed for a summer, long way back. Said the crops died and the virgins of the village got themselves in a family way, down to the girl. Not to be crude, you understand."

"I think me heart can take it," Jack said. Aside from the tick of the spirit heart and the whistle of the wind, the only sound was his breath and the rustle and hiss of ghosts at the edges of his mind. They didn't like Lovett getting all the attention. Jack had to finish with Lovett before their attention turned to demands.

"After . . ." Lovett shivered, tucking his several chins down into the collar of his uniform. "After I got into this state, I didn't wander far from the churchyard. That Naughton place is cold, and the moors will blow you all to pieces, scatter you every which way. There's a bad thing in those groomed gardens and fancy turrets, my son. Hungry, howling, and cold."

"Cold?" Jack thought of the sucking quiet that surrounded the house—when it wasn't trying to drown him in a wellspring of the Black. "Second time you've said cold. Cold how?"

"Ice cold and rotten," Lovett murmured. "Spreading out black fingers, feeling in the dark for anything it can catch. All knotted up in the bones of that house, that cold. Such an awful feeling. Burns, it's so cold."

Jack's skin prickled in sympathy, even though he was shielded from the wind by the wall of the church.

"Didn't used to be this way." Lovett sighed, his form flickering like dirt on celluloid. "But now there's badness gathered there, and blackness. And the cold, always the cold."

Jack stopped the spirit heart, metal running cool and dimpled under his fingertip. "Much obliged, Officer Lovett."

"Wait!" Lovett wavered, losing cohesion as Jack's spell spun to a stop. "My wife . . . she never found the necklace. My mother's necklace. It was Valentine's Day." Lovett reached for Jack and Jack took a fast step, nearly tumbling over another headstone. "The day I died . . ."

"Sorry, mate." Jack snapped the spirit heart shut and shoved it into his pocket. "Guess us Northerners are all the same."

Lovett faded with a sigh, just another formless silver shade drifting among the tombstones and weeds, and Jack made his way back to the iron gate, which hung open at an angle that imitated a cheap paperback gothic.

"Shame on you, Jack Winter." The voice was far too smug and solid to come from a spirit throat. "Leaving that poor soul with his noncey unfinished business."

Jack turned sharply, saw nothing. "Leave off your games," he snarled. "If you've got something to say, look at me face. If not, bloody well fuck off. I still have time."

"Do you really?" the demon purred. He was there, in the slice of shadow cast by the gate, same suit but sporting white on black this time and the same black, black eyes. "Or do you only have as much time as I give you?"

Jack jerked his chin. "This how all you gits dress in the Pit? Or did you lose your way en route to the *Clockwork Orange* fancy-dress party?"

The demon narrowed its eyes. "You should take care how you're speaking to me, Jack Winter. What's that the little black book says? *As above, so below?* Show me fealty now and I could perhaps find some little time to spare you. Time with Miss Caldecott, just for instance."

"You're not screwing me with that particular dildo, not again," Jack snapped. He turned to walk away, because he knew it would slag the demon off. Demons were creatures of ritual and respect to the point of compulsion. Jack tipped a salute over his shoulder. "Do give my regards to the other droogs."

"You don't want her?"

Jack stopped in the middle of the road that ran by the church, looked back. The demon smirked, rocking back and forth on the balls of its feet like it was waiting for the punchline of a joke. Jack sneered in return, contempt he didn't feel except as a nervous boil in his guts.

"You know exactly what I want, you bastard."

The demon smiled, tongue flicking out between its teeth. "I suppose that's why we're here, isn't it, Jack?"

"It is," Jack agreed. "But the difference between you and me is that me, I don't care about my moth-eaten old soul. But I'll be thrice-damned if I drag Pete down with me, so if you show your face again before it's my time, I'll exorcise you so far back into Hell you won't even have a name."

"Ohhh." The demon shut its eyes and breathed deep, nostrils flaring, as if Jack's belly-deep, sweaty fear was a heady perfume. "Jack, Jack. You shouldn't threaten me so, old son. You know that I can visit you any time I like. Can do anything to you that might come into my little head."

"Fuck. Off," Jack said plainly, putting the rest of the road between the demon's grin and his person.

The demon raised its hand as if to say farewell, and Jack felt the breathless, vertiginous sensation of magic, demon magic, too late as it gripped hold of his mind and dug its claws in deep.

Pete shivered in the night air, the rain causing the torches at the edge of the stones to spit and smoke. Her hands tugged against the iron restraints, small delicate fingers begging to return the gesture as Jack's hands searched over her stomach, her ribs, coming to rest on her breasts. His finger pads stroked her nipples, smearing the blue paint in time with his thrusts.

This was raw magic, how it had always been, since the first druid and the first Weir long ago. Layers of power wrapped Jack, sweat grown cold against his skin. Pete circled her legs about his waist. Her heels dug into his thighs and her lips parted, panting wordless cries that urged him on to finish, to bind the spell their bodies wove, to take her magic as his own, by force. . . .

Jack raised his face from the pavement, feeling small pockmarks where grit had wormed its way into the flesh of his jaw. A car horn sounded from somewhere far off.

"Jack?" Pete's voice drew closer and small hands felt his pulse, checked his pupils, and then sat him up.

"'M all right, luv," he managed. "Just wanting tea, I expect. Low blood sugar."

Pete favored him with her *Don't pull my bloody leg* eyebrow.

"Alien abduction?" Jack offered. "Overeager and/or amorous sheep?"

"Don't think we won't discuss this when you're not sprawled in the dirt," Pete said, offering him a hand up.

After what the demon showed him, Jack knew better this time than to take it and expose himself to her talent.

Even so, he swayed like he'd downed six pints when he managed to pull his shivery legs under him and stand. "But?" he said as Pete climbed back into the Mini.

"But I found something at the council that you need to hear about," she said. "So loosen your corset and try not to swoon again, Mr. Darcy."

Jack collapsed into the passenger seat with a grateful sound, rather like someone had punctured him and let the air out. "That's hurtful, that is. I'm far better looking than Colin Firth."

Pete steered them back toward the estate, even though it was the second-to-last place in England and the Black that Jack wanted to go at that moment. He kept that to himself. He had pride.

"I looked at old newspapers and provincial records, trying to find any deaths that might be our four," Pete said. "And fended off a sweet old thing who kept trying to give me a biscuit and send me out on a date with her grandson."

"Oh yeah?" Jack leaned his head back. "Any potential there?"

"He stuffs lamb sausages for a living, so no."

Jack grinned with his eyes closed. He didn't have to look at Pete to make her blush. "You know you could never give me up, luv. I'm in your blood like the Black."

"The hell you are." Pete snorted. "Like cheap vodka, maybe. Give me a fag and a coffee and I'm well rid of you."

Jack opened his eyes then. Wanted to say, *I could be. If you let me.* But he'd just told off a demon, claimed he was the white knight who wanted for no strength or nobility.

It was a fucking nightmare, being the knight. No small wonder white witches always looked like they had poles up their bums.

Pete stayed quiet while they rode back to the estate, and she handed him a sheaf of photocopies when they were in the kitchen. She plugged in the ancient and calcified electric kettle and found two mugs, as well as a box of loose tea. "I'm thinking eating anything in this kitchen is asking for us to join the ranks of the gloopy dead upstairs," she said.

Jack lit a fag and offered the last of his pack to Pete. She took it, but he pulled back before their fingers brushed. He didn't trust himself, not because of the demon's interference with his sexual energy and by extension his talent, but because watching Pete move assuredly about the manky kitchen, making tea, her petite limbs moving under torn denim and an ancient jumper with moth holes in the elbow, fag dangling between startlingly plump lips, was nearly more than he could take.

"Fancy lighting me up?" she said, leaning over. Jack called a bit of power and touched his finger to her fag. Pete grinned and exhaled through her nose. "Cheers. Look at the clippings."

Jack scanned the cramped lines of print, none too clear when they'd been churned off a drum press, further decayed by microfiche and a cheap laser printer.

The man with the slit throat was Gilbert Naughton, found on the moor behind the estate in the summer of 1927. No suspects, no witnesses. The burned woman and the mangled boy were a maid and a stable boy, the victims of a barn fire in 1893 that had also killed *Ten fine head of horseflesh*.

The little girl was last. She'd gone missing just after the war's end, and the papers said her name was June Kemp. June was from Limehouse, sent by her family to the Naughton's largesse to avoid the furor of the Blitz as it rained down on the factories and shipyards of the East End.

June Kemp had walked away from the estate one afternoon and gone missing. A manhunt larger than any yet formed in Princetown went out after her, but the girl's body was never found.

Jack stubbed his fag out viciously against the table. "Fuck."

Pete looked at him over the rim of her tea mug. "I'll take that to mean you figured out who or what did this."

"Necromancer," Jack said, crumpling the A4 sheet so June Kemp wouldn't stare at him any longer. Even without hollow eyes and black magic pouring off her, she was an eerie child. "That's not the bad news."

"What is?" Pete broke off the end of her cigarette and tucked the unused bit away for later.

Jack massaged his temples. Ghosts, demons, and now plain aggravation. His headache returned, swift and vicious as a Staffordshire terrier latching on to a postman.

"I can undo the necromancer's bindings. But to get the ghosts out of the house, I have to find their gravesites and set them to rest and if I can't find little Creepy June's remains I can't bloody do that, can I?"

Pete sighed. "Let me see if I can call in a favor with Ollie at the Met. They've got some toys for sniffing out cadavers that are quite good."

"Cadavers that have been under a log for seventy years?" Jack said. Pete sighed.

"Must you shoot down everything I say?"

Jack spread his hands. "It's called being a realist, luv. Worked well for me so far."

Pete slammed her mug into the sink. "It also makes you a sod."

He went quiet, the elaborate apathy that drove Pete up the wall in full force as he slouched at the table and smoked.

"Tell me about necromancers," Pete said instead. "And why one would do something like this."

"Not just one," Jack said. "Even if he ate his veg and gave up smoking, no sorcerer would live to be a hundred and thirty years old on his best day." Usually, they died well before their time. Sorcerers were like roaches—a vile existence and a short life expectancy. Not that Jack and his ilk had any better hope. If you were made of flesh, the Black was predisposed to be fatal to your health.

Seth had said that human beings were never meant to touch magic, but that it was a good joke while it lasted.

"Who knows why a bone-shaker would do something like this." Jack sighed. "And more important, who bloody cares? Bound spirits keep everything that was with them at their moment of death—all the fear, all the pain, all the rage. That's why you need a violent death. Aunt Martha going peacefully in her sleep makes a crap poltergeist."

"And the binding?" Pete said. "We need *something* to show Nicholas, otherwise we won't get a bloody shilling out of him. It'll be the Pooles on repeat."

Jack pushed back from the table. "Need some supplies. Assuming we can keep the ghosties out of our hair long enough, binding's not a difficult thing to undo."

He waved her back when she started to follow him. "We have to wait for sunset. What I need's best done in the dark, at midnight."

Pete snorted indelicately. "Are you quite serious?"

"Have you ever known me to put one over on you, luv?" Jack held up a hand when Pete started to answer. "Never mind. This time I'm not. We'd do better at a new moon but tonight'll have to do."

"We've got a few hours," Pete said. "No telly, no internet service . . . what do you suggest we do until then?"

"I've got a few ideas," Jack said, winking at her. He could stop touching her, stop letting his eyes linger on her, but to ask him to stop flirting was akin to asking him to hold his breath for the next ten years. It wasn't bloody happening. Jack had few joys left, and making Pete blush and smack him in the head was one of them.

"If that's all that's on your mind I'm going for a walk," she snapped.

Jack sobered. "I think after that *cu sith* showed its lumpy face we'd be safer together, luv."

Pete sighed, fingers twitching up to scratch the back of her neck. "I just feel so . . . *locked up* in here. It's not a good place to be."

"You feel the binding," Jack said. It niggled him as well, the subtle sting of black magic crawling up and down his back. It was like a cold draft, the scrape of a thorn against his flesh, not painful but not pleasant either. Jack jerked his chin at Pete. "Come on, I'll teach you something to take your mind off it."

She folded her arms. "If this is another excuse to be a pervert . . ."

"Luv, I never need an excuse. Move your little arse into the parlor and I'll teach you a trick. With me clothes on."

Pete's lips twitched up. "Promise?"

Jack made a poor attempt at crossing himself. "Cross my heart, Petunia."

She followed him into the parlor, where Jack lit on a music box—a dreadful Rococo concoction of pink enamel and gilt scrollwork. It had a lock, though, and it was the lock that interested him.

"Here." He set the thing on the table and gestured Pete into the armchair opposite. An occasional table, his mother had called these things. All spindly legs and round top. She'd kept figurines on the one in their flat. Kev liked to kick it over during their fights.

"That is hideous," Pete said. "Are we transmogrifying it into tea and biscuits? Please say we are."

"You don't need a key to open a lock," Jack said. He put his fingers against the small metal opening and whispered a word of power. The music box sprang open and a snatch of "Greensleeves" drifted out of the musty interior before Jack snapped the lid shut again.

"Magic isn't all circles and chants, Pete," he said. "Magic

is the ability to bend the world to your will. That's why it's frightening and that's why it's powerful. Magic means the rules of the human race don't apply."

Pete shied away from the music box. "I don't like the rules any more than the next human, but the way you put it makes you sound like a bloody sociopath."

"Oh, no, luv," Jack said softly, opening and closing the box again. There was a tiny ballerina figure in a satin dress that danced when her gears spun. "Magic isn't freedom. There's another set of rules entirely, and they're swift and immutable as a guillotine blade."

"So why do it?" Pete said. "Why not just live a normal, human life?"

Jack shrugged. "It's my blood. Yours, too. You can't ignore the Black once it's chosen you, Pete. You can just try to exist."

He turned the box to face her. "Try it. Open the lock."

Pete's brow crinkled. "Thought you said that was black magic."

Jack drummed his fingers on the edge of the table. "You wanted to learn, and I shouldn't have put you off. Open the lock."

Her jaw set, Pete admitted tightly, "It doesn't work that way for me."

Jack folded his arms. "You open doorways to the Land of the Dead. You pull power through you when I do me spells. How is this any different?"

"It just bloody *is*!" Pete snapped. She shoved the box back at him. "I can't do fancy tricks. I just have this awful, deep, dark hole inside of me and sometimes the monster inside it wakes up. I can't *control* it, Jack. I'm not touched with magic like you. I'm stained with it and it doesn't wash off."

"Pete . . ." Jack wanted to reach for her and stop the encroaching tears he saw in her too-bright gaze, but he held himself in. "Pete, you need to listen to me now. You have to learn a few things. Enough so the Black doesn't swallow you alive." He took one of her hands, put it on the lid of the music box. "You're not a monster, Pete. You're something rare, and there's them that will come for you and try to abuse your talent."

"Look." Pete sighed, pulling her hand back into her lap. "I know that I can't hide behind Jack Winter. My whole sodding life has been self-reliance, ever since my mum walked out and left me in charge of my sister and our da." She gave a shrug. "But this isn't me."

Jack felt his jaw begin to twitch. How did you explain to the only person who mattered that you wouldn't be there, wouldn't be able to help her, so she had to help herself?

"Just try it?" he said finally, softening his frown and giving Pete one of his smiles. "For my humor, luv?"

When Jack had nothing else, he still had his snake's charm, even if it made him feel like a low-down hustler to use it on Pete. He reverted back to the clever animal he'd been on the streets, fixing, with the false face and the predator's smile.

And Pete finally nodded, and touched the music box again. "I feel stupid as anything."

"Don't think about that. Don't trouble yourself over anything," Jack said. "Just feel. Bend the lock to your will, and say the words. Tell it *oscail*."

Pete's lips pursed and she shut her eyes. In the curious void that the necromancer's magic left around the house, her power sent out waves like a stone in a pool, like a bell in misty dawn air. It played across his skin like the light drag of fingers and Jack shivered.

After a moment, Pete blew out a breath. "It's no good. I feel it but every time it gets away from me. Like trying to grab a greased cat."

Jack set his hand next to hers. But not touching. Not when her magic was up. He didn't fancy sending either of them into a coma. "Try it again. It takes doing but if you can open a lock, you can call flame and if you can call a flame you can . . . well . . . do practically anything."

"Make someone spit toads?" Pete's lips parted in a smile but her eyes stayed shut.

"I suppose, if that's what gets you off," Jack said.

"I've a few old schoolmates who deserve to cough up an amphibian or two," Pete said.

Jack nudged her foot with his. "You're supposed to be concentrating."

Pete went quiet again, and after ten minutes opened her eyes. "It's no good, Jack. You're a fine mage but you're a lousy Mr. Miyagi."

"So I am," he said. A part of him, small and traitorous, was happy that Pete hadn't mastered in an afternoon a cantrip that had taken him weeks to perfect when he was with the *Fiach Dubh*. A larger part just felt the deadening pressure of his final days, rushing headlong, faster and faster. Too much to tie up, too little bloody rope to do it with.

"When it goes dark we'll try the flame," he said. "For now, keep practicing."

"I do know how to pick a lock," Pete said. "The old-fashioned way." She stood up and put the music box back on the mantle. "And hotwire a car, and cheat at cards."

"Why, DI Caldecott," Jack said, feigning shock. "What a wicked, wicked woman you are."

"Wicked, yeah." Pete laughed. "That's me."

"More than you know," Jack told her. He lit a fag and watched her cheeks color pink at the comment, before she ducked her head and pretended to be interested in the expanse of dead and muddied lawn outside the front window.

Jack watched her until she noticed, and then looked away. The sun was beginning to set behind the moor, and soon enough it would be time to go to work. For now, all he could do was sit and think about Pete, his wicked, wild Pete, and the running hourglass of time ticking off his moments with her.

Chapter Seventeen

After sunset, and too many fags to count, when his throat felt raw and scraped and his heart thrummed uneasily in his chest, Jack shrugged into his leather and opened the front door.

There was a mean sliver of moon overhead, but blowing clouds covered and uncovered it, like the blinking iris of a predatory bird riding the air currents high above his head.

He slung his kit over his shoulder and turned to look at Pete. "You don't have to come along."

"Don't be silly," she replied, small body hunched inside her jumper and overcoat against the cold.

Truthfully, Jack was relieved she'd decided to come along. At night, against a waxing moon, the raw energy of the moor curled around his ankles and echoed in his head, whispering tales of blood and lust and moonlit hunts.

Jack was reminded, as he squelched through the mud, of why he was a city boy and would remain so. The brush of the Black, always so close and present, was like living next door to a slaughterhouse and hearing the animals scream day and night, smelling the flesh and offal. He missed London, stone under his boots and the Black tucked away in hollows and crannies where he could see it coming. Not to mention there wasn't a decent pub or curry stand for miles in any direction.

Jack muttered, "I'd murder for a beer and a chicken tikka."

"Coffee and a *pain au chocolat*," Pete murmured back, sticking close and just behind him as they left the semblance of civilization offered by the long grass of the estate's lawn and crossed a barely flowing stream into the moor.

He flashed her a grin in the moonlight. "We'll be done after tonight, luv. Once we find little Junie and lay her to rest."

"No word from my friend at New Scotland Yard," Pete said. "But he'll come through." Ollie Heath, Pete's rotund former desk mate at the Met, excelled at coming through. Bulbous and sloe-eyed as a Yorkshire sheep, Ollie and Jack had only one brief exchange, but he came away with an enduring dislike for the man.

"You take care of Pete, you hear?" Ollie's Midlands brogue reminded Jack of a council worker who'd sneaked about in the dead of night and shagged his mother for a reduction in their electric bill. *"Lord knows, she deserves better than you."*

Jack didn't know if he disliked Ollie because the man was a prick or because he was right. Most likely both.

He pulled out the crinkled tourist map of the Dartmoor that Pete had procured on her visit to the archives and breathed onto his palm.

Witchfire blossomed, blue and spectral, from his skin, the gentle burn-off of extra magic against the night air. The flames drifted lazily into the twilit sky, the silvery glow lighting the map, just. Jack turned west. "Not much farther."

"What are we looking for?" Pete asked. Wind swept down from the crest of the hill and lifted her hair like a flight of black feathers against her cheek. Rain followed it, in a soft ice-cold sheet, and Jack cursed as it dribbled into his eyes.

"A road."

"Jack," Pete grumbled, "there's a bloody road running right in front of the bloody house. Fuck me."

"Not that road." Jack felt his feet sink into mud as his boots found another ditch, and then gained a roadbed that was little more than gravel and dirt turning rapidly to sludge.

Pete cursed and stumbled against him. Between the witchfire gently bathing them in a bubble of blue and the sideways rain, Jack was none too balanced, but he caught her. She didn't weigh much, but she was undeniably present.

Pete looked up at him, skin translucent and eyes black pebbles in the light. "Thanks."

"Just up here," Jack said, as the moor whispered to him, licked at him with teasing tongues of power. It wanted him to join in the wild celebration, in the mud and the rain. The Black here teased him with memories of what the demon had made him see. Such a place as this was made for the oldest rituals of the *Fiach Dubh*. The deep magic, the old magic that had fallen to the wayside as the people and their power hid in cities, curled up behind iron walls, in front of tellys instead of bonfires, and no longer needed to spill blood into the good soil to procure crops, children, and rebirth.

"This feels wrong," Pete said, dropping her voice so that it blended with the rain. Jack also felt the urge to be silent, creep like a mouse under floorboards. The wild magic around him rose, gathered, and in the back of his consciousness he sensed the prickle of warning that had kept him alive as long as he'd managed the trick thus far.

"We should go back," Pete said, more forcefully. She'd stopped walking, her gaze roving beyond the confines of the witchfire, too much white about the pupil. Fear-white. Her hands clutched her jacket at the neck, knuckles tight.

Jack's heart sped up, warned him that they *should* go back, that they weren't wanted here, that whatever was hunting on the moor tonight was bigger, older, and hungrier than he.

Cold, Jonathan Lovett's ghost hissed. *Always the cold.*

"Fuck off," Jack growled under his breath. The day he turned tail was the day he might as well take a razor to his own wrists. It was the single quality that he could lay claim to as a mage—he might not be as strong or quick as a sorcerer but he'd fight. And the fight he gave would be dirty and mean.

The crossroad loomed out of the rain and the gathering mist, a road sign knocked onto its side in the dying grass the only signal of human occupation.

Jack knelt and opened his bag, pulling out a battered tin and unscrewing the top. He pulled out his flick-knife and scraped up a layer of damp dirt, another. He filled the tin halfway, more than enough for the unwinding spell, but proper crossroads dirt, touched by no human hand, was difficult to come by and he could sell it. When he was back in London. Home.

Pete shivered and she hadn't stopped looking around, but she crouched and watched him. "MG said once that you bury things at the crossroads and a demon comes to grant you a wish."

"They buried murderers at a crossroads," Jack said. "Couldn't have them in a consecrated cemetery. The demon story is a load of shit." Like so much of what MG said. Just enough truth in the lie to be destructive.

"Demons exist, though," Pete murmured. Jack slapped the lid back on the tin with more force than he needed.

"Yes, they do. And calling them is much, much simpler than burying some ruddy box in a crossroads at the dark of the moon."

He shoved the dirt into his bag and folded up the knife.

They were walking a dangerous edge, and he needed to steer Pete away. "Now if we're done talking about it, may I suggest you don't try to summon anything from the crossroad, and that we get the unwinding over with so we can find June Kemp?"

Pete sighed. "My sister said a lot of things. I'm not messing about with Hell, Jack. You don't need to worry."

He breathed in, out, tried to get the panicky tremors in his hands to stop. This deception deep under his skin was like detoxing all over again, shaking and stuttering and freezing to death even in a warm bed. "I'm not worried for you, luv. You're much brighter than me and mine."

Pete smiled, but even that couldn't warm him. "I'm soaked. Let's get back and get this nasty business done so we can go home."

Jack's witchfire faded as his concentration stuttered and they were swept up into the blue-black of moonless night and rain. He shoved his hands into his pockets as he watched and tried to keep the rain off, not succeeding. Mud worked its way into his boots, water between his toes, rain down the sides of his face.

Pete stumbled and cursed. "Hold on." She felt in her pockets. "I've got my light here somewhere."

Jack looked back to the crossroads as a thin beam of weak gold sprang to life from Pete's penlight. In the witchfire, which gave everything deceptive sharp edges, he might have missed a section of shadow peeling off its fellows and padding forward into the roadbed, but he didn't miss it now.

"*Fuck*," he hissed, as the wild magic rose to a roar in his head, drowning out even the rain.

"Jack?" Pete spun around, training her light on the spot where something moved.

"Pete," he said softly. "You need to listen to me now." His brain clicked over like he'd just snorted a straight hit of crystal—it was too far to the house, they'd never make it in time. Not both of them, at any rate. His bag just held herbs and the odd tin of dirt, not salt, not iron.

All he had was his flick-knife. He was fucked.

"It's . . . it's that thing from this afternoon," Pete whispered as the *cu sith* advanced on them, inexorably, the limpid glow of its eyes like a lamprey floating through the soft sheets of mist and rain. "The black dog."

"Caught our scent," Jack muttered. The black dog drew back its lip to reveal blade-sized teeth. "Pete," Jack said. "When I tell you, you have to run. Really run, this time. For your life, and don't look back. Get inside the house. Salt the doors and windows—every entrance."

Pete's fingers clutched his arm as the black dog snarled, a sound that vibrated through the soles of Jack's boots. "Why the fuck are you telling me all of this?"

"The same reason I taught you the lockpicking charm," Jack said, prising her grip off his jacket. "Because I might not be there when you need it."

Pete tried to grab for him again but he held her at arm's length. He hated letting go of her, hated the expression of utter bone-deep betrayal on her face. But he had practice calling whatever outward expression he needed in the moment to his face, too much practice, and he kept his features calm. "Go, Pete. Salt the doors."

She hesitated for an instant, and Jack pushed her. "I said *run*, you stupid bint!"

Pete ran, her footsteps crunching on gravel and fading as they joined the grass of the moor.

Jack faced the black dog.

The thing stopped a few meters from him, scenting the air. It chuffed, large head swinging from side to side.

"You're too late," Jack told it. "Too late for anything except scraps. She's gone."

He squared up his shoulders. This wasn't what he'd

imagined—a creature of the Black doing the demon's work—but he supposed it was fitting as anything. "Get on with it, then. Lock your jaws on me and drag me down under the hill, if you would."

The black dog cocked its head. It took another step and Jack's body, the traitorous thing that craved a fix and Pete and life, took a jerky step back in return.

"You heard me!" Jack shouted, dropping his bag and spreading his arms. "What are you waiting for? Come the fuck on!"

He waited for the cold, deathless sensation of a Fae creature sinking its teeth into his magic, into his very soul, but it didn't come. The dog just snarled, swiping at the air with a paw. Its claws looked like carving knives.

Jack held his ground, heart slamming fit to break his ribs. He stared into the black dog's soft candle-flame eyes, and the black dog stared back. For a shred of eternity, Jack and the Fae creature shared the moor, the wild magic flowing around them, over and through Jack, filling him up with the desire to let go of his earthly burdens and step into the grasp of the *cu sith,* to give in to the inexorable pull of the Bleak Gates and admit that unless he found a way to get free of the demon, Death waited beyond every breath.

We don't want the crow-mage, the black dog purred in the sibilant bell-voice endemic to the Fae.

"I'm what you're getting," Jack gritted, but desperation was birthing a frantic plan in his hindbrain. The black dog was hunting, not feeding. It wanted something.

Creatures that wanted something could be bargained with.

They could be tricked. The sure and swift fate of those marked by the *cu sith* might not be his, after all.

We seek the blood-born messenger of the old voices, the girl on the owl's wing, the dog rumbled.

"Can't help you there, mate," Jack said. "Kiss me or kill me, but you're not getting Pete."

Crow-mage, in your arrogance do not make the mistake of thinking we will mind the Hellspawn's bargain, the dog whispered, and Jack's stomach went sideways.

"How do you know about that?"

We guard the doorways and the byways, the secret places and all who pass. We see much. We see you.

The dog let out a howl that could bleed eardrums, that rolled and echoed off the hillside.

"It's not Pete you want," Jack said, the edge of frantic making his voice ragged. "You have to *leave*, do you understand? Leave her alone."

We are not seeking harm, crow-mage, the dog hissed. *We are seeking to keep her from the taint of death, the mud and blood and carnage of the crow. We do not expect you to understand.*

Jack felt his temper fray, a curious physical sensation akin to standing up too fast when you'd gone and tied a few pints on. His shield hex grew in front of him before he was even aware he'd whispered "*Cosain*," and he felt witchfire curl across his exposed skin as his fury burned in the night.

Gone was the fear. Now he just wanted the thing in front of him to hurt, burn, and cower before his magic.

The black dog crouched, nails digging into the mud. *You think I fear a flesh-and-blood thing such as you, crow-mage? Bitch of the war-hag?*

"You're one to talk about bitches," Jack said. "And I think you're scared enough to keep away from me, to skulk around in shadows like a shade. If you want to kill me, you're welcome, mate. Here's your open chance. Take your fucking try."

The black dog reared, charged, and Jack braced himself for the psychic impact on his hex. It felt like nothing so much as sticking your head inside a great bloody bell and ringing the clapper, loud and riotously painful.

Something streaked into his vision from the left, a small form with a silver weapon. Pete swung the crowbar over her head and down, landing it squarely on the black dog's spine.

"Go back where you sodding came from!" she shrieked.

The dog howled at the touch of cold iron, and stumbled. Jack spun out of the way, going on his arse in the mud and avoiding the thing's claws by inches.

Cease! The dog howled. *We mean to take you as our own, Weir. . . .*

"Not bloody likely." Pete clutched the crowbar, her breath rasping in and out like a saw, lips parted and body trembling. "Now I'm no mage and I'm no sure hand at this but if you come near me again I'll send you back to the fucking Dark Ages, you mangy git, so take the chance and *fuck off*!"

She swung the crowbar again, catching the dog across the snout, and it yelped and cowered, eyes fading to a sick shade of orange.

That, it told Pete, *was a grave error in judgment, girl.*

"Wouldn't be the first," Pete said, her voice icy as the aura surrounding the black dog. "Won't be the last."

Jack gripped Pete's arm, causing her to lower the crowbar. The black dog skirted around the edges of his hex, wary now of the iron, its breath leaving great dragon puffs of white in the freezing air. "We need to go," Jack told Pete. "We need to go *now*."

"Couldn't agree more," Pete said. She dropped the crowbar and backed up until she was pressed arm-to-arm with Jack, and as one they turned and ran.

Jack felt his lungs protest after the first few steps, a cutting sensation sawing against his breastbone. For the first time in his adult life, he wholeheartedly promised any higher power listening that if he survived past the next few minutes, he'd seriously consider cutting back on the fags.

They pelted down the hill, Jack snatching glances into the night behind him, watching for the black dog.

The baying started when the estate was just within reach, a few hundred meters across the muddy grass.

On the crest of the hill, Jack saw the black shadow ripple and re-form as the dog stopped to scent him, and then two other shadows join it, all of them raising their snouts to the hidden moon and offering their blood oath.

"What d'you know," he panted. "I thought it was just being a pretentious git using the royal *we*."

"Less talk!" Pete snapped. "More moving!"

The house lay so close, back door open, a slice of light spilling forth like the Heaven that the priests of his childhood assured Jack he'd never see.

Behind him, the black dogs bayed and he felt their breath, heard their pants as he ran through the rain, dug in his toes, and really pulled for the line. He wasn't going to die in the mud, brought down like a rabbit.

Jack didn't have much, but he was better than that.

Just when he thought he was going to drop, when black closed in at the edges of his eyes and his breath felt like a rusty bayonet ripping through his chest, he hit the door, tripped over the threshold, fell hard on the shoulder the poltergeist had bollocksed.

Pete stumbled after him, slamming the door and sliding the bolt home. Jack felt the wild magic following them, like a cloud of toxic smoke, and he pointed at the kitchen. "Salt!"

In the fetid kitchen, Jack snatched up the big tin he kept in his kit and Pete grabbed for the leather packets laced with thongs, jerking one around her neck and tossing one at Jack. He put it on as he flung a line of white crystal at every window and door he passed. With each application, the magic retreated a bit, loosening its bony grip on his heart. The baying of the hounds faded, and finally, as Jack salted the front door, all that remained was the gentle wash of the rain against the glass and discordant drip of water from a leak somewhere high above.

Jack realized his hands were shaking as he closed up the salt tin, and it took a few tries to shut it tight. He leaned his forehead against the front door and fumbled for a fag. His pack was flat and empty. "Shit," he muttered. It never rained but it poured.

The shivering wasn't just from coming so close to the *cu sith* and its mates a second time—he was soaked to the bone and the mansion was erratically heated at best.

"Pete?" he shouted, checking the salt lines one last time. Nothing from the Black was coming into the mansion. Nothing was getting out, either. Jack hoped the poltergeist of Danny Naughton would hold off from smacking him about until Jack'd managed to put a ration of whiskey and a cup of tea down his throat.

Until he stopped shaking, stopped betraying the bottomless fear that had crept up when he saw the black dog again. When it *spoke* to him. Fae creatures, other than the Unseelie, didn't speak to humans, and they certainly didn't threaten them like the black dog had.

"Kitchen, still," Pete called. Jack put the salt away in his bag, and pushed his hands through his hair before he left the front hall. It was damp and frozen at the tips, and started him shivering again.

Pete had poured the last of a cloudy bottle of whiskey into two jam jars. She took hers, mounting the servants' stairs. "I'm freezing. I'm going to get dried off."

"Are you all right?" Jack said as she started up.

"Of course," Pete said. "Shaken, a bit. But fine."

She didn't meet his eyes, and Jack took her gently by the wrists, drawing her close. "Why did you come back? I told you to stay inside. Stay behind the salt."

Pete still wouldn't look at him. "Jack . . ."

"Why, Petunia?" He gave her a small shake. "Do you realize what could have happened?"

"Of course I do!" Pete flared. "I'm not bloody stupid!" She shrugged him off with an angry slap. "I'm not fine, Jack, and I don't know precisely what happened but I *do* know that you don't get to give me orders. Not about things like this. I won't let you fling yourself on a sword for me. *No one* gets the right to do that, you understand?"

Jack grabbed her again, pushing her back against the door, her skull and his knuckles rattling against the wood. "*You* need to understand, Pete. I won't always be able to tell you what to do, so you have to *learn*, now. Before . . ."

He trailed off, letting go of her, scrubbing the heels of his palms into his eyes. The secrets crowded close in his brain and his skull throbbed like it was going to shatter.

"Before what?" Pete said, softly. She took his hands, pulled them down so she could look at his face. "Before what, Jack?"

It was her touch that undid his resolve, because it was gentle. Pete could be hard—Jack'd experienced it firsthand when she'd handcuffed him to her bedpost and forced him to detox from the heroin.

But she held his hands gently, and squeezed them. "Jack . . . just tell me."

He looked at his boots. They were crusted with mud and salt, drying now, the battered leather stained. "I can't," he whispered. "I can't, Pete."

Her touch went away. "If that's how it is then we can't be anything, Jack. We'll do the job and we'll collect the pay but if you can't tell me something even when it's eating you up, then this can't go on."

She mounted the stairs and she was out of sight before Jack found his voice. "I'm sorry, Petunia," he murmured. "I am so, so sorry."

Chapter Eighteen

He followed her after a time, found her stripped down to her undershirt and denim. Her muddy clothes were in a heap on the carpet and she'd lit a small fire in the smoky grate.

Jack held out a mouse-nibbled pink towel. "Peace offering?"

Pete sighed and then snatched it from him, using it on her face and hair. "Only because I'm like a drowned rat."

"No," Jack said, using his own manky towel to dry his hair. "You're never that, luv."

"Jack," Pete sighed. "Do me a favor and don't try and make this better by coming on to me. It's just horrid and confusing at this point."

He turned his back so Pete wouldn't see him looking gut-punched, because what sort of a hard and wicked mage would he be if he got sour over a girl shooting him down?

"My apologies," Jack said. "In a platonic and boring fashion, is it all right if I share your fire until me clothes dry out? I have a feeling if I fall asleep damp I'll wake up with some horrid Victorian disease."

"That's fine," Pete said. Her posture unwound when she realized he wasn't going to push her.

How he wanted to push her. He wanted to touch cool milky skin with his fingers, feel hot breath on his neck, crush her with the desperate pressure he felt whenever she came within a meter of him.

Jack stripped off his shirt, the sodden thing landing with Pete's clothes, and unlaced his boots, setting them on the hob. His tattoos licked up the firelight, and he was surprised when Pete sat next to him on the edge of the bed, blocking the dancing shadows.

"I trusted you, you know," she said. "When we met again. I trusted you even though it nearly killed me."

Jack lifted his shoulder. "Trust isn't a commodity that has any value in this life, Pete."

"But it does between us," she said. "And the fact that you won't trust me speaks buckets."

He stayed silent. There was nothing to be said, and Jack valued silence, always had. When one grew up with screaming, crying, and soft whimpering day and night, silence was worth more than gold. And when there was nothing to be said that didn't bring fury on your head, you shut the fuck up and you took your lumps.

"And the real pisser of it is that I like you," Pete said. "If this were some bloke at work, or a regular, normal, dull-as-dishwater boyfriend, I wouldn't care. I'd move on. But you, Jack. You had to make me take the plunge into *this life* with you, and now you won't trust me and that's just bloody shit of you, isn't it?"

"Can't," Jack corrected her, voice barely more than a cigarette rasp. "Not won't. Can't trust you."

Pete's lip curled. "Well, Jack Winter, tell me: what *can* you do?"

Jack felt the weight of the secret, in his gut like a stone.

He felt the demon's secret as mercury on his tongue, cold and slippery and begging to be spilled.

Instead, he grabbed Pete by the nape of her neck and pressed their lips together.

She let out a small sound, her cheek going flush and warm against his as their bodies met, and her hands searched up his bare chest for his shoulders, finger pads digging in and holding fast.

As he slid his tongue between her lips, and they parted warm and willing for his advance, Jack thought to himself that he should stop. If he had any kind of decency left, he'd stop. He'd remove himself from temptation then and there, and never see Petunia Caldecott again.

But Jack knew the story of him and temptation, knew it by rote. The bright, hot, shining things always tempted him. And sooner or later, Jack always gave in.

Pete climbed into his lap, slim strong thighs pressing against his legs, breaking the kiss long enough to tangle her hand in his hair, dig the other into the flesh of his back, press her tits against his chest and her core against the swell of his cock, which grew harder, nearly painful, at even the hint of her touch.

Jack wasn't naive enough to think he held any control over himself any longer. He put his lips against Pete's neck, the deep-down reptile memory expecting the taste of sweat and sex and woad from his vision.

She tasted cool instead, a few raindrop still clinging to her skin, her pulse fluttering under his mouth as he frantically drank down as much of her as he could. It was his last chance, his only chance, and Jack breathed her in instead of air as his hands searched out the hem of her shirt and tugged.

Abruptly, Pete pulled back, away from him, and Jack came back to himself with a vertiginous jolt. He was too warm, the air was too cold, and his hard-on scraped painfully against his jeans.

Of course she'd stop him. This was Pete he was with, not some coke-addled Bastards groupie or blissed-out junkie girl fucking him for a bed in a squat.

Pete put her finger under his chin, drew his gaze up. Every touch sent waves of the Black echoing through him, their magics twining even now, as Jack struggled to keep himself from simply grabbing her and doing what every fiber in his body demanded.

"Jack, what are we doing?" she whispered. Her voice was rough and her breaths were heavy, in time with Jack's own throbbing heart. Pete was spinning out as badly as he was, and for some reason the knowledge filled Jack with a giddy joy. He might as well have chased a handful of downers with a shot of espresso.

"I don't know anymore," he whispered back, pressing his forehead against hers, their lips close enough to share any secret.

Except one.

Pete swallowed hard, the enticing alabaster length of her throat flexing. "Fuck it," she said roughly. "I don't care."

Jack stroked down her neck, over her clavicle, feeling the rise and fall of bone and skin beneath his fingers. His sight made everything silver tinged as the power gathered around him and made him fly, made him float, the only high he'd felt that was better than the needle could ever be.

Still, the small bit of him that whispered when he couldn't sleep, when he saw things a man tried to bury with fags and booze and easy companionship, made him speak. "I do. I don't want to be your mistake, Pete."

"Too late for that," she murmured. "I told you you're in my blood, Jack." She shut her eyes, and Jack saw silvery tears shimmer at the corners. "You're in my blood like poison."

Jack took her face in his hands, stroked the tears away with his thumbs. "Petunia, no. Don't cry, luv."

Pete opened her eyes, and her hands crawled around his neck, her body insistent against the bulge in his trousers, hip bone on hip bone. "You're in my blood like poison," she repeated, her voice scraped. "And I'd die because of you."

Jack saw it in her eyes, that reckless feral desperation he recognized. He'd seen it on his own face, in cracked bathroom mirrors and shards of glass for cutting lines, too many times.

He grabbed Pete by her hair, pulled her mouth down to his, answered that he felt the same as she.

Pete moaned, and Jack slid his other hand down to her arse, lifting them both from the bed, swaying with her added weight and going down hard on his knees on the threadbare Persian carpet in front of the fire.

He let go of Pete, barely gave her time to catch her breath before he pushed her to the floor, nudging her knees open with his own, capturing the sweet expanse of skin just above her collarbone in his mouth.

"Jack," Pete whimpered. "Jack, I need . . ."

"I know," he said into her skin. "Me, too." He moved, though he could have stayed in the spot forever, and fumbled with her undershirt, trapped as it was against the floor. Pete's hands found his belt buckle, tugged it loose with far more skill. The pyramid studs made a dull *thunk* as they hit the floor and Jack muttered, "Fuck it." He grabbed the neckline of Pete's top and yanked. The lacy fabric gave way and Jack tossed it aside, pausing to appreciate the sight of Pete's small but impressive tits encased only in a black lace bra. The blush of her nipples was visible in the firelight, and Jack grinned.

"Petunia, you wicked, wicked girl."

She reached behind her and unhooked the strap in response. "I told you, didn't I."

The bra joined the undershirt, and Jack dropped his

mouth to Pete's nipple, skating over her breast and taking the nub between his teeth. Pete cried out, her hips swaying under him, and Jack decided to hell with taking it slowly or softly. Slow and soft was for ponces and virgins. This was Pete. He was making it count.

He undid the fly of her jeans, helped her wriggle until they were halfway down her legs. Pete grabbed his hips, pulled him up to her lips, and kissed him deeply as her hands worked at his cock, stroking him length and breadth, teasing his balls with her fingertips, and grinning against his mouth.

"You like it, luv?" he murmured, rubbing circles against her tits with his thumbs, coaxing the soft high moans from her that made his cock leap in her hands.

"Yes." Pete drew back and eyed him seriously. "I may faint from sheer awe."

"You *slag*," Jack growled, hooking his fingers in her panties and jerking them down to mid-thigh.

Pete let out a gasp as his hand found her, parting the thin stripe of black hair at her pelvis and sliding from her clit to her opening.

Jack felt wet against his fingers, enough of it to tell him that Pete wasn't waiting. A rub of his thumb against her clit confirmed his theory, as she gasped, her back going rigid and pushing her bare tits against him.

"*Fuck. Jack.*"

He pushed into her with his fingers. She was still tight, soaking wet but not quite ready for him. Any other time, with any other woman, Jack would have been happy to give the assist, but he felt that if he didn't put himself inside her in the next few seconds he was going to combust.

The tip of his cock had stroked the outer fold of her when she stopped him.

"My overnight bag," Pete murmured thickly, palms against his hips. "The outside pocket."

Jack braced himself on his arms, looked down at her. "You have *got* to be sodding kidding me, Petunia."

"Jack," she said, still panting. Mussed and flushed as she was, Jack knew she wouldn't stop him if he simply fucked her with no further chatter.

"Now who doesn't trust who?" he said peevishly as he snagged the bag and found the packet of rubbers where Pete said it would be.

"Not you," Pete said, grabbing them from him. "Just all of the other women you've been fucking."

She tore the packet and flung it to the side, and although her movements were frenetic they were still too slow. "Pete," Jack said, the hoarse note in his voice entirely involuntary. "Do you want to drive a bloke into cardiac arrest?"

She took his cock and slid the rubber over it, biting her lip in such a fashion that Jack was nearly blinded by the urge to make her come, so she'd repeat the gesture while she screamed his name.

"There," she said. "Was that so . . ."

The last word lost as Jack shoved her thighs akimbo and drove himself into her, Pete let out a gasp, half pain. Jack gave a groan of his own as she closed around him, and even though he'd resolved to make it last, to lose himself, he kept moving, hard and rhythmic as the drum line of a Bastards song.

Pete, for her part, arched her back upward, digging her nails into his back and meeting his thrusts. It was nothing like his vision—it was hot and frantic and *present*, and their magic wasn't colliding but combining and nearly sending Jack off-balance as he edged closer to the finish.

He watched as Pete dropped one of her hands between her own legs while Jack drove himself faster as the telltale heat waves spread across his vision.

"Oh, Petunia," he growled, the sight nearly sending him over then and there. "The things I'm going to do to you."

"Do it, then," Pete dared him, her cheeks flaming. "I want to come, Jack. Make me."

Even though his base instinct snarled in protest, Jack pulled out of her, and Pete gave a cry of protest. He grabbed her hips and flipped her easily onto her stomach on the carpet—one of the benefits of fucking such a petite little thing.

His left hand dug into the firm, yielding flesh of her arse. His right reached down into her curls and found her clit as he re-entered her, his cock finding its deepest purchase yet.

Pete gave a small scream, shocked and hoarse, and Jack fingered her in time with his thrusts, her cries driving him harder and faster with every movement of his hips.

"Jack," Pete whispered. "Jack . . . *Jack* . . . "

She shuddered around him, the first hint of release, and her breath was little more than ragged sounds. "Stop," Pete begged. "Stop it . . . I can't . . ."

"No," Jack said. "No, my sweet, I'm not done yet."

But Pete was, and with the next stroke of his fingers she lost herself, her pussy closing around him and fluttering along the length of his cock as he moved.

"Oh, *fuck*!" Pete screamed out, trembling as another wave took her. Jack pushed her back down as she started to rise, gripping her shoulder and using it to lever himself for one last thrust.

Jack felt himself come, and it bent him over, gasping, as he spent himself and spent himself again inside Pete. When he'd finished he stayed still for a moment, the two of them crouched, his chest touching her back and his arms around her waist.

Pete moved at last, gently distancing herself and rolling over to pull up her panties. Jack sat back on his heels, his sight roiling and his heart speeding along at two hundred kilometers.

"Fuck me," he said finally. "I'd murder a fag."

Pete let out a shaky laugh. "Here." She fished in her bag and handed him a new pack. Jack lit one for himself and offered one to Pete. She took it, her hand still shaking.

"That was . . ." She inhaled too deep, coughed, exhaled a cloud of blue. "I never know what to say."

"Don't say anything," Jack said, unkinking his legs and stretching out in front of the fire. He shot Pete a grin. "I'm just getting started, luv."

Pete's lips parted, and her next draw on her fag was positively pornographic. "Are you?"

"Do I ever make a promise I don't keep?" Jack asked her. For just a moment, the length of his burning cigarette, he allowed himself to believe he hadn't made a royal mess of his good intentions, that Pete was still safe and that he could stay with her long as he pleased.

Then Pete flicked away her fag and moved into his lap again, and it didn't matter any longer.

Chapter Nineteen

Thin gray morning light lay across his face when Jack woke, fingerlets of silver reaching through the moth-eaten drapes. His neck was stiff from passing out against the hard feather pillows, but the rest of him was warm and content to float between sleep and waking.

Slowly, so he wouldn't wake her, Jack twisted to look at Pete. She slept curled on her side, one hand tucked under her cheek and her bare shoulder exposed where the coverlet slid off.

Jack pressed his lips to the spot and then levered himself out of bed, grabbing Pete's pack of fags on his way to the loo. He lit one, took a piss, and looked out the uncurtained window at the morning. Mist hugged the grass and moisture filmed the windows of the Mini. He couldn't see beyond the gates. The moor had vanished in the fog.

A reflection moved behind him in the window glass and Jack looked sharply at the bathroom door. Smoke stung his eyes as it drifted.

The demon grinned at him. "Caught you with your

knickers down, Winter." It held Jack's denim on the crook of its index finger.

Jack tugged on the rusty chain of the ancient loo and flicked his fag butt into the water. "See something you like, mate?"

"Don't play the happy sod with me, Winter," the demon purred. "Your lady-love is asleep in the next room, after all."

"If you touch her you'll be dust before you draw your next breath," Jack promised. The fear had fled with the light and left in its place a flat, hard resolve. The detritus of a retreating tide, sitting jagged in his chest.

Jack Winter wasn't a man who got dragged to Hell and tortured. Not when the Black was trying to devour a friend, because friends were a rare enough commodity in his life as to be practically mythic.

"You think you stand a chance?" the demon asked, head tilting to catch the beam of morning on its waxy skin, like sunlight touching the face of a corpse with a torn shroud.

"I may not beat you," Jack said, pulling a little magic to him from the bones of the house. "But I'll fight you, tooth and nail." The magic slithered and thrashed, unwilling to be caught. Jack grimaced. It might be a short fight. Many poor sods had the idea just before the end to fight, to cheat, to wriggle free of their bonds, but Jack wagered that none of them were quite as desperate as he. Desperation counted for much, when you dealt with demons.

"You're a bit peevish, aren't you?" the demon said. "Not even a proper hello, just moaning and whingeing as usual." Its gaze drifted past Jack and landed on Pete's form in the bed, her bare skin pale as the morning light and hair dark as ink spilled on it. The demon's lips parted. "Was the little Weir slut not everything you hoped for?"

"I'm only going to say this once," Jack told the demon. Posturing with citizens of Hell never ended well, but acting the hard man was natural camouflage when he was backed against a wall. "Your business is with me, not with Pete. Stop threatening her, and stop sending your fucking Fae emissaries to chase me all over creation. I'm not some bare-breasted twit in a B-grade horror movie, so don't think you can frighten me with a few loose ghosties in a train station and some chatty cunt of a *cu sith* on the moor."

The demon frowned. The expression was unnatural on its face, like watching a dead body try to frown once its muscles had seized in rigor mortis. "I have no idea what you're babbling about." It tossed the denim at him. "Put your pants on, mage. You and I have matters to discuss."

The demon stared out the window, breath making wing-shaped patterns on the glass, while Jack dressed and splashed water on his face. Post-coital warm fuzzies lasted exactly as long as it took him to either realize his girl of the night was three pints south of shaggable or for a boyfriend to burst in.

Or demon, as the case might be.

"This place," the demon murmured. "It's a dead place. How do you stand it?"

"Not planning on being here much longer," Jack said. "Doing what needs doing and going home to London."

"Enjoying what time you have," the demon murmured. "Most people would call you a bright lad."

"Why are you here?" Jack leaned against the sink but he didn't relax. "You appear to me in the loo to have an idle chat, or, let me guess—you're lonely."

"I wanted to speak with you, Jack," the demon said. "Not as an adversary but as a mage. Can you do that? Put our dealing aside for the moment and listen?"

"You prepared to rescind your claim on me?" Jack asked. "Because I'm *not* putting anything aside, and if you're not prepared to offer something, you can fuck right off back to the Pit."

"Jack." The demon sighed. It folded its arms, and back-lit against the glass it looked almost angelic, if angels had existed. "I could have left you to die that day when you called for me, and instead I reached out my hand. So I think maybe, just maybe, you should leave off your complaints and show me a bit of fucking respect."

The air around the demon's form flared with power, and Jack grabbed his forehead. The demon stretched and grew, a black shadow robed in smoke, the same black stone eyes boring into him like drill bits.

Jack shut his eyes. He let the old mantra pound through his skull. *Not there. Not real. Not real. Not real.*

The demon gave a soft chuckle. "Just remember who you're dealing with, boy. Do you want to hear my proposition or not?"

Jack massaged at the throb in his temples, ineffectually. "All right, then," he said. "Talk. Thrill me."

"When we met," the demon said, "I chose to bind a bargain with you because I sensed something of the demon in your nasty, soot-stained little soul."

"I think your crystal ball needs adjusting, mate," Jack said. "I'm just plain old flesh and blood."

"Mostly blood, as I recall." The demon chuckled. "Jack, in spite of your mouth and that sullen mien, I do like you, boy."

Jack braced himself on the sink. "So you came to me for a lift, is that it?" The door was only two feet from him—if he needed, he could be through it and to his bag of tricks before the demon had time to worm its way past his shield hex.

"I know that even though you've got a weakness for flesh and a bigger one for drugs, you're one of mine, boy." The demon regurgitated the phrase with a sneer. "You're a liar and a cheat and you think you're far cleverer than you actually are—"

"And I am, really," Jack interjected. "Quite clever. Cause of and solution to all me problems, cleverness."

The demon gave him the blade edge of a smile. "If you were *that* clever, Jack, we wouldn't be talking."

"If you didn't have the pressing need to hear your own voice, we wouldn't be talking either," Jack muttered.

"Don't think I don't know you would wriggle out of my bargain in a moment if you *were* clever enough," the demon purred. "Or that I don't know your little mind is whirring away even now, wondering, *How can I flip and flop and squirm out of yet another tight spot?*" It reached out and patted Jack on the cheek. "You can't. And the fact that you haven't openly tried any foolishness is the only reason you're still taking up oxygen, Jackie boy. Believe me."

Jack fished another fag out of the pack. He could only take so much inane chatter from Hell's denizens before the craving for nicotine made him more than a shade rude. He sucked in smoke, relished the burn as something real to cling to while the demon's smoky, musky aura swirled around him, poisoning the air breath by breath.

"I sense this is going somewhere," he said. "In the slow and meandering manner of a London bus in rush hour. Care to cut the journey short? I've better things to do, like go downstairs and drop a tire iron on me foot."

"There's another," the demon said. "Another man. Equally desperate when we met." The demon bared its teeth. "But he fancies himself far, far cleverer than you, Jack Winter, in the most odious way possible." The demon gave its tie an irritable stroke, smoothing out all its wrinkled edges and glaring at nothing.

Jack grinned around his fag. "I don't believe it. This bloke found a way to cheat you?"

"That's a bloody lie!" The demon flared, and the witchfire in his eyes moved, slick and oily like ripples across a pool of runoff.

"All right, he didn't." Jack shrugged. "No skin off me that you're in denial."

"Oh, but it will be," the demon said. "If I lose one of my charges, I will lose all of my charges, and the one who takes them from my cold, lifeless hand will not be a sweet forgiving old sot, like me."

"I'd hate to see who's unforgiving in the Pit," Jack said. "If you're the nice old granny of the lot."

"Someone must go among the pagans of his hiding place," the demon said. "Someone must return him to my patch to face his trial."

"And this someone can't be yourself . . . why, exactly?" Jack exhaled. He'd swear, if demons could look put out, his would at that moment.

"It's not my land," the demon said stiffly. "It's not mine to trespass on."

"Someone bigger 'n' badder than you runs the patch!" Jack laughed, and it turned into a cough when he sucked smoke down the wrong pipe. He hacked for a moment, eyes watering. One of these days, he should really slap on some of those patches Pete was always buying and abandoning around his flat.

"You're treading on thin fucking ice, mage," the demon hissed. "Be mindful of the next step."

Jack watched his fag ash for a moment. He could smart off all day long but it didn't change the fact that he would have to give the demon an answer. A yes would bring him that much closer to the bosom of Hell. A no would only start his clock unwinding again, the number growing alarmingly low as the days passed.

"Maybe you should abandon this cryptic shite and tell me what you want," he said finally. "Because I'm bored, mate. Dead bored, of your mysterious appearing and your riddles and your fucking *Saturday Night Fever* wardrobe."

"What an apt choice of words," said the demon. "You

always had a facility, didn't you?" It scratched its chin and then said, "Go to the pagan city and bring this man home. That's all you have to do, Jack. He's a mage, like you. He even plays a bit of music. You two lads should get on famously."

Jack shifted his posture, only a little. Shoulders forward, arms folded. Every smallish boy turned skinny bloke learns how-to-make themselves look bigger, if they don't want an arse-pounding or worse. Jack had the advantage of height on the demon, but he still felt its magic like a boot on his chest. Made him defensive, like the demon had come in and pissed all over his belongings. "And if I bring your little lost lamb to the fold? What then?"

"I suppose I'll owe you a favor, won't I?" The demon showed its teeth.

Jack returned the gesture. "Not good enough. I want your word. I want something tangible."

"Oh?" The demon raised its eyebrows. "Conditions. And specifics. The little Weir's taught you well, my son."

"I'm not your fucking anything," Jack snarled. "Let's get that straight, at the outset. I'm not your rent boy, I'm your hired gun. Condition the first."

The demon's eyes barely flickered. "Accepted."

"Condition the second," Jack said. "I agree to fetch this arse-monkey for you, I get something for it. Something *I* choose."

The demon's posture stiffened and it licked its lips. It liked Jack setting the pace far less than simply invading his head with visions of Pete. Jack watched its face carefully, even though looking the thing in the eye hurt at the bottom of his forehead, the space where hippie gits said your third eye rode.

This was the litmus test. If the demon agreed, it needed him badly. And it wasn't telling him the whole truth. If demons even understood the concept.

Finally, the demon exhaled, a sharp irritated huff of air. "All right. Agreed." It sneered. "State your grand terms."

Jack felt a cold snatch of excitement in his belly. The bloke who'd slagged off the demon must really be on to something, and the thing guarding his hideout must have sharp fucking teeth indeed. Two things in his favor. It might as well have been fucking Yuletide.

"If I find him and bring him back," Jack said, stubbing out his fag on the edge of the sink. "I get your name."

The demon hissed, sucking the breath back through its razory teeth. "Impossible."

"Suits me," Jack said, making for the door. "Have a fine time getting your naughty boy back home, and while you're at it, go stick a cactus in your bum, you great tight-arsed poof."

"*Stop.*" The demon's voice rattled the mirror and the windowpanes, although it didn't raise it.

Jack put his hand on the doorknob. Small acts of defiance let them know they weren't in control, not fully. It sent them off, made them stupid and grasping. "Those are my terms," he told the demon softly. "Take them or leave them."

During the long moment of silence that followed the words, Jack watched a fat crow land on the windowsill and peer inside, at him, at the demon.

The crow preened and then stared at Jack, head cocked as if to ask him what exactly Jack thought he was on about.

"It seems I have no choice," the demon said, at last. "And how you'll chew over that bit of victory, Winter, I'm sure. Savor it. You won't have another."

"I don't care about you," Jack said, and had never meant anything more. "If there's a chance for me to get your name, I'm taking that chance, mate."

The demon felt inside its coat pocket and Jack felt the rotten snap of its magic. It produced a small blue folder, stamped with red.

"This will get you where you need to go," it said. Jack

took the ticket, inspected the destination. BANGKOK stared back at him, the ink blurred and off center on the line.

"I haven't a passport," he said.

"Explain to me how, exactly, that's my problem?" the demon said mildly.

Jack spread his hands. "You want me to go fetch, you give me the ball, mate."

The demon sighed and produced the square red wallet from another pocket. Jack found his likeness inside, and his vitals. The passport photo was even hideous and badly lit.

"Think of everything, do you?" he grumbled.

"You have a week, Winter," the demon warned him. "The time of your bargain. After that . . . we go back to spinning the same old records until the lights go down."

Jack turned his back, yanked open the door. "Yeah, don't twist your knickers. I'll find him."

"His name is Miles Hornby," said the demon. "He's white, American, he's twenty-seven years old, and he disappeared into Bangkok after he got the notion he could fuck me about." The demon pressed its finger into Jack's bare chest, over one of his eye tattoos. The ink lit up like a house fire under the demon's touch. "He can't. And neither can you, so be the good boy and bring our Miles home to me."

With a puff of displaced air, the demon blinked out, leaving Jack alone, with his flesh crawling.

The crow took flight, cawing, and disappeared as well, swallowed by the mist.

PART II

Dead Men

Sing me a song of the winding road
Sing me a song of the dying day
Rivers of tears down from my eyes
And miles to go before dead I lay

—The Poor Dead Bastards
"Stygian Road"

Chapter Twenty

Jack crammed his few clothes, his lighter and fags, and an ancient Bastards master tape that he carried for luck into his bag, and slipped out of the Naughton house before the sun roused itself.

He'd left plenty of women abed, women with whom he was on varying terms of civility, but he'd never felt quite so much like a fucking cunt about it as he did walking down the muddy lane to the B road.

Leaving Pete a note had nearly been his undoing—he could have sat for hours at the sticky kitchen table holding the pen, trying to find just the right way to say, *Sorry I'm a fuckwit* in language that wouldn't make his darling Petunia borrow a pistol from her good friend Inspector Heath and blow Jack's balls off.

In the end, he'd settled for simplicity—*Don't worry. I'll be back.* He wasn't sure yet if it was a lie or not.

The road was deserted in the early morning, and Jack walked, listening to the peculiar stillness of a winter dawn, water flowing in some hidden culvert, things rustling in the hedgerow but not seen, the slow sleepy twine of magic around his senses as the sun came up and the moor retreated into itself in the face of the witch's domain, the sun and the hare and the deer, the psychopomps of what little was pure and good about the Black.

A lorry rumbled in the distance, silver grille flashing intermittently as it dipped behind the curves of the road and found the sun again.

Jack waved the driver down, had to jump aside as the lorry rumbled to a stop with a *swish-hiss* of air brakes.

"You fancy giving me a ride, mate?" he called.

The youth behind the wheel eyed him with an air of great distaste. "Sure, man. I pick up riders all the time in the arse-end of nowhere in my company truck."

"I'll make sure you get taken care of," Jack assured him. Just a little push, just a little tickle of magic to make him sound truthful, to convince the surly bloke that what he wanted—be it ass, cash, or grass—would be waiting for him at the end of the line. Jack was a gifted liar, and gifts that came naturally were easy to turn into magic.

"I'm going down into Tiverton," the driver grunted. "After that, you're shite out of luck, friend."

"Close enough," Jack said. He climbed aboard and the lorry driver examined him more closely.

"What are you running away from, then?"

Jack leaned his throbbing forehead against the passenger window as the lorry pulled away.

"Nothing you need to worry about, *friend*." He didn't want to imagine Pete waking up alone, dressing, finding the note. "Nothing at all," Jack repeated. They left the moor behind, the wild magic with it, and the road smoothed out, taking Jack back to what he supposed was some version of civilization.

Chapter Twenty-one

London bustled and howled and rumbled underfoot like an old friend when Jack got off the train at Paddington. The rustle and caress of the city's magic felt awkward to Jack's mind, like a lover you hadn't seen in weeks, with the perfume of the bird you'd been cheating with still clinging to your collar. After the assault of the ghosts, the primal scream of the moor, the feeling of his and Pete's magics touching so close and hot they could kindle flame . . .

Jack kicked traitorous thoughts from his head and found a pay phone near the taxi line at the station.

"Yeah, Jack." Lawrence sounded resigned, like one did when their skint uncle called asking for a loan, again.

"Stop answering the phone like a bloody clairvoyant," Jack told him. "It's just showing off, isn't it?"

"You back already, then?" Lawrence said. "Thought you had a big bad exorcism afoot out there in God's country."

"God has a sick fucking sense of humor," Jack said. "Listen, Lawrence. Cancel your stitch-and-bitch or whatever you have on for today and meet me at Paddington."

"No. 'M busy, Jack," Lawrence said. "Got me own life, shocking as I know it be for you to hear."

"Make it now," Jack snarled into the phone. "Move your arse. I don't have a lot of time."

While he waited for Lawrence, Jack paced back and forth in front of the National Rail boards, and he paced to the ticket machines opposite, and he paced from the Boots to the coffee stand and back, until the transit copper began to look at him like Jack might be contemplating his chances of blowing something up.

Jack sat down and stared at the stains on the floor, islands and peninsulas attesting to the passage of human glaciers. His sight showed him old ghosts, older bodies, flickering in and out of sight as Paddington flowed around him. The Blitz, the bad old days of Thatcher and New Labour, muggings and murders, blood snaking black and gray across the tiles under his feet. Always, the dead came to be with him, just out of sight but never gone.

At length, Lawrence loped up the steps from the tube lines on the lower levels, dreadlocks tucked under a knit cap and his long form encased in a navy coat. He stalked over to Jack and stood, hands shoved deep into his pockets. "All right, man. Here I am. What's got you so twisted you drag me away from a payin' client?"

Jack stood up, casting an eye around the crowd out of habit. No one immediately averted their gaze, but that didn't mean nothing was watching. "Not here," Jack murmured. "Loo."

"Fuck off," Lawrence said. "You want them train cops to think we a pair of rent boys?"

"They can think I hail from Suffragette bloody City for all I care," Jack said, snatching his friend by the arm. "Now come along."

The men's loo in Paddington smelled like bleach and was only half lit, fluorescent tubes spitting when Jack passed under them. He locked the door to the outside and faced Lawrence. "I need to talk to you, and I need you to listen and not give me any of your usually granny nonsense, all right?"

Lawrence blinked at him. "What happened since I saw you last, Jack? This shifty business ain't like you."

Jack ignored the question, casting about in his leather for a key to his flat. He pressed it into Lawrence's hand. "My grimoire is on the mantle in the sitting room. Everything I bothered to write down, every spell, every spirit, it's there." His pulse pounded, feverish against his temples, and the lights flickered again, casting Lawrence into shadow for a split second. "I have about fifty pounds in a sock in the top drawer of the bedroom dresser. You should give that to Pete. Haven't anything else, except the flat, and I suppose you and she can decide what to do with that."

Lawrence held up his hands. "Jack. I know you think the devil's bargain be pulling you down into the Pit, but it ain't sure yet. You're scarin' me, true."

"It could be. You know that, too." Jack fixed Lawrence with a stare that he hoped was penetrating enough to prick his friend's denial that Jack Winter was fucked, indeed. "Lawrence, if I don't see you again, I trust you to do what needs to be done. It's that bloody simple."

When mages kicked off, there were rules. Rituals, and incantations. A thousand small assurances that your dearly departed friend would not become a plaything of the creatures in the thin spaces, things that were neither Fae or ghost. The mourners of a mage ushered the spirit through the Bleak Gates, locked it up tight where it could never trouble the living.

So if Jack didn't return, and he admitted it was wholly possible, Lawrence would burn his grimoire, dispose of his assets, and take his body—if there was one—to its final rest, in the tradition of the crow.

Lawrence started shaking his head immediately when Jack stopped speaking, his eyes panicked. "Won't do it, Jack. You ain't going through with whatever foolishness you think you up to . . ."

"It's not foolishness," Jack snarled, perhaps more harshly than he needed to. His voice echoed off the tile of the loo. "And you're the only person I fucking trust to do right by me if it is, so shut your gob, take the key, and say you'll look after Pete if I don't come back."

Lawrence screwed up his face, but he tucked the key into his coat pocket. "I don't like this, Jack. You still thinking you can beat that demon, aren't you? Still thinking you the wickedest man in the world."

Jack faced his gaze to Lawrence, staring a hole in the other man until Lawrence squirmed. "I'm fucking rubbish at a lot of it," Jack said quietly, "but I am the crow-mage and it wouldn't kill you to have a little fucking faith, Lawrence."

Lawrence dropped his eyes, giving the small victory to Jack. "I save me faith for the devils and the saints, man."

Jack felt his fists curl. An ego was something a man of his age and situation could ill afford, but there was still a bit of the flame left in his chest, enough to burn small holes in other people's good intentions. "You want to say different? Want us to have a little mage's duel right here in the loo?" Jack set his feet. Lawrence had height and weight on him, but he was a white witch with white witch charms and spells in his arsenal, and Jack wagered he could knock Lawrence on his arse before the magic ever started flying.

"I don't want to fight wit' you, Jack," Lawrence sighed. "I want me best friend in the world not to be dragged into Hell. But me a day late and a pound short on that score."

"Too right," Jack said. He left off his planted feet and solid fists, and went to unlock the door and leave. Lawrence could piss and moan the hind legs off of a horse, but he'd do what Jack asked. He always had, from the first day they'd met, in a squat straddling the edges of the Black and a horrid dump in Peckham. Lawrence was a deejay from Birmingham. Jack was a skinny nineteen-year-old git still wearing a Dublin hospital bracelet around his wrist, no more possessions than that and an outsize ability to slag the wrong people off. They'd gotten along immediately.

"You can't cheat a demon," Lawrence said softly. "No living soul can manage that. You going to die, Jack, and the best you can hope for is to go with your head up."

Jack's guts twisted up. "Thanks. Nothing like knowing my mates are expecting me to come marching home with a smile on my ruddy face."

"You're good, Jack," Lawrence said quietly. "But you're not that good. I'll say my farewells, and if you come to your senses . . ." He flashed the flat key, made it disappear again. "You know where to find me."

"Cheers. And fuck you, Lawrence." Jack shoved the door open, let the sound and light of the station engulf him once more, like dropping into an ocean of bodies and sound. High above him, on the same rafter, the crow watched. Jack stilled, glaring at it. He'd been seeing entirely too many nosy birds of late. It was like being trapped in one of those insipid talking-animal films, laced with a hit of bad acid.

Lawrence came to his shoulder. "You got a fetch on you, boy."

Jack rolled his eyes toward the crow. "That animal companion shite is for your type, Lawrence. I call it a bloody obnoxious pest."

The crow hopped from one foot to the other, flexing its wings to their full length. It stared at Jack. Jack flipped it two fingers.

"Treat your fetch better, Jack." Lawrence clapped a hand on his shoulder. "Never know when you need that old boy to carry your soul home."

"Like you said," Jack told Lawrence. "Too little, too late."

Lawrence knocked one booted toe against the ground. "Take care of yourself, Jack."

Jack lifted one corner of his mouth. "You going to miss me, you great pair of knickers? Going to have yourself a cry once I'm gone on my way?"

"I ain't saying good-bye," Lawrence told him hotly. "It is what it is. You don't listen to no demon's lies and you don't get yourself in more trouble than you already carrying."

Jack threw Lawrence a salute. "Just as you say, guv."

Lawrence gave a nod. "Then I see you later, Jack."

"Yeah," Jack told him as Lawrence joined the line of people descending back into the tube. "Much later."

A garbled call for the Heathrow Express echoed over the PA, and Jack's headache joined his nervous stomach. He joined the line of people boarding the sleek dove gray train car, passing his fingers over the ticket machine to open the gate to the platform.

The magic tingled, ran through him from head to toe like he'd just grabbed a live socket. Such a small trick shouldn't send pain up and down his nerves, but then his sight shouldn't be going haywire and he shouldn't be dreaming of a ritual that had gone out of fashion with painting yourself blue and chopping the heads off of Picts.

Shouldn't be feeling the pull of Pete's Weir talent even when she was miles away. Shouldn't be going to bloody Thailand on a fool's errand. Jack would have traded with a demon all over again in that moment to be back in Naughton's smelly, lumpy bed with his arm over Pete's waist and her slender leg wrapped around his.

Pete's leg dug into his thighs, urging him harder, urging him to take what he wanted, needed.

"Oh, fuck off," Jack gritted as the Heathrow train rolled out of Paddington, gathering speed as it slid through the junkyards and council estates of south London. Not that any vision he'd ever been subjected to had been chased off with a bit of bad language.

"Jack . . . ," Pete gasped, back arching, body stiffening around him, driving him to the edge. "Jack, stop . . ."

He wouldn't stop, couldn't stop as the chanting crested, the onlookers watching the pair on the stone, faces blank and eyes glistening with desire.

"Jack." Pete stilled herself and looked into his eyes. "You have to stop, Jack."

The chanting fell away and the circle closed in, and Jack saw for the first time the white robes, the silver masks, and the crowns of horn hiding the circle of mages from his view.

Not the Fiach Dubh. Not his brothers. These were strangers, and all at once, the rain and the mist froze against Jack's skin. Cold. Always the cold.

Pete tried to put her hand against his cheek, stopped at the end of the shackle, and sank back to the stone. Jack saw the bruises blossoming under the woad, saw Pete's starvation thinness and the chafe marks at her wrists from her time on the stone. "Stop, Jack," she whispered. "Stop running. Stop fighting."

Jack placed his hand against her cheek. "Can't, luv. I'm doing it for you."

She shook her head, a bitter smile thin as a line cut on broken mirror growing on her face. "You don't know what you're doing, Jack Winter. And you don't know me. Not really."

The circle of mages closed in, their hands snatching at Jack, trying to drag him away, and Pete strained to hold him. "Wake up, Jack," she whispered. "Open your eyes."

"We are now arriving at Heathrow, Terminal Three," the train robot announced. The train jolted, and the doors slid open. "Please mind the gap as you exit the train."

Jack managed to rise, collect his kit, and leave the car with the rest of the foreigners and travelers shuffling through the dank gray tunnel with their luggage. Then he took a quick turn around the rear of the train, leaned over the edge of the platform, and vomited his guts out. There wasn't much, just coffee and a few biscuits he'd nicked from the dining car of the Tiverton train.

Jack felt the gnawing ache of an empty stomach, the jittery sick dance of his heart. Jack wanted Pete with him. She'd have made sense of the vision, helped him quiet his sight and his magic. He could talk himself out of the truth, if Pete were with him.

His talent was going haywire. He couldn't control his sight. As the anniversary of his bargain crept closer, Jack's power was unwinding. He'd seen mages go off the rails before, when some curse or malice of the Black caused their mind and their talent to diverge, shredding one another as they fought tooth and nail inside the unlucky mage's meat sack. Those mages ended up in Velcro pajamas. The ones that didn't top themselves outright.

Wake up, Pete had said. *Open your eyes.*

"She sees you, Jack Winter, and she says that you can run. . . ." Pete grinned, half with the pain of her shackles and half with malice. *"She says you can run far and fast, but you can never hide."*

Chapter Twenty-one

Jack dug his fingers into his armrest when the Malaysia Air plane took off from Heathrow, and kept them there as the jet bounced from cloud to cloud, each jerk designed specifically to keep his guts somewhere in the vicinity of his tongue.

"Bad flight?"

The girl in the middle seat was one of those self-conscious hippie types made of natural fibers and henna dye, who did things like joining the Peace Corps and handing out condoms to third-world Catholics, urged through the poverty-drenched mud and shit because of some deep moral compulsion brought on by not enough hugs from Mummy.

"'M fine," Jack said. When was the last time he'd flown? American, 1994? The ill-fated trip to Belgium when Lawrence got himself mixed up with the Stygian Brothers and Jack had to go to their necropolis and bargain back Lawrence's death?

Too bloody long, and he hadn't liked strapping himself inside a giant lipstick tube and getting suspended five miles above the earth any better in the bad old days.

"You don't look fine," the girl said. She eyed the flight attendants in their colorful vests and neckerchiefs moving in the galley and then dipped a hand into her hemp bag. "Here."

Jack narrowed his eyes at the small round pills. "What's that, Xanax?"

"Darling, do I look like I carry mother's little helper?" the girl scoffed. "Take it. You'll have a nice ride, I guarantee."

Jack eyed the little pills when she tipped them into his palm. Then the jet bounced again and turned, skimming west over water and on into southern Europe and the Middle East.

The girl unscrewed her complimentary in-flight water bottle and handed it to him. "I'm Chelsea."

Jack debated for only a moment, until turbulence bounced him against his lap belt once more, and washed the chalky aftertaste of the pills down with nearly half of the water. After months off, his throat had forgotten how to accept copious handfuls of pharmaceuticals.

"I'm Michael," he said. "Mick." Giving a fake name was a reflex, when you couldn't know who you were speaking to. Names were kept back, used for currency and passage, not given out like Chelsea's mystery drugs. Jack pressed his tongue against the roof of his mouth. He could still taste the pills.

"Why Thailand?" Chelsea asked after they'd watched an announcement about the in-flight films and blood clots that could be forming in one's legs at this very moment.

"Why did your parents name you after a fucking neighborhood?" Jack returned. She laughed, and washed down her own pills. Three, Jack noted. He must have lost that scraggly addict's aura, the one that telegraphed he needed at least twice the doctor's dose of any medicine you chose.

"They loved it there. We couldn't afford it, of course—they lived out in Chiswick, and I left when I was about fifteen and went wild for a few years before I settled down and got into activist work."

Sometimes pegging people dead to rights in the first go was extraordinarily boring, Jack reflected. If Chelsea had said she was going to Bangkok to recruit an all-castrato chorus line for the musical production of *Trainspotting*, the flight wouldn't be dull, at least.

"You rescue prostitutes and bums, then?" he said. "Turn them into useful members of the human race?" The pills were making themselves known. His head and legs felt swimmy and his heart and lungs felt slow.

"I rescue anyone who asks me," Chelsea said with a thin smile. "But what happens after that is up to them." She put two fingers over his eyelids. "Go to sleep, Michael. I'll wake you up when it's time."

Jack tried to say "time for what," but he had a feeling he only mumbled vaguely before he drifted into a cotton-wool floating sleep. Chelsea's image flickered once in his sight, gold lion's eyes and twin shadows sitting on her shoulders. The Black caressed her sharpened cheekbones and full lips, and her hand that stroked his face was full of talons.

"Oh," Jack slurred. "Fuck." Before he could really look at Chelsea, put a barrier of power between her pointed black teeth and himself, a dream opened its jaws and swallowed him down. He saw Irish hills, English cities, Pete's eyes, and then nothing, until it was much too late to do anything at all.

Chapter Twenty-two

Jack woke, suddenly and with the sensation of falling. He saw long metal arms out of the airplane porthole, metal carts manned by drivers in orange vests. It was a bit like waking up after you'd fallen asleep, stoned and watching something from the sixties about robots.

"Come on." Chelsea nudged him. "It's always better if you walk it off."

Jack stood with her help and every joint in his body from his neck to his ankles protested. "The fuck did you give me?" he mumbled. His tongue was thick and furry, a remake of too many mornings when he'd been on the road with the Bastards. That had been the nicest thing about the heroin—you never got hungry enough to feel the sick afterward.

"Dreamless sleep," Chelsea said. She stepped into the aisle and shouldered her fuzzy bag. "That's what you wanted, isn't it?" She gave him another one of those small half-smiles, the ones that didn't express anything close to comfort or joy. "That's what you ask for, Jack. When you think no one can hear you. Not to see."

Jack watched the way her eyes changed, from pleasant gray to iron slate to gold, pupiless and staring.

"Who are you?" he slurred. "Actually, strike that bollocks—what? What are you?"

Chelsea leaned back and squeezed his hand. "The guardian of the gateways sends her regard, Jack. She grants you safe passage through this land."

Then she was gone, moving lithely through the crush of people disembarking from the jet where there should have been no space, just elbows and bags and snorts of "Move it!" from the American in the Hawaiian shirt, lugging two roller bags and a camera case.

Jack moved to the side and caught the bloke in the ribs as he chugged passed. "Sorry." He shrugged. "Bit close in here."

"Up yours, fuckwad," the American said, and shoved on down the jetway, tossing smaller Thais and Brits out of the way with a casual swing of his luggage.

"Thank you for flying," said the flight attendant manning the door. "Have a lovely stay, now."

"Listen," Jack said. "The girl sitting next to me on the flight—which way did she go?"

"Girl?" The woman's eyes flicked toward the cockpit and the phone on the wall next to the tamper-proof door.

"Yes," Jack said, shifting from foot to foot in an effort to force his blood to expel the drug expediently. His vision still swam in slow circles and his arms felt like logs, but at least he could talk without sounding like a Mancunian Joey Ramone. "Reddish hair, manky clothes, nice face. I need to find her."

"Sir." The attendant reached for the handset. "You were alone in your row."

"She said her name was . . ." Jack rubbed a hand over his face. "Never mind. Put the phone down, luv, I'm not crazy or trying to blow you up."

The attendant set the phone down reluctantly. "Then what are you on about, sir?"

Jack sighed, trying to keep his balance on the gently listing jetway. "Nothing, it seems. I'm simply having a royally shite fucking day."

When Jack backed away from the wide-eyed attendant and joined the concourse of Suvarnabhumi Airport, it was as full of people as a riverbed after a flash flood. The light scattered through the thousands of windowpanes that entombed Jack in glass as crowds shoved to and fro all around.

"Like bloody Snow White," he muttered, watching a 747 take off overhead. The ground under his feet shook.

Jack let the crowd push him for a bit, drifting while he got his bearings. The demon knew where he was and what was happening, so who'd send the hippie girl on the airplane? The girl with lion eyes, and fingers like fossilized claws that could reach inside him and pull out his dreams like a photo album. The girl who wasn't a girl at all.

It could be any number of people—or not-people, Jack reflected. Anyone he'd slagged off in the last twenty years. Any vulture circling who'd heard about the demon and wanted his pound of Jack Winter.

Or the demon could be a liar, could be stringing him up like a puppet and sending its cronies in the Black for its own amusement. Offer everyone a bit of the crow-mage, soften him up before the day came around so Jack wouldn't fight, wouldn't scheme, and would beg the demon for his life like every other stupid fuckwit who'd bound a bargain before him.

Jack knew this was likely as anything else, but he still let himself join the line for customs and presented the passport the demon had given him. Miles Hornby had tricked the demon, and Miles Hornby was in Bangkok.

"Reason for visit?" The Thai behind the glass couldn't

have been more disinterested if Jack were a cardboard cutout.

"Vacation," Jack said, and fought to keep from laughing.

"Duration of stay?" The Thai clicked at his computer.

"Less than a week," Jack said. "One way or another."

His passport slid back at him through the slot. "Very good. Next," the customs agent said, and the crowd swallowed Jack up again.

Chapter Twenty-three

Jack boarded a train for the thirty-kilometer ride to downtown Bangkok, pressed in with Thai citizens, their luggage, visiting backpackers, and their burdens. Jack stood and let the gravity of the train pull him from station to station.

In a crush of people, Jack had always felt the most secure. He could create a bubble of solitude out of the ebb and flow of bodies, and he could find silence while everyone else talked and laughed and shouted. The living could shut out the dead, at least to a degree. The press of overlapping souls was like listening to traffic on the motorway, or the rush of blood through your own ears. Normal people felt like passing a hand through flowing water—gentle and present, but never cold or dreadful, like looking at the Black or standing in a group of other talents.

In this crowd, though, Jack just felt alone, overwhelmingly so. The air was foreign and the magic was foreign, and it left a hole in him, the gaping black pit of his sight without anything to catch him at the bottom. Thailand's air was close and hot enough that it felt like a hand over his mouth, and the snatches of smell that Jack caught as the train drew closer to the central city certainly weren't winning any prizes. The cacophony of voices speaking half a dozen languages rang in his still-fuzzy head, and his abused stomach lurched with every bump on the track.

If Pete were here, he could lean into her as the train rounded a curve, steal a touch and pretend it was only gravity and not any desire to be against her. *But she's not*, Jack told himself, *so leave it alone and smarten up*. It wasn't Pete that he needed to be thinking of now. What he needed was further back, memories that he'd rather not stir even in his most pissed, most sorry, or most high-as-a-fucking-kite moment. Jack needed his memories of the time before Pete and the fix, before anything except the dead.

The train rattled on, never disgorging a passenger, only packing more in as they wound deeper and deeper into the veins of Bangkok's heart. Jack found himself pressed against the window, watching the world flow by in snatches of color and stain, high-rise skin reflecting a water-slicked image of the train and slums that stared at him with broken glass eyes.

A female face grinned at him out of the blur of twilight buildings, and his sight showed him a bloody slick on the ground underneath her, her body a mass of sticky meat and her teeth filed to sharp points. Bangkok showed him its Black, clawed at his sight, a teeming and frantic energy that was foreign to his senses as the Thai alphabet that delineated the train's stops and starts.

Jack blinked and looked away from the woman's reflection. Sometimes, it was all you could do. Avert your eyes and pray to your gods that whatever It was hadn't noticed your insignificant scrap of heartbeat and talent.

The train rumbled into Silom Station, and Jack shoved his way off, relieved to finally be able to at least lift his arms. He fished in his pocket and unfolded the scrap of vellum, worn shiny. The remains of a penciled-in map were barely visible. His handwriting in the bad old days had been shit—it was a wonder any of his cantrips or incantations had ever worked the way they should.

On Silom Road, he stopped to get his bearings before plunging into the eternal stream of foot and motor traffic traversing the street between Jack and the crush of Patpong.

In Patpong, the Black was different—it spoke to him much like Whitechapel did, as he crossed with a knot of Japanese men in blue polo shirts, some kind of tourist group, cameras and fat rolls of *bhat* bulging in their pockets and cases. The red-light district was a crush of smell and sound and blurred expanses of flesh glimpsed through streaky nightclub windows, garnished with torn posters advertising sex shows years out of date.

The same dark heartbeat bent and whispered through the tourist and the barkers attempting to entice Jack upstairs to see the girls, or the boys, or the boys dressed as girls take their clothes off, lay themselves upon the altar of sex magic, and send up painted and pierced and fragrant offerings to the gods of such things. The bloody bones of Whitechapel were here, but tinged with sex and spices, the ambient power of the place rolling over Jack's skin like honey.

A peddler in the night market choking off a street signed as PATPONG 1 ahead of him stretched out a handful of gold chains and watches. "American? Good discounts for Americans."

"English," Jack said. "I still get a discount?"

The peddler laughed. "English, I charge you double. See anything you like?"

Jack scanned the table, covered with nylon and anchored at each corner by a statue of the Buddha. There was the usual assortment of knockoff jewelry, but he passed his finger over a chain with a coin attached. His sight returned a thread of magic, small white flames rising off the coin in the Black.

"This one," Jack said. "It has something."

"You have a good eye," the peddler said. "That's a passage coin—in your culture, you use it to pay the ferryman. To your next world?"

Jack felt his mouth curl up at the corners. "You know what you're talking about."

"Around here, mostly tourists," said the peddler. "But I see enough of you to make it worth my while."

Jack picked up the necklace, felt the weight of the copper coin on the end of the cheap chain. "How much?"

"Depends on what you have, mage." The peddler folded his arms and smiled. Jack laughed.

"What's your name?"

"Banyat. But everyone around here calls me Robbie." The peddler made a show of counting his money roll. "I'll sell it to you for a story. Tell me why you're here."

Jack slid the chain around his neck. Stories were a good currency, provided you had them to tell. Much better than names, or dreams. "Why do you care?"

"This is my corner," Robbie said. "I keep my eyes open and if something slithers up from the Black that's a wrong thing to be walking in this side of the veil, I whisper in the right ears. You, mage—you're a wrong thing."

"So for your silence, you get to know my business?" Jack knew when he'd been manipulated—usually it was by flexible and willing girls getting back at their ex-boyfriends after a Bastards gig, but the feeling of vague unbalance was the same.

"That I do," Robbie said. His English wasn't accented with American, and Jack turned the coin over his fingers, made it disappear, reappear.

"Fine. I'll tell you my business here if you tell me why in the hell you're called Robbie."

"I did some time in the UK," Robbie said. "For robbery, get it? As for the chain, Irish bloke lives up on Patpong 2 pawned it to me for some crematory ash and a bootleg of the Stiff Little Fingers."

"I'm in Bangkok looking for someone," Jack returned, because a bargain was a bargain whether you were speaking with a demon or a street hustler. "And I have a feeling your Irish friend and I will be meeting over that someone soon enough. That slake your burning curiosity for you, Robbie with the posh boarding school accent?"

Robbie snorted. "What poor bastard got them after you? I saw you coming, I'd turn the other way so fast I'd whiplash meself."

"A clever boy," Jack said, echoing the demon's words even though thinking of those blank black eyes and crimson mouth made him nauseous. Or it could be the comedown from the pills. Treacherous bitch. If he found out who had set these specters of ill fortune on him, they were going to be short their balls.

"Can't be very clever after all, if you found him," Robbie said. He jerked his chin at the coin. "Take that. For safe passage wherever you need to go."

Jack fingered the coin, but he kept the chain around his neck. The weight felt right, solid and warm against his chest, and precious little was solid in this tilting city where the Black screamed rather than hissed. "Cheers, Robbie."

"This man you're after," Robbie said, as he flashed a smile at a passing tourist couple. "What's his name?"

"Miles Hornby," Jack said. "You heard of him?"

"Can't say I have." Robbie rearranged his fake watch display with the speed and efficiency of a card sharp. "But then again, aren't you *farang* all supposed to look alike?"

Jack gave a snort. "Good one. The cranky Irishman, what's his building?"

"The *kathoey* bar with the pink flamingo sign down on Patpong 2," Robbie said. "Got apartments upstairs. Mostly for the ladyboys and their . . . friends, you understand? But he moved in there. Said he liked it. Had a good . . . it's Chinese."

"*Feng shui?*" Jack supplied. Robbie nodded, and Jack shook his head, feeling a true smile grow for the first time since he'd climbed onto the airplane. That was Seth—he took the piss by the bottle, and setting up shop above a transvestite sex club would be his idea of a right long laugh. "Got any idea which apartment? So I don't interrupt any of the gentlewoman's business, you understand."

Robbie returned Jack's crooked grin. "He's . . . number three, I think. Don't blame me if you bust down the wrong door and get an eyeful, though."

"Furthest thing from me mind." Jack tipped Robbie a salute and found his way through the night market, past a set of enthusiastic barkers outside a sex show featuring a dancer billed as "Around-the-World Sue," past a knot of smoking fans and drunks outside a music bar. The band inside wasn't half bad—a fusion of rockabilly and electronica that'd do well in London. The quintet played with the sort of easy harmonies the Bastards aspired to and never quite found.

If he'd been less wrapped up in trying to be the largest, wickedest mage in London and paid more attention to his music, he might be in that club now, Jack thought. Or he might still be on the floor of a rotting squat in Southwark, with the cold kiss of a needle against the crook of his arm. In his lighter moments, Jack thought that seeing the future would be even worse than seeing the dead. At least the dead couldn't shake their heads at you and tsk with disappointment for ambition and dream crushed beneath boots and heroin.

Club Hot Miami sat halfway down Patpong 2, nestled like a gaudy tropical bird among swampy trees. Pink flamingos and palm trees described in neon danced across the facade, and a barker grinned at Jack, waving a happy-hour flier under his nose.

"No, thanks," Jack said. "Just looking for the *farang* who lives upstairs." Even though he'd taken pains to remember nothing of Seth McBride, the description rolled out with no pause. "Irritable sod, a little shorter than me. Black hair, blue eyes, got a mouth on him that'd strip the gears on a lorry."

"Oh yeah, we know him." The barker looked as if he wished emphatically that he *didn't* know anything of the sort.

"He at home?" Jack said. "If not, I could be convinced to come in. Murder a drink of anything, honestly. It could have an umbrella and a goldfish swimming in it after the day I've had."

"He's always home," said the barker glumly. "Never goes out. No friends."

"That sounds right." Jack mounted the outside stairs of the flat block. The stairs were even more precarious than his fire escape at home, if such a thing were possible. They groaned under his weight, the bolts grinding against cement.

The landing on the second floor was little better, close and closed in by mosquito netting, bug lights fizzing as Jack passed. The doors were unmarked, and moans and pants from behind the thin wood confirmed Jack's theory that nearly everyone in Bangkok was having a better night than he was.

At the third door, he detected no sound. Jack's eyes traveled up out of habit—you never crossed a mage's threshold without looking—and found an iron nail, bound in hair and tied to a crow feather soaked in blood.

Not taking his eyes from the hex, Jack reached out and rapped thrice on the bubbly painted wood with his knuckles. They came away sticky. The city itself was alive in Bangkok, breathing and sweating.

A voice rattled the thin door from within. "Fuck off!"

Jack knocked again. "Open the door, Seth."

He heard scuffling, as if not Seth but a herd of enormous rats resided behind the door, and half a dozen locks clicking.

An eye, watery blue like a cloud-covered sky, peered through the crack. "How'd you know that name?"

Jack spread his arms. "Like I could forget, you Irish bastard."

Seth's eye widened, and his broad flat face went slack. "Jack Winter. Fuck me sideways."

"I'll pass, thanks," Jack said. "You never were my type."

"And you always were a mouthy little cunt, weren't ya?" Seth demanded. Jack lifted one shoulder.

"No denying it. You miss me, Seth?"

Seth's hair still stuck up wildly and a pack of Silk Cut still rode shotgun in his front shirt pocket, but he was tan and carrying more weight than the last time Jack had clapped eyes on him. "Yeah, I missed you," he growled. "Like a case of the clap the peni didn't chase away."

"Going to invite me in?" Jack said. "I'm not keen on that hex chewing me up."

"Right. Worried about the hex." Seth dropped his shoulder and moved, and pain exploded across Jack's right cheek. He stumbled, felt himself lose balance and go down in a tangle of mosquito netting.

"You've got a lot of nerve, boy," Seth rasped, sticking a cigarette in his mouth. "Remind me why I shouldn't just kill you now." He touched his finger to the end of the cigarette, and smoke curled up.

"*Fuck*." Jack sat up, shook the cobwebs from his head, and touched the spot where Seth had hit him. It was pulpy and tender, and blood trickled down into the hollow next to his mouth. It left the taste of iron and salt on the tip of Jack's tongue. "Got it out of your system?" he asked Seth.

The Irishman shook out his fist. His knuckles were pink and pulpy, like a bunch of grapes. "Not hardly. You never did know when you weren't wanted, Jackie."

Jack grabbed the rusty rail and pulled himself to his feet. "And you never could throw a punch worth fuck-all, McBride."

Seth bared his teeth around the Silk Cut. "Why're you here, Winter?"

Jack pointed up at the hex. "Let me in and I'll tell you."

"Shit." Seth threw his butt down on the cement and stamped on it with one sandal-clad foot. "I wouldn't invite a fucking demon into my home, so explain to me why I should invite you."

"I'm looking for a bloke called Miles Hornby to void a bargain with a Named demon of Hell and I've got precisely shit to go on, so I've come to you, oh wise and generous mentor, for your help." Jack folded his arms and concentrated on keeping on his feet. His head didn't ring from the blow, it tolled—slow and rolling, over and over, waves of pain like waves on a shore, threatening to drown him.

"Well." Seth tipped his head to the side. "Jack Winter asking for my help. I've had this dream before." He looked up and down the walkway.

Jack followed his glance. "What?"

"I'm waiting for Stephen Fry and the talking monkey to come in," Seth said. "That's the next bit."

"Fuck off." Jack prodded his cheek again. It was roughly twice its normal size and would bear the impression of

Seth's knuckles when the bruise solidified. "I mean it, Seth."

"So do I, Jack," Seth snarled. "I don't want a thing to do with missing bastards, your dodgy troubles, or you. I'd take the talking monkey any fucking day."

He retreated into the shadow of his flat, and Jack felt the swell of desperation in his chest like Seth had hit him all over again.

"I don't have anywhere else to go."

Jack had admitted the same truth to Seth close to twenty years ago, when Seth had found him turning conjure tricks on the streets of Dublin, sat him down, gave him a fag, and asked him where he'd come from. The crow spread her wings over Jack that night, folded him into her purview, but he felt no such darkling comfort now.

Seth grumbled out a string of curses, but he moved to the side, jerking his head at Jack. "Fuck it. Come in, then."

Jack shouldered his bag and stepped cautiously over the threshold. Half expecting to feel the teeth of Seth's warding hex lock into his skin and his sight, he only relaxed when McBride snorted at his tension. "I wanted you face down, Jackie, you'd be swallowing your teeth now and you know it."

Jack itched at the back of his neck as his talent prickled at another's encroachment. "Suppose that's true."

"Fucking right, it's true. I am sorry about that belt, though," Seth said. He stubbed out his fag into an over-flowing ashtray that lived in the belly of the ubiquitous Buddhas that grinned out at Jack from every corner of Patpong.

"No you're not," Jack said. He went in Seth's minuscule freezer and found a packet of frozen mixed veg that was dated three years past. Sticking it against his face helped with the dull ache, but not the sting. "You haven't been sorry for a thing since the doctor slapped you on the arse and made you cry."

"All right, probably not so very much," Seth admitted. He settled himself in a cracked vinyl armchair in front of a telly crowned in rabbit ears, lines of color wavering up and down the pocket-sized screen over a Thai cricket match.

Jack looked out the back window, down into an alley. Grinning white tourists led along a pair of underage Thai girls, their smiles as pasted on as their plastic dresses. Laughter bounced off the concrete and the air thickened with curls of wayward power as the girls fell behind the pair of men, heads bent together like painted, predatory sharks. Jack caught their extra arms as they passed from street lamp to shadow, the scales that painted themselves onto skin like emerald and onyx tattoo ink, the forked tongues. Served the two wankers right.

"Now," Seth said, leaning his bulk forward and turning down the volume of the telly. "What the fuck are you babbling about, you owe a demon a bargain?"

Jack talked, keeping the packet against his face. The telly burbled underneath his voice, discordant counterpoint to the story of the demon, the *cu sith*, the fetch, and Miles Hornby. Seth stayed quiet for a time after Jack finished the whole sordid mess. He changed among four equally distorted channels on the telly, scratched the back of his neck, and finally said, "So what you're telling me is, you're buggered and you want old uncle Seth to kiss it and make it go away. Is that it?"

"I just need your help finding the bloke," Jack said. He wanted to keep his tone even, truly, but he felt restless and itchy inside the cramped little flat that had to be over a hundred degrees even with the arthritic fan in Seth's window bringing in cooking smells and the low-pitched roar of the city outside.

"Always a *just* with you, boy." Seth sighed. "Just needed a little training. Just needed to translate the sorcery grimoire. Just needed to make deals with fucking cock-sucking Hellspawn *demons . . .* "

"Oi!" Jack dropped the frozen packet on the counter and slammed his hand down with it. "You're no paragon of virtue, Seth. I saw you do things in the bad old days that would have curled the hair of any respectable sorcerer, so cut out this Catholic schoolboy act and either throw me out on my arse, or get off of yours and sodding *help me.*"

Seth heaved himself out of his easy chair. "You don't want help, Jack. You want a fuckin' miracle."

"Is that so wrong? Your people pioneered that sort of thing, least that's what you were always bending my ear on." Jack touched his cheek again and winced. "You know, for an old man, you're quite violent. Better watch that. Might break a hip."

Seth pointed a stubby finger in Jack's face. "Don't tempt me to make your other cheek match, you Limey arse-jockey."

"Like you could land a hit on me again, you cabbage-swilling altar boy–fancier." Jack sighed. "Does this mean we're all right?"

"You will never, ever be 'all right,' Jack Winter," Seth growled. "But you and me—that's for another day." He grabbed a bottle of cheap scotch with a Thai label from his cabinet and two cloudy glasses. "You take water?"

"'S like asking if I take piss," Jack said. "Has it really been that long?"

Seth poured Jack two fingers and himself four. Some things never changed. "I heard you've bypassed the bottle entirely of late," he said, tossing back most of the whiskey and wiping a hand across his lips. "Moved on to a more direct method of getting yourself pissed."

"No," Jack said, cold crawling over his skin in spite of the damp, close heat. His sweat turned to ice at the thought of the pinch of a syringe, the cool presence of the needle and the hot, sweet rush into his blood when he pushed down the plunger. *Can't ignore me forever,* the whisper came. *You'll come home, one day.*

"No," Jack repeated. "I'm clean." Even true, it sounded like a lie.

"Good." Seth dropped his glass into the sink, causing a scattering of something alive and gifted with an excess of legs. "You were never that stupid when I knew you, Jackie."

"That's because I could still tell what was real and what was a phantom," Jack muttered. "Those were the fucking golden years, for sure."

"I don't know this Miles Hornby, but I'll make some calls," Seth said. "Meantime, I suggest you take what time you have and enjoy our fair city."

Jack took a seat in the only other chair in the room, a suspicious wicker contraption that creaked under his weight. "No offense, mate, but I think the nightlife here might be a bit carnivorous, even for me."

Seth cocked his eyebrow. "Got someone back home? That's a new one."

"No one special." Jack finished off his whiskey. It burned like drain cleaner going down and no doubt tasted like it coming back up.

Pete would be awake, would have weathered an entire day and night with him gone. Or started a torch brigade to find and burn him. Pete wasn't sentimental, but she was vindictive. She wouldn't simply slap him across the face and be done with it.

"If you're not going to find something to fuck or get pissed, you should sleep," Seth's voice broke in. "You look like seven kinds of shite dragged across Dublin, boy."

Jack looked around the single room and dinette that made up Seth's mildewed, sweaty flat and felt his skin crawl up the back of his neck. Magic had nothing to do with it—the years of sleeping rough voluntarily were behind him in his twenties and the place reminded him of nothing so much as a squat. Add in a dozen or so junkies and a bucket in the corner and the experience would be authentic.

"On second thought," he said quietly, "I could use some company."

"That's my Jack," Seth hooted. "An eye for the ladies and a taste for the underbelly." He slapped Jack on the shoulder. "Enjoy yourself, mate. I'll send someone for you when I find something out about this Hornby."

Chapter Twenty-three

Jack walked back through the tourists to the bar with the music. The band was packing up, and a deejay had taken their place. A pair of drunk Scots were howling a karaoke version of "My Heart Will Go On" in front of a fuzzy monitor scrolling lyrics.

Jack knocked on the bar. "Drink."

"Anything special?" The bartender was tattooed, and to Jack's surprise, female.

"Something that will convince me I don't want to stick a fondue fork in me ear," he said, giving the Scots a baleful glare.

She laughed, and set him up with a bourbon with a neat flick of her wrist. "You're not a tourist. Why you in a tourist bar?"

"Waiting on someone," Jack told her. "Looking for someone else. Running away to join the circus. Take your pick."

"You're funny," the bartender said. She flicked her towel over her sculpted shoulder like a proud Fae creature flicking its tail.

"You're nosy." Jack drained his glass. He wasn't drunk,

yet. Just floating a few inches off the ground. "What's your name?"

"People around here call me Trixie," she said.

"Like Speed Racer's girl?" Jack snorted into his glass. "Cute."

"You probably couldn't pronounce my given name," Trixie said. "Or my Thai nickname. Trixie gives the *farang* something to relate to. They think they know me, I get bigger tips. Simple."

Jack drained his glass and nudged it back toward her. "You're not . . ."

"A dancer?" Trixie shook her head. "You guys like the skinny girls, the My Asian Barbies." She held up one arm, the full sleeve of her tattoos rippling. "I do not come in a pink box."

Jack turned his glass between his fingers. "I was going to say you're not a prozzie, actually, but now I'm a bit intimidated."

Trixie shrugged. "I get asked a dozen times in a night to put tab A into slot B. I'm not going to knock you in the head."

"Stranger things have happened." Jack watched the last trickle of bourbon slide down the side of his glass, like sweat on skin.

Like a raindrop in the hollow of a throat . . .

"You know . . ." Trixie cocked her hip. "You look familiar to me."

Jack favored her with a incredulous smile. "You say that to all the mysterious good-looking foreigners."

"No." Trixie tapped her full lower lip. Coated with waxy pink gloss, it looked swollen, plastic. "I've seen you somewhere. In a photograph."

"Never hit Bangkok in me touring days," Jack said. "Can't imagine where you'd know me from, luv, unless you'd spent time in the UK." Even then, Trixie would have been no more than eight years old when Jack was playing music and getting his mug slapped on posters up and down Mile End Road.

"You're Jack Winter!" Trixie shrieked, slapping her bar towel down. "You sang in the Poor Dead Bastards!" A huge grin lit up her face. "I have your records, man!"

Jack felt an entirely different kind of buzz grow in his chest. "You're putting me on."

"No shit!" Trixie insisted. "I got your *Suicide Squad* LP off of eBay, signed. Cost me two weeks of tips, and I make fat tips."

Jack fished in his wallet to find the last of his English money. "Well, you're very kind, luv, but that was a long fucking time ago indeed."

Trixie waved off his payment. "On the house, for as long as you're in Patpong. I'll take my trade in stories."

Jack started for the door, but turned back. "There is one thing, luv." He scratched at his chin. He wanted a shave again. Pete would have reminded him.

"Anything," Trixie said. "Except what everyone else is giving up around here."

Jack rocked on his heels. Stay casual, stay charming. Don't act like you care. The liar's rules to making others tell the truth. "You know music, yeah? The local scene?"

Trixie nodded. "Most nights off, I'm far from here. There's a great hardcore club over on Silom if you're ever in the mood to see the real Bangkok."

"Miles Hornby," Jack said. The name was beginning to sound like an epithet. "He's apparently a musician. You ever heard of him?"

"Well, sure," Trixie said. "His band was the Lost Souls. Played around here a few times before he got a legit gig. Not bad—sort of an early Nick Cave thing going on."

Jack's heart beat faster, cutting through his fatigue and

the pleasant slack warmth of the cheap bourbon. "You've seen him."

"Sure," Trixie said. "Lots of people saw him. He was pretty good. Not as good as you and the Bastards on *Nightmares and Strange Days*, of course. But he might have gone on a label with a few years of gigging."

"You said his band was the Lost Souls?" Jack was talking faster now, leaning in close enough to smell Trixie's cherry perfume and a hint of salt beneath, to see the eyes on the curling dragons of her tattoos. It couldn't be this easy, not after what the demon had told him. "What d'you mean *was*?"

"Past tense," said Trixie. "They're not anymore."

Jack gripped her wrist. Her skin was warm and her pulse was fast, and she didn't try to pull away. "Why not?"

"Because . . ." Trixie's bee-stung lips turned down. "Miles Hornby's dead."

Chapter Twenty-four

Jack found his way back into the street in a haze of bourbon and disbelief. Dead. Hornby couldn't be dead. The demon wouldn't have sent him. . . . He slumped against the outside of the Club Hot Miami, head scraping the bricks. Hornby could very well be dead, and the demon still would have sent him. It was exactly the sort of thing the demon would do.

He wanted to sink into the ground, to slip through the layers of the Black and find himself back in his flat, in London, before any of this shit had ever gotten started.

But if he sank into the ground, the only thing he'd find would be the Land of the Dead, the howling of lost souls, the clanging of the Bleak Gates.

The want for a fix crawled up from Jack's guts with a burning, frenetic intensity like his stomach was going to come up along with his craving. He scanned the passing crowd, found the youth with greasy hair and a bowed head, the thin girl in the bikini top and ripped denim skirt standing on opposite corners of the intersection, like two poles on a globe. The boy's slouched gait and Phish T-shirt promised weed, LSD, perhaps peyote, while the girl's bony legs and bruised arms promised exactly what he needed.

Sweat ran down his chest under the frayed fabric of his Stooges shirt, and Jack shut his eyes, his sight rolling over him in silvery waves. The pavement of Patpong 2 faded, the sound, and he saw a dumpier, seedier, more dangerous road—GIs in uniforms thirty years out of date on the arms of girls doped out of their minds as they teetered on platform heels, pimps in Western suits and sharp-brimmed hats watching from the shadows like sharks under a reef.

A GI with a knife wound in his gut stared at Jack. *"Say, brother, can you help me out? I lost my wallet and I . . ."*

Jack scrubbed at his eyes, trying to make it stop. To make it all stop—the sight and the need and the deep, sucking void in his chest that they combined to create.

"Just a few bucks for a cab," the GI coaxed. *"Just a few . . ."* Bloody hands grabbed on to Jack, smearing the black miasma of the dead across his skin and up his arms, blotting out his scars and tattoos.

"You know you're just like us," the solider pleaded. *"Lost and lonely and walking that dark road. Just walk with me, buddy. Just for a few minutes . . ."*

Hands yanked him away, and knuckles freshened the bruise on his cheek with a backhanded blow. Jack let out an involuntary yelp. "Fuck me!"

"Not drunk enough for that yet," Seth said, setting Jack on his feet again. "You all right, Jackie? Looked like you had the ghost on you."

"I just . . ." Jack's eyes wandered to the corner of the street again, against his will. The girl was gone. The boy was bobbing his head to his iPod. Everything was right and real and normal about the scene, except him.

"I'm fine," he breathed out. Seth grunted.

"Look worse than you did when I found you, boy. You keep up like this, you're going to be under the ground before the week's up. Forget the demon and all his plans, you're doing a fine job of it yourself."

"About that." Jack sighed. "I talked to that bird bartender in the music club. Hornby's dead."

Seth felt in his pack and came up empty. "Got a fag?"

Jack passed him a Parliament. "Did you hear me? I said that Hornby's dead."

"I'm old, not deaf, you sod," Seth snapped. "Came to tell you I made a few calls and heard the same thing."

"That's it, then." Jack looked at the toes of his boots as he walked. He'd come a long way in these boots. Steel peeped out where the leather had worn away at the toes and the mismatched laces had been broken and reknotted like a map of a B road at home. "The demon played with me. I came here for nothing."

"Hell." Seth exhaled into the face of a passing female tourist, who coughed dramatically and then shot him the bird. "*I* could have told you that, boy. What was lesson one, after you came to me?"

Jack chafed, Seth's tone snapping him back like a rubber band to when he was young and stupid. "I didn't come here to be lectured on your musty old crow magic, McBride."

"Demons lie!" Seth spat. "Lesson. Fucking. One." His face hardened from anger into something more permanent. Jack decided that if he cared, he'd call it disappointment.

"You were my best, boy," Seth grumbled. "You had the spark, the talent, and look at you. Pissed it all away, didn't you? Bloody waste."

"You're one to talk," Jack said. The passing urge to ball up his fist and hit Seth in the jaw to even up his bruises gripped him, but he forced it down. "Look at you—hiding here, living like a retarded pensioner, bored out of your skull. You might as well top yourself and join Hornby, because this ain't a life, mate—it's just a prolonged, sweaty death." He lit a fag of his own and sucked down the smoke, relishing the burn. "Hornby would probably be far better company."

"You're so hung up on him, go find his grave and lie on it," Seth returned. "And good riddance to you." He turned his back and stomped up the stairs to his landing.

Jack stood for a moment, fuming, before he followed Seth. "That's it?" he shouted. "You're just tossing it in? That's all Seth McBride is good for?"

Seth turned back, his eyes lit from within with witch-fire. His magic was pure white, the white of cleansing fire and sacred incense. "I can't help you, boy, you understand? Hornby's beyond our reach."

Jack rubbed the back of his neck.

The demon had told him to bring Hornby home. The demon had lied. The demon had made the new bargain for his name.

Names had meaning, in the Black. They had power and currency in the great tide of magic that swept along the underside and seeped through the cracks of the waking world.

The demon wouldn't promise a name, even idly.

"He's not beyond all reach," Jack said.

Seth narrowed his eyes, the sun-drenched wrinkles in his redly tanned face bunching up. "What are you on about, boy?"

"If Hornby's kicked it," Jack said, "then why was the demon so keen to have him brought back? He's alive, I understand not coming onto another demon's patch. He's a stiff, I'd collect me debt and cross Hornby off the books. I wouldn't send my arse halfway around the world."

"Jack." Seth held up his hand. "Leave it alone. Leave Hell to Hell's concerns and go home."

"I can't do that and you know it," Jack growled. "Come on, Seth. You can't say you're not curious about this. About why a demon would ask me to reel in a dead man."

"If there's one thing I know," Seth said, "it's that I don't give two shits about the wherefore and the why of the Black any longer. That's why I retired." Seth pushed into his sweltering flat.

"The demon should have collected its debt," Jack insisted. "It shouldn't have sent me here. It still needs Hornby." Jack massaged his temples. "I still have to bring him back."

Seth tipped his head back, and his eyes went narrow, as if Jack had just suggested setting fire to his own hair.

"I hope you're talking about a body bag and a slew of customs forms and not what I think you are."

Jack took up Seth's seat in the sticky plastic armchair. "The demon was very clear. He wants Hornby. Not just a bag of dead flesh."

Seth flicked on the telly and sat on the edge of his futon, kicking aside a pile of dirty football jerseys. "Jack, you're talking about raising the dead. Necromancy. Not just a dip of your toe into a little sorcery, but a full-frontal fuck with the dark side."

"Spooky," Jack commented. "You going to scold me, or help me?"

Seth snorted. "As if I'd let you die on me again, boy."

Jack tipped his head back. "Bloody wonderful. After I catch a few hours of kip, we need to find ourselves Hornby's corpse."

Chapter Twenty-five

Pete opened her eyes, staring a hole in Jack as he moved in her. The chanting of the watchers rose. The rain ceased, leaving the air snapping cold against his bare skin.

He could stop, or he could die at the watchers' hands. The stone would have its blood this night, and Jack's blood was as sweet as a Weir's.

Pete's lips moved, her words lost in Jack's breath and the sounds of the bespelling song.

Jack bent his head closer as they coupled, and as the ritual flowed toward completion—toward the circle of power that bound him surely as the shackles bound Pete, toward the vile and unnatural completion of a dead ritual, itself a ritual of the dead, Pete's voice cut through the haze of power and down to his thudding heart.

"Wake up, Jack."

Jack bolted from his rest. His back and neck screamed at him for passing out, yet again, at odd angles in a chair better suited to employment as a medieval torture device.

"You got that look again," Seth commented. The light outside the flat was hazy dawn, and the telly had changed from cricket to a Thai cooking show presided over by a cheery woman in a neon pink apron.

Jack cracked the tension from his neck with a sound like a rifle. His head echoed. "What look's that?"

"Haunted," Seth said. "You were anyone else, I'd say you'd caught ghost sickness." He pottered around the kitchenette until he'd installed coffee and filter in an ancient carafe and switched it on. "That you'd got a spirit feeding off you, like you were a fuckin' milkshake."

"I've seen ghost sickness," Jack said. "'S not what I have." Ghost sickness ate a person slowly from the inside. It had showed in Pete's eyes first, in the haunted cast of her gaze and in the dreams of death that came any time she shut them. She'd carried Algernon Treadwell's spirit like a black rider on her back, her slight body pale and papery as Treadwell drank of her life.

"Oh?" Seth rummaged in the fridge and found a few eggs, which he cracked into a frying pan. "Always thought it was a load of bollocks, myself. Who'd you know got it?"

"Someone in London," Jack said, and ended Seth's probing with a flick of his hand. "We need to find out where Hornby is buried. Dig him up and get on with it."

"You're gettin' ahead of yourself, Jackie," Seth told him. "Unless, in the intervening years, you've taken it upon yourself to learn the ways and means of calling back the dead."

Jack shoved his hands into his hair. It was flattened on one side and he attempted to muss it equally again. "You know I'm no fucking sorcerer, Seth. But if we have no body, no necromantic spell we try will do one bit of bloody good, so let's start at what we do know."

Seth shook crystallized sugar into his coffee, sipped, and winced. "Fuck me. Can't brew a cuppa in this country worth shite."

"Just point me at the cemetery," Jack said. "I'll do it myself, since you're feeling delicate." As the sun rose, gray-yellow like an old bruise through the haze of smog that hung over Bangkok, Jack felt his time of reprieve slipping away, little by little, like sand against skin.

"It doesn't work like that here," Seth muttered.

"Explain, then," Jack snapped. "Because this might be a bloody amusement for you, but this is my life, Seth. *My* fucking life and someone else's besides if I can't do what the demon wants from me."

"And who's fault is that, exactly?" Seth demanded. "You didn't have to call him, Jackie-boy. You didn't have to reach out."

"I suppose you would have had me die." Jack's headache began with a renewed vengeance. He wasn't damply sweating any longer, but cold. Cold like the day he'd lain on the floor of Algernon Treadwell's tomb and felt the slight warmth of his own blood spread across his chest, his stomach, soaking through his shirt and dribbling onto the stones.

"Yes," said Seth shortly. "I would have." He dumped the sludgy coffee down into the drain and slammed his mug onto the porcelain washboard. "But that's the past and this, unfortunately, is me present so after I find a bite to eat we'll go see about finding your dead man."

Chapter Twenty-six

"Hornby couldn't've picked a worse city to die in," Seth said as they walked down Patpong 2. The road and its citizens lay much subdued in daylight, as the district nursed its hangover. "You got any idea where and when he kicked it?"

"No," Jack said, spying Trixie unlocking the door of her bar. "But she does." He raised a hand. "Oi! Luv! Got a minute?"

Trixie smiled when she caught sight of him, but the expression dropped just as quickly when she saw Seth. "I know you. You're the *farang* who puts curses on people from your balcony."

Seth puffed up. "Is that what they say about me?"

"And you had the nerve to jump on my back about black magic?" Jack muttered.

"Shaddup," Seth told him congenially. "Like you're bein' fitted for a halo, boy."

Jack had almost forgotten how much he wanted to punch Seth in the mouth, but the desire came back sharp and twinging between his knuckles. He looked to Trixie instead. "Luv, we need to know how Miles died. And where."

"He bit it out on Silom Road." She jerked a thumb. "Got hit by a taxi walking to the train station after his set. About two weeks ago."

"Happens a lot around here," Seth said to Jack's questioning look. "Taxi drivers willy-nilly, drunk tourists pushin' and shovin' . . . recipe for a pavement pancake if I ever heard of one."

"Yeah, well . . ." Trixie pursed her lips. "He took a long time to die. He was still screaming when the corpse collectors got there."

"Corpse collectors?" Jack cast a glance up and down the street, sunlight diffused by buildings closing in overhead. He wasn't looking for a pissing contest with a host of necromancers. If they were thick on the ground in Bangkok, he might have to accept his fate with grace and go home. Which was as bloody likely as Seth joining the Riverdance.

"Bangkok doesn't have a city ambulance service," Seth explained. "So when there's a dead bloke lying in the street, whoever can snatch him up first gets the fee from the hospital morgues. Bloody business, that—quite literally."

"He's right," Trixie said. "But Miles died soon enough after that. They probably took him to Patpong Hospital." She put one hand on her hip. The forearm bit of her tattoo was a pair of dancing geishas, peering from behind their fans. "Why d'you want to know?"

"Pure academic curiosity," Jack assured her. "Cheers, luv. Who's playing tonight?"

"Unicorn Euthanasia," Trixie said, opening the door into the bar. Jack frowned.

"They any good?"

"They're shit," Trixie said. "Good luck finding whatever it is you're looking for, Jack." She shut the door on him, and the space where she'd been filled up with a poster advertising go-go dancers and free drinks.

"I know a bloke," Seth said slowly. "At that hospital. He works in . . . well . . . corpse delivery."

"And?" Jack cast a look at Seth. He'd never remembered the man looking reluctant to plunge into any sort of dealing with the Black, but Seth was tapping his sandal on the road, eyes darting everywhere but Jack.

"And, nothing," Seth said too quickly. "He's a skin trader. Knows words, spells. Things for you to use, to bring Hornby back. Which is still a royally shite fucking idea, by the way."

Jack stopped at the crush of traffic on Silom Road. "I'll take me chances." If he opened his sight he could feel it now, the splashes of blood in the gutters, the shrieks of the dying, the mosquito buzz of small engines carrying motorists right on by. Bangkok's Black was like a pile of corpses—dead at the core but crawling with layer upon layer of new life.

"This way." Seth walked through the crush of people on the pavement, and Jack followed, riding the small space of his wake. They passed shops, shoppers, tourists, locals, gangsters covered up with tattoos and Buddhist amulets, and housewives haggling over the price of vegetables.

Once, a crowd of monks passed, and every woman on the street backed up against the nearest wall, allowing them to pass.

"They can't touch women," Seth murmured. "Seems a hellish old lot in life, you ask me."

"Hellish is a word some bastards use entirely too lightly," Jack said, watching the monks wend their way down the road. They were the only ones who didn't have to shove, elbow, and shout to make way.

Jack could think of worse lives.

Chapter Twenty-seven

Patpong Hospital resided in a squat brown building that smelled of sickly-sweet cleaning compounds and buzzed with a nervous system of flickering fluorescent tube lights. The air conditioning made an effort, but the black celluloid strips taped to the vent above the doorway into A&E barely fluttered when Jack passed beneath them.

Seth stomped down a narrow corridor past a nurse's station crowned by a bouquet of wilted daisies, past rooms filled with patients in steel beds surrounded by white mosquito netting.

Jack thought of spirits, floating above their beds, white and lacy, while the ebb and flow of the Black plucked off pieces of their souls and tossed them on the current.

Seth turned through a swinging door marked in Thai. Jack didn't have to read the language to know a NO ADMITTANCE sign when he saw one. The smell here was different—cloying, heavier. A smell that wasn't pretending that life was still possible, just covering up the stench of death. The floor under Jack's feet ran with cracks and water the color of mud dribbled into rusty drains.

One door sat off the narrow corridor, under a broken light that blinked arcane semaphore in shadow and bright. Morgues around the world were the same—silent, stinking, and filled up with the psychic energy of the dead.

"Be easy in here, yeah?" Seth said. "He's a bit of a skittish bloke and you don't speak the language anyway, so don't go off shouting and pitching a temper fit like you do."

"I'll be polite as a vicar at a church picnic," Jack promised.

In the morgue proper, Jack spied a body lying on the single steel table in the center of the room. He'd been around plenty of dead things—both recently deceased and long-rotted—but seeing the man on the table, half-covered by a sheet as if he were about to receive a shady massage instead of an autopsy, made him itch all over, under the skin. Jack didn't like corpses, and neither did his stomach.

"Heya," Seth shouted, knocking on the edge of the table. The man under the sheet jumped, limbs going akimbo at his ministrations.

"Christ," Jack muttered, turning his back on the corpse.

"'Ey, you were the one who's so keen to truck with these rotters," Seth said. "Chin up, little camper. It's not going to bite you."

Jack cast a baleful eye at the corpse. "That's a matter of opinion."

A figure backed out of a small wash closet on the other side of the morgue. The space was spare, just a steel counter covered in surgical instruments and a black nylon doctor's bag, the washroom, and a row of freezers near it. A hose dangled from the ceiling, fitted with a spray nozzle for washing bodies. The quiet *drip-drop-plip* of water and blood was the only sound, beyond the humming of the freezers.

"Jao," Seth said, giving the small pathologist a nod. "Been keeping yourself well, mate?"

Jao looked from Seth to Jack. He fired of a rapid sentence of Thai and Seth spread his hands.

"No, no. He's a friend. He's one of us."

Jack gestured at the dead man on the table. "Hell of a centerpiece, mate. Your work?"

Jao slipped on a pair of blue nitrile gloves and picked up a scalpel and forceps, peeling back the skin of the man on the table. His cuts bifurcated tattoos, sutras and dragons tangled together in the hurried flurry that Jack recognized as prison ink.

"So?" he growled finally, hands never pausing as he lifted out a section of sternum that a Stryker saw had separated. "What you want?" Jao wore white at his temples and a scowl on his face like battle scars, and he glared up at Jack from under a thatch of black hair. He resembled more than anything a troll, something small and scuttling that lived under a bridge. Jack knew from hanging about Pete and her work with the Met that it happened when you spent your days prodding dead bodies.

"You had a bloke come in about two weeks ago," Seth said. "Dead bloke, obviously. *Farang* who got himself pasted in a man vs. taxi spat. White, probably pale as this cunt right here." Seth jerked his thumb at Jack.

"He was a singer," Jack supplied. "And talented."

"Talented, right." Seth fingered his packet of Silk Cut, tapped out a fag. Jao curled his lip back.

"Ain't no smoking in the surgery."

Jack took the fag from Seth's fingers and stuck it between his own lips, touching his finger to the end. "Brilliant. You see this dead bloke or not?"

"No," Jao said instantly. He opened the nylon bag and pulled out a bunch of herbs. "We ain't had nobody here like that."

The herbs went under the dead man's skin and Jao

rummaged in his supplies until he found a wide-gauge needle and rough cotton thread.

"That's hawthorn," Jack said, puffing out a cloud of smoke and breaking off the burning tip of the fag, for later. "Recognize the leaves." He poked at the pile of herbs in the dead man's chest cavity. "Not a lot of hawthorn trees in this part of the world, eh, mate?"

Jao slapped his hand away. "Not for touching."

"I'm really couldn't give a flying fuck what you're doing to this poor bastard," Jack said. "Although according to Seth here, you people got a real problem with ghost sickness. Seems maybe you're not so very skilled at your chosen discipline, Jao."

Jao's massive eyebrows drew together like a thorny hedgerow. "What you mean 'you people'?"

"Skin traders," Jack said evenly. "Necromancers. Liars."

Seth rubbed a hand across his forehead. "Jack . . ."

"You recognized the description," Jack said. Jao's hand, moving the needle in and out of the seam of his Y-incision, burying the hawthorn in the dead man's chest, missed and he stabbed himself in the thumb.

"You know who he was," Jack told Jao. He snaked out his hand and snatched the hawthorn bundle from the corpse's chest. "And now you're going to tell me what happened to the body."

Jao's lip curled. "You think you can order me around?"

"Bet your lying arse, I do," Jack said. "I've come too far and I've staked too much. *What* did you do with Hornby?"

Jao heaved a dramatic sigh and cast a look at Seth. "Don't look to me," Seth said. "I'm not his bloody keeper."

Jao extended his hand to Jack. "Give it back."

"Nope." Jack twitched the hawthorn out of Jao's reach. "Quid pro quo, mate. Where's Hornby?"

Jao's jaw muscle knotted under his skin, and his eyes blazed with the sick bruise-purple witchfire endemic to sorcerers. "I make your skin into a handbag, you miserable white bastard. I pull your teeth one by one and string them for conjure necklace . . ."

Jack held up the hawthorn twig. "Too much chatter. Not enough information."

Jao's lip pulled back in a sneer. Seth rubbed his forehead. "Jackie, I warned you. . . ."

"I'm waiting," Jack intoned, pulling his lighter from his pocket and flipping the top. He held the flame just under the hawthorn. "I don't hear an answer."

"I can look up," Jao muttered after a long moment when Jack wasn't sure if Jao would cooperate or come after him with a scalpel. "Get my log book." He shuffled over to the steel table and pulled a battered ledger from his bag, flicking over the pages with irritable twitches of his fingers. "Here," he said finally. "Come here."

Jack approached but stayed clear of arm's reach. "You find him."

In response, Jao spun around and lashed at him with a blood-coated scalpel. Jack slipped on the slick floor, went down, lost the lighter and the hawthorn twig along with his balance. His elbow cracked the concrete and pain radiated from his arm into his chest, hot fingers of flame.

Before he could manage a fresh breath or to take inventory of his smashed bits, Jao lunged for him again, and Jack slid backwards, banging into the surgery table. The corpse shifted, and the whole thing toppled over.

"Seth!" he shouted. "Grab this crazy cunt!"

Nothing answered him except Jao's hysterical gasping as he raised the scalpel and bore down on Jack. Jack whipped his gaze at the spot where Seth had last stood.

Seth had vanished.

Jao was screaming, face swollen and red as an overfilled balloon. As with the signs on the door, Jack didn't need to speak a lick of Thai to know hysterical fear when he saw it.

The silver tooth of the scalpel struck. Jack raised his hand and spit out a word of power, throat contracting like there was a cord about his neck.

"Cosain!"

The shield hex didn't stop Jao, since he was flesh and only tangentially magic, but it slowed him down. The blade slid neatly along the outside of Jack's arm as the necromancer stumbled and fell over the toppled surgery table, into the embrace of the corpse. Pain sparked in Jack's muscle and bone, warm blood dripping down his forearm onto the floor to join the dead man's.

Jack's hammering heart and blurred vision told him that he didn't have more than thirty seconds before the blood loss and the blow put him out, and Jao was already up. Panicked and awkward as he was, he was faster than Jack on Jack's best day.

"I'm not going back!" Jao shrieked. "Not into that mouth! No more!" He slashed at Jack, and Jack felt air part in front of his eyes as the scalpel missed his face by millimeters.

Jack considered that he was an all-right brawler, when the weapons were bottles, fists, or chains. He'd spent enough time in dodgy clubs populated with skinheads looking for a bruising to be fair with his fists. Against a crazed necromancer with a blade, though, he was rubbish.

Jao wouldn't sit still long enough to be hit with any kind of paralysis hex, and a spell to steal breath or eyesight wasn't the sort of thing you conjured empty-handed.

Jack had his sight, a flick knife, a pack of cigarettes, and the necklace Robbie had given him. No kit, no spell materials. Jack Winter, mage, had precisely shit.

Jao came for him again, his magic cutting a roiling wake through the Black, and Jack ducked his swing, nearly falling over the corpse. The corpse, lying still, waiting for its fate as the instrument of the necromancer's black magic.

Or his.

Jack felt his lungs seize as the fags had their revenge, and he let himself fall back, landing next to the clammy sack of flesh on the floor. He clapped one palm on the corpse's stiff leg, fixing on Jao as the panting necromancer poised over him for the killing blow.

Black oily power floated behind Jao's gaze, like a burning slick of gasoline on a river. Jack opened his sight to the energies of the morgue, pulled all of the power into him that his body would allow.

When you cast a curse, second chances weren't given. Curses worked in triads, the words of power, the energy of the mage, the conductor medium. All three balanced exactly, or the curse could snap back and do worse to you than you'd conjured, thrice.

Curses weren't worth the trouble, by and large, when the same problems could be solved with a boot to the teeth or a cricket bat to the guts. But Jack had seen what they could do when they were applied properly, and he needed to stop Jao, for sure and for good.

He drew in his last bit of air, held it, and expelled it in a fury, putting all of his panic and rage behind it, pushing every ounce of his energy into the words of power while he grasped the corpse hard enough to leave a handprint on the dead man's splotchy skin. "*Cosbriste!*"

The corpse jumped under him as its leg bone cracked, and Jao let out a scream. His left leg twisted under him as the curse sprang across the distance between Jack and the necromancer like a starving dog and sank its teeth into his soul. Jao's leg bone snapped with a clean, crisp sound in the small room, and he dropped.

The scalpel tinkled out of his grasp and landed close to where Jack sat, fighting to pull his heart back under control as it thundered along fit to snap his ribs.

It always took a few seconds to realize you were still

alive, when Death put out a hand and clapped it against your face, forced you to look it in the eye.

Seth came pelting through the door with a security man in a blue uniform, and stopped short at the scene before him. "Jackie boy, what the fuck is this?"

"Leg-breaker curse," Jack said hoarsely. His feet slithered under him on the wet concrete, but he used the slimy tile wall and got to his feet. "What's it look like, we danced a samba?"

The security guard asked Seth if things were all right, and Seth waved him off in Thai, pressing a few hundred *bhat* into the man's hand before he shoved him out of the morgue. "Jesus, Mary, and Joseph in a ménage à trois," Seth growled. He slammed the door and locked it. "He came after you like a fat schoolboy on a custard cake. Told you not to open your big mouth."

Jack flipped Seth the bird. "Up yours." Air passed across his extended arm with a sting. His cut was pumping blood, and the slash neatly bisected his tattoos. Jack grabbed a towel from the wash closet and wrapped it around himself, vines of crimson soaking through the cotton. "That cunt. If I get some sort of infection that makes bits of me fall off . . ."

"You need stitches," Seth said. "I'm not mopping up after you again, Jackie."

"After we find Hornby." Jack took a deep breath through his nose. Willed his heart to stop pumping his life out of the gash Jao had left. Wrestled the magic in the room back under control. It was rough and ugly, like a waterfall from a polluted stream, as his power and the magic left over from the sobbing necromancer's attack commingled.

He tied off the towel tight as he could stand it, and righted the surgical table with his good hand. "Get him up," he told Seth, jerking his chin at Jao.

"Jack, he's a good bloke," Seth said. "He's a scared bloke. Whatever's happening here, it's not his fault. . . ."

Jack pointed at the table. "Get him up and put him on the fucking table, McBride." He didn't have any spare panic now, just a tight black feeling in his chest. He was alive. He'd looked at the blade coming down and he was still standing. Jack didn't think he'd ever become accustomed to the weightless, breathless feeling of still taking up space in the world when he should be on his way through the Bleak Gates.

Seth wrestled Jao's limp form onto the table with a grunt. "Jack," he said. "I'm asking you, properly now . . ."

Jack slammed his good hand down onto the metal next to Jao's head. The clang echoed round the small room and Jao whimpered.

"Right," Jack said. "I ask again: where's Hornby's fucking corpse?"

Jao's throat worked. "I can't . . ." he rasped. "I can't . . . tell you . . . that."

Jack turned his back, went to the instrument tray, picked up a rib spreader. "Five seconds and I loosen your jaw, mate. The old-fashioned way. No curses involved."

"Jackie . . ." Seth looked at him askance. "This is a far cry from you, Winter."

Jack put the rib spreader against Jao's lips. "I'm a far cry from meself right now, Seth," he said. "I'm a desperate man and this cunt is standing between me and my dead vocalist, so either hold him fucking still or walk out now." He cranked the spreader one turn. "Where's Hornby?"

"I can't say it!" Jao screamed. "I can't!"

"Can't, or won't?" Jack ratcheted spreader another turn. "Where's Hornby?"

"I'm not afraid of you," Jao quavered, his voice distorted by the metal fingers in his mouth.

The pounding in Jack's head increased to blackout levels, and his hands quivered. He knew the rage. He'd watched it belt him across the mouth, pour whiskey down its throat, and kick him with steel-toed boots for fourteen years before he left Manchester.

And he wanted Jao to share the knowledge, wanted to crank the fucking rib spreader to the maximum and break the sneaky wanker's jaw.

Instead, he leaned close to Jao's ear, close enough to smell sweat and the last vestiges of cologne. "You should be," he hissed.

"*You* should be," Jao shouted. "You think you the worst thing to come through my door? You think I'll tell you when he's . . ."

Jao choked, and then his face went slack after a moment of struggle. Cloudy, bloody spiderweb drifted into the whites of his eyes, and his body slumped against the table, still.

Seth shoved two fingers against Jao's sweaty neck. "He's dead. You've fucking killed one of my best customers, Jack. Bloody cheers."

Jack dropped the rib spreader. "That wasn't me."

Seth threw up his hands, like an aggravated mother. "Who the fuck was it, then? Darth fucking Vader?"

Jack wheeled and grabbed Jao's kit bag, dumped out the necromancy supplies atop Jao's surgical instruments. "By my guess," he said, "whoever Jao was afraid enough of to take a slash at me." Baggies of herbs, a tin of salt, a child's knucklebones in a velvet sack, a silver dagger blunted on the edge, and a bit of lint fell onto the steel.

Jack slammed his fist into the table. The pain brought him back to himself, a bit, but the rage was still pumping through his veins like cold fire, racing his heart and splitting his skull. "Fuck. He doesn't have a grimoire." Jack pressed his hands over his face. He was smeared in blood, his eyes were gritty, and he wanted nothing more than to put his head down and sleep for roughly a decade, until the world made sense again. As much as it ever had.

"Who's next?" he said instead, dropping his hands to look at Seth. "Who's the next necromancer you know? One who might actually have some corpse-raising spells lying around instead of trying to cut me fucking throat?"

"Forget that, boy," Seth said. "After what you just did? You aren't in any shape to be working magic of this caliber. Can see it right in your face."

"For fuck's sake, Seth!" Jack scattered the instrument tray with a sweep of his arm. "This isn't an academic exercise, this is my fucking *life*!"

"And what god decrees your life weighs more than his?" Seth pointed at Jao. "Or Miles Hornby's? What makes you so bloody special, Jack Winter?"

"No god," Jack snarled. "I belong to a demon, remember?" Jack wished, viciously, for something to take the edge off his panic and pain.

"'S what I thought," Seth sighed. "Always had to be the chosen one, the one for whom the rules didn't fucking apply, didn't you, Jackie?"

"If you've got something to say, spit it out." Jack unlocked the door and slipped out into the hospital corridor. Seth followed him, digging a Silk Cut from his pack and lighting it with a vicious snap of his power.

"You know you shouldn't be here, Jack. You stole some time from the crow woman by cutting your deal, but her claws are sharp and her gaze is sharper. We all reach the road's end. There's nothing you can do to change *that*."

"My road doesn't end here," Jack snarled. "Unlike you, sad old bastard, I haven't given up."

"Why now?" Seth demanded. "You had thirteen years to cheat the demon—why now, at the end, does it become the thing you're willing to murder and torture over?"

Jack rounded on Seth, fists turning to knots of bone. *"Because I have something to live for."* His cut started bleeding again, soaking the worn towel.

Seth gave Jack a wire-thin, resigned smile. "What's her name?"

Jack started walking again. The A&E suite had filled while they were with Jao, tourists and locals sitting where they could find space on the floor and the metal benches. "You don't get to know her name."

"I guarantee the demon does," Seth said. "The demon knows that she's your soft underbelly, and that's why he's sent you on this doomed errand." Seth exhaled, sharp, an arrow of smoke. "Don't do something you can't wash off for a piece of skirt, boy. Take it from me, it all comes down on your head in the end."

"In the end," Jack said quietly, "she's the only person who gave a *shit* about me, who held out a hand, who even pretended to care if I lived or died, so if you say one more word about her I swear to the crow woman I'll bleed you where you stand, Seth. I mean it."

"You've changed, Jack." Seth shoved his hands into his pockets. "And though I didn't think it was possible, not for the better."

"Same to you, mate," Jack said. "And a big cheery thanks for all of your nonexistent help."

"Help? Anyone who helps you ends up dead or broken, boy. I learned my lesson on that score twenty fuckin' years ago." Seth shook his head. "I'm finished with you, Jackie. You shouldn't have come to me, caught me up in this. It's not considerate and it's not bloody fair."

"Fair?" Jack rounded on Seth. "Don't you talk to me about fair, old man. I suppose to you fair is dumping out an apprentice so addled with the sight he'd put out his own eyes to stop the dead coming. Fair is knowing your friend is wandering the street with skag for blood. Fair is sleeping nice and tight every night because you're lucky enough to be able to forget your sins." Jack hissed as his arm throbbed.

"If that's what you think, Seth, then you're right—it was right fucking unfair of me to expect any help from the likes of you."

Seth took his hands from his pockets, flexed his fists. "You really want to walk this road, Jackie?"

"No, Seth," Jack sighed. "I want to find Miles Hornby. I want to find him, and give him to the demon, and go home."

Seth's posture slumped, and he passed a hand over his face to clear it of sweat. "You were always so bloody stubborn, Jackie. Always had to be right, even when you missed it by a mile."

"It's one of me charming traits," Jack said. "Ask anybody."

Seth shook his head, his gaze shifting to a point over Jack's shoulder. "You won't change your mind."

"Can't," Jack shrugged. "The demon wants Hornby and I want what the demon promised me. I suppose I don't want to die, either. Silly me."

Seth dropped his eyes to the stained vinyl floor. "Then I'm sorry, Jackie. Dead sorry."

Jack only became aware of the two men in sunglasses when they approached from the entrance of A&E, their dark suits and slacks and gold chains giving them away as a creature not normally found in the bowels of a hospital waiting room.

"Help you, gents?" Jack smiled as they glided up on either side of Seth, like two shadow spilling into a lit doorway.

The man on the left smiled at Jack. "Mr. Winter?" His accent was London, and not the part Jack had spent most of his life in. This accent reminded him more of Nicholas Naughton than it did a gangster. The man was surely that, though—gangsters looked the same the world over, once you got past the superficial costumes. Blank eyes, shark smiles, energy too big and pulsing with malice for the space their bodies occupied.

They always thought they were the worst predator on their patch, and the shit bit of it was that outside the Black, they were nearly always right.

"I'm Jack Winter," Jack confirmed. No point in lying about his name if they already knew it.

"Then we are to extend you an invitation, Mr. Winter," Lefty said. Rightie was silent. His hand clutched a string of what looked like Buddhist prayer beads, at first glance, but what Jack saw were really tiny skulls, carved from black stone. A fetish or a focus—Jack wasn't keen to find out, and even less keen to know the gangsters had some talent for sorcery.

"Sorry, mate." Jack held up his bloodied arm. "I've had my dance for today. Unless your invite is for a stitch-up and a stiff drink, thank you but please fuck off."

The man inclined his head. "Perhaps I wasn't clear. This is not a request, Mr. Winter."

Jack felt the electricity up and down his spine that signaled another mage was close. "You said it was an invitation."

"It can be," said the one with the beads. "It can be something else if you don't feel like being sociable."

Their magic was thick and hard, like scraping your knuckles against stone, leaving blood and skin behind. Jack favored them with a wide smile. Keep smiling, keep the gangsters calm, and work out how the bloody hell he was going to extricate himself from the situation before someone used that hard, ugly magic on him. *Think, Winter,* the fix mocked him. *You're so clever. Bright boy, always a quicksilver mind.*

Jack spread out his hands, so the gangsters could see they were empty and that he was no threat, just another hapless *farang.* "Who do you work for, then? Or do you run about like superheroes in chavvy gold chains, striking down wicked men like me where you find them?"

Lefty sighed. "Mr. Winter, don't make this difficult."

"Difficult?" Jack shook his head, slow and pitying. "Difficult would be me taking the two of you by the bollocks and tossing you headfirst through the waiting-room window. Difficult would be me cursing you into small, bloody smears in front of all of these nice people. I have not *begun* to be difficult yet, mate."

Jack felt the light air-brush of witchfire start to spread from his fingers and anywhere his skin was exposed. Everyone in the waiting room had averted their eyes when the men stepped up, but Jack didn't care. He was never coming back to this bloody city, with its slick snakeskin magic and its crowded, whispering Black.

Lefty's hand shot out and clamped down on the spot where Jao had cut him. The pain was deep and dull, a rusted blade in his skin, and Jack ground his teeth to keep from yelling. "Mr. Winter," Lefty said. "I don't want to do this, but I have my instructions. You need to come with us. Right this moment."

Righty clicked his beads. The power around the two mages swelled. Jack felt blood from his wound start to drip again, hitting the linoleum floor with dull splats. Blood was a powerful cantrip. A mage could use blood as a conductor, a channel, a focus for almost any magic. If he had the control, and the skill. If he didn't lose that control, let himself get taken over by a hungry ghost, and end up bleeding to death on the floor of a crypt. There was always a catch with magic. Limitless power, if you didn't let it burn you alive.

"Jack," Seth said quietly. "You should do as they say."

"Thanks, Seth," Jack said, keeping his eye on Lefty. "But I'm about through taking your advice."

"Your friend is concerned for your well-being," Lefty

intoned. "And rightly so. You've been here less than two days and already you've managed to end poor Jao's life."

"Wasn't me, I said," Jack snarled. "And by the look of poor fucking Jao, he'd had it coming for miles."

Lefty glanced at the blood on the floor. "You are not in an enviable position, Mr. Winter. You can fight me, it's true." His grip tightened, driving iron barbs into Jack's arm. "You'll lose."

Jack watched the blood pool grow, crawling by degrees across the linoleum, adding a new stain to the battered gray surface. He didn't reach for it with his talent, didn't grasp the shimmering well of power waiting to fend off the gangster's ministrations. "I'm not some nonce who'll fold at the hint of a few hexes."

Lefty heaved a sigh as if he were being entirely unreasonable, and pulled up his shirt to display the silver butt of a gun—a .45, by Jack's reckoning. "We already know you bleed, Mr. Winter. Now, walk in front of us out to the car waiting at the curb, and don't cause a fuss."

"Magicians who go strapped," Jack said. "Very Wild West, mate. Phallic, really. Suppose it's true what they say about you Thais and your love of the ladyboys."

"It's loaded with pig-iron bullets," Lefty said, pleasant smile affixed to his face as if he were a housewife on Valium. "It will rip your insides to shreds and your magic along with it and I will enjoy watching you die slowly. Walk."

Jack turned around and walked. You didn't fuck about when someone threatened to shoot you in broad daylight in a hospital. Spells and hexes, he could give as good as he got. Bullets weren't the same thing at all—and iron bullets, fuck it. You didn't stick your hand in a spinning fan because you fancied a cooling off.

The gangsters seemed reluctant to damage him, and that

worked in his favor. He could kick up a row, and get himself gut-shot, or he could play the cooperative sod and see who, exactly, had fixated on his presence in Bangkok, and why.

"All right, lads," he said as the doors to A&E swished back, dropping the damp blanket of Bangkok's heat over his skin. "I can be sweet as custard if the occasion calls. No reason to be shirty."

Lefty shoved him across the tide of people on the walk and into the street. "Stay quiet and move your arse."

At the curb, as promised, a smooth black Lexus idled like the riverboat of Charon, waiting to whisk Jack away to the Underworld.

Lefty rapped on a tinted—and to Jack's eye, bulletproof—window and the boot popped with an oiled *click*. Righty took out a black cloth sack and unfurled it with a snap.

Jack's headache returned as if some vicious sod had bounced a bowling ball off his skull. Eight or nine times.

"You're not bloody serious."

Lefty put his hand on the pistol again. "Quite, Mr. Winter. I believe the expression is 'dead serious'? "

Jack shot Righty a glare. "That thing better not have other people's spit on the inside."

The bag slipped over his vision, and Lefty put a firm hand on his shoulder—his power was different from Righty's. Smooth and cold rather than rough. Lefty had some black magic training, while Righty was crude muscle who probably had little more than what the Black spilled into his blood when he was conceived. Jack put it away for later.

Lefty shoved, and Jack banged his forehead on the boot lid. "Fucking hell!" he exclaimed, muffled by the hood. "You want me cheery, stop treating me like you're moving fucking furniture!"

Another shove, and Jack was forced to tumble forward or break his neck. He landed in the boot, which stank faintly of cigarettes, just to add insult to injury.

"Have a comfortable ride, Mr. Winter," Lefty said, and then the boot lid slammed above him, and what light there had been through the hood vanished, leaving Jack alone and in the dark.

Chapter Twenty-eight

Being locked in the boot allowed Jack plenty of time to think. His thoughts didn't travel anywhere he particularly wanted to be, but all the same, the situation was what it was and there was no point in crying about it.

He'd stopped bleeding, and Jack forced himself to think like Pete, who certainly wouldn't have gotten herself locked in a boot by a pair of manky sorcerers. The facts unfurled thusly:

Seth had sold him down the river to whoever in Bangkok resented a nosy mage on their turf.

Seth was a cunt, but Seth wasn't the one who'd kidnapped him.

Seth was in thrall to the same being who'd put the god's fear in Jao and snuffed out his life.

The car slowed, and Jack tried kicking at the lid of the boot. His heel skidded off of solid metal. Smashing his way out of this was becoming less possible by the second.

"Solve it, you stupid nonce," he grumbled to himself. He got a mouthful of head-bag for his trouble. It tasted sour and stale. Who put a bag on your head when you were already stuffed in a boot?

You could tell a lot about a bloke by how he threatened people. Lefty had been polite to a fault, and that posh speech didn't come from growing up in a place like Manchester. Lefty had some education, and more than a bit of talent, and yet he was an errand boy.

Whoever or whatever had Lefty and Seth in its thrall was worse than the demon. Fiercer. Harder. Someone who knew he owned his patch and fed trespassers to rabid dogs.

The master of Bangkok. The demon that belonged to every city and its Black, just as the city belonged to the demon. Knots of life and death and magic called to demons, some lost and searching for Hell, some coming willingly from the Pit to reap a harvest of human misery.

Jack tried to take a breath, and didn't manage much more than a gasp of carbon monoxide. If the demon of Bangkok knew who he was, the demon was halfway to knowing why Jack was in its fair city.

At least the errand boys hadn't tied his hands—and where would he go, if they had? Even if he popped the boot, he'd land in the middle of the thrice-cursed crush of Thai traffic and end up pavement mulch, just like Hornby. If he was lucky enough to avoid getting a necromancy curse shoved up his arse and used as a bizarre Yuletide gift in some sorcerous feud.

He ripped off the stifling hood as the Lexus rolled around a corner and smacked his head against a sharp edge again. Jack cursed the mages, the car, the powers that be, and when he was dizzy from sucking in tainted air, he saved one last curse for that treacherous cunt Seth McBride.

The Lexus inched and bounced through the streets of Bangkok, Jack's sense of time liquefying and lengthening until it might have been years that he'd spent crushed into the boot rather than minutes or hours. His arm was bound up with dried blood. Jack didn't bother peeling back the towel. Cuts were like bad memories—aggravate them with enough prodding and they began to hurt and bleed again.

At last, the car jerked to a stop as abruptly as Lefty and his companion had appeared in the waiting room, and light from the outside world dazzled Jack into blindness.

Righty's hands grabbed him by the front of his shirt. "He took the fucking bag off."

Lefty sighed. "Like it's a secret fortress around here. Get him out of there."

Jack caught a quick snatch of crowds and noise before he was hustled onto his feet and indoors, Righty stopping their procession in a shadowed vestry. Jack chanced a glance backward, into the outside. The small slice of city he could see consisted of stacked flats and Thai faces, devoid of the English signs and foreigners that overran Patpong. Jack was the only white man that he could spy, and curious faces peered from the greasy windows of the flats at the Lexus and the gangsters, the only clean things in the street. Clean, shiny sore thumbs.

Righty jerked him along and Jack lost his view. He watched a corridor lined with Japanese-style Shoji screens speed by, alcoves full of gold statues, until they came to a jerky halt again under a gilt archway, beyond which a pair of doors studded with iron nails waited.

"Bit Las Vegas, if you ask me," Jack said. "The gold paint isn't doing it any favors." He couldn't make out fuck-all in the dimness of the place, but air came from somewhere above and the smells drifting in were of sewage and chili oil and sun-warmed concrete, wound up with the cloying musk of *nag champa* incense.

"We are in Khlong Toei," said Lefty. "It is . . ."

"A slum?" Jack guessed. Manchester or Bangkok, poverty-ridden streets all smelled the same.

"And a port, and a holy place, among other things," Lefty said. "*Farang* assume because a place is one thing it must be only that thing."

"It smells like one thing," Jack muttered. "Shit."

Lefty pointed at Jack's feet. "Take off your boots." When Jack didn't immediately comply, Lefty put a hard, knuckle-ridden fist into his kidneys.

"You poisonous bollock-pustule!" Jack wheezed. "What was that for?"

"I grew up in Khlong Toei," Lefty said softly. "It's my home. Just because you see a face does not mean that face is not wearing a mask."

"Yeah. Many faces, mystical Far-East shite, blah blah blah," Jack said. He stuck his fingers in his bootlaces and yanked them off. "No offense to your lovely home, mate, but I didn't ask to be here and I don't fancy spending any more of my life in slums. Had enough of that already."

Lefty's stony face didn't flicker. "He's waiting for you. Go through the door and show him the proper respect. Or you can choose not to." The gangster took the nickel-coated .45 out of his waistband and let it dangle loosely in his hand. "Frankly, I'd like it if you did."

"Subtle," Jack told him. "You tell all your dates exactly how long your pan handle is, as well?" Jack's toes curled on the cool stone seeping through the holes in his socks.

"He is the master of Bangkok," Lefty said. "And you'll address him as such. You are a maggot, not fit to get crushed under his foot."

"I've got a fucking pronoun, at least," Jack said. He'd wanted to be wrong, to have merely fallen in with necro-mancers, but Seth had set the master of Bangkok on him and Seth didn't pull punches. McBride always did have a talent for note-perfect screwings-over. Jack fancied that if

Seth hadn't been magically inclined, he would have made a bang-up divorce barrister.

"Get moving," Lefty said. "He's not patient."

"That makes a pair of us," Jack grumbled before putting his hand on the door within the arch.

The interior of the building whispered with cool shadows, sunlight filtering through cracks in the roof. Votives flickered in lanterns hung from roof beams and a small gold Buddha glowed in the low light at the far end of the room.

Behind the Buddha, the shadows moved. They crawled across the floor and re-formed, spilled into cracks and slithered out again, and at last they twined and formed into a man, who folded his hands at the small of his back and tilted his head to examine Jack with fathomless eyes.

"Hello, Mr. Winter," the shadow said. "Thank you for your promptness."

"Well, if you want promptness nothing assures it like stuffing me into a bloody boot," Jack said.

The shadow laughed. The power that crawled off the man's shape told Jack it was not a man at all. The magic was not the magic of a human. Thick, cloying, prying at his defenses and his sight with relentless claws, it slipped in around all of Jack's frayed edges and tried to fill him up with the hot, dry winds of Hell. Jack didn't like things that he didn't know how to work over with his talent, or how to exorcise. The master of Bangkok wasn't an energy he'd felt before, and Jack gave a violent shiver. He was a control freak; he admitted it, owned it, wore it with pride.

That comes from being beaten and spit on and raped by the sight your whole life, Seth had said. *Use it, Jackie boy, don't fight it.*

The only voice he'd ever wanted in his head was the one that bent him over and fucked him in the end. Jack let out a small chuckle.

The shadow flowed toward him. "Something amusing to you, Mr. Winter?"

"Just thinking." Jack shrugged. "If I didn't have shite luck, I'd have no luck whatsoever."

"Very apt," the shadow agreed. "But today, your luck is good. You're here."

Jack caught a glimpse, just a flash, of a blackness that went on and on, and a horned figure with a protruding tongue riding on the back of a black ox while behind him came every dark and wretched thing that found refuge in the Black. He tried to shut his sight against the creature in front of him, but the tattoos on his shoulders began to burn and his head felt as if it would split. He ground his teeth together and drew blood from his tongue while the creature laughed, a smooth, velvety sound that made Jack's skin prickle.

"You can't stop seeing, Jack. I'm not like one you've met before."

"D'you want me to stick a star on you?" Jack said. He focused on the pain in his arm, the lump forming on his head. Physical pain could hold the sight back—for a little while. Long enough for him to either talk his way out of the temple or find out exactly how deep he was in the shit.

"Introductions, then," said the creature. It held out a hand, and with a ripple of power its body became flesh. Its hand floated in front of Jack's face, slim and unscarred, adorned with silver rings and black fingernails. "I am Rahu."

Jack didn't take the proffered digit. "You'll forgive me, but I'm not fucking stupid."

Rahu lifted a shoulder. "Your friend Seth did pass that tidbit on." At Jack's sneer, Rahu grinned. "You've noticed a change in your old friend."

"Seth hasn't been me friend in a long time," Jack said. "You're so all-knowing, you must know that."

"It doesn't change the fact that he values his new life here, and if one values life in the currents of the Black river of Bangkok, one eventually crosses paths with me."

Jack pushed his hands through his hair. It curled around his temples. The heat killed any hope of his usual mess of spikes. "If you're going to kill me, could we kick on?" Jack said to Rahu. "I've never been so damp and miserable as in this city."

"I'm not going to kill you," Rahu said. He whipped out his hand and closed it around Jack's scalpel wound. "I'm going to tell you two facts: this isn't your city. And it isn't a scheming demon's, either. I don't know why your bargain-binder sent you here, but you'll tell me. How quickly determines whether you go back to London in a bag or on your own two feet."

Jack met Rahu's eyes, and refused to flinch as the creature kept a death grip on his wound. "I didn't come here to move against you. I just came here to bring Miles Hornby home."

Rahu's eyes were black, pupilless. They flickered with power, like Jack's own eyes when his magic was up. Jack tugged against his grip, but the creature held fast. "I smell it on you, Jack," Rahu hissed. "I can taste it in the air around you. There's demon taint on your skin and in your blood. You're a dog, following a command." He let go of Jack. "And you've just walked into a wolf den."

A dark handprint stayed in the dried blood on Jack's arm, and the skin was freezing and burnt, frostbitten from a touch. Fingertips of shiver worked their way across his skin, searching through nerve and tissue and blood.

"Go home," Rahu said again. "Go back to your demon and tell him whatever coup he sent you to conduct failed. This is your only chance."

Jack rubbed the burn. Pain could be managed. Pain meant his heart was still beating. Pain was a friend. "I can't," he said.

Rahu's lips drew back. His profile was striking—sharp nose, sharper cheeks, the barest hint of crystalline white fangs protruding over his lower lip. "I don't think I heard you," the creature said.

"You did." Jack swallowed. "I know you're the master of Bangkok, that the demon won't step foot here because of you, so I reckon you're a hard one, but right now I'm something worse."

Rahu's perfect eyebrow raised, wrinkling his perfect golden forehead. If the nasty, oily smirk wasn't in place, he could have been a ringer for the Buddha. "And what are you, Jack?" he purred.

Jack balled his fists. "I'm desperate." Feeling his rings dig into his flesh and his tattoos flex gave him a grounding, a bit of the real against the vast whirlpool of magic Rahu commanded. "Miles Hornby is a dead man who tricked a demon. The demon sent me to bring him home, and I said I would."

Rahu twisted the rings on his fingers, methodically, one after the other. "You are not making a compelling case for your continued life and breath, Jack."

"I have to find Hornby," Jack said. Telling a demon the truth was always a risk, because most demons wouldn't know truth if it sat up and offered them tea and a biscuit. "I'm going to make him tell me how he got out of his bargain." Jack locked his eyes onto Rahu's, even though staring at the creature made his sight scream. "And then I'm going to do the same thing."

Rahu ran his fingers along the gilt altar supporting the Buddha. Gold paint curled in flakes under his fingernails. "Ridiculous. I don't believe you."

"I don't particularly care," Jack returned. "I'm going to break my bargain, and to do that I have to find Hornby."

Rahu merely smiled. Some men Jack knew could smile and make it a thousand times worse than any curse, hex, or blow. Kev. Seth. Treadwell's ghost.

"You don't know who you're bargaining with, Jack. Your demon is older and cleverer than most." Rahu's face went jagged, all planes and rage. "I once was master of the whole of the Floating World, the lands beyond the sea and to the mountains. Do you know who took that from me? Do you know who resigned me to this fetid, sweltering trap of an island?"

"We both have something to hate it for, then," Jack said. "I'd think you'd be dancing in place to help me."

Rahu's smile went sharp and cold as the rusty edge of a razor. "And yet, for *some* odd reason, I don't trust a man sent to me by the very demon responsible for this misery of an existence."

"Believe it or not"—Jack lifted a shoulder—"I really don't give a fuck, mate. May I go?"

"Not yet." Rahu's voice stopped Jack as he started to walk away. "You say you're a desperate man. Desperate men bargain. Am I to understand you correctly?"

Jack cursed inwardly, sensing he'd walked right onto the big red X and let Rahu drop an anvil on him. "I suppose."

"And you wish the possession of the dead man Hornby." Rahu tapped his chin with one black-painted nail. "Which explains why you attacked poor Khan Jao." Rahu tipped Jack a wink. "No sort of necromancer, are you?"

"Call me a madman, but my mum always taught me to leave the dead be," Jack said.

"Did she?" Rahu advanced on Jack, laid a hand against his temple before Jack could backpedal. Ice crystals sprouted on the spot, feather-light on Jack's skin and hair. "Or was she a whore and a junkie who abandoned you to a life of terror and misery while she crawled inside her pill bottle?"

Jack laughed. He smiled wide. And then he snapped his forehead down against Rahu's perfect smirk. He caught the creature in the nose. Black blood fountained, hissing where it hit the stone, smoke curling as if the effluvia were liquid nitrogen.

"Don't bait me," Jack said. "You won't like what you find in the trap."

Rahu cracked his nose back into place. The sound of cartilage scraping echoed against the domed roof of the small temple. The creature didn't flinch. "Mage, I am going to send you back to your demon in a box with a bow if you're lying to me."

Jack massaged his forehead. There was a lump growing. "And if I'm not?"

"If you're not," Rahu purred, "then you need what I have."

"I sincerely hope it's not wit or charm." Jack rubbed at the sore spot on his forehead. Rahu had a skull like a cricket bat. "Because you're skint on that score."

"Before this city grew from the mud and the filth of the river's bank," Rahu said, "I was a keeper of knowledge. I supped with beings you can only imagine, and I took their secrets as my own. I am the forsaken knowledge of the Black, mage. I can give you the spell that awakens Hornby and delivers to you the means to slip your bargain's bonds."

"And in return?" Jack spread his hands. "Let me guess, you just want a little something, a little shred of soul or a little pinch of flesh?" He sat down on the prayer cushion opposite the altar, weary all at once, down to his bones. "I haven't got anything left for you, mate. I'm spoken for, head to toe."

"I have a grimoire that will get Hornby home for your task," Rahu said. "All you have to do to get it is tell the truth."

"I don't know how to tell you this," Jack said. "But I'm not a liar. Yes, I am when it suits me but you really think I'm shining you on at this moment, over this matter? You're a paranoid git, Rahu."

"You irreverence no longer diverts me," Rahu said. "Do you want the grimoire or not?"

"Do you think I'm that stupid?" Jack demanded. "That I'll make another bargain with the likes of you?"

"No," Rahu said with a blinding flash of teeth. "But you said it yourself—you are desperate."

Jack conceded with a kick to the floor that he had a point. His jackboot rang off the stone. "Show me the flaming hoop, then. I'll jump like a good boy."

Rahu's eyes glowed blackly. "No need, mage. He'll be dying to meet you."

Chapter Twenty-nine

The world faded from Jack's sight and hearing, and he saw the temple as it was half a century before. The windows were empty of glass and open, sutras hanging on faded ribbons drooping over the altar around the Buddha. Planes droned overhead, the high-pitched whine of single-prop engines. Jack craned his neck and caught sight of three Zeroes flying in formation, the suns on their noses fresh and bleeding red as if they'd just come off the line.

His sight had shown him slices of the past before, but nothing as vivid. He could smell the smoke, hear the rumble of traffic, shouts, and horn honks from the street outside.

It's real. The voice slid from the stone and the air, blanketing Jack in pinprick chills.

"You a war buff, then?" Jack asked. He tucked his hands in his pockets, rocked back and forth on the balls of his feet. "I have to say, I'm more of a 1970s retro man, meself. Go to the 100 Club, walk around Chelsea, see Zeppelin. That sort of thing."

This is the time I prefer. In other lands, with other men,

I have shown them the Crusades, the burning times, the Inquisition. But this place, in a war beyond memory, is where I began.

A shadow hit the floor as one of the planes flying overhead flicked across the sun, and it spread and grew, twin pinpoints of flame snatched from the altar candle becoming eyes. A body twitched forth next, scaly wrinkled skin like a shar-pei dog, paired at an oozing stitch line with the head of a lion. The thing tasted the air with a black tongue.

"You're an elemental." Jack fought the urge to bury his face in his hands. "That fuckwit Rahu thinks I'll piss myself at the sight of an elemental?" He met the thing's eyes. "Don't take offense, mate, but you lot were the first thing I exorcised. Practice, like."

I am not a golem of anger or terror or pain, mage, the thing said. *I am not those pieces of child's play that haunt your isle.*

Jack sighed. "Then thrill me. What are you?"

I am all things black and hopeless, it whispered. *I am the Kartimuhkha.*

When it breathed the name aloud it grew and solidified, the small details of its body resolving like Jack's gaze had been blurry from a long night of pints, fags, and mood-altering chemicals. The thing in front of him sported long claws that scraped flakes from the stone floor, strings of spittle hanging from its jaws and blazing flames dancing in its sunken eyes.

Jack stopped smiling. He felt a bit as if someone had just wrapped a rope around his neck and the other end around a gallows pole. "You have a name."

I have yours as well, crow-mage. Your soul is bare before my eyes.

Elemental demons were scavengers, the carrion birds of Hell. They clung to human emotion, to sin and sadness and pain. They didn't have names of their own.

Jack hissed through his teeth. "What do you want, then, Karti? Begging? Crying? To play fetch?"

Feed me your pain, Kartimuka whispered. It padded closer on bare human feet, its long tongue snaking out to lap at Jack's skin. *Feed me your terror.* Where it touched him, a numbness started, one that Jack recognized too well as the paralyzing bliss of a high. *Feed me your nightmares*, Kartimukha purred, and Jack fell to his knees and felt his sight peel back the layers between his consciousness and the Black.

Tell me the truth, Kartimukha rumbled in his ear. *Show me why you've come.*

He managed to scream once before his mind was stripped bare and Kartimukha plunged his claws in.

Jack saw everything, everything at once, and it overwhelmed his sight like a flash flood. His skull throbbed and filled up with the sensory overload of touching Kartimukha until he was sure it would split wide open.

Kartimukha watched him impassively, one foot planted on his chest. *Show me the secret dark and shame inside of you, mage. Feed me. Fill me.*

Jack couldn't breathe. His limbs were lead. His lungs were flat. This was the drifting place, the twilight sliver between life and the Bleak Gates, the place of overdose and suicide, of regret and despair. His heartbeat slowed, a watch with a loose spring and faulty gears.

Yes, Kartimukha breathed. *So many memories. So much pain.*

Jack felt the claws tighten around him like razor wire, around his sight and his magic and the things—the memories—that made him Jack Winter were sluicing away as the Kartimukha fed.

"You can't have them," he whispered. Kartimukha tilted its head.

They cause you pain, mage. I can rid you of them. Why would you keep them?

Jack shut his eyes against the horrible burning gaze. "They're mine," he said. "They're my scars, not yours."

You have been brave for a long time, Jack. Kartimukha caressed his face with its hot, sour breath. *You don't need to be brave any longer.*

"Brave?" Jack wheezed. Drawing a breath was agony. He felt as if someone had put a jackboot into his ribs. "I shoot smack into my arm to forget the things I've seen. I wake up screaming because of the things I've done. I can't even look the only person who gives a fuck about me in the eye. I'm not brave, I just survive better than most."

Then why do you fight? Kartimukha sounded genuinely puzzled. *Why not feed me those bleeding dreams? Why live with the scars?*

Jack forced himself to look at Kartimukha again. "That's all I have, mate. Scars. If you want memories, if you want to see that I'm being truthful, then take a look inside my head if you can stand it." He raised his head. An inch was all he could manage. "I'm not afraid of my own memories."

Kartimukha snarled. *Even now, you lie.* The thing raised its paw, brought it down, and struck into Jack's mind with its power and its magic, stripping him down to the core.

Jack blinked and found himself staring at a stained plaster ceiling, neon light blinking Morse code across the ceiling from the sign bolted to the wall outside.

He was warm—warm from whiskey in his gut and warm from blood dribbling down his arms. A hooked rug, lumpy underneath his body, soaked up the red, stain spreading.

Jack's blood was black under the blue neon. His fingers went slack, and the razor blade tumbled to the carpet.

Around him, the dead crowded in. A severe man in a celluloid collar and Windsor tie. A mod girl in a leather minidress with handprints on her throat.

They touched him, hissed at him. Stared into his soul with their black eyes and waited for him to be one of them.

This is how it ends, the girl whispered, *but her voice wasn't the strangled rasp Jack remembered. The voice was Kartimukha's. This is your last moment of life. Come to me, Jack. Leave your misery with your life.*

Jack drifted, dreamy. Soon it would be over. Soon he could forget his sight, forget his failed time with Seth and the Fiach Dubh.

Soon, he would be one with the dead instead of fighting them.

The ghost girl stooped and brushed her fingers across his forehead, moving aside strands of sweaty hair with icy fingers. This is how it ends, she breathed. *Let go, Jack. Come to me.*

This was how it ended. Life bled onto the floor of a cheap hotel room. A razor blade in a straight line up his forearms. The end of Jack Winter.

Faintly, Jack felt his breath slow and the warm, floating sensation of blood loss engulf his senses. A maid would find him, and he'd lay in a freezer for a few months, an anonymous body among the anonymous dead of Dublin, until he was sent to the potter's field.

He was with the dead. With the dead he would stay.

A sense of wrongness overtook Jack, the last flicker of his magic. This was not how he died. He didn't lie down and give up. He cut his wrists deep with a shiny new razor and he felt his life draining onto the floor but he didn't die, he didn't go over even when the ghosts begged him to join their ranks. . . .

No one's coming for you, *the ghost girl breathed.*

Jack turned his face away from her, watching the hotel

sign blink outside the glass. Raindrops clung to the win-
dowpane, refracting the blue light, blue like witchfire. A
crow landed on the sill outside, flapped its wings. The
bird's profile beat against the glass, beak leaving starburst
cracks as it wrecked itself trying to get inside.

The pain of his cuts crawled inside the numbing sensa-
tion of the ghosts, the ache from the floorboards and the
burning of whiskey in his empty stomach.

Hush. *The ghost girl stroked his brow again.* Rest, Jack.
None of it matters now.

The crow beat at the window, its own black blood smear-
ing the glass.

A pounding started outside the hotel room door. "Jack!"
Fists and boots shook the wood. "Jackie, you stupid bastard! Open the fuckin' door!"

Seth's voice was the hand that dragged Jack away from
the Bleak Gates.

Seth came in. Seth called 999.

Jack curled in on himself, struggling with nerveless fin-
gers to stanch the bleeding from his arms, and the crow
watched him, stock-still now. Beak broken and bloody as
his own body. Croak sad and empty as Seth's echoing
voice as he wrenched Jack's arms above his head, tore his
own shirt to stop the bleeding.

The crow waited for Jack, waited for his soul until the
emergency responders came in, their codes rapid-fire into
their radios.

"Attempted suicide. Six minutes out . . ."

"Hang on, Jackie," Seth whispered. "You stupid prick.
You hang on. None of the crows get to check out that
easy."

Jack retched violently. Blood ran from his nose and his
guts twisted.

Kartimukha gave a cry. No! Feed me!

Jack struggled to his knees, and then his feet. Breathing

was a task, but he could hear the sounds of a modern street, and he felt the Black ebb away, letting go of the stranglehold on his sight.

Kartimukha stamped its feet, its tongue flapping and its eyes blazing as it snarled. *Feed me!*

"Oh, fuck off," Jack panted. "It'll take more than raking up tattered old nightmares, my son."

Kartimukha hissed, and tensed to spring. Jack braced himself. Violence, at this late date, would almost be welcome. He was itching to use his fists and feet on something, to take the fight into the tangible world where he could make the creature in front of him hurt and bleed.

"That's enough."

Rahu's voice cut the air, and Kartimukha bowed his head. Rahu ran his hand over the mangy lion's mane, and turned his eyes on Jack. "Kartimukha ate your memories. What was it like?"

Jack swiped at the blood on his face. "Tickled."

Rahu sighed. "It appears that you did tell the truth. You are attempting to trick your demon." He opened the cubby beneath the altar and removed a cloth-bound scroll tied with silk cord. "This is my personal necromancy grimoire. Take it. Your plan won't work, but take it."

Jack took the grimoire and shoved it down into his leather where it rested snugly against his ribs.

Rahu inclined his head. "May I ask you a question, mage?"

"After I ask you one." Jack backed away, so that he could touch the doors of the temple with his palm. "Where's Hornby?"

"The Christian cemetery north of the city," Rahu said. "We burn our dead, but Hornby's bandmates paid for him to be interred. What was left after the taxi finished with him, at any rate."

Jack shoved the door akimbo, letting in the sounds and scents of Khlong Toei. "All right. Ask yours."

"Why did you promise yourself to the demon?" Rahu folded his arms. "I'm curious, because your fate must have been beyond imagination to risk challenging Hell so."

Jack thought of Pete, of the demon's covetous smile when he said her name. "I had someone needed looking out for," he told Rahu.

Rahu chuckled. "Lucky them."

"Take care," Jack said. "And good luck with the whole memory-eating bit." He stepped through the door, and back into the light.

"I'll see you again, mage," Rahu called. "And next time, Kartimukha will feed."

"Yeah," Jack called back. "Shaking in me boots and all that. Virtually pissing in fear. Cheers, Rahu."

The door shut, and he stood on the street. The Lexus had vanished, along with Rahu's boys, so Jack began to walk back to the train line, to catch a car to Patpong. He would get his kit, take the grimoire, and go dig up Miles Hornby.

He would make Hornby tell him how he tricked the demon and he'd take the poor sod home so that Jack could get close enough to do the same.

But first, he was going to have a few choice words with Seth McBride.

Chapter Thirty

After the train dropped him at Silom Road, Jack found his way down Patpong 2 and up the stairs by Club Hot Miami. He leaned his head against Seth's door, and listened for three beats of his heart. Sounds of the telly emanated from within, along with Seth's voluble cursing against the parentage of the goaltender on the screen.

Jack braced on the railing. He put his boot against the lock and after two kicks the flimsy, rotted door flew inward to dent the damp plaster of the flat wall.

Seth leaped from his armchair, lager can tumbling to the floor and spilling a sticky amber puddle across the boards. "Jack?" he exclaimed. "Crow and cross, boy."

Jack closed the space between them and hit Seth in the jaw, sitting him down hard in the puddle of lager. "Thought you got rid of me, Seth?"

Seth's eyes bled to white, and a shield hex rippled at the edges of Jack's vision. He leaned forward and pulled Seth up by the front of his T-shirt, so that any hex the other mage threw would disintegrate Jack, but put Seth on his arse as well. "*You sent them to kill me.*"

"Rahu wouldn't kill you," Seth scoffed. "He's the master of Bangkok, not some thug fresh from the Pit. He was supposed to teach you a lesson and send you on your way."

"You have no idea what he did to me," Jack snarled. He wanted to smother Seth with magic, break his bones, call a demon to feast on his entrails. But that was the old days talking, the old hates.

Seth had found him, in the end. He'd kept Jack from passing through the Bleak Gates. For that, Jack dropped Seth back into his chair and paced to the window. The sun was setting across Bangkok, lighting the clouds on fire, orange tongues of airy flame scraping the iron sky.

"He did it to me as well, you know," Seth said after a time. "When I arrived. He judged me worthy to live in this city under his protection."

Jack leaned his forehead against the sticky glass. "What did he show you?"

"'S not important," Seth muttered. "A girl, some bad magic, a mistake. It was all a very long time ago."

"Well, mine wasn't," Jack said. His scars were itching, like they hadn't in a decade. The thin lines were dessicated and covered over by track scars, but they burned now, like a hot razor was parting his flesh all over again.

"Jack." Seth sighed. "Here's the truth—you burn things down. After you tried topping yourself and finished disgracing the brothers, I had to leave Ireland. I lost my life because of you, Jack. But I'm content here, and if you come in throwing your weight about, everything will go to ashes because Jack Winter doesn't leave anything but death in his wake." Seth stood and held out his hand. "Give me the grimoire."

Jack shot a glance at the open door, judged the distance, and then folded his arms. "Not in the cards, mate."

"I'm not letting you bring your feud with Hell to me doorstep," Seth insisted. "Give me the grimoire or I'll take it from you."

Jack spread his hand. "Come on then, old man. Make your best effort."

A flutter of magic, like feathers across his cheek, and Seth balled his fist. A hex, a black flight of crow's wings, flew toward Jack.

He'd never been one for duels—silly, antique things for mages who still wore frock coats and wallowed their days away in absinthe halls. Winning a magic slap fight didn't depend on how much power you commanded or how refined your hexes—it only depended on being the man who could duck faster than the other.

Jack let himself fall, stumbling out the flat's front door. He rolled to a stop against the railing and Seth's hex flew overhead, magic screaming against his sight.

Panting, Seth chugged after him, raising his hand again. Seth might be old, but he was mean and tenacious, and fear only made him meaner.

"You stupid sod," Seth wheezed. "Can't accept your fate, leave them what still have a life to it and die like a normal bugger . . ."

"Not in my nature." Jack pulled his own power to him, the slimy magic of the Black slipping between his grasp, shield hex forming and fragmenting before he could cast it. "You of all people know that, Seth."

"Knew it would come to this, somehow. Always." Seth's magic flew to him, settled about his shoulders like a mantle of swirling black energy. Jack felt the cold, spindly fingers of a death curse reach out for him. "Sorry as hell, too. I did like you, boy. You can take that with you when you go."

A shadow fell across Seth's face as he raised his hands, and before the death curse flew free, there was a *clang* of metal on bone and Seth crumpled.

Jack sat up and shook off the first vestiges of the curse, his skin prickling. A figure crouched, and he saw Trixie's bruise-colored eyeshadow and plum-painted Bettie Page lips, masking an expression of dire worry. "Are you all right?" she demanded.

"Fine." Jack tested his shoulder, his ribs. They hurt, but he'd survived worse. "Thanks for the assist, luv."

"Wasn't me," Trixie said. She helped him up and jerked a thumb over her shoulder. "She came looking for you, and we saw Seth about to do you in."

Jack looked at the person behind Trixie and felt his guts drop into his boots.

"Jack," Pete said. "Glad to see you're still making friends."

Chapter Thirty-one

Trixie set Jack up with a whiskey and retreated to the far end of the bar. Pete picked at the label of her Thai-brand beer. "Who was that on the landing, then? Jealous boyfriend?"

"Cute." Jack watched her, and grimaced when Pete's expression went stony and blank. Her copper expression, used on suspects and scum. Jack drained his glass. "How'd you find me?"

Pete's expression darkened. "You aren't as mysterious and unfathomable as you might think, Jack."

"Seth used to be a friend," he offered. The warmth of the whiskey burned some of the aches and pains out of his body, but not his mind.

"Your passport tripped a security alert at Heathrow," Pete said after a time. "I had you flagged. Ollie's mate at Interpol." She turned on her stool and faced him, fingers tapping the wood of the bar. "So I knew you came here. Still waiting on the why."

Jack tipped his empty glass to her. "Sightseeing."

"Right, that's fine," Pete agreed. "Keep treating me like

I'm stupid and that your honeyed words are all I need to hear." She leaned in, close enough that Jack could see the furious pulse beating in her neck. "I thought something had happened to you. That morning, when I woke up alone. I thought you'd gone and gotten yourself killed. I was frantic. I cried, Jack. Over *you*."

"Pete . . ." Jack slid his hand over her rattling fingers. "I had to go. I freely admit it was shit of me to leave you like that, but it couldn't be helped."

"Very well," Pete snapped. "Because lord knows your secrets and lies are more important than anyone they might leave behind." She jerked her hand out from under his, the friction warming his palm. Pete glared. "Put your hand on me again and you're going to discover exactly how sorry you can be, you ruddy son of a bitch."

She drained her beer and slammed the bottle on the bar. Jack watched her, rememorizing her hair, the set of her mouth, the way her fingers drummed unconsciously on the bar. Even furious with him, Pete was the best sight he'd clapped eyes on during this whole miserable journey.

Pete sighed, at last. "But as usual, anything I might be feeling gets shoved aside in favor of Jack Winter's latest disaster. So who's Seth, and why was he ready to take your head off with a hex?"

Jack shot a look at Trixie. She was too far away to overhear much of anything, and from the vicious way she was rattling glasses about, thought that Jack's girlfriend had come to reel him back in from his carefree sexual exploration of the exotic Orient. "It was a curse, not a hex," he told Pete, "and it's complicated."

Pete reached behind the bar, snatched another beer from the ice bucket, and banged the cap against the bar edge to take it off. "Ah. I see. Far too complicated for those of use who aren't Jack Winter."

Jack avoided her gaze by staring at a bruise forming on

his knuckles from where he'd hit Seth. He said, "Luv, it's nothing for you to worry over," and would have said more, except Pete hit him.

Her palm left a burning impression on his cheek and snapped his teeth sideways, blood coating his tongue. The last vestiges of the whiskey stung.

"*Fuck* you, Jack," Pete said. Her cheeks were bright with blood roses. "You no longer have the privilege of dictating when I bloody worry over *anything*."

Jack put his fingers against the spot. It was rigid and tender with a forming bruise. Pete had been kind—if she'd hit him closed fist, she would likely have broken his jaw. And he would have deserved it.

"Well?" she demanded. "Got any other excuses before I walk out of this dump and go home to somewhere the air doesn't cling to you?"

"I'm out of them," Jack promised. "I did wrong, Petunia. I'm not arguing." He wiggled his jaw. His entire skull rang from the blow. "I shouldn't have left."

"And you think that makes it all right?" Pete demanded. Jack pressed a hand over his eyes.

"I don't think it will ever be all right, Pete. But what's done is done, and I'm glad you're here."

Pete sat back on her stool. She looked wrung, sweat forming a V in the front of her cotton shirt. "First truth you've told me since I got here."

"Let's start over," Jack said. The lies made his tone smooth and easy, and he felt his throat and guts blacken. *This is the only way to save what you have*, he reminded himself. *This is the only way to keep Pete out of it*.

"Seth is the man on the landing," Pete said. Jack nodded. She swigged her beer and made a face, shoving it away again. "And he tried to knock you off why?"

Jack got a towel from behind the bar, dropped some ice into it, and put it against his face. "We had a disagreement."

Pete sighed. "Have you ever met someone you didn't slag off, Jack Winter?"

He lifted a shoulder. "Not yet. But there's always a thin ray of hope."

"God help us all. Why it was imperative you leave without so much as a word and run off to Bangkok? Tell me that."

"I'm looking for a bloke named Miles Hornby," Jack said. "Actually, found him."

Pete spread her hands. "So? What about Naughton? What about our job? You can't just chuck me when it's convenient and swan off."

"Believe me," Jack muttered, "there is nothing about this situation I'd consider 'convenient.'"

Pete rubbed her thumb over the center of her forehead. Jack saw dark half-moons under her eyes and a drawn thinness in her cheeks. He resisted the urge to reach out and push her lank black hair away from her face, wipe her skin free of sweat, take her back to her hotel, and put her to bed until she felt right.

Those weren't things Jack Winter did for anyone. He wasn't the sensitive, loving boyfriend with the kind word and the assurance that no, your arse did not look big in those trousers.

"Tell me," Pete said. "Tell me everything."

Jack waved at Trixie for a replay on his drink. "Miles Hornby is dead," he told Pete. "He has something I need, and to get it I have to perform a necromantic spell on his corpse. A black magic spell. It'd be dangerous for a sorcerer and for me it'll likely end with me vomiting my lungs out me arse. So if you're planning to stay around, I could use your help."

He exhaled. Sipped the new glass of whiskey. Watched Pete, and waited.

"Will you answer one more question for me?" she said

at last. Her face wasn't overtly hostile, her wide eyes guileless. Jack tensed, sensing a trap.

"If I can, luv."

"When, exactly," Pete said, "did you become a raving nutter?"

Jack set his glass down. "It's the truth, Pete. I'm going to dig up his body and raise him from the dead."

Pete rolled her eyes at Jack. "Bollocks."

"I dunno what else to tell you, luv."

Pete slapped her hand on the bar. "How about the bloody *truth*? What does this Hornby have that you need badly enough to just . . . to just . . ." Her face went red and her eyes took on a sheen. "To just *leave*." Pete swiped at her eyes. "Shit."

Jack reached for her hand, but Pete yanked it away. "You have to believe me," he whispered. "I wouldn't run out on you, Petunia. I . . ."

"You would, because you did," Pete said. Her voice was low and vicious. "It's exactly the kind of thing you do, Jack. A rough patch comes and you bolt for the bloody hills."

Jack threw back the last of his whiskey Now it only burned, didn't numb. "It's life and death, luv."

Pete chewed on her lip. "Whose life?"

"My life."

Pete put her elbows on the bar and her forehead in her hands. "Jack, what have you done?"

Jack reached over and lifted her chin with one finger. The spark of her talent rang sweet along his bones.

All at once, he felt the weight of every lie. Crawling inside his mind, deadening his talent, and hollowing him out until there was no Jack Winter, junkie, mage, or otherwise. There was only a memory of Jack Winter, liar and dead man.

Another lie would twist him irreparably, start a psychic hemorrhage that Jack knew he wouldn't be able to stop.

He dropped his hand. "I will tell you absolutely everything, Pete, but I am running out of time. Help me raise Hornby's corpse, and then I'll tell you anything. Me favorite color, the name of the girl who beat me with her lunch box in first form, why I possess an irrational phobia of John Gielgud. Anything you like."

Pete blinked away the last of the tears. Her mascara made miniature deltas down her face and Jack ran his thumb lightly over her skin, returning it to pale and pristine. Pete reached up and grabbed his hand, trapping it against her cheek. "You swear?"

Jack nodded. "On me life. What little of it I have left."

Chapter Thirty-two

The Bangkok Protestant Cemetery was overrun with roses and long grass, the paths barely wide enough for Jack's boots side by side. No lights watched over the graves, and the dank, ripe smell of the Chao Phraya River mingled with the smell of turned earth.

Pete shone her light at the crooked rows of tombs and graves. "Where is he?"

Jack saw the hump of a newly buried body under the beam, wooden cross stuck crookedly in the earth a few feet ahead of him. "Let's start there."

"And if we get the wrong grave?" Pete muttered.

Jack swung his spade to and fro, the iron weight moving like a divining rod. "Then I imagine we'd say, 'Oh, so sorry, let me just tuck you up and shut your coffin again, guv. Lovely weather we're having.'"

Pete waved him quiet. "You're a wanker."

Jack heard a rustle from the bushes and detected silver eyeshine. The small owl stared at him, head twitching back and forth. Jack curled his lip.

"Never liked those things."

"I don't mind them," Pete said. "They used to show up in our garden when I was a girl. Da said they were there to take the bad dreams out of the air before they got to me and my sister."

Jack prodded the earth over Hornby's grave and tried to ignore the gaze of the owl. Owls came on an ill wind, harbingers of things that even Jack, with his visions of the dead, didn't want to imagine too closely. Not psychopomps, like the crow. Only watchers, keepers of the shadows that lived beyond the Black and beyond even the grasp of Death.

"Hold the light steady," he said to Pete, shoving the spade into the grave mound. The earth was loose and soft, warm still from sunlight. It took him fifteen minutes and a few gallons of sweat to uncover the elongated hexagon of the pauper's coffin.

"Never liked this," Pete said. "Exhumations. When I was with the Met, it always seemed wrong, somehow."

"That's the Black," Jack agreed. "Once a soul's flown from a body, the body has a nasty resonance. Necromancers feed on it."

"How do they stand it?" Pete brushed her arms off with her hands, as if she were beset by ants.

"They're evil, foul-smelling necrophiliac idiots," Jack said. "Reasonable folk know better than to trouble something that belongs to the Bleak Gates." He swiped the rivers and waterfalls of sweat from his face, and braced himself for the sight of Hornby's ghost. Magic users, mages particularly, didn't often go into the underworld quietly and with lack of fanfare. Algernon Treadwell, his worst spook, had been a sorcerer who died bloody and tortured at the hands of witchfinders.

His sight tingling, Jack tapped his spade against the coffin lid. Nothing sprang from the earth in answer. No flutters or cries echoed from the Black. The graveyard was curiously silent, holding its breath in the dense night air of the river. Jack threw the spade aside.

"Be a love and hand me the prybar," he said to Pete. His bag, at the edge of the grave, pulsed with the loose ingredients to the necromancy spell written out in the grimoire. Trixie had translated the Thai for him, and Robbie had sold him most of the ingredients that weren't already in Jack's kit. The spell elements hungered for flesh, to dig into skin, for a corpse to weave their magic around even resting separate in his canvas bag.

Black magic felt like cobwebs, like sticky drying blood and the spongy, soggy flesh of a drowned man. Like wearing a wool sweater next to bare skin. Jack's sight flared, and the graveyard was bathed in silver for a moment before he ground his teeth and felt the sting of his tattoos holding back the dead. It wasn't an active boneyard like St. Michael's, but there were bodies under the earth and lately, with Jack's sight flying haywire at the slightest touch, it was still too much.

Pete handed him the small prybar, wordlessly, and stepped back from the crumbling edge of the grave.

Jack straddled the coffin and shoved the metal in between the wooden seams.

From its branch, the owl watched, unblinking. Jack flicked it off before he bore down on the prybar, straining to open the coffin lid. Nails shrieked, and Jack's sore shoulders and hands complained as he strained against the coffin lid. It lifted with a dull *thud*, the release throwing Jack down hard in the dirt.

Pete flashed her light on the contents of the coffin. "Well. He's a handsome git, isn't he?"

Jack struggled up, and looked into the coffin.

The figure within stared back at him with empty sockets, blackened skin stretched tight across a skull rife with rotted teeth.

"He's been dead a lot longer than two weeks," Pete said. "Even in this heat. Hasn't got any flesh on."

Jack leaned down and picked up the gold chain around the figure's neck, the same gold he'd seen on the gangsters in Patpong, cheap and bleeding to green from moisture. "It's not Hornby." His voice echoed from the sides of the grave, hollow.

Pete half-slid down the pile of earth to stand next to him. "Then who is it?"

Jack felt the want of a fix claw into his skull, vicious and sharp. He heard the demon's laughter. He felt the cold of the Underworld, even in the oppressive heat of Bangkok, like a finger of ice down his back.

"Jack?" Pete touched his shoulder. "Who's in this grave?"

Jack dropped the pry bar. Over the Chao Phraya, thunder rumbled and twin tongues of lighting licked the underside of black smoke clouds.

The owl took flight as rain started to fall, fat warm droplets the temperature of tears splashing on Jack, on Pete, and over the stone and dirt of the graveyard.

"He's nobody," he said finally.

Pete turned her light on his face. "You don't look well, Jack."

Which followed, because Jack felt like run-over shite. Felt numb, cold, and nerveless even in the warm rain. "I'm going back to Patpong," he said. His boots slipped in the graveyard dirt but he pressed on, leaving Pete behind him.

Chapter Thirty-three

The rain fell, steady sideways lines of water, blurring the neon of Patpong into a fever dream. Thunder crashed and rolled above the city like a Sham 69 drum line, and lightning licked forked tongues between skyscraper and cloud.

Jack stalked through puddles, heedless when water seeped into his boots. The girl was still on the corner near Trixie's bar, hunched under a roof overhang. The tourists had taken cover, and she was virtually alone in the street.

Jack wove through the push of traffic down Patpong 2 and approached, ducking his head against the rain.

"Hey, traveler." The girl peeled herself away from the wall, her plastic skirt and nylon top slicked with water. "You want something?"

Jack cast a glance over his shoulder out of habit. He wasn't caging for coppers as much as for Pete, but the few damp pedestrians in evidence hurried on their way and studiously avoided looking at Jack, or the girl. They might as well have been two more oil-slicked stains on the pavement.

"Something sweet?" the girl persisted. "I got party, I got good stuff. You want something?"

Jack dug into his leather and pulled out a crumple of pounds and *bhat*. "Give me a dose. Of the sweet."

The girl fished in her voluminous knockoff handbag, and Jack heard the shifting scrape of cellophane bags against bags, the clack of pills. She palmed him a twist of plastic with a nub of brown inside, and made Jack's money disappear like a magic trick.

"You want a sharp?" She titled her head, hair curled up from the rain. Her makeup was smeared, and she looked a bit like a thrown-away doll.

"Yeah," Jack muttered, shoving the smack into his pocket. "Give it to me."

The girl passed him a disposable needle in a sterile wrapper, stamped with a hospital name in English and Thai. "You have fun," she said, closing his fingers over it. "And come back soon. I'm here every night."

Jack walked away without answering. He ducked through the door of Trixie's bar. She was busy serving a trio of Australians who in turn were busy gawping at a pair of go-go dancers divesting themselves of their gold bikinis on the stage. A DJ spun house tunes, and the lights were low and blue.

Jack went straight through the kitchen and into the back alley. The alley was piled with crates and metal garbage cans, quiet except for echoes of raindrops and faraway laugher. Neon signs spread fingers of pink and red and blue across Jack's skin, turning him from a Fae to a demon to a corpse in the span of a heartbeat.

Demons lie. Lesson. Fucking. One.

He'd been so close. So fucking close to working it all out. Find Hornby, find his secret, find his way out of Hell. At the worst, absolute rock bottom, he'd have the demon's name.

But there was no Miles Hornby in the grave.

Jack leaned his head back against the slimy exterior wall. The neon beat a heartbeat against the back of his eyelids.

He could run, he could run far and fast, but the sight always caught him. The bargain would never be unwound.

He could pretend that he was clean, an ex-junkie, an ex-liar, and an ex-bastard, but Jack knew who he was. He was Jack Winter.

Junkie. Liar. Sinner. Dead man.

As he unrolled the baggie between his fingers, Jack realized that nothing had changed from the moment he'd bound the bargain in the first place.

The motions came back, like playing a D chord or putting a record on a turntable. Automatic, rote, familiar.

Drop the smack into the spoon. Find your lighter, buried underneath a ball of vellum and an ancient packet of crisps in his jacket pocket. Cook the shit, mindful of your fingers. Jack's callused fingerprints weren't only from playing guitar.

He used his teeth to rip open the sharp and his belt to tighten up his arm. The studs cut into his bicep, dull hot pain, but Jack ignored it as he drew the cloudy gold into the belly of the needle. Like watching a mosquito feed, he'd thought the first time. Feed and bloat on the sweetest blood there was.

Jack let the spoon drop into a puddle and he sat himself on a crate, out of the rain.

Slap your arm. Watch the bruise-blue map of heart's blood float to the surface, pulsing and quivering under the skin. Try to find a spot that will still take a sharp, the black blots of collapsed veins like impassable terrain.

Jack wriggled his arm and slotted it comfortably against his thigh. He bit the cap off of the sharp and spat it out, flat plastic taste on his tongue.

Prime the needle, force all the air out. Embolism will

ruin your day, and earn you a stint in rehab when you get found and taken to A&E. If you get found in time.

The tip of the needle bit into his skin, and it hurt a bit, like passing your hand through a lighter. It hadn't hurt in a long while. Being clean had started a new season in his body, nerves and blood renewed.

Jack tilted his face up to the rain, put his thumb on the needle's plunger, and pressed down.

For a moment there was nothing, just the slightly foreign sensation of a sharp under his skin. Then the warm tide ran up his arm, across his chest, over to his heart.

It was good shit, pure and strong, and it hit Jack's brain like plunging into a river of fire, kissed his skin so that he was surprised it didn't begin to steam under the rain.

Jack felt his head go back and scrape brick, and felt the sharp tumble out of his fingers. He wiggled the belt loose so the dose could work its magic unfettered.

Welcome home, the fix whispered as it wrapped a million fingers of oblivion across his sight and his mind. *I've missed you.*

Jack let the numbness steal over him and didn't fight. The storm cooled his skin, but inside was warmth and forgetfulness. He slipped beneath the waters of the fix, and let himself drown.

When he opened his eyes, lids heavy with the desire for a nod into the opium dreamland he knew too well, the demon was in front of him.

It wasn't the demon, not really. His sight didn't flare and his blood didn't chill, but seeing the wavering outline in the white suit, black coal eyes boring into him, sent Jack reeling. Acid boiled up in his stomach and he doubled over. *Not yet, not yet. Need to sleep, need not to dream.* He couldn't vomit, couldn't come down so soon.

"Poor little Jack," the demon purred. "Figured out that you've lost, at last."

"Go . . ." Jack choked down bile, his throat blazing. "Go away. I haven't yet."

"No Hornby, no name." The demon's tongue caressed its lips like it could already taste Jack. "No name, no saving yourself. Demons lie, but I wouldn't lie to you. You're a special soul, Jack. I wouldn't insult you that way."

"You're not real," Jack groaned. "You can't be here."

"I will be." The demon leaned close. Rain fell through him, hissing as it hit the pavement. The heroin was playing hell with Jack's sight, his neurons exploding against his eyes, allowing the Black to twist and distort into something it wasn't. The fix was his only shield against his sight for over a decade, and now it was showing him this. If Jack hadn't felt like he was close to passing out facedown in the garbage-choked puddles at his feet, he might have laughed.

"Go," he gritted again. "I don't see you. You're not . . . you're not real."

"Has that ever worked?" The demon chuckled. "I *will* be real, Jack. I'll wrap a hand around your heart and the Weir will watch. She'll weep. And she'll die along with you, every time she remembers how you tried to change fate and didn't."

Slow heavy swells of the fix rolled over Jack, made his speech slow and thick. "Fuck . . . off."

The door banged, metal on brick, and the demon was gone. In his place, small strong hands propped Jack up and a face dipped into view.

"Jack!" Pete shook him, slapped his face. She peeled back his eyelid and he batted at her. Her touch spread warm tendrils through him, down to the core and the place that got him into more trouble than it got him out of. If he'd been able to stand with any reliability, he would have grabbed Pete in return, put her against the rough brick, and let the rain slick their bare skin.

"'M fine," he muttered.

"You're so bloody far from fine I can't even say." Pete's voice shook, her fingers echoing the tremor. She jerked his chin to look, and she was holding the needle. "You went and did it, after everything? Everything I did to get you clean?"

"Pete . . ." He exhaled. His lungs were slow and hot. The air was wet, too thick to move on its own. "You don't understand."

Pete tossed the needle away and crouched in front of Jack, gripping his arms. "Make me understand. I want to have followed you here for something worthwhile, Jack."

Pete's tears mixed with the raindrops on her skin, cutting furrows in her face. Jack tried to reach for them, wipe them away and make her smile, but he missed her cheek, letting his hand land on her shoulder again, tilting her slight frame under his weight.

"Go home," Jack said. "You don't have to see me like this, Petunia. No need."

Pete brushed him off and Jack's stomach opened like a pit. He fell sideways, retching, his gut rebelling against the onslaught of skag.

"Fair warning," Pete said. "Don't order me about. I'm two seconds from kicking seven colors of shit from you, you bloody idiot."

Jack tried again to apologize, but his vision tunneled, then spiraled, then became black. When he sat up, scraping a hand across his mouth, the world had started to creep back in. His clothes were soaked and deep-muscle aches had worked their way up his arm from the tie-off and the sloppy injection. Pete watched him silently, crouched on her heels.

She hadn't left him even now, when he was doubled over puking his guts out in the rankest alley he'd ever found himself in. She hadn't helped him, either, but if Jack were in her position he would have pushed his head into his own sick and held him there until he drowned.

And he'd lied to her. He'd used the danger of the demon

to lie to Pete, likely the only person who wouldn't leave him in the gutter at the truth. Jack wrapped his arms around himself as shivers wracked him, his stomach bucking again even though there was nothing left to bring up.

"I'm sorry, Pete." His voice came out a rasp that barely lifted over the rain, and his ruined throat clenched.

Pete scrubbed her hands over her face, blending the rain and tears. "What?"

"I'm sorry," Jack said. He reached out and had more success capturing her hand this time. "Please don't go, Petunia." He dropped his head back, shut his eyes. His sight was empty, and the bright blazing place where it lived in his mind was cold. "Don't go," he said to Pete, so that he could barely hear himself over the drumming rain. "I need you."

Pete let him close his hand around her palm, but she wouldn't look at him. "If you really mean that, Jack, and you don't want me walking away right this moment, then you'd better give me an explanation that isn't a complete load of bollocks."

Jack gripped Pete's hand. "Luv, I never meant to . . ."

Pete slammed her fist into the concrete. "For once in your fucking life Jack, let go of your sodding pride and *talk* to me!"

Jack jumped at her voice echoing from the alley walls, sat up and pressed the heels of his hands into his eyes. Sweat, vomit, rain. Wasn't he the picture of recovery. "Fine, luv. Haven't got any pride left, anyway."

Pete spread her hands when the silence between them stretched thin.

Jack swallowed down the last lump of nausea in his throat, to put off speaking for another clock-tick. To speak was to confess, and to confess was to lay bare all the black and rotten bits of himself to Pete.

"I'm waiting," she said.

"So am I," Jack murmured. The rain was a solid sheet of

mist and droplet. You could almost discern faces in it, ghostly passengers on the fog that rolled in from the under- world on nights like this one. The neon lit everything, pink and black and blue and black over and over again like a macabre circus. The ghosts pressed close around him, but the fix didn't let them find a way in. Another twenty min- utes, thirty at the outside, and things would be usual—the onslaught of the dead and the new strange makeup of his magic.

But in this moment, his sight was still and the Black was silent. "I guess I've been waiting all the time you knew me," Jack said. He held out his hand to Pete and tilted his head in pleading. "At least let me cage a fag if I'm going to spill me guts, luv?"

Pete sighed as if she were being asked a great service, but she passed him one and gave him a light. Their fingers brushed. Hers were warm and wet, reminders of furrows dug in his shoulders, Jack's sweat on Pete's skin.

He coughed as he drew too sharply on the fag. "All in all, I guess I've been waiting for thirteen years."

"Waiting for what?" Pete stubbed hers out and let Jack take up the mantle of polluting the immediate vicinity. A door down the alley opened and a bag of garbage sailed out, along with a snatch of "All Along the Watchtower."

Jack smiled at Pete and felt the stiffness of it. The smile was the last lie, the only one he had left in him. "For Hell, Petunia."

Pete's eyes darkened and widened, like she'd spied a London bus bearing down on her. One last lone curl of smoke drifted from her nostril, and then she blinked and she was a hardened copper again, wearing a hard plastic mask.

"Right," she said. I think you'd better finish your story."

Chapter Thirty-four

When the ghost of Algernon Treadwell stuck its hand into his chest on the spring day thirteen years past, Jack was surprised to feel nothing. Not pain, not cold. Just the absence of feeling, a bit of cool wet on his skin from blood, and a glaze of silver across his sight.

Pete was screaming. She was standing on the other side of a tomb a little bigger than a minicab, and she was screaming. Blood dripped from her palms, trickled down her wrist like she'd drawn her veins on, and she was screaming.

Treadwell hissed, wordless pleasure as he filled Jack up with his icy poison. Jack fell, cracking his skull against the tomb floor. Treadwell smiled down at him, an angel borne out of the Land of the Dead.

Keep the ghost from Pete. Treadwell had sunk his claws into her, into the raw Weir talent that lived behind her too-serious face, those drowning-pool eyes. Pete didn't count him a lover, or fuck, even a friend as far as he knew, but Jack didn't care. And all that mattered now was keeping the ghost from her. She was innocent in the Black and she was here for him. Because of him. Pete was screaming because of him.

A black candle from the summoning sailed past Jack and broke into three pieces against the tomb wall.

"Go back!" Pete shouted. "Go back!"

Treadwell bared his teeth, and the awful pressure on Jack's heart intensified. He felt Treadwell grab hold of his magic, of his power, and meld his burning cold corpse energy to it. Blackness filled Jack up like Thames water, until he couldn't breathe and nothing but feedback screamed in his airs.

Not water.

Blood.

In his lungs, spilling down his chest, spattering a fine mist across his face. Blotting out the logo on the chest of his Replacements shirt. Draining his life onto the stones of Treadwell's tomb.

As the summoning seal drew Treadwell back to the underworld, the ghost scraped ice fingers down Jack's face, a final caress. *I'll see you very soon, mage,* the ghost hissed. *And we'll share this embrace again.* A whisper of the Black, a flux and flow of power, and Algernon Treadwell was gone, exorcised from the world of the living.

Jack's senses folded in and narrowed down to one point, beyond sight and beyond pain. He floated, a rudderless drifting into nothing. There were no pictures from his life before his eyes. No grand parade of memories. Just Jack Winter, dead man, dissolving little by little like wreckage at the bottom of the sea.

The crow woman came to him. She bent and touched his face, and all of Jack's instincts flared to life again. The crow woman was never a cause for celebration, or calm, even at this moment. She appeared for one reason and one only.

"No . . . ," he croaked. "No, I'm not finished."

The raven woman grinned at him. Blood dripped from between her teeth, painted her lips black-red. *I'll wait.*

The blood galvanized Jack. He couldn't die. He couldn't slip away because of Treadwell, a fucking ghost, a piece of vapor. He was the crow-mage. When he died, he became the crow woman's.

"Wait as long as you like," he rasped. "I have time. I have a life yet . . ."

All warriors meet their end in my arms, the Morrigan whispered. *All battles have a loser. Come away to the field with me, Jack. Take your place in my ranks.*

"I'm not . . . yours . . . yet . . ." It was getting hard to speak, becoming an effort to suck in anything besides blood. Pete had fled, and the bar of light from the open tomb door lit the Morrigan from the back, casting the shadow of her wings across Jack's eyes. Outside, in the light world, he heard the flutter of wings, the hollow croak of a crow.

You are my favored son, Jack, she whispered. *You are the crow-mage. Called to the Land of the Dead from his day of birth.*

"No . . . ," Jack choked, black borders swirling at the edge of his vision like slowly sinking into a deep well. "I left them. I left you."

The Fiach Dubh *are a construct, Jack. Men and flesh and petty concerns wrapped in the illusion of power. I am Death. I am eternal.* Her fingers brushed his cheek, her nails digging into his flesh. He felt nothing except the chill of the stones.

"I won't go," he croaked. "Not willingly."

It is the field, crow-mage, the Morrigan hissed. *Or it is Hell. You are a sinner in life, Jack Winter, but I could make you a god in Death.*

Jack dipped his shaking fingers into his own blood, felt

a clear rough patch on the stones. "Never . . . never wanted to be a god. Just wanted to live me life. . . ."

The pages of the grimoire he'd stolen from Seth's library floated before his eyes, blurred and half-remembered.

It was enough. It had been enough to expel him from the *Fiach Dubh,* and it would be enough now.

Jack drew from memory the invocation and the pentagram, the devil's gateway. The calling card of the Triumvirate. The invitation for Hell on earth. A sorcerer's knowledge, for a mage who had nothing left but a slow ebb and flow of blood and magic.

You fool! The crow woman spread her wings, screeched, spectral wind chilling Jack's wounds. *You can only prolong. You can never escape.*

"Yeah, well." Jack coughed and more blood coated his tongue. That was a bad way to go. His time was slipping down to the last few grains in the hourglass. "Guess it's Hell for me, hag. So until my time's up . . ." He extended his two fingers into the crow woman's face. "Fuck off."

He let his eyes fall shut, his fingers move across the blood-slicked stone. The words fell from his lips with surprising clarity, words of power from his long-ago glance at the mildewed linen pages Seth kept locked in a metal trunk from his days in the Irish army. Locked with a bespelled lock and a set of hexes, until the clever boy Jack Winter had slipped them.

Mages didn't deal with demons. Only sorcerers invited the denizens of Hell to their threshold. Only evil men.

Desperate men.

"I call the servants of the Morning Star, the tainted princes, the jackals of judgment," he whispered. "As your servant, I humbly call."

He opened his eyes with a struggle, the ceiling of the tomb wobbling and distorting as he stepped to the threshold of dying. It hurt less this time, was colder, stiller than the hotel in Dublin, but dying itself always felt the same. Cold. Always cold.

"With my blood on the stone," Jack whispered, "I call."

A shimmer of black in the shadowed air, a thickening of the darkness in the corner of the tomb. Jack listened to his heartbeat, felt the cobweb kiss of black magic across his bloody face.

"With lies in my heart," Jack rasped. "I call." This was where a name was supposed to lay, a race of demon or a word of power to bind the encroachment of Hell to the sorcerer's will.

Jack didn't know the names of demons. Seth hadn't taught him. Had expelled him from the order when he'd tried to learn. Had left him to the mercy of his sight.

"Somebody," Jack rasped. "I'm Jack Winter. And I sodding need your help."

He didn't see the demon come, but it was there when his gaze roved back to the floor of the tomb, black suit and dark hair, so ordinary as to cause tears of disappointment.

The demon took a step toward him, and cocked its head. "And what, little mage, is so dark in that heart of yours that you summon whichever of Hell's Named that feels like making a human a plaything today?"

Jack met its eyes, those dreadful black button eyes that spoke of flayed skin and burnt char, breaking and bleeding and screaming.

"I don't want to die," he whispered. "I can't, yet . . ."

The demon crouched, laid a hand on his wound, Jack's blood growing vines of red up the immaculate French fold of its white shirt as it ran a finger down his cheek.

"A mage who's afraid of the afterlife. That's interesting, that is."

"Not . . . afraid," Jack managed. "I can't. I can't . . ."

"All right, be still," the demon purred. "Don't drain

yourself dry before we have a chance to chat with one another."

"I'm . . . the crow-mage. . . ." Jack managed. "If I die . . ."

Laughter floated around him, dark and poisonous as a sip of cyanide laced into port wine. The demon sat on its heels. "Say the words, mage, and I'll consider what I can do to help you." It smiled, and Jack knew he should be scared, terrified, pissing in his shorts.

If he had any sense, he'd be frightened.

If he had any balls, he'd be dying on the floor alone, last words taken away only by the ghosts of Highgate.

But the mages who decreed *Thou shalt not bargain with demons*, Lawrence and Seth and the rest, they'd never been here. Never felt cold stone under their back and warm blood on their skin. They'd never seen the crow woman, watching and waiting for them to join the ranks of her corpse army.

"Say it," the demon coaxed. "I want to hear it from your sweet throat, mage."

The words crawled up with Jack's last breath. "Please," he said to the demon. "Save me."

Chapter Thirty-five

A litter of cigarette nubs lay at Jack's feet when he finished talking, tiny corpses borne on the rivulets of rain.

Pete wrapped her arms around herself, didn't look at him, didn't speak.

Jack exhaled. He felt as if he'd been kicked in the ribs by a jackboot, a fair few times, and left in a gutter to be pissed on. "You're too bloody quiet," he muttered. "Say something."

Pete sniffed, and uncurled her arms. "How long?"

"Thirteen years," Jack said. "Thirteen years from the day I died."

"And Hornby? What's he to you?" Pete chewed on her bottom lip.

Jack stood, worked the kinks from his back. He didn't used to knot up, to feel the bruises from fights until the day after. Now he felt all of it, down to his worn-out bones. "He's me chance," he said. "All I have to do is bring him home."

Jack climbed up, swayed only a little, decided it was safe to walk inside and find himself a stiff shot of whiskey.

Pete caught his hand. "I should be furious with you. You've kept everything from me."

"I know," Jack said. "If you weren't furious, I might think you were some kind of shapeshifter and go looking for an iron needle to kill you with."

"I just don't understand why you felt like you couldn't tell me," Pete said. " Were you just going to let me wake up one day and be alone forever? Is that how little you care, Jack?" Pete sniffed hard, the only hint the red in her eyes and the flush in her cheeks.

Jack felt in his pocket for his bandanna, held it out to her. "I suppose I was afraid, Pete."

Pete's expression sagged. "Jack, you're not afraid of anything."

He felt the ends of his mouth curve up. "I'm a good liar."

Pete grabbed the bandanna from him and dabbed at her face. "You know I should bloody kill you."

"I'd deserve it," Jack agreed.

"Only it won't do any bloody good and I'll still end this alone in the Black," Pete said. After a moment, composure returned to hers features and she blinked the last of the moisture from her eyes. "But if you give Hornby to this demon, you're free?"

"If I find Hornby, I won't have to worry about the demon," he said. "Because I'm not making the mistake of trusting it twice." Jack got a fresh fag and lit it. "But the thing's just been playing with me. Hornby wasn't in that box. He's not anywhere." He exhaled. "I'm fucked. It just wanted a laugh. Let's go home."

Pete drew in a breath. "Why would the demon promise you something like a name? Why give you a chance at breaking this awful deal if Hornby isn't who the demon says he is?"

"This is a guess," Jack said, "but perhaps because it's a fucking demon and they wank off to human suffering?"

Pete shook her head. "Never saw a gangster at the Met who didn't keep a promise when there was respect or honor involved. Never saw a hard man who risked his own reputation to make another look bad." She smiled to herself, eyes narrowing. "Miles Hornby exists. And he's in this city."

Jack shook his head, scattering raindrops from his hair. "If he's alive, he's going to be even harder to find than dead."

Pete pushed a finger into his chest. "Then you'd better hope you're as good as you say you are, hadn't you?"

He flashed Pete his smile, the one he used on stage and in situations where something larger wanted to beat the shite out of him. "I am that, luv. Every bit as bloody good. 'S how I stayed alive for thirteen years."

Pete opened the door back into the noise of the bar. "Good to hear. Now let's find Hornby, because I want to go home."

PART III

Lost Souls

Take the secret to my grave
I'm not your tale to tell
Not your salvation, not your lost boy
I'd rather burn in Hell

—The Poor Dead Bastards
"Soul Currency"

Chapter Thirty-seven

Trixie watched Jack and Pete carefully when they came into the bar. Her hands worked over drinks and glasses, but her eyes stayed on him. *You all right?* she mouthed. Jack waved her off.

"Seems a silly thing to bargain your life over," Pete murmured as they came to the street. "A name."

"Not among demons," Jack said. "Names have power—a name is the only thing that separates a demon from the ravening horde, down there in the Pit. Names given by Lucifer are Hell's currency."

"And souls are what, Hell's bus token?" Pete shook her head, lip curling up. "I hate bloody demons. I hate every last one. Cold bastards."

Jack didn't correct her. Demons knew the value of cold bastardry better than any being in the Black. He'd taken most of his lessons in merciless self-service from demons. They were good teachers.

"I suppose I can call up some contacts," Pete said as they walked through the night market, the tide of Patpong parting around them. "Use Ollie to get in touch with Interpol, see if Hornby's turned up anywhere besides the grave he was supposed to be in."

"He won't." Jack shuddered as the last of the good feeling the fix had brought ran out of him. Now was just roiling guts and headaches and cravings all over again. "Hornby's too clever to get caught up by the coppers. He's gone deep underground."

Pete lifted a shoulder. "Faked his death? That's never as simple as the telly makes it seem."

"Simple enough," Jack said. "Come to a city where the demon's not welcome, spread around a story of a taxi accident that probably really happened, shove an anonymous gangster's corpse in the grave in his place, and *poof.*" He spread his fingers. "No more lightly talented, unlucky musician with a short lifespan for the demon to find."

Pete pulled a face. "First thing we learn in the Met—people don't just vanish."

"No," Jack agreed. "Even mages." You could get a new face and a new identity with varying degrees of magic, but to erase other people's memories of you—that was the trick. Memories were the spine upon which the Black rested its weary flesh and blood. Memories were the only thing truly a man's if he moved among the creatures of Faerie and Hell.

"People don't just disappear," Jack echoed.

"I said it," she agreed. "Who here might know? What about that git Seth?"

Jack held up his hands. "Not Seth." His scalpel cut was healing crookedly, puffy and red around the edges. He needed a real hospital, real stitches from a real doctor. "Seth shot his bolt," he said. "He thinks I've gone over to sorcery, and I think he's a fucking cunt. It's safe to say we've reached an impasse."

"He did try to kill you." Pete folded her arms in such a

way that Jack knew Seth would be eating through a tube if Pete had reached the scene a few seconds earlier.

"I'll see him again someday, settle it, probably have to put the mad old man down." Jack sighed. "Selling me out to the demon of Bangkok . . . I swear. He's gone senile."

"Who, then?" Pete stopped walking as her stomach rumbled. "Bloody hell, I'm starving."

Jack realized they were near Robbie's stall at the edge of the night market and gestured. "Oi, mate. You got anything to eat around here?"

While Robbie troubled his neighbor, a noodle cart, for two pasteboard containers heavy with spice, Jack rubbed the back of his neck. His head and his muscles ached. His arm hurt at the slash and at the injection site. Pete's mouth twisted nervously.

"You all right?"

"Falling apart," Jack said. "I'm discovering that I'm not as young as I once was."

"Fuck me, I could have told you that," Pete scoffed. Jack nudged her in the ribs.

"Oi. Watch that mouth, missy."

"Or what?" Pete cocked her eyebrow, corners of her mouth dancing with a grin. Robbie handed her the noodles and she sucked down a mouthful with her chopsticks, watching him over her food with a hooded gaze.

"Or I might just take it into my head to show you the error of your ways," Jack said. He was decently sure that Pete, the dedicated and driven inspector, had no idea the effect she had on men. Especially when she gave them that wicked come-hither look while smiling her arse off at their expense.

"I'd like to see you try," she teased. Jack tasted the noodles, felt his stomach give a warning gurgle, and passed them to Pete.

"There's a way we might find Hornby," he said, to distract himself from sicking up all over Robbie's stall. "It's not pleasant or easy but it's a pretty reliable scry if you can get past that."

"Good." Pete finished both portions and chucked the cartons in a bin. "When can we do it?"

Jack tilted his head, found the sound of sirens and screaming on the night air. "As soon as I find a corpse."

Chapter Thirty-eight

The accident was a scooter accident, and the man in the street was broken nearly in half. A lorry idled nearby, the driver arguing with police. *Bhat* changed hands, and the police returned to their vehicle, inching away from the scene through traffic.

Crowds on the pavement pressed close. A camera flash added its punctuation mark, bleaching the dead man's skin paper white.

The corpse collectors carried a canvas field stretcher of the type used by the Territorial Army, and they set it on the damp street. Rain water and blood mingled in the gutters, slick black flowing down into the sewer and out to the river.

Jack stepped into the street, boots splashing in the current from the rain, and approached the corpse collectors. "Oi. Speak any English?"

One of them nodded, so Jack produced his wad of *bhat*. "There was a bloke died earlier today, in the hospital up the road. Name of Jao. Where'd you take him?"

The man shrugged. "I didn't pick him up. Lemme ask

my friend." After an exchange, he pointed at Jack's money. "Give us that and you can ride along."

Jack nodded, but pulled it back when the man reached for it. "Her, too?"

Pete made a face at the small ambulance. It was an ancient Cadillac, insignia blacked out with spray paint, the low chassis and dented fins giving it the visage of a shark. "In that? With the corpse?"

"It's that or I give up, go home, and get to know the more intimate crevices of Hell," Jack shrugged. Pete's jaw twitched, but she nodded.

"All right."

The ambulance pulled away from the accident site with a jerk that moved Jack, Pete, and the corpse to the left as if they were on strings. Pete let out a breath as the corpse's bloody hand flopped into her lap. "Jack, when this is over I am going to shove your head so far up your arse . . ."

Jack nudged the corpse back onto the canvas sled with his boot. "Get in line, luv. I'm popular on that score."

They rode through newly rain-washed streets, neon bouncing off the dew and refracting Bangkok into a thousand shards of glass.

The hospital was larger and newer than Jao's lair, and Jack caught a glare from a nurse when he and Pete walked through A&E with the corpse delivery.

Morgues, as far as they went, were not Jack's favorite places on earth, along with police stations and shops that sold a lot of glass figurines. Morgues were cold and their magic was spiky, the layer between the Black and the light world thinned by death and the dead themselves, who crowded in close as he crossed the threshold.

Jack saw ghosts, the first other than the dead GIs since he'd arrived in Bangkok. Most were still and silent, wearing their Y incisions and their last injuries like permanent black and silver tattoos. A few bore the twisting cloaks of ethereal malignancy, pain and rage spilling across the tiles from their sunken black eyes and gaping black mouths.

Jack fought against the nausea that boiled up in his guts. The fix was having its revenge.

At least the dead told him they were in the right place. Jao's spirit would draw every scrap of dead magic within the vicinity, a necromancer's soul an irresistible morsel.

If Jao had been a different sort of person in life, Jack might have felt a bit of pity. Then again, his arm was still throbbing and swollen, so perhaps not. Jao and Rahu and the lot of them—they could rot in their miserable little city on their corpulent, stinking river.

The corpse carriers deposited their bundle and the one who spoke English eyed Jack. "You still want to see him?"

Jack cast his eye at the tray of instruments waiting for the return of the unlucky charnel worker in the morning hours. "I want to do more than that."

The corpse man rolled out a tray, and Jao's milky, suffocated eyes, shot through with pink spider veins, stared up at the ceiling. The corpse man held out his hand. "I can't just leave you alone in here, you know."

"Yeah, yeah." Jack shoved the last of his *bhat* into the corpse carrier's hand. "I know the score, mate. Give us a moment for my trouble?"

The man nodded and he and the partner retreated with their sled. Jack pinched the sanitized plastic covering off the instrument tray and picked up the Stryker saw, the whining darling of B-horror directors everywhere.

Pete frowned. "Jack, what are you doing?"

"Something sacrilegious in nearly every way you can think of," said Jack. "Learnt from a Stygian Brother back when they'd stolen Lawrence's death—you want to find something, nothing homes in faster than a piece of black magician."

Pete pressed a hand over her mouth. "Please tell me you're speaking in terms of a vial of blood or a lock of hair."

"Petunia, he's dead," Jack explained as he gave the saw an experimental rev. "And he was a nasty bugger when alive, so if you're going to lose your supper over this of all things, go wait outside."

Pete's eyes narrowed. "Just because I can stand some of the things you get up to doesn't mean I like them."

"Fair enough." Jack slipped on a cotton mask and a pair of goggles that pinched at the temples. He flipped the switch, and lowered the Stryker saw to Jao's neck. The blood mist against his goggles was fine, coagulated, and nearly black. The salt-iron tang of it filled the air.

The saw faltered when it reached the spine, and Jack pressed down with all of his strength. He was rewarded when Jao's head flopped back, nerveless, the skull thunking on the metal tray like Jack had dropped a bowling ball.

Jack looked at Pete, who had backed up against the far wall. Her pulse was pounding in her neck like a jackhammer. "Find me something to carry this in," he said, indicating Jao's head.

Pete moved stiffly, and got him an orange biohazard bag, which Jack in turn stuffed into a tote left behind by a morgue worker. Pete's color hadn't improved. "I'm going to be sick."

"If you're dealing with bastards, sometimes you've got to get dirty," Jack said. "Be a bit of a bastard yourself."

Pete put as much distance between herself and the bag as possible. "Jack, I don't think I could do what you just did. Magic, fine. Demons, very well. But things like this . . . I just can't."

"You could, Pete." Jack zipped the bag closed. "Just pray you never have to."

Jao's head was leaden, and Jack felt the tendrils of bad magic seeping into the air around him. The ghosts crowded after Jack, Pete, and Jack's burden as he crossed the threshold back into the hospital, watching him through the swinging doors, their whispers teasing his sight until it felt like a thin needle piercing his brain.

Jack exhaled, massaging the center of his forehead. Pete eyed him. "What is it now?"

"Nothing," Jack said. "But sometimes, I think I made the wrong bloody deal."

"By most people's definition, any deal with a demon is a wrong one," Pete grumbled.

"Here it comes." Jack shouldered the bag. "The self-righteous tongue-lashing from your spot of Catholic guilt. Go ahead, luv—I'm ready."

"I'm not saying a word," Pete told him, and kept her promise while they left the hospital and found a motorbike taxi. Jack told the driver, "Nearest river bridge, and hurry it up."

Pete stayed silent while they poked inch by inch through the crush of motorbikes and cars converging on the choke point of the river's edge. She stayed silent when Jack paid the driver with pounds sterling, and she stayed silent when he walked to the center of the pedestrian walkway and peered into the river.

"How long are you going to be in a snit?" The sewage stink of the river, mixed with salt and cooking oil, wafted up to put greasy little fingers all over his face.

Pete sniffed. "As long as I bloody well please."

"Look." Jack let out a sigh. The river was crowded with long boats and water taxis, but this spot looking toward the skyscrapers and away from the slums would do. "Whatever you want to say, let it out and have done. This silent treatment is for twat couples on the telly. It's not for us."

"Oh." Pete's tone bit down hard and let Jack know that his usual style of git with a bit of arsehole mixed in might have landed him in uncharted territory. "There's an *us* now, is there?"

Jack stopped, his hands knotted in the plastic wrapped around Jao's head, and shut his eyes. "Pete, what do you want me to say? Want me to run into the street and declare me love? Burst into song? I don't know what we've got any more than you do."

"If I have to tell you what we've *got*, Jack, then fuck it anyway. It's not bloody worth it." Pete paced away a few steps and leaned on the railing. "Never was."

Jack set Jao's head back in the bag. "You think I don't know, Pete?" He stood up, went to her, grabbed her arm. His hand slipped against her sweat. "That I've been stupid and reckless and deserve what I've got coming because I'm a coward and a liar? You think it doesn't follow me like shadow wherever I walk on this earth?" His fingers pressed down, and they would bruise, but Jack couldn't stop himself. He'd frayed, and worn, and now he'd broken. "Tell me, Pete. Tell me what exactly you don't understand about my wasted, wrecked existence, because from where I'm standing it's not that fucking complicated."

Her eyes filled but her fist came up, thumped against his chest like a second heartbeat, over and over. "How you could do it!" she shouted. "How you could do it when you're Jack Winter!" She slumped against him, her fist unclenching. They'd traded bruises, now. Stood square and equal. Pete gave one shuddering breath and drew herself upright. "You're not supposed to be the one with scars, Jack," she whispered. "Because if you can be broken, that means I have to pick up the pieces, and it terrifies me, knowing what I know now, to think you won't be there beside me someday soon."

Jack conjured a smile. Pete didn't need to see the dark, twisted, terrified mess inside his chest. She needed to see his armor, the Jack she'd met a dozen years ago. "They haven't got me yet, luv. And if this goes right, they won't."

He passed the backs of his knuckles down her cheek. They came away warm, wet, and salty.

Pete looked down, sniffed like she hadn't let the tears come at all. "You promise me?"

"Promise," Jack said. And he meant it, for fuck-all a promise from him was worth. For Pete, he'd kick and fight and bare his teeth until the demon dragged him into Hell with claws in his hide. "Now, I need to concentrate on scrying, so what say we kiss and make up?"

Pete choked a laugh. "Because nothing's romantic as a head in a plastic wrapper. You sweep me of my feet, Jack Winter. Truly."

He dipped his head and planted a light brush of lips on her forehead. "I do me best."

Jao's head still stared at him bug-eyed when he unwrapped it, lips swollen and tongue threatening to pop out from the mouth. Jack forced the jaws open with his finger and dug in his bag for herbs. He stuffed in his scrying mediums, a flat black stone, a twist of feather, and a clump of sage. He gathered Jao's hair in a clump, attaching a length of linen string in a hardy knot.

Jack cradled the head in his arms and stepped up on the rail, toes hanging into space, black water flowing under his feet like the tide of souls into the Bleak Gates.

He held the head out in front of him like a rugby ball, wrapping the string around his knuckles. He lowered the thing by degrees, until it dangled a few meters above the water, and the feedback of black magic traveled up his arms and across his skin, burrowing deep.

"Someone's going to see us," Pete warned.

Jack rocked against the weight of the head, and the heady rush of energy all through his nerves. "'Course they will. However, I wager no one's going to bother the crazy *farang* and his severed head."

Pete made a face, like she'd report him to the coppers

herself if she had a choice. "Just be quick. That head is absolutely creepy."

The string in his fist gave a twitch, and Jack held up his free hand to Pete. "Hush."

Scrying wasn't like summoning or exorcism. It was a quiet art, precise and delicate, requiring a steady hand and a steadier mind to keep the sharp pinpoint of focus on whatever it was you sought. Mages used ink, mirrors, or plain stone pendulums to find nearly anything. White witches stared at crystals and sorcerers used the writhing, sticky energy of necromancy to scry with human bodies.

Mages could find ghosts, missing things, lost people, but to find a human being who wanted to stay hidden and cemented their chances with magic—that was the realm of the darker arts.

The head moved. It swayed back and forth in a parabolic arc above the river water. Water, the great current that bound the spirit world and the light one, channeling the sorcerous energy into Jack's search.

Jack said, "Miles Hornby."

The head came to a stop at an angle, rigid, white eyes staring north. They rolled back toward Jack.

He felt the magic squirm from his grasp, winding down the string to take up residence in Jao's skull. Jack's skin crawled, like it was trying to separate from his flesh and bone.

The sorcery spoke, in a voice that was older than bone and more wicked than any demon. It filled Jack up until it spilled over, and as he watched the head's jaws began to work, the swollen tongue flopping with the effort needed to form a word.

Jack's stomach and his balance lurched as the scrying spell gripped him, and he strained to hear the worlds borne on the spell. For a moment, there was only the rushing water and the hiss of the long boats poling underneath the bridge, and then his arm jerked as the spell snapped home.

"Kâo Făn Wat," the head gasped, and then the string broke and the thing plunged into the river with a splash, disappearing beneath the dark and oily waves.

Jack let go of the string, felt it slip through his fingers and follow the spell down into the depths. The long boats passing by paid no notice to the slowly dying pool of ripples on the river. They paid even less attention to one lone white nutter standing on the rail.

Pete grabbed him when he swayed, and Jack jumped down. The heroin had left behind a feeling of being hollow on the inside, a carapace around a dusty left-behind set of innards, owner long since moved on.

"So?" She let go of him quickly and put an arm's length between their bodies. They may have made up the fight but he wasn't forgiven.

"Kâo Făn Wat," Jack said. "Whatever that means."

"A *wat* is a temple," Pete said. "Learnt that from *Tomb Raider*. What direction?"

Jack pointed to where the head had come to rest. "That way. Never heard of Kâo Făn Wat. No idea what it is."

Pete grimaced. "Fantastic. Now what do we do?"

Jack sighed, the feeling of inevitability clenching at his stomach, forcing him to step out to the road and hail a motor taxi. "Now we go and ask someone who does."

Chapter Thirty-nine

"I have to say, I would have laid a bet that you wouldn't come back here." Rahu smiled at Jack, at Pete. Outside, the nighttime smells and sounds of Khlong Toei rose and fell and tantalized, thick and dreamy.

"Not by choice, mate." Jack fought the urge to remove the smirk from Rahu's face. Not that he could manage it, but the effort would be cathartic.

"Seth McBride is in the hospital," Rahu said. "It seems someone fractured his skull."

"Good," Pete shot back. "Never met anyone who deserved it more."

Rahu clucked. "Out of respect for your mistress, Weir, I'll let it pass. But don't think I'll turn my head a second time."

"The crow woman? She's not mine." Pete snorted. "Talk to Jack."

Jack stepped in, closer to Bangkok's demon than he would have strictly cared for. He only moved so close to show that after the last time, he wasn't afraid. "Kâo Făn Wat. Hornby's hidden out there."

"And this concerns me how?" The night was wet and

warm as saliva on skin, but Rahu neither sweated nor for-
went his all-black head-to-toe getup. Jack had learned long
ago that you didn't trust things that didn't sweat.

"You want me gone, you tell me where he is," Jack said.
"Simple. You want me to hang about, bothering your necromancers and your arse-boys like Seth, getting drunk,
pissing in your gutters, and generally making a great fat
nuisance of meself, then by all means. Pull the other one."

"Kâo Făn Wat is the Temple in Dreaming," said Rahu.
"And I can't tell you where it is, mage, because no one
knows. No one who knows the location of Kâo Făn Wat has
lived in the last five hundred years."

"I'm not mistaken," Jack growled. "I scryed for Hornby.
I asked the Black."

"Then perhaps you've forgotten that the Black can lie
and deceive," said Rahu. "Just as a treacherous mage can."

"Fine," Jack said. "What *can* you tell me? Or are you
useless, like all the other pit-spawned wankers I've come
up against?"

"Jack, I'm surprised at you." Rahu beamed. "After what
Kartimukha saw in your head, insulting a demon is the last
thing you want to play at."

"I swear," Jack said, and felt witchfire grow around him
like a blue cloud, "I'll burn this rathole slum to the ground
to get what I want."

Rahu sighed. "Threats are the last refuge of the weak
and fearful, Jack. You should know that, too." He twitched
his cuffs straight. "Now, I'm very busy. Have a pleasant
evening, Jack."

"I'll make a deal." Jack's voice came out too loud, rattling the Buddhas and the faded paper sutras that suffocated Rahu's temple. Pete knocked him in the ribs with her
elbow.

"Jack! For Christ's sake, enough already!"

Rahu, for his part, tilted his head back to gaze at Jack.

"You have nothing to deal with, Jack. You're a scrap that's already been picked over."

"You tell me where to find Hornby, and my demon is gone," Jack said. "The demon who sent you here. I'll trick him out of my bargain and he'll fall from favor in Hell. You can go home."

Rahu shut his eyes. His nostrils flared and a smile played on his lips. "Home, yes. If I thought you could do it, Jack, I'd help you within the beat of my heart." Rahu opened his eyes. "But you can't. You're a rare breed, mage, but you're not a messiah for the likes of demonkind."

"I'll do it," Jack said softly, "or I'll die." Wind came through the open sides of the temple, swirling a cloud of candle-flame shadow and incense. Pete watched him, her eyebrows drawn together. Jack watched Rahu, the demon's unmoving face like wax in the low light.

"I have not been home in a very long time," Rahu whispered.

Jack looked at his boots. The exposed steel shone like something precious. "Neither have I, mate."

Rahu blinked, decision made. "The Kâo Făn Wat supposedly lies in the jungle north of the city. The last to see it were a company of soldiers during the Vietnam War. They disappeared to a man."

"There, now," Jack said. "That wasn't so hard, was it?"

Rahu showed his teeth. "Good-bye, Jack Winter. Go and find your way home."

Chapter Forty

"What's a Kartimukha?" Pete said, when they'd sat for an hour in silence on hard plastic seats that stuck to the back of Jack's pants, the train from Bangkok rattling them north. The closest village to Kâo Făn Wat that Pete had been able to find on a map was Grà-jòk Baang, and their tickets, stamped in bleeding ink, held that as a destination.

"Rahu's pet." Jack shuddered. "It eats your memories. Picks them over like bones."

Pete watched him as the train chugged slowly through the city outskirts, pity in her gaze. "What did it take from you?" she said softly.

Jack leaned his forehead against the glass. Bangkok sprawled for miles, a great slumbering organism of light and wire and tumbledown tenement flats. "When Seth offered to instruct me in the *Fiach Dubh*, I was young. Stupid. I thought I knew better."

"And?" Pete's voice held none of the edge she'd had earlier, but she wrapped her arms around herself, like you would at a scary movie.

"I stole something of his, and I got myself into an arseload of trouble," Jack said. The soft vellum pages of the demonology book had crinkled under his fingers like skin. "I ended up in a hotel room in Dublin, tormented by the dead." Jack scratched at his scar. "I cut my wrists to get away and it wasn't until I'd almost bled to death that I saw my fate. I'd become one of them—the ghost who saw ghosts." He shrugged. "Seth tracked me down and I got stitched up. I went home, I learned how not to be a precocious git on my own, and there's nothing more to talk about."

A warm, dry touch joined his own and Jack looked over to see Pete tracing the faint old scars under his fresher tracks with a slow, almost reverent touch. "I never knew."

"It's not something I shout from the rooftops, luv. It takes a special kind of stupid cunt to top himself."

She moved her hand into his and shut her eyes, leaning her head on his shoulder. "That's right it does. Wake me when we get to this stronghold of mysticism. I'm knackered."

Jack let himself relax a bit, on this moving iron snake, but he didn't let himself sleep. To sleep now would just invite dreams, screaming nightmares of the deaths that had nearly been his own, and what waited for him when the one with his name finally came to roost.

He watched the lights of the city wink out one by one, the beast shutting its thousand eyes as the train rolled on through the night.

Chapter Forty-one

When Jack woke, dawn had unfolded over the world. Pete nudged him. "It seems we've arrived."

Jack pulled himself to his feet and grabbed his kit, seeing a snatch of gray, cracked train platform sprouting out of a swath of intractable jungle. "Grà-jòk Baang. Somehow I pictured it as being more . . . alive."

He followed Pete from the car, down the steps onto the platform. The conductor slammed the door and the train whistle hooted as soon as his feet touched concrete.

In a matter of a few moments, they were alone, the train only daytime thunder in the distance.

The heat in the jungle was worse than the city, contained and damp as the canopy closed in air weighted with decaying leaf mold and orchids. A dirt track led away from the train platform and a pocket-sized station house with boarded-over windows. Jack saw curls of smoke and the faint sheen of hazy sun off tin rooftops.

"There's the village," he said. "We can ask about the temple."

"Of course," Pete muttered. "Because two foreigners walking into a shady village has never ended badly in any of the Indiana Jones films . . ."

They walked down the track in silence, Jack feeling the heat crawl across his skin. The air was thick and it hummed with the same wild magic as the Dartmoor, undercut with sorcery that brushed against his face like sticky fingerprints.

Jack didn't walk willingly into situations where he knew he was properly fucked. That was for white knights, and he was no kind of knight—white, black, or any other shade.

Pete trailed Jack by a few feet, eyes twitching nervously from trees to path to the hunched shape of the huts ahead. Jack slowed so they walked side by side.

"You hear it?" he asked after a moment. Pete shook her head.

"I don't hear anything."

"Nothing," Jack agreed. Sweat coursed down his neck, rivulets meeting and mating to become rivers. "No birds. No beasts."

Pete pointed her chin toward the village. "No people."

Jack's boots squelched in the mud track as they reached the village outskirts. There were no animals in the pens made of corrugated tin and mesh, no smoke rising from the crooked chimneys that poked among the shacks like a cluster of broken finger bones.

Pete cupped her hands around her mouth. "Hello!" Her voice bounced back, but no one replied.

The village square was populated with footprints, sodden newspaper, and one half-deflated soccer ball. An enterprising soul had staked out tarps to collect water, and cloudy clusters of mosquito eggs drifted across the surface.

Jack had already turned to go back to the train platform and call Kâo Făn Wat another dead end when he saw the crows.

The crows sat in a straight line on the sagging telephone

wire, eyes unblinking, wings unruffled. They stared at Jack, and he stared in return.

Three black bodies, three sets of feathers gleaming in the hazed-over sun. After two heartbeats the crow on the right turned his head, met Jack's eye with one made from a bead of black lava glass. The fetch and the mage stared at one another for a few slow, hot breaths.

"Jack." Pete's voice floated to him from far off, but the tone was flat and hard as a tombstone. "Jack. You need to see this."

She stood in the doorway of the largest shack at the square's edge, a rusty Quonset hut with the markings of the American military thirty years past. Pete was pale, and the sweat on her skin stood out like crystals.

Jack didn't ask what was inside the hut. The sweet, weighty scent of rotten orchids rolling out from the narrow door answered him. Still, he came to Pete's shoulder and he looked inside.

The bodies were one or two high, three in the corners. Flies were thicker than air under the arch of the roof. The dirt floor had become mud, darkened with sticky blood that refused to dry in the heat.

Under cover, the smell became a presence, a physical hand that shoved its fingers down Jack's throat and coated his tongue with sticky offal.

"There's got to be thirty people here," Pete said. She clapped a bandanna over her face and pressed a canister from her overnight bag into Jack's hand. He looked at it. "Makeup remover?"

"Under your nose," Pete said. "Trust me."

Jack dabbed the pink cream under his nose and the sharp scent of toner and artificial strawberries cut the cloud of decay. "Thirty people," he agreed, as Pete clicked on her pen light and flashed it over the corpses. The blank smiles of cut throats stared up at Jack.

"Thirty-three." The voice spoke from behind him, from the outside, and Jack spun. His heart jumped against his bones, a betrayal that he knew had escalated to his face when the figure smiled.

"You're here to kill me, you'll end up like the rest."

The dark hair, gravelly voice, and stained Radiohead shirt told Jack all he needed to know. "Miles Hornby."

Hornby ran his hand through his lank mass of brown hair. "I knew they'd send someone with his head pulled out of his ass next time, but I didn't know it would be Jack Winter." He sighed, rubbing his forehead. "Heard a lot about you, man."

"Likewise." Hornby was taller and wider than Jack himself, but he had a slithering, fey quality to his features that put Jack in mind of a predatory animal skulking through brush.

"You've left a very unhappy demon behind in England, mate," Jack told him. "But I think you know that."

Hornby instead looked at Pete. "Didn't expect you." He held out his hand. "You shouldn't have to see this. Wait outside, will you? Your boyfriend and I will be over in a minute."

"Fuck off," Pete said. "That shirt of yours is the most frightening thing in this hut."

Hornby's jaw twitched. "Aren't you the little pistol."

"Oi." Jack put himself between Hornby and Pete. "You don't talk to her. You talk to me."

Hornby took a step toward Jack. He was unique in that—most backed away, and still more simply ran when they confronted him. "I'm not going back," Hornby said.

"Oh?" Jack popped the knuckles in his right hand. They'd separated long ago, at eighteen or nineteen, a club brawl that he could have avoided, or at least won, if he'd been less pissed or less of an arrogant little sod. "I beg to differ, Miles. I think you're coming with us. And I think you're going to do it with a smile on your fucking face."

"You haven't even asked about the dead bodies," Miles

mused. "Only care about me. Makes you a sick man, Jack. Priorities all screwy." Underneath the scent of decay and the heat, Jack felt another sensation rise. Older, wickeder. The thrilling pull of black magic.

"You know what did this to them?" Jack jerked his thumb at the corpses. "That's wonderful. Really fantastic. You can have a cry about it on the plane ride home."

"Of course I know," Hornby said. "It was me."

Pete touched Jack on the wrist. "Maybe we should reconsider this . . ."

Jack didn't take his eyes off Hornby. It was a gunfight now, as the other man's magic rose, an ambush he'd walked into. Hornby was playing at the dark arts and Jack hadn't been ready. "I beg your pardon?"

"The demon sent *vargr* to take me back," Hornby said. "So I killed them. Didn't like it, but there you go."

Pete leaned toward Jack. "*Vargr*?" she murmured.

"Hellhounds," Jack said. "Demon's scent dogs." The *vargr* were shadow, formless, but Jack saw the twisted faces of the villagers, the long black teeth and claws that had begun to grow and usurp their human forms.

"They possessed the village," Hornby said. "It was them or me and I chose myself."

Jack shook his head. "Thirty-three people. Cross and crow, you're cracked. Too much time in the sun."

"What I am is not going back to England," Hornby said. "I don't want to hurt you, Winter, but I will."

"For fuck's sake," Pete said. "You really think you can cheat a demon and get away with it?" Jack wasn't sure who the question was directed at.

Hornby considered. "Yes."

"All right, all right." Jack held up his hands. "I'll make you an offer—you tell me how you cheated the demon and I won't drag you out of here with your weasely little head shoved up your arse."

Hornby let out a small, hysterical laugh. "You think you scare me, Winter? I told you, I'd heard of you. Maybe twenty years ago you were something, but you've lost your step. Got on some bad drugs and some badder company and now you're just another sad old bastard grasping for the glory days."

"Right, that's it." Jack pulled energy to him, prepared the word of power for a hex. "I'm going to kill him."

"Jack!" Pete snatched his arm down. "For God's sake."

"He listens to you?" Hornby shifted from foot to foot. "Good thing. Tell him I'm not going back, and that if he tries that again I'm going to make him number thirty-four on the pile, okay?"

"Sorry." Pete's smile narrowed into something unpleasant. "I'm rather fond of Jack, and I think that if you've really got this miracle cure-all for demons, you'd better turn it over, or *I'll* kill you."

Hornby sighed. He wasn't more than twenty-five or -six but his skin sagged under his eyes and the pale cast of his skin even in the tropics gave the impression of him being sickly, wasting away from the inside out. "I really don't want to keep doing this, but if it's the only way he'll leave me alone . . ." His hand came up, joints knobby from playing guitar spreading in the half-moon of the hex.

Jack didn't stop to think, to calculate his odds of advance and retreat. He threw his weight between Pete and Hornby, yanking a hex from the well of power inside him. Drawing only on yourself hurt, hurt like peeling your skin off with a dull, hot razor. The hex shimmered, wavered, held as a black tide rushed outward from Hornby's fingertips.

The jolt of magic knocked Jack on his arse, the mud splashing up to coat him in a gummy mix of dirt and blood. The corpses he landed against gave like deflated rubber rafts, and the smell choked him again.

Jack made it to his knees, wheezing and retching, before Hornby stepped closer and kicked him in the gut, hard and precise, with one trainer-encased foot. Jack's air went out of him, along with the bile in his stomach. His tongue burned, and he gagged, trying to draw in air.

Pete launched herself at Hornby, putting her full weight into the maneuver. Hornby spun halfway around, staggered, cuffed Pete on the side of the head. "I said to stop! I don't want to hurt you!" He hit her again, and Pete sat down in the mud next to Jack. Hornby shook out his hand. "Gods. You'd think someone as talented as you're supposed to be could do more than smack me around, Winter." Hornby prodded the spot where Pete had hit him. "But then again, what do I know?"

Jack grabbed for Pete when she tucked her legs under her to go at Hornby again. "Not this way. Stay down." He kept the grip, felt the well of Weir power fall away beneath him. The breathless, weightless feeling of falling into the Black, cut with the heat of the wild magic of the jungle around him. He didn't think or fret over what touching the Weir could do to him, he just let the hex spill forth.

"*Aithinne*," Jack rasped. The second hex he'd learned. The strategy in any mage's duel was the same: block a spell and then fling one back hard as you could.

Except when the bastard across from you bounced the hex off his protection magic and sent a jet of wild magic-fueled fire bouncing around the shed.

"Shit!" Jack exclaimed, as the clothing of the nearest corpse caught on fire. "Pete, move your arse!" He bolted for the door, and Hornby turned tail as well, the three of them spilling out into the abandoned village square.

Hornby panted, swatting at the soot on his clothes as the fire consumed the hut and the bodies inside. "Fuck, man. You're strong."

"And you're clever," Jack told him. "The demon was right."

As Hornby gasped, Jack closed the distance between them and put a fist into the younger man's nose. "But you're not that clever."

Hornby yelped and went down, mud splashing up around him. Jack pulled his magic back under his control, and aimed a paralysis hex at Hornby. "*Sioctha.*"

The mage jerked, veins throbbing at his temples, but his body was rigid as a board. Jack crouched next to him. "Let's try this once more: I'm Jack Winter, I'm the worst thing your skinny arse has ever clapped eyes on, and you're going to tell me how you cheated the demon before I do something more than make your legs not work."

"This village," Hornby gasped. "This village is in the shadow of the *wat*. They massacred the villagers during Vietnam. Thought I was safe here. Ghosts and feedback from the massacre . . . like a radio jammer . . ."

Jack clapped his hands above Hornby's face. "Oi. Not wanting your life story, mate. Just tell me how you did it."

Hornby let out a misery-laden sigh, and then his eyes rolled back into his head. "Fuck it," Jack muttered. Pete came and crouched beside him.

"He dead?"

Jack jammed his fingers against Hornby's neck. "No. Just a coward for pain." He stood, leaving Pete with Hornby. "Watch him. If he wakes up, give him another tap on the gob."

Jack prowled through the small houses around the square. Most were covered in layers of dust and mold that spread like fans along the walls, flies and maggots thick on spoiled food left sitting when the *vargr* took over the residents. Only one house showed any signs of recent occupation. The bed was rumpled, the sheet stained with sweat. Water dripped from a rusty pump in the kitchen in time with Jack's heartbeat.

He walked back to Hornby and grabbed him by the

shirt. "Help me," he said to Pete. She took Hornby's other side and they dragged his dead weight into the house, where Jack dumped him unceremoniously on the bed, found a length of cord, and tied Hornby up like a kidnapped teenager in a sex dungeon. For good measure, he stuffed the muddy kerchief from his pocket into Hornby's mouth.

"Now what?" Pete said, fanning herself with an ancient, wrinkled copy of *Rolling Stone* printed in Thai.

Jack sat on the single chair in the tiny room, across from Hornby, and stared intently at the other man. Sleeping, he looked like any hapless washed-up musician, in want of a shave, a shower, and a recording contract. Jack thought it was a good thing he knew better.

"We wait," he said. "And when Sleeping Beauty here sees fit to stir, we make him talk."

Chapter Forty-two

Night came to the world again before Hornby did anything but twitch and snore on the mattress. Jack had exhausted his supply of both fags and patience.

"Welcome back," Jack said when Hornby stirred. "You have a pleasant nap, Princess?"

Hornby bucked, struggling like a trussed pig. "Let me go."

Jack grinned at him. "Tell me how you cheated the demon."

"Fuck you!" Hornby shouted, loud enough to echo through the village square.

"All right then," Jack said, standing. "We'll be off to catch the last train. Pete, remind me how long a body can stand being without water?"

"Thirty-six hours," she said promptly, from where she leaned against the sill of the open window.

"Thirty-six hours," Jack murmured. "Less, in this heat. Lose water like a sieve in this country, me. It's a trial for skinny blokes like us."

Hornby snorted. "Go ahead and leave me. I'll just bespell the knots."

"Ahead of you on that score," Jack said. "I already be-spelled them. To stay tied." He'd done no such thing—a spell like that would have taken supplies and time—but Hornby didn't know. Jack crouched, taking Hornby by the chin. "Face it, Miles—you may be a hard lad, but I'm older and I've had more time to learn how to be a dirty low-down bastard."

"Just go," Hornby groaned. "Every minute you're here, he's closer to finding me."

"Should have thought of that before you made the deal," Jack said, picking up his kit and starting for the door. He fully intended to follow through on his threat if Hornby didn't cooperate. Jack would be fucked, then, and Hornby might loose the knots in time to survive. Or he might not. Jack would be in Hell either way.

"My sister had lukemia," Hornby muttered when Jack and Pete reached the door. "My baby sister. I promised to keep her safe and they tell me she has two months to live."

"So you bargained with the demon," Jack said. "Not the first sob story I've heard, mate."

"I never did a black magic spell in my life, I never even dabbled in scrying or cursing, until I made the deal." Hornby sighed. "I used to be a decent guy."

Jack sighed, grabbed up a kitchen knife, and went back to the bed. "Miles, mate. Take it from me, we all used to be decent sorts." He sliced Hornby's ropes and sat him up. "No adorable little curses, now. Just tell me how you got out, and we'll be on our way."

"Tell me what you did it for, first," Hornby insisted. "Because somehow I don't see you sacrificing your soul for a poor dying kid. Was it for fame? Sex?"

"Mine was for being a fuckwit," Jack said shortly. "Which is exactly the same as you. Dress it up how you like, but we're both here because we made a shit choice."

Hornby shut his eyes, slumping back into the mattress like a puppet. "Suppose I did."

Jack wasn't sure whether Hornby moved or whether he merely lashed out with magic and sent Jack sprawling, but he came up with an oblong black shape from under the mattress. "The difference between you and me is," Hornby said, "I can fix my choice."

Jack called a shield hex, not fast enough. Hornby swung the gun to bear on Jack, causing Jack to scrabble backward. Hornby didn't shoot, though. He snapped the pistol up, tucking the barrel under his chin.

"I told you I'm not going back."

"Miles," Pete said at the same time. "Don't do that . . ."

"Don't be a wanker," Jack supplied, their voices blending and tripping over one another like tangled strings.

"I will never be free," Hornby murmured. "I ran but it will find me. I know why I went to it in the first place and you're right—shitty choice, shitty result." Hornby met his eyes. "The difference between you and me is that I'm done running." Hornby sighed, and Jack saw his shoulders relax, all of the tension and fear trickle from his body.

"Miles," he started. "You stupid fuck . . ."

"And I take back what I said before, Winter," Hornby told him. "You're still pretty good. But I'm done now."

Jack made it a single step before Miles squeezed the trigger, and the gunshot echoed and rolled back from the buildings around the square. In the jungle, birds and creatures took flight with a cacophony of screeching and warbling.

Hornby's body hit the floor, landing faceup. The gun thumped on the sisal matting next to him. Pete let out a small scream that blended with the jungle birds.

In Jack's moment of paralysis, a shadow bent over Hornby. Not the same shadow that had come to him thirteen years ago, not the crow woman. Not the demon, either.

This shadow had a lion's mane, teeth, and a twisted body that bled and flowed indistinctly when Jack tried to look at it.

"Don't . . . ," Jack croaked, but there was nothing he could do aside from protest. The demon of Bangkok had a new soul. The demon who owned Jack's had lost it.

And then the sound faded and the world sped up again and Jack realized he was shouting, wordlessly, and that the floor was pitching beneath him as dizziness and nausea and the realization that he, too, had lost came.

Jack followed Hornby down, down to his knees. "You stupid bastard," he whispered. "You ruddy, stupid bastard. What the fuck am I supposed to do now?"

Chapter Forty-two

The hospital ceiling had gone yellow, acoustic tiles stained with the familiar tinge of nicotine. Taped above his bed, a curled-up poster sporting a monkey would, were it in English, have encouraged him to *Hang in there!*

Jack groaned and pulled the hard foam pillow over his face. It smelled of bleach and the rough casing tickled his nose.

"You're awake." Pete herself looked barely that. She was curled in the plastic chair next to his bed, the black circles under her eyes speaking to days, if not weeks, of nights spent in the same place.

"After a fashion." Jack cast the pillow aside. Sound came back, the chatter of busy people outside the door of his room, the whoop of sirens from outside the walls, the hum and rattle of an overworked air conditioner blocking most of his window. Jack tilted his face toward it and let it dry his sweat. "Fuck me standing up, that's nice."

"Brought you in after Hornby killed himself," Pete said. "You were a bit shocky. That cut of yours was infected with god knows what. Doctor said it's a miracle you didn't lose your arm."

Jack felt himself over. He wasn't tied down, so he hadn't been raving crazy when he came in. There was an IV, and the pleasant cotton-wool feeling of sedatives. Jack laughed. "You didn't tell 'em I'm a smack addict?"

"In this country?" Pete rolled her eyes. "The very last thing I need at this moment is to spring you from some Thai prison, Jack."

Jack tried to sit up and the wallowing dizziness from the painkillers put him back down. Pete came to his side, laying the back of her hand against his forehead.

"You all right?"

"No," Jack muttered. "I'm about seven shades of not right at the moment, luv."

Pete got him a cup of water and a straw and stuck it between his lips. "You're dehydrated, too. Drink."

Jack obeyed, because even dubious city water seemed sweet at the moment, and when he'd emptied the pink plastic cup he sank back against the pillow, which gave not a whit. "Hornby's dead, Pete."

"I was there, Jack." Pete settled herself back in her chair. "Precious little to be done. We've got a flight home as soon as the infection is out of your system. I didn't think you wanted to be around when police started asking questions about the dead *farang*."

"Hornby did the right thing," Jack said. "He knew what he was in for and he topped himself. He made sure his soul stayed here. That's the proper thing to do."

"Christ, you do say stupid things when you're on drugs," Pete said archly. Jack waved his hand. The IV needle scraped against the underside of his skin.

In Jack's mind, Hornby put his finger in the trigger of the gun and squeezed.

Why had a mage had a gun, anyway? Didn't he know they were for amateurs?

Stupid sod.

Jack pushed back the itchy coverlet and swung his bare feet to the floor. They stuck to it, and he fished under the bed. "Where are me boots?"

"Jack, don't be stupid. You need to stay in that bed," Pete said. She rose, but Jack yanked out his IV needle before she could summon a nurse.

"I need to go home," he said. "My time's almost up, Pete. It'll go badly if the demon thinks I'm trying to do a runner like Miles."

"Jack . . ." Pete caught him as he swayed. Standing up too fast on downers was like pouring all of the blood out of your head.

"I don't want to think about what I'm doing and I don't want a lecture, because I know it's low and I know it's fucking weak," Jack said. "But I haven't got a better idea, so I'm getting out of this fucking hospital and doing what I must."

He found his boots, yanked them on with difficulty. He couldn't begin to manage the laces, so he let the tongues flop free. He was halfway down the corridor when Pete caught up with him.

"Jack, wait!"

"Not changing my mind, Pete," he said. "You can argue if you like."

Pete shoved a plastic shopping back into his hands. "You forgot your jacket and your kit, idiot. I think you might need them if you're intending to challenge this demon of yours."

"Cheers." Jack slowed, subdued. "Pete, you don't have to come with me, you know."

She sighed, brushing past him to the nurse's station. "Him. The stupid bloody *farang*. He needs to sign out."

After their business with the hospital was complete,

Pete walked with him to the street outside, where she hailed a motor taxi. "Let's get one thing straight, Jack: I'm here until the end. One way or the other, I'll be with you. So the next time you suggest I might want to preserve my delicate sensibilities, I'm going to punch you right in the gob. Clear?"

"Crystal," Jack said as he opened the taxi door. The demon waited for him in England. Hornby's soul was planted here, sure as the stones that paved the bones of Bangkok. His innocent's soul, which had made his shit deal for the right reasons and not out of paralyzing fear.

Jack wasn't sure which he regretted more.

Chapter Forty-three

England rose up to meet the jetliner gray and lacy with mist, the kind of silver-green day that poets scribbled about and tourists lost their wits over.

Jack could have gone down and kissed the oily tarmac of Heathrow when the plane touched down, but the chill in his chest wouldn't allow him that much happiness.

He'd tried to cheat the demon. And he'd lost. He'd doomed Miles Hornby to his time in Hell and himself to go toe-to-toe with the demon.

Pete sat beside him, but silent on the Heathrow express into Paddington. She'd stopped looking at him by the time they boarded the Hammersmith & City Line back to his flat.

Pete thought he was going to die.

Jack didn't know that she was wrong.

The tube rattled on its way and Jack mounted the steps, past the street market selling *hijab* and knockoff purses and kebab, past the White Hart pub, the closed-down shop fronts and shady money-changing kiosks, through the ebb and flow of the dark energy of the only place he'd ever really called home.

The demon was waiting for them when they stepped through Jack's front door.

"Look at you," it purred. "Home safe and sound, tanned and rested." It rubbed the fingers and thumb of its left hand together. "I trust you brought me what I need, Jackie boy."

Pete fetched up against his shoulder, propelling Jack into the flat. His protection hexes hung in useless tatters from the demon's passage.

"This is him?" Pete said. Her fists curled into small knots of knuckle and bone.

"It," Jack said. "Not him, no matter what it chose to make itself look like."

The demon ticked its tongue against its teeth. "I'll ask again, Jack—where's my soul?"

Jack ignored the feeling that the floorboards had dropped away from him, ignored that his heart was thudding so loudly it nearly drowned out his own voice. "Did you check the last place you had it? Or—hold up—behind the sofa?"

The demon cocked its head, and Jack was on his knees. Blink, crash, pain. Jack's air rushed out of him, but he didn't make any sound. Didn't let the demon know that it hurt. That was the first thing you learned—never show them that it hurt.

"Where. Is. My. Soul?" The demon knelt and put a finger under Jack's chin. He felt the nail sink in, and a trickle of blood work its way into the hollow of his throat.

Pete's shadow fell over them both. "Let him go."

The demon's black pits of eyes flicked away from Jack, looked to Pete, and came back to rest. Tiny flames danced in their recesses. "Got a better offer for me, my dear?" He licked his lips. "You offered yourself to Treadwell. You nearly died. Won't be a near miss with me, I promise you."

"Pete," Jack managed. "This isn't your problem, luv. Get out of here."

"No," she said. "It can't have you."

The demon's lip curled back. "If she keeps sassing me, Winter, she's going to be joining your arse in the Pit. Am I quite clear?"

Pete grabbed Jack's arm, clung to him, and for once her power didn't stir him up. The demon's cold, inhuman, lizard-brained magic curled back from the onslaught of the Weir, and Jack's sight quieted.

"You can't have her," he echoed Pete. The demon laughed.

"I don't need her, Winter. I've got you."

"No." Jack raised himself up from the floor with Pete's help. The demon's nail scraped across his jaw as he yanked away. "You don't have me, either."

The demon stopped smiling. "What are you saying to me, boy?"

Jack shook off the pain of the demon's magic, made himself stand straight. "Your fucking soul is in Hell, one of Rahu's charges. He had the right idea—shot himself in the face. You wanted Hornby, that's where Hornby's gone to. He didn't cheat death in the end but he cheated you, right enough."

The demon's eyes flamed to twin points. "This is *not* what we agreed on, Winter."

"It's not," Jack said wearily. "But it's what you're getting. You want him, you go and tangle with Rahu. I find myself curiously unmotivated to do anything else you ask."

He crossed his arms and waited for the demon to absorb the fact that his prize soul had slipped away.

The demon lifted a shoulder. "Ah, well."

Pete shot Jack a glance. He bored his gaze into the demon. "Well? What?"

"Dead, isn't he?" the demon said. "Old Rahu is a bitter sod, but I'm sure I can find something he wants for one marginally talented musician who sold himself out of noble selflessness. Fuck me, it's so boring when they do it for altruism." It grinned at Jack, as if they shared a secret. "I told you that no one cheats me, Jack."

"You did," Jack agreed, trying to ignore the sickness in his throat. The crow landed on his sill, stared in at the proceedings. It opened its beak silently, bared it at the demon.

"Can't say it hasn't been fun, Jack," the demon intoned. "I'll be seeing you in, oh, about thirty-six hours, yes? Three-thirty p.m. on the day."

"Not so fast," Jack snarled. His shakes had started again, withdrawal or simple fatigue he couldn't tell, but the thing he knew for sure was that this time, it wasn't fear.

"I think you owe me something," he told the demon. "We made this bargain for your name."

"And the bargain was for a whole soul, not a scrap I have to wrestle away from another member of the pack," the demon said. "I was quite clear. Too bad, Jack. You failed. I'll see you soon."

The demon opened the door of the flat, began to exit. Pete and the crow watched Jack with frantic stillness, panic raging through Pete's eyes.

Jack stepped toward the demon. "*Wait.*"

The demon turned its head back, mouth flicking in amusement. "Yes, Jack?"

In Jack's mind, the pages of the grimoire that he'd copied before Seth had ripped it from him floated. The summoning. The safeguards a sorcerer could use.

"I'm calling our bargain before the Triumvirate," Jack said aloud. The pain from the demon's magic increased, vibrating through his blood and his bones, making his head ring as if it were made of brass, but Jack held on. "I challenge you before the rulers of Hell for your name, you shite-talking speck of soot. For your name."

The demon's face cracked, its expression going waxy and plastic, a lifelike doll with the batteries run down. "Don't do this, Winter. Your pride is going to eat you alive, boy."

Jack decided it was his turn to laugh, even though it hurt. "I'm not scared of you, or dying. Not anymore."

The demon shook its head. "Then you should be, Jack. Because you're going to Hell, and all that you've left behind is bad memories and a broken heart."

"I challenge you in the view of the Triumvirate," Jack repeated. "For your name."

"I heard you the first time," the demon snarled. "You are making a bad, bad mistake, Jack. I liked you before this, but now you've begun to irritate me."

"You can't refuse," Jack said quietly. "You and every other demon of Hell are bound by the same laws."

The demon rolled its eyes heavenward, a move that Jack would have found infinitely amusing were he not bartering for his life. "Fine. Name the time and place of me thoroughly teaching you the error of your ways."

"The Naughton manor," Jack shot back. "One day from now."

"Very well." The demon grinned at Pete. "Enjoy the day with him, Weir. It's your last."

It was gone when Jack looked back, the Black rippling in its wake. Jack made it to his sofa and slumped. Pete sat next to him, brows drawn together in vast concern.

"Jack, what just happened?"

He put a sofa pillow over his eyes. There had never been sofa pillows—or saucers, scatter rugs, or napkins made of cloth—until Pete had come to live with him. A sofa pillow was good. You could tuck it under your head for a quick kip, or use it to smother yourself when you'd just become the biggest bloody fool you knew.

"I made the shit choice," Jack said. "To willingly go to Hell and challenge the demon to learn its name before the three ruling members of the Triumvirate."

Pete chewed on her lip. "Can you win?"

Jack took the pillow away. "Not a chance."

Pete let her air out, slumping back to mimic his position. "Oh."

She went to her travel bag, found her fags and lighter, lit one. She offered it to him when she'd taken a drag. Jack accepted it and polluted his lungs for a long breath.

"Cheers."

"And the Naughton mansion?" Pete asked. Jack scratched under the edge of his bandage, where the cut from Jao was beginning to itch like a particularly virulent venereal disease.

"Blank spot in the Black. Energy is so bollocksed up from the necromancer fucking about I thought it might give me an edge."

Pete curled against him, surprising him with her weight, and Jack moved to make room for her in the crook of his body. "Thought you said you'd lose," she whispered.

"Yeah." Jack put his lips on the top of her head. "But that doesn't mean I won't go down kicking."

"Jack." Pete rotated her head to look at him. "I don't want you to go."

"Not keen on visiting Hell myself," Jack said. "But unless you've got a corker, luv . . . I'm out of ideas."

Chapter Forty-seven

Jack fell asleep with Pete's breath rising and falling against his chest, setting the pace for his heartbeat and his thoughts.

Everything took on a sharp-edged quality when he woke. Washing up, making tea, having a fag, and restocking his kit to put in the Mini were acts of incredible significance, rife with color and meaning.

The drive to the Dartmoor was no longer arduous and too long. The colors of the moor, the wild magic that embraced him like a prodigal son, it was all irrefutably alive, sharp and vivid enough to pain his senses.

Pete set the brake in the Naughton's circular drive. "Here we are."

Jack tried to shake off the hyperawareness, but he couldn't quite manage it. Death had ripped the veil from his eyes, shown him exactly what he would be seeing no longer, if the demon had his way.

Death, Jack reflected, was a bit of a cunt that way.

While Pete put up her overnight bag and laid in a tea in the Naughton kitchen, Jack laid out his kit on the long table in the formal dining room.

Salt, chalk, herb bags. Black and red and white thread, his scrying mirror, and a butane lighter for starting herbs in his censer.

It wasn't much, in the scheme of things, but the battered canvas satchel had kept Jack alive thus far.

None of it would do a bit of good against the demon. Jack swept his things back into the satchel and left it on the table. His reflection in the polished wood twisted, distorted and ghostly, pale face crowned by pale hair with sunken black pits for eyes, just as a spirit.

A shape shimmered in the reflection behind him, and Jack snapped his head around. He was prepared for the ghost of June Kemp, or the mansion's poltergeist, but it was only the owl.

It sat on the branch of the tree near the drive, staring at Jack with unblinking eyes. The sunlight skipped through the clouds on the moor, dark and light slashes across the ground. The owl should be far away from the light, asleep somewhere, but it watched him and when Jack merely stared, twitched its head and wings in irritation.

Jack tilted his head in return, and the owl spread its wingspan wide. A cloud rolled across the sun and the afternoon plunged into iron-gray dark. The owl took flight, alighting at the edge of the garden near the fallen stone wall that bound the estate, kept it from the encroachment of the moor.

Jack went to the wide front doors, left them open in his wake, and crossed the sodden lawn to the tree by the stone wall where the owl had flown.

When the sunlight fell through the clouds again, a woman stood under the tree. Though her hair was gray, her face was young, with the round, pale, unlined freshness of a pubescent girl.

She extended her hand to him, fingers wide, as if tasting the air before his passage.

Hello, Jack. A bar of light fell through her, gray and diffused where it scattered through her form.

A few steps from her, Jack caught a hint of the wild magic that rolled over the moor, the wild magic that had summoned the *cu sith* and distorted his sight. The power wasn't coming from the moor this time, though. It came from the gray-wrapped figure in front of him.

She regarded him with her golden creature's eyes, while the gray mist that clad her pale form writhed and shifted in the Dartmoor's changeable wind.

"You," Jack said. "That was you on the airplane."

Yes. You asked for safe passage. I granted it. She smiled at him, with a coquettish tilt of your head. *You're not an easy man to deny, Jack. I can see why she stays with you.*

From behind the tree, in the shadows, Jack heard a rumbling snarl and two *cu sith* blossomed from the dark spot on the ground, coming to stand at the girl's flanks. On the tilt of the moor, a herd of *sluagh* drifted with the wind, howling and grasping at the wild magic of the earth. All around Jack, the world faded as the Black swelled and spilled over the edges of his unconscious, staining his sight like ink.

"Why?" he said, keeping his eyes on the black dogs. "Why send this lot? What do you want from me?"

Nothing. The girl laid a hand on each *cu sith's* head.

"I'm confused, then." Jack shoved his hands into his leather. "You've been following me since Paddington, for what? A laugh? Got a crush? Tell me, because I'm out of ideas, luv."

The girl stepped toward him, and though her countenance was calm and far less terrifying than either the demon or the Morrigan, Jack took a hasty step back.

Her magic wasn't something he wanted touching him, not a feeling he wanted to remember over and over again in nightmares that shot him screaming back into the waking world.

You feel it, she whispered. *You've felt it for months, since you found her again.* This time she was faster, and she pressed a hand to his cheek, pulling Jack down to her eye level. The gold burned, roiling with liquid witchfire as magic flared in the girl's gaze.

"Don't know what you're talking about," Jack said flippantly. "All I've felt is a great and overwhelming desire to stab meself in the forehead to end the visits of things like you."

Her nails dug into his cheek. *Watch yourself, mage. You may be able to speak to the hag so, but I'm a different breed.*

Jack flinched, blood dribbling down is jaw. "I know." He sighed. "I know what you are."

The girl's smile curved up at the ends, became predatory. *Say it.*

Jack shut his eyes, to close off that burning gaze, the triad of youth, magic, and death that marked the girl for what she was. "You're the Hecate."

The girl's tongue flicked over her pale lips, and she withdrew her hand, running her fingers through Jack's blood and painting streaks down his cheek, covering his scar.

I am the guardian of the gateways. And you are the crow-mage, so I have come to give you this courtesy. She stepped back, cradling the head of the black dog against her. *Don't tell me you haven't felt it, Jack. Your magic curdling within you. Your sight is clawing your mind to pieces.*

Jack looked out toward the moor. The sun was falling, slowly but surely, painting the tops of the hills with pale fire.

"Yeah," he said. "I noticed it. Same shite, different day, you know?"

It is not the same, crow-mage. The Hecate sighed. *The Black is in turmoil. The ways between the worlds are choked with corruption. You know what is coming, Jack, and what you must do.*

"I haven't the faintest, darling," Jack said. "All you old ones can never just spit it out, can you? Always got to dance in circles until your feet bleed."

There is war coming, the Hecate whispered. *There has been war before, war at the beginning and war since, but this will be the vastest, the bloodiest. The old gods and the old ways are rising, parting the layers of the spirit worlds.*

Jack felt a long, slow crawl of unease down his spine. "And I'm supposed to do what about your war, exactly?"

The Hecate bared her teeth. Her canines were pointed, like her dog servants'. *You will do nothing. You will stand aside, crow-mage, and you will keep your meddlesome fingers out of what is coming.*

Wind stripped the mist from her figure in a sudden gust, leaving her bare before Jack's eyes. *The one who must act is Petunia.*

"No," Jack said instantly. "Pete has nothing to do with any of this."

You cannot protect her, and to presume is a grave insult, the Hecate snarled. *She is a Weir, crow-mage. She is a servant of the gateways just as you are a servant of the dead.*

"Pete is an innocent," Jack snarled. "She doesn't belong in the Black. She doesn't deserve your attentions."

Petunia was a Weir long before she was your consort, the Hecate snapped. *She will stand at the head of my army. She will lift us from the hidden place of dreams and place us on the path.*

"Like fuck she will," Jack snarled back. Pete's talent brought her under the purview of the Hecate, true, but she'd never had a sign. Never seen her fate, like he had with the Morrigan. "You've made a mistake," he said, softer. "It's another Weir. Not Pete."

The Hecate's eyes flared. *The Black is rotting, crow-mage. The hag and her consorts, the demons and their* bargains, spreading filth through the worlds like poison in a river. *Even now, demons dance in anticipation of the world's end, and necromancers create offerings to their old gods. Sorcery and sin gnaw the bones of magic, of the druid and the Weir and the hearth witch.* The Hecate looked away from him, and a tear slipped over her translucent cheek. *The world I was born into is gone, crow-mage. But in the fires of war I will rebuild it from ash, and Petunia, my Weir, will open the way. I do not make mistakes.*

She turned back on him, and Jack saw the full glory of the Hecate, her triple face and her owl's wings and the vast, breathless space between the worlds that the girl's form walked. *And if you value the world you live in, crow-mage, you will stand down. You will retreat, forget that you know such a thing as magic, and stay away from my Weir until it's all over.*

Jack felt his jaw twitch. Orders were orders, whether they came from a headmaster or the goddess of the gateways. "Can't do that," he said.

You will, the Hecate hissed, *or you will burn the world.*

Jack turned his back on her, started for the Naughton house.

"If I had a shilling for every time I've heard that bollocks."

Chapter Forty-eight

"Jack?" Pete called to him when he came through the door. "Jack, where'd you go?"

"Having a conversation," Jack called. The Hecate's eyes still burned in front of his gaze.

Stay away, mage. Or you will burn the world.

"You left all your things on the table," Pete said, when he came into the kitchen. She handed him a plate of biscuits. "Expect you'll be needing them."

Jack shook his head, putting the biscuits down on the table, stealing one. "Those are yours now."

Pete's face tightened. "Jack, no . . ."

"Listen, Pete." Jack placed his hands on her shoulders. "I haven't time to explain properly, but suffice to say that there are people and gods in the Black who want you, dead or otherwise. They always will, because of what you are. I'm giving you me kit because you're going to need it. To defend yourself and not be made to serve someone or something that you don't want."

Pete's mouth quirked. "Fuck off. Who'd want my service besides musty old ghosts like Treadwell?"

"Your patron," Jack said quietly. "The Hecate. The guardian of the gateway. Weirs are her purview, like the Fiach Dubh are the Morrigan's."

Pete sat down hard at the table. "Why does she want *me*? I haven't done a thing!"

"You've got power," Jack said. "And there's some bad shite coming down the road, Pete. Power will be in short supply." He closed his hand over hers. "Take the satchel. If nothing else, there's still an unwinding spell needs doing and it's high time you learned how to cast." Jack felt about for a fag and lit it, blowing smoke to the ceiling. "And you should probably call that sodding Ollie Heath and have him arrest Nicholas Naughton."

Pete's eyebrow crawled upward. "Nick? Why?"

Jack watched the ash grow on the end of his fag. *Necromancers make offerings to their old gods.* "Because he killed his brother."

Pete set down her mug. "That's quite a leap, Jack."

"This house is the work of a necromancer," he said. "A line of necromancers. Nicholas Naughton said it was just himself and his brother. One of them's dead. So, by your very own copper logic, the one that's still kicking round London in a nonce suit is the necromancer. One who owns a great big country house and estate on which to bury the dead he's bound."

"But Naughton is the one who demanded that we cleanse the house!" Pete cried.

Jack stubbed out the end of his fag. "Naughton's an idiot. You don't get a poltergeist from a binding ritual. He knew I'd see it. We were probably sent here to be the next juicy mage offerings to his bone gods, seeing as how he'd run out of hapless family members."

Pete pressed her hands together, put them against her mouth like she were making a brief bid not to smash something. "I can't believe it. I can't believe I sat there and took that git's money and *smiled* at him, for fuck's sake."

"You're not the first person he's fooled," Jack said. "Think of how poor Danny must have felt swinging from that beam . . ."

"All right." Pete placed her hands flat on the table. "I'll keep the kit, for now. And I'll have Naughton taken care of. But that doesn't mean you aren't coming back." Sheen blossomed in her eyes, and Pete sucked in a long breath. "Tell me you're coming back."

Jack got up and pulled Pete up with him. Pete wrapped her arms around his neck and pressed her cheek into his shoulder. Jack put one hand on her neck, the silken ends of her hair tickling his palm.

"I'm coming back," Jack whispered. It wasn't a lie, really. Just an unknown quantity. "I should go back to work, luv," he said. He would do what he always did when he was at a loss—smoke, curse, consult his books, and pace until something shook loose and he came up with a way to weasel out of his problem. He was a clever boy, after all.

Pete pulled him back against her instead, small body warming his skin. "No." She ran her thumb down the scar on his cheek. "I don't want you to go."

Jack slid his hands across her waist, pressing his fingers into her hip bones. If he had the chance to look back, he supposed, he would call himself an idiot for spending time with musty books when he could be with Pete. "I suppose it can wait. For a bit."

Pete pressed her lips against his, firm and warm and insistent. "I suppose it can. Just for a bit."

Chapter Forty-nine

Jack's eyes snapped open, and he snatched up Pete's mobile from the bedside table. Pete stirred next to him, groaning and pulling her pillow over her face.

The numerals spelled out 10:13, and Jack slumped back, forcing his heart to stop pounding.

He had hours. Hours until he faced the demon in Hell.

"Jack?" Pete curled into him, her leg sliding up his thigh to drape across his waist. "Don't leave yet." Her hands brushed down his abdomen. "Haven't had a chance to say a proper good morning."

Jack's cock jumped as Pete's hand wandered into unsafe territory, and her lips brushed over his earlobe. He rolled over and pinned her frame beneath his weight, causing Pete to yelp. Jack grinned. "Good morning, Petunia."

"I called Ollie Heath while you were sleeping," she said.

"Ohh, yeah. Nothing's more erotic than talking about your work mates," Jack said, nuzzling into her neck.

Pete slapped him on the back of his head. "Don't be awful."

Jack sighed, coming up for air. "What did he say?"

"Nicholas Naughton's done a runner," Pete murmured. "Cleaned out his flat and his accounts and he's gone."

Jack levered himself onto his elbows. "I'm sorry, luv. Looks like he's not quite the idiot I thought."

Pete lifted one bare shoulder. "It's a problem for another day, Jack." She pulled his face down, and Jack followed willingly.

He kissed her for a long moment, letting his fingers roam over her, memorize her. If it was the last touch he had, it needed to count. Memory was all that mattered, in the Black.

Pete pushed him off gently after a moment, rolling her face to the window. "Jack, there's a bird watching us."

Jack followed her eyes and saw the crow nestled on the sill, staring at him.

"Creepy thing," Pete muttered. Jack rolled over on his back, throwing a hand over his eyes.

"It's a fetch. A psychopomp."

Pete quirked her eyebrow. "What's it fetching?"

Jack laughed. "My soul, if I'm lucky. Everybody has a fetch. All the citizens of the Black."

Pete shrugged. "I don't."

Jack put his feet on the floor, winced at the chill, and reached for his pants. "'Course you do."

"No," Pete insisted. "Never had anything like the crow in my life. I don't have anything that's stayed with me." She propped herself up on her elbow and ran her free fingers down Jack's spine. "Except you."

Jack shuddered when her fingers, her magic, made contact with his skin. "I can't say I've been that great about sticking around," he told Pete. "In fact, I've been shite."

"If anyone is going to take my soul down into the Land," Pete said softly, "I'd rather it be you."

Jack looked at the crow again. Its eyes gleamed, and it

stared back at him, unblinking, piercing him down to the core of his magic.

You know what's coming, the Hecate whispered. *The fires of war.*

Jack raised his hand, staring at the crow through splayed fingers, an inkblot on the pristine dawn.

Something uncurled in his chest, behind his sight. It didn't ache and pound against his mind as it had in recent weeks, it just stayed in his head, heavy and present.

"I meant it, you know," Pete said. She sat up and wrapped her arms around him, her bare breasts pressing into his ribs.

"I know, luv . . . ," Jack murmured.

You're gonna die, Jack, Lawrence whispered. *Best you can do is go with your head held high.*

Jack stared at the crow. The crow stared at him. Watching, the way it always watched him. Waiting for his soul to float free of his body, so it could carry it to the Land. The way he'd watched Pete, since the first night they'd laid eyes on each other.

"Jack?" Pete said as he got out of bed and pulled on his shorts. "You're quiet. What is it?"

Jack put a fag in his mouth and started for his books "Don't you worry. I think I may not be going anywhere."

Chapter Fifty

The demon was on time.

Jack stood under the tree in bare feet, denim, and his tattered Supersuckers shirt. He smoked a fag slowly, letting the burn travel all the way down his throat and warm him against the cool air.

"You ready, Winter?" the demon said. The grass under its polished shoes withered and died, fading away to bare salted ground. "No more excuses. No more tricks. You and I, down into Hell."

"If you're that eager to give up your name," Jack said, flicking his fag away, "then let's get on with it, mate."

The demon's smile twitched into life like a worm on a hook. "Why do I sense another card up your sleeve, Jack?"

Jack lifted his shoulder. "Maybe 'cause I've got one."

Pete stood on the stoop of the Naughton house, watching. Far enough away not to get caught in the edge of a hex. Close enough for what Jack had thought of as he sat with her in bed, watching the crow.

The demon let out an irritated huff. "Let's see it then, Winter. I'll kill you that much quicker."

Jack gave Pete a small smile of reassurance, and she lifted her hand in return. She trusted him, though he hadn't told her what he intended to do. On the off chance it didn't work, and the demon peeled his skin off.

Fuck off chance. There was a very good bloody chance it would all go pear-shaped. But Jack wasn't going to hold his head high. He didn't have the dignity left to accept his fate, so he might as well fucking fight.

He might live.

And Margaret Thatcher might hop on a broom and do a lap around the Houses of Parliament.

The demon grabbed him by the shirtfront, pulling them close enough to kiss, if Jack were that sort of man. "What the fuck are you grinning at, Winter?"

Jack turned his smile on the demon, and let the spell that he held in his mind unfurl. No kit this time, no salt or iron. Just his talent, coiled in his mind starving and stinging, like a snake.

Jack stared into the demon's eyes, at the flame dancing there.

"Everyone has a fetch," he said.

The spell unfolded, caught the wild magic of the moor, and faster—far, far faster than he expected—Jack and the demon tumbled into the whirlpool of his sight.

Everything is black. Everything is pain. Jack is aware that the screams echoing are his.

Light burns through his eyelids, light blotted out by a man's shadow, and when he opens his eyes, he's in Ireland. Seth is leaning over him. He's fallen asleep on the grass, trying to read one of the interminable Latin diaries the older mage foisted on him. He throws the mouldering thing at Seth.

"This is a great load of shit."

" 'Course it's shit," Seth tells him. "But it's shit that might save your wee arse one day, boy, so you best read

on. *Conjugate some verbs if that will break up the monotony.*"

Jack watches a crow land on Seth's roof, and stare at them. Seth sees it, and his smile grows sly. "You've got a fetch, Jackie boy."

Fetches aren't something Jack believes in. Jack believes in what he can see, touch—the magic in him that responds to liquor and rage and cigarette burns. The sweet taste of a fag and the sweeter taste of skin under his lips. "Old wives' tale," he tells Seth. "It's probably seen something dead in the field."

"Old wives could learn you a thing or two, as well," Seth tells him, and retreats indoors.

Jack shuts his eyes against the sun and he's on his knees in a circle of stones, wearing the white raiments for the first and last time in his career as a Fiach Dubh. In a few weeks, Seth will catch him with the grimoire. This is the first nail in his coffin.

Seth and his brothers stare in horror, Seth's athame held at half-mast, as the crows land one by one, on the top of each stone, and before Jack the crow woman stands with her hair made from feathers and her face spattered in blood.

Stare as she touches his forehead, where the white witch gits say the third eye lives.

Stare as she whispers to him, in a language that Jack should not be able to understand, "My mage. Crow-mage."

Nausea and dizziness grip him as he sees bonfires in her gaze, smells the smoke of funeral pyres, and hears the clash and scream of battles fought up and down the length of the land on which he now kneels. He smells blood and decay, smoke and char, and he sees the spires of the Bleak Gates piercing the fire-lit night.

Jack shuts his eyes as his dinner of mediocre bangers and mash has its revenge while the brotherhood reviles him with whispers and fearful stares.

Opens them, and sees Pete Caldecott. She's skinny, and hides inside a school uniform that's at least a size too large. She has her sister's eyes and hair, but both her face and her gaze are sharper. She looks far more like Inspector Caldecott than the woman Jack supposes was their mother, the one who gave MG the soft face and generous tits. Pete is sixteen, and she's still all planes and angles. Her eyes are decades older, and they don't miss much.

When he touches her, he smells the night of the initiation, the scent of battle-wracked earth. The calling card of the crow woman.

Jack Winter vows to stay away from Pete Caldecott, until he's tempted beyond resistance, breaks his vow, and he's in the tomb, the cold stone at his back, the demon looking down at him, lips curling back from pointed teeth.

The demon speaks. "Wake up, Jack."

But Jack holds on to Pete. Holds on to the feeling of the first time he touched her, across the circle in Highgate Cemetery. When Pete has called out to him, Jack has come.

When Pete lay dying on the graveyard earth, Jack was with her. As long as Jack has Pete, nothing can steal his soul away. Jack is bound to her surely as the crow is bound to him. Jack Winter, fetch of the Hecate's Weir.

Jack presses his face into Pete's hair, smells the sharp smoky scent of autumn in the graveyard, the penny tang of her blood.

Jack will never leave her, and so he moves in the memory, even though he didn't on the day, nearly dead from blood loss himself, and takes her face in his hands. "Body and soul," Jack tells Pete. "I'm yours. I'm the fetch you never had. You and I are bound, by blood and by stone. Bound for all the turns of the earth."

Pete smiles at him. Reaches up.

Wraps a clawed hand around his throat.

Pete's face is full of fang and malice. Pete's smile is the demon.

"Nice try," the demon hisses. "But you should have woken up when you had the chance, boy."

Its hand closes down, and Jack can no longer breathe. The demon draws him close, the demon that looks like Pete, and presses its lips against his. "By the by," it whispers. "The name's Belial. And you, Jack Winter . . . you've tricked me for the last time."

It releases him, the places where it touched burning Jack up from the inside.

He falls.

And is awake.

Jack thrashed up from the visions of the Black, gasping for air and clawing at his throat. The demon stood over him while Jack lay on the grass. It folded its arms and shook its head. "You failed, Jack. You tried, and you failed."

It picked his chin up with the toe of its shoe. "You tried to bind yourself to a living soul. Cheat me. That's trickery, and your challenge is void under those laws you're so fond of." The demon grinned, a smile of pure pleasure splitting its waxy face. "So that's the end for you, bright lad."

Jack stared up into the demon's face. Its tongue flicked over crimson lips. Somewhere in the distance, Pete was shouting, and the demon moved its gaze to her.

"She's trying to save you, Winter. She's going to throw herself on your pyre, surely enough."

"I'm her fetch," Jack said. "Spell or not, I'm hers. You can't take me if my soul is bound to an innocent's. It's the rules."

"Jack." Belial crouched, elbows on knees, genuine confusion on his face. "I'm a fucking demon. What makes you think I play by any bloody rules but my own?"

Pete reached them, panting, and launched herself at Belial. The demon spun, caught her about the neck, and shoved her against the tree, lifting her feet off the earth.

"Look what I've caught," he murmured. "A little Weir, very far from hearth and home."

Jack got to his feet, even though the breaking of his fetch spell had chewed him up and spit him out. With nowhere to go, the wild magic pounded in his head, expelled itself like poison into his muscle and bone. "Let her go," he warned.

Belial glanced back at him. "I could, Jack. I could let her go and take you instead, as you're bound by the bargain." He turned back to Pete, leaning close and scenting her, running his nose and lips up and down her neck. "Or you could try to break the bargain, and I could kill you and take my time with your sweet, sweet piece of meat."

He dropped Pete to the ground, where she choked. Belial straightened his tie and cuffs. "Your choice, Jack. What do you say?"

Jack looked down at Pete, tears of rage hovering in her eyes. He looked down at his own hands, pale and veined from the feedback of broken magic.

You burn things down, Seth said. *Wherever Jack Winter goes, death follows.*

Thirteen years to agonize over his shit decision, and suddenly it was no decision at all.

"Pete," Jack said. "I'm sorry. But I'll see you again."

"No, Jack!" she screamed, scrabbling to her feet. "No! You promised!"

Jack looked at Belial. "I go with you and you never, ever come to her or anyone I care about again. Clear?"

Belial snorted. "I couldn't bear less interest toward your little found family, mage. I care about you."

"*Jack!*" Pete's shriek rang against the moor. "What are you *doing*?"

Jack stepped up and faced Belial.

You can't cheat Death, boy. You just got to go with your head up high.

No escape. Not for you.

You know it's coming, mage. The fires of war.

He smiled at Pete. That was the only kind of knight he was—beaten and broken, lying in the mud. "What I should've done thirteen years ago," Jack said to Pete. "You be good to yourself, luv. And don't waste one moment crying over me."

Belial put his hand on Jack's cheek, and leaned close to his ear, whispering the ways and words of the secret passages into Hell. Jack didn't flinch, as his sight screamed and the magic around them flared. He watched Pete, on her knees by the great tree, arms wrapped around herself, face slick as glass with her tears. He watched her scream, wordless and lost, into the air.

Jack wished he could speak to her, tell her the truth, but before he could do more than raise his hand in farewell, the Dartmoor vanished under an onslaught of the sight.

When his eyes opened, Jack found himself looking up at three triple spires crowned with a lightning-etched sky. Hot wind snaked across his face and brought with it the smell of charnel fields. In the distance, across a blackened marching ground, a thousand pyres burned under the watchful eye of the spires. Thorns tangled around Jack's bare feet and cinders landed on his skin, leaving fresh red burns.

Next to him, Belial took a deep breath of his native air. "Welcome to Hell, Winter," the demon said. "We've missed you."

EPILOGUE

Hell

The places I see in my nightmare
Ain't nothing compared to what I see each day

—The Poor Dead Bastards
"Strange Days and Nightmares"

Chapter Fifty-three

Jack lay on a damp concrete floor, the floor of his flat in Manchester, the council flat where he and his mum had lived until he'd lit out for London.

He spat a little blood. His jaw wasn't broken, or maybe it had been. Here in Hell—or Manchester—time lengthened and bent and folded back on itself. What was true today would not be true tomorrow and could be true yesterday. He wouldn't know until he got there.

Belial made him see. All of the guilt, all of the lies. The beatings and the bar scuffles and the betrayals, from Seth down the line to Pete.

The demon showed it all to him, like a movie reel, and when it was over Belial wound the reel and showed him again.

The pain was physical. It wouldn't last. Belial was tenderizing his meat, softening Jack for the main event. The memories were what would continue, for all the term of his bargain.

Jack rolled onto his back, stared up at the stained ceiling. He'd memorized the maps of past residents, the water stains, leaks, and billowing clouds of petrified nicotine in the plaster.

He would stay here for a while, curled on the floor with blood dribbling across his vision.

Then the workings of Hell's clock would wind backward, and Belial would start over.

A shadow fell across Jack's gaze, changing the landscape of the ceiling. The familiar whispers crept in around the edges of his sight.

He didn't shy away from the crow woman as she crouched above him. Even if he'd wanted to move, he couldn't. His ribs were broken, at least one of his hands. Head swimming with concussion. Her touch was, for once, the least painful thing about his body.

So far you've fallen, the crow woman intoned. *Has this torment salved your conscience, Jack? Has it saved your soul?*

"Do I bloody look like my soul is saved?" Jack muttered.

Her skirts floating around her in a rain of feathers, the crow woman placed her lips against his forehead. *I can make it stop, crow-mage. I can lift you from this perdition and elevate you to salvation.*

"No thanks, luv," Jack said. "I've had my fill of bargains." The pit was as low as he could go. The endless loop of his life was the end.

Not a bargain, my child. The crow woman sighed. *A duty. The duty you were born for.*

The Hecate came to Jack's mind. It was a memory Belial never showed him, because Jack thought of it often enough on his own. "No," he said to the crow woman. "I have to stay away. Pete . . ."

The Weir has her fate and your fate is twined with hers so tightly that your trees have grown together. You share

*the same soil, crow-mage, the same air, the same life. You
sacrificed for her and still you cannot pull away.*

She stood, her shadow spreading across the room, across
the prison of Jack's memories.

You can stay in Hell, Jack Winter, the crow woman said.
*Or you can take your place on my field, and stand in my
ranks as it always should be.*

Jack tried to sit up, failed as his ribs stabbed him with
pain like a rusty blade. "I don't belong to you anymore. I
belong to Belial now."

Belial is a pitiful, scrabbling cockroach, the Morrigan
hissed. *I am Death's walker, the raven of war.* Her wings
scraped the walls, rained plaster dust down on Jack.

What do you think will happen to your Weir? she asked.
*When war rips the Black asunder and you are here, locked
willingly in Hell? How long will she remain if you are not
at her side? Mage and Weir, Jack. As it has been since the
beginning. Without you she is bereft, one half of a broken
pair of wings.*

Jack hadn't let himself think of Pete, when he could think.
Pete would survive. She was made of tension wire underneath the skin, and she could be battered and stripped, but
she'd survive. Everyday life, even living life in the Black,
she'd survive.

I speak the truth, the Morrigan intoned. *She will not see
the end of what is coming if she is alone.*

Jack swallowed, tasted blood. "What do I have to do?"

Come with me, the Morrigan said. *Stop your running
and your hiding from your fate as the crow-mage. Burn the
world down and rebuild it in the image of Death. Spread
your hand across the sun and turn my enemies to ash.*

She held out her hand to Jack. *You only have to agree,
crow-mage. Take up the mantle of your fate.*

Slowly, with a dull popping in his knuckles, Jack

grasped her hand and held on tight. He saw the battlefield, smelled the blood, heard the screams. Felt his feet sink into bloodied earth. Saw the way spread out before him, spires of London drifting with smoke while sirens wailed and screams twisted in the wind. War and death. The twin desires of the Morrigan, his to bring to the world. Jack Winter, the pale rider. The harbinger of war.

A war that Pete would face alone, as long as he remained under the yoke of Belial's bargain. A war that he knew, deep in the small part of him where truth was still alive, that she wouldn't live survive.

Not unless Jack finished what he'd started in Seth's circle. Until he acknowledged the touch of the crow woman on his life, and his sight.

You are dead, Jack, the Morrigan whispered. *With the dead you should stay. As the crow-mage's fate always cycles.* She stroked his blood-caked hair from his face with her free hands, claws tracing his skull. *Will you stay, Jack?*

Jack squeezed the Morrigan's hand, until his broken knuckles creaked. "Take me," he told the crow woman. "I'm ready."

Tv Kinder: The Embrace

Book Vampire Macabre

author by

Martin Rein-
Hadger